DARK REVELATION

"Oh, Quentin. Your life has been in danger ever since you had a claim to this heritage. It terrifies me." Germaine flung hat and whip on the table and came to him. "Let it go, Quentin. Let them have it who covet it, who will do murder to possess it. Go back to England. Do this if you love me."

Quentin was aghast. "Surrender my rights because I am threatened? Should I bow before evil rather than stand to defend what is mine?"

"There is something else." She hesitated, averting her glance. "They . . . they do not believe that your title is sound."

"What?"

"Oh, Quentin. Must I be plainer?" She was almost in anguish. "They do not believe that you are your father's son."

And as she spoke these words it was as if a knife had slashed her own heart. For whatever their truth or fiction, she realized that she'd unwittingly forced the man she loved into a battle that would surely cost his life . . .

Master-at-Arms

By
Rafael Sabatini

BALLANTINE BOOKS • NEW YORK

Contents

BOOK I

BOOK II

Contents

BOOK III

BOOK I

CHAPTER 1

Master-at-Arms

THERE IS, you will come to agree, a certain humour to be discovered in the fact that Monsieur de Morlaix accounted himself free of the sin by which the angels fell, took 'Parva domus magna quies' for his motto, accounted tranquillity the greatest good, and regarded as illusory and hollow the wordly prizes for which men sweat and bleed.

That was before the sight of Mademoiselle de Chesnières came to disturb his poise. It was also at a time when, living in a state of comparative affluence, he could afford such views. For he enjoyed an income greater even than that earned by the famous Angelo Tremamondo, whose show pupil he had been and a part of whose mantle had descended to him. And he enjoyed, too, the benevolent aid of Madame Fortune. She had spared him the years of arduous toil by which men usually climb to their ultimate eminence. She had lifted him at the very outset to the summit.

The manner of his becoming thus, *per saltum,* London's most famous and fashionable master-at-arms was demonstrably of her contriving.

This Quentin de Morlaix, whose peculiar mental equipment and steady nerves enhanced the natural aptitude of his spare, vigorous body for the exercise of arms, was encouraged by Angelo—too well established and prosperous to be apprehensive of competition—to adopt swordsmanship as a profession, so as to supplement the very meagre income of his mother.

But there were other masters-at-arms in London who could not view a fresh arrival in their ranks with the same complacency; and one of these, the well-known

3

Rédas, carried resentment so far as to publish a letter in the *Morning Chronicle* in which he held up to cruellest ridicule the youthful newcomer.

It was the more unpardonable because Rédas himself was in flourishing circumstances, and next to Henry Angelo's his school was the best attended in Town. His criticisms were accounted of weight; and crushed by them, it might well have followed that Morlaix would have accepted the dismissal from the ranks of fencing-masters which that abominable letter was calculated to pronounce. Fortunately, the generous-hearted Angelo was at hand to inspire confidence and dictate a course of action.

'You will answer him, Quentin. You will not waste words. You will accept his description of you as a bungling dilettante, and you will inform him that this being so he will the more easily defeat you in the match for a hundred guineas to which you have the honour to invite him.'

Quentin smiled his regrets. 'It would be amusing so to answer him if I disposed of a hundred guineas and dared to risk them.'

'You misunderstand me. That is the sum for which I will back you against better men than Rédas.'

'It's a flattering confidence. But if I should lose your money?'

'You won't have done yourself justice. I know your strength, and I know Rédas', and I am content.'

So the challenging letter was sent, and its appearance in the *Morning Chronicle* produced a mild sensation. It was impossible for Rédas to refuse that trial of skill. He was caught in the trap of his own malice. But he was so little aware of it that his acceptance was couched in terms of scornful insult and garnished with assertions of the phlebotomy he would perform upon his rash challenger if his profession did not preclude a meeting with unbuttoned foils.

'You will reply to this bombast,' said Angelo again, 'that since he desires phlebotomy, you will gratify him by using the *pointe d'arrêt*. And you will add the condition that the match shall consist of a single assault

4

for the best of six hits.' The old master answered Morlaix's look of astonishment by laying a finger to his nose. 'I know what I'm doing, child.'

After this jactancy Rédas could not refuse either condition without rendering himself ridiculous, and so the matter was settled.

The courtly old Angelo, acting for Quentin, made the necessary arrangements, and the meeting took place in Rédas' own academy in the presence of his pupils, their friends, and some others drawn by the correspondence, making up an attendance a couple of hundred strong. The thrifty Rédas had been inspired to charge a half-guinea a head for admission, so that whatever happened his stake would be fully covered.

It was soon apparent that this fashionable crowd came with intent to heap ridicule upon the presumptuous young fool who dared to measure himself against so redoubtable a master, and to embitter with their laughter the humiliation which they perceived in store for him. For there was laughter and there were some audible jeers to greet his appearance, in contrast with the applause that had hailed the entrance of the formidable Rédas.

Added to the memory of the taunts in his opponent's published letters, this insultingly expressed partisanship filled Quentin de Morlaix with anger. But it was of a cold and steadying kind, which determined him in the scrupulous observance of the plan that Angelo had laid down for him, the plan at the root of the insistence upon a single assault without respite until the best of the six hits had been delivered.

Old Angelo, still youthful of figure at sixty and a model of grace and elegance in an apricot velvet coat above black satin breeches, acted as his pupil's second, and conducted Quentin to the middle of the fencing-floor, where Rédas and his second waited.

The audience, composed mainly of men of fashion, included also a few ladies and some early French *émigrés;* for this happened in the year 1791, before the heavy exodus from France. These spectators were ranged along the sides and at the ends of the long barn-like room. It was a morning of early spring, and the light, from four windows placed high in the northern wall, was as excellent as could be desired.

As the two swordsmen faced each other, stripped to the waist in accordance with the conditions Quentin had made, the general chatter rippled into silence.

The advantages of wind and limb were certainly with Morlaix. Lean and long, his naked torso, gleaming white above his black satin smalls, seemed muscled in whipcord. Nevertheless Rédas, for all that at forty-four he was twice the age of his opponent, looked formidable: a compact, swarthy, hairy man of obvious power and vigour. It was a contrast of mastiff with greyhound. Rédas had discarded his wig for a black silk scarf in which his cropped head was swathed. Morlaix wore his own hair, dark chestnut in colour and luxuriant, tightly queued.

Formally the seconds examined the adjustments of the arresting point with which each foil had been fitted. It consisted of a diminutive trident, strapped over the button, each of its sharp steel points being a half-inch long.

Satisfied, they placed their men in position. The blades were crossed, and for a moment held lightly by Angelo at the point of contact. Then he gave the word and stood clear.

'Allez, messieurs!'

The released blades slithered and tinkled lightly one against the other. The engagement was on.

Rédas, determined upon making an end so speedy as to mark the contemptible inferiority of the rash upstart who ventured to oppose him, attacked with a dash and vigour that seemed irresistible. That it should be resisted at all sowed in the onlookers a surprise that grew steadily as the resistance was protracted. Soon the reason for it began to appear. Morlaix, as cool and easy as he was determined, ventured no counters, not so much as a riposte that might give his adversary an opening, but contended himself with standing on the defensive, concentrating his play in the deflection of every thrust and lunge whirled against him in fiercely swift succession. Moreover, by playing close, with his elbow well flexed, using only his forearm and the forte of his blade, he met an onslaught that was recklessly prodigal of energy with the minimum exertion of strength.

The counsels of Angelo had determined these tactics, calculated to avenge as signally as Morlaix's powers might permit the insults of which he had been the butt. The aim was not merely to defeat Rédas, but to make that defeat so utter as to leave him crushed under a recoil of the ridicule which he had used so lavishly. Therefore, whilst taking no risks, Morlaix made use of his every natural advantage, the chief of which were his youth and greater staying power. These he would carefully conserve whilst Rédas spent himself in the fierce, persistent attack which had been foreseen. Morlaix calculated also that these tactics, and his opponent's impotence to defeat them and to draw him into counter-attacking, would presently act upon Rédas' temper, driving him to increase the fury of his onslaught and thus hasten that breathlessness and exhaustion for which Morlaix was content maliciously to wait.

It came as he had calculated.

At first Rédas, whilst fencing with unsparing vigour, had yet preserved the academic correctness to be expected in a *maître d'armes*. But with the growth of his irritation before that impenetrable defence, which nothing could lure even momentarily into an offensive, he descended to tricks of swashbuckling, accompanying feints by exclamations and foot-stampings intended to deceive the opponent into mistaking a false attack for a real one. When by such devices he had merely succeeded in the further wastes of an energy of which he had now none to spare, he fell back and paused so as to give expression to his anger.

'What's this? *Morbleu!* Do we fight, or do we play at fighting?'

Yet even as he spoke he was conscious that this verbal attempt to save his face did him no better service than his fencing. Even if he should still prevail in the end—and that, at least, he had not yet come to doubt—his could no longer be that masterly overwhelming victory upon which he had counted. Too long already had his crafty opponent withstood him, and in the utter silence that had now settled upon the ranks of the spectators he perceived as astonishment that humiliated him.

Worse than this, there were actually one or two who laughed as if in approval of Quentin's answer to his foolish question.

'It is what I was asking myself, *cher maître*. Do not, I beg you, be reluctant to make good your boasts, since I am here so as to afford you the opportunity.'

Rédas said no more. But even through the meshes of his mask the baleful glare of his eyes could be discerned. Enraged by the taunt, he renewed the attack, still with the same unsparing vigour. But it did not last. He began to pay for the hot pace he had made in his rash confidence that the engagement would be a short one. He began to understand, and enraged the more because he understood, the crafty motive underlying the condition that the combat should be limited to a single assault. His breathing began to trouble him; his muscles began to lose resilience. Perceiving this in the slackening speed and loss of precision, Morlaix tested him by a sudden riposte, which he was barely in time to parry. He longed desperately for that pause, be it of but a few seconds, which the conditions denied him.

He fell back in an endeavour to try to steal it. But Morlaix was too swift to follow him. And now Rédas, half-winded, weary, and dispirited, found himself giving ground before an attack pressed by an opponent who was still comparatively fresh. It broke upon him in answer to an almost despairing lunge in which the master had extended himself so fully and with such disregard of academic rules that he employed his left hand to support him on the ground. A counter-parry swept his blade clear, and a lightning riposte planted the prongs of the arresting point high upon his breast.

A murmur rippled through the assembly as he recovered, with the blood trickling from that superficial

wound. He fell back beyond his opponent's reach in
another desperate hope of a respite for his labouring
lungs.

Actually Morlaix allowed it him, what time he
mocked him.

'I will not further tax your patience, *cher maître*.
Now guard yourself.'

He went in with a feint in the low lines, whence he
whirled his point into carte as he lunged, and planted
the trident over the master's heart.

'Two!' he counted as he recovered. 'And now, in
tierce, thus, the third.' Again the points tore the master's flesh. But crueller far were the words that tore his
soul. 'Pah! They told me you were a fencing-master,
and you're but a *tirailleur de régiment*. It's time to
make an end. Where will you have it? In carte again,
shall we say?"

Once more Morlaix thrust low, and as Rédas, grown
sluggish, moved his blade to the parry, the point
flashed in over his guard. 'Thus!'

And there, as the fourth hit went home, so violently
that Quentin's foil was bent into an arc, the seconds
intervened. The master's ignominious defeat was complete, and from the spectators who had come to mock
him Morlaix received the ovation earned by his concluding supreme display of mastery.

Rédas plucked the mask from a face that was grey.
He stood forth railing and raging whilst the blood
streamed from his labouring chest. '*Ah ça!* You ap-
plaud him, do you? *Quelle lâcheté!* You do not perceive how base were his methods.' Passion strangled
him. 'That was not to fight, that. He has the younger
heart and lungs. He used the advantage of those. You
saw that he did not dare attack until I was tired. If this
coward had played fair—*crédieu!*—you would have
seen a different end.'

'And so we should,' said Angelo, intervening, 'if you
had fought with your tongue, Rédas, or with your pen.
Those are the weapons of which you are really master.
In swordsmanship Monsieur de Morlaix has shown that
he can give you lessons.'

It was the common opinion, as the immediate sequel proved. For after that assault-at-arms scarcely a pupil remained to Rédas. Those who had come to jeer at Morlaix were the first to transfer themselves to his school, whilst such was the stir made in Town by the affair, so swiftly and widely did it spread the fame of the new fencing-master, that he found his academy overcrowded almost from the hour of its establishment.

This instant, fortuitous flow of prosperity compelled him to engage assistants, justified his removal to handsome premises in Bruton Street, and enabled him to bring the ease of affluence into the closing years of his mother's life.

In the four years that were sped since its foundation the Académie Morlaix, under royal patronage, had become fashionable not only as a fencing-school, but as a resort. The long, austerely bare *salle d'armes* on the ground floor, the gallery above it, the elegant adjacent rooms, and in fine weather even the little garden where Morlaix cultivated his roses, came to be frequented by other than fencers. The continuing and ever-increasing flow of French emigrants to London in those days was largely responsible for converting the academy into a fashionable meeting place. It may have begun in an assumption that Monsieur de Morlaix was, himself, one of those fugitives from the Revolution who were compelled to apply such aptitudes as they possessed to the earning of a livelihood. By the time this misapprehension had been corrected the character of the fencing-school had been established as an agreeable rendezvous for *émigrés,* and one in which these exiled nobles were under no necessity of spending any of the money that was so painfully scarce with them.

Morlaix encouraged them by the affability that was natural to his easy-going temperament. Reared from infancy in England, and an Englishman in tastes and outlook, yet his French blood lent him a natural warmth of heart for his compatriots. He made them welcome to his well-appointed establishment, encouraged them to frequent it, and out of his prosperity—for his school was reputed to earn upwards of three thousand pounds a year, which was affluence indeed in the days of King George III—he dispensed a liberal hospitality, and eased the financial embarrassment of many an *émigré* in those days that were so dark and grim for the French *noblesse*.

CHAPTER 2

Mademoiselle de Chesnières

IT IS, as I have hinted, from his meeting with Mademoiselle de Chesnières that he dates the awakening of ambition in him, that is to say, of discontent with a lot which hitherto had fully satisfied him and of desire to fill in life a loftier station.

That historic event is placed some four years after the founding of his academy. Its scene was the mansion of the Duc de Lionne in Berkeley Square. The young Duke, having married soon after his emigration the heiress of one of those upstart nawabs who had enriched himself with the plunder of the Indies, had been so far removed by this matrimonial opportunism from the indigence afflicting so many of his noble compatriots that he was enabled to live in a splendour even surpassing that of which the Revolution had deprived him in France.

His house, and to a limited extent his purse, were at all times open to his less fortunate fellow exiles of birth, and once a week his good-natured Duchess held a salon for their reception and entertainment, where music, dancing, charades, conversation, and—most welcome of all to many of those half-famished aristocrats—refreshments were to be enjoyed.

Morlaix owed his invitation to the fact that the

11

Duke, with ambitions to excel as a swordsman, was of an assiduous attendance at the Bruton Street academy round the corner. For the rest it came to him chiefly because the Duke had fallen into the general habit of regarding Morlaix as a fellow *émigré*.

In shimmering black and silver, with silver clocks to his stockings, paste buckles to his red-heeled shoes, and a dusting of powder on his unclubbed, severely queued hair, Morlaix's moderately tall, well-knit figure, of that easy deportment which constant fencing brings, was of the few that took the eye in an assembly that in the main was shabby-genteel.

To many of the men he was already known, for many of them were of those who attended his academy, a few to fence, and more merely to lounge in his antechamber. By some of these he was presented to others: to Madame de Genlis, who made a bare living by painting indifferently little landscapes on the lids of fancy boxes; to the Comtesses de Sisseral and de Lastic, who conducted an establishment of modes charitably set up for them by the Marchioness of Buckingham; to the Marquise des Réaux, who earned what she could by the confection of artificial flowers; to the Comte de Chaumont, who was trading in porcelains; to the Chevalier de Payen, who was prospering as a dancing-master; to the Duchesse de Villejoyeuse, who taught French and music, being imperfectly acquainted with both; and there was the learned, courtly Gautier de Brécy, who had been rescued from starvation to catalogue the library of a Mr. Simmons. Thus were these great ones of the earth, these lilies of the field, brought humbly to toil and spin for bare existence. None of it was toil of an exalted order. Yet that there were limits imposed by birth to the depths to which one might descend in the struggle against hunger, Morlaix received that night an illustration.

He found himself caught up in a group of men that had clustered about the Vicomte du Pont de Bellanger. It included the corpulent Comte de Narbonne, the witty Montlosier, the Duc de La Châtre, and some *émigrés* officers who subsisted on an allowance of a shilling or two a day from the British Government. These Bellanger was entertaining in his rich, sonorous voice with the scandalous case of Aimé de La Vauvraye, on whom sentence had that day been passed. Bellanger's manner, pompously histrionic and rich in gesture, went admirably with his voice and inflated diction. A tall man, of a certain studied grace, with hair of a luxuriant and lustrous black, eyes large, dark, and liquid, and lips full and sensuous, he carried that too handsome head at an angle that compelled him to look down his shapely nose upon the world. Arrested and sentenced to death by the Revolutionary Tribunal of Saint-Malo, he had saved his head by a sensational escape, which made him famous in London *émigré* society, and procured him in particular the admiration of the ladies, of which, having left a wife in France, he accounted it due to himself to miss no advantage.

Tonight he was more than ordinarily swollen with importance by the part he had played in the case of Monsieur de La Vauvraye. That unfortunate gentleman, a Knight of Saint Louis, had so far forgotten what was due to the order of which he had the honour to be a member as to have taken service as valet to a Mr. Thornton, a wealthy merchant of the City of London. It was a scandal, said Monsieur de Bellanger, which the order could not possibly overlook. The Vicomte and three general officers had constituted themselves into a chapter of the order. They had that morning attended as a preliminary a Mass of the Holy Ghost, whereafter they had sat in judgment upon the unfortunate man.

'We found,' Bellanger declaimed, 'and you will say, messieurs, that we were right to find, that the state of servitude with which this unhappy man did not blush to confess that he had stained himself left us no choice but to condemn him. Our sentence was that he surrender his cross, and that he never again assume any of the distinctive marks of the Royal and Military Order of Saint Louis, or the title or quality of a knight of that order. And we are publishing our sentence in the English news-sheets, so that England may be made aware of what is due to so exalted an order.'

'What,' asked one of the listeners, 'was La Vauvraye's defence?'

Bellanger took snuff delicately from a hand that first had been outflung. 'The unhappy creature had none. He pleaded weakly that he accepted the only alternative to charity or starvation.'

'And so far forgot himself as to prefer dishonour,' said an officer.

Narbonne fetched a sigh from his great bulk. 'The sentence was harsh, but in the circumstances inevitable.'

'Inevitable, indeed,' agreed another, whilst yet another added: 'You had no choice but to expel him from the order.'

Bellanger received these approvals as tributes to his judgment. But meeting the fencing-master's eyes, something in their grey depths offended his self-satisfaction.

'Monsieur de Morlaix is perhaps of another mind?'

'I confess it'—Morlaix spoke lightly. 'The gentleman appears to have been moved by too scrupulous a sense of honour.'

Bellanger's brows went up. His full eyes stared forbiddingly.

'Really, sir! Really! I think that would be difficult to explain.'

'Oh, no. Not difficult. He might have borrowed money, knowing that he could not repay it; or he might have practised several of the confidence tricks in vogue and rendered easy to the possessor of a cross of Saint Louis.'

'Would you dare, sir,' wondered the Duc de La Châtre, 'to suggest that any Knight of Saint Louis could have recourse to such shifts?'

'It is not a suggestion, Monsieur le Duc. It is an affirmation. And made with authority. I have been a victim. Oh, but let me assure you, a conscious and willing victim.'

He possessed a voice that was clear and pleasantly modulated, and although he kept it level, there was a ring in it that penetrated farther than he was aware, and produced now in his neighbourhood a silence of which he was unconscious.

'Of Monsieur de La Vauvraye,' he continued, 'let me tell you something more. He borrowed a guinea from me a month ago. He is by no means the only Knight of Saint Louis who has borrowed my guineas. But he is the only one who has ever repaid me. That was a week ago, and I must suppose that he earned that guinea as a valet. If you have debts, messieurs, it seems to me that no servitude that enables you to repay them can be accounted dishonouring.'

He passed on, leaving them agape, and it was in that moment, whilst behind him Bellanger was ejaculating horror and amazement, that he found himself face to face with Mademoiselle de Chesnières.

She was moderately tall, and of a virginal slenderness not to be dissembled by her panniers of flowered rose silk of a fashion that was now expiring. Her hair, of palest gold, was piled high above a short oval face lighted by eyes of vivid blue that were eager and alert. Those eyes met his fully and frankly, and sparkled with the half-smile, at once friendly and imperious, that was breaking on the delicate parted lips. The smile, which seemed to be of welcome, startled him until intuition told him that it was of approval. She had overheard him, and he felicitated himself upon the chance use of words which had commended him in advance. From which you will gather that already, at a glance, as it were, he discovered the need to be commended to her.

Delight and something akin to panic came to him together in the discovery that she was speaking to him, in a soft, level, cultured voice that went well with her imperious air. That she ignored the fact that he was a stranger, which in another might have been accounted boldness, seemed in her the result of a breeding so sure of itself as to trust implicitly to the boundaries in which it hedged her.

15

'You are brave, monsieur,' was all she said.

The ease with which he answered her surprised him. 'Brave? I hope so. But in what do I proclaim it?'

'It was brave in such company as that to have broken a lance for the unfortunate Monsieur de La Vauvraye.'

'A friend of yours, perhaps?'

'I have not even his acquaintance. But I should be proud to count so honest a gentleman among my friends. You perceive how fully I agree with you, and why I take satisfaction in your courage.'

'Alas! I must undeceive you there. Perhaps I but abuse the disabilities under which my profession places me.'

Her eyes widened. 'You have not the air of an abbé.'

'I am not one. Nevertheless I am all but debarred from sending a challenge, and not likely to receive one.'

'But who are you, then?'

This may well have been the moment in which dissatisfaction with his lot awoke in him. It would have been magnificently gratifying to announce himself as a person of exalted rank; to this little lady with the airs of a princess to have answered her, 'I am the Duc de Morlaix, peer of France,' instead of answering, as truth compelled him, simply and dryly, 'Morlaix, *maître d'armes*,' to which he added with a bow, *'Serviteur.'*

It produced in her no such change as he dreaded. She was smiling again. 'Now that I come to look at you more closely, you have the air of one. It makes you even braver. For it was your moral courage that I admired.'

To his chagrin they were interrupted by an untidily made woman of middle age, large and loose of body and lean of limb. An enormous headdress, powdered and festooned, towered above a countenance that once may have been pretty, but must always have been foolish. Now, with its pale eyes and lipless, simpering mouth, it was merely mean. A valuable string of pearls adorned a neck in scraggy contrast with the opulent breast from which it sprang. Diamonds blazing on a corsage of royal blue proclaimed her among the few Frenchwomen who had not yet been driven to take advantage of the kindly willingness of Messrs. Pope and Company, of Old Burlington Street, to acquire for cash—as advertised in the *Morning Chronicle*—the jewels of French emigrants.

'You have found a friend, Germaine.' He was not sure whether there was irony in the acid voice, but quite sure of the disapproval in her glance.

'A kinsman, I think,' the little lady startled him by answering. 'This is Monsieur Morlaix.'

'Morlaix? Morlaix of what?' the elder woman asked.

'Morlaix of nothing, of nowhere, madame. Just Morlaix. Quentin de Morlaix.'

'I seem to have heard of a Quentin in the House of Morlaix. But if you are not a Morlaix de Chesnières I am probably mistaken.' She announced herself with conscious pride: 'I am Madame de Chesnières de Chesnes, and this is my niece, Mademoiselle de Chesnières. We find life almost insupportable in this dreary land, and we put our hopes in such men as you to restore us soon to our beloved France.'

'Such men as I, madame?'

'Assuredly. You will be joining one of the regiments that are being formed for the enterprise of Monsieur de Puisaye.'

Bellanger, arm in arm with Narbonne, came to intrude upon them. 'Did I hear the odious name of Puisaye? The man's astounding impudence disgusts me.'

Mademoiselle looked up at him. Her eyes were cold. 'At least he is impudent to some purpose. He succeeds with Mr. Pitt where more self-sufficient gentlemen have failed.'

Bellanger's indulgent laugh deflected the rebuke. 'That merely condemns the discernment of Mr. Pitt. Notorious dullards, these English. Their wits are saturated by their fogs.'

'We enjoy their hospitality, Monsieur le Vicomte. You should remember it.'

He was unabashed. 'I do. And count it not the least of our misfortunes. We live here without sun, without fruit, without wine that a man may drink. It is of a piece with the rest that the apathy of the British Government towards our cause should have been conquered by this Monsieur de Puisaye, an upstart, a constitutionalist, an impure.'

'Yet the Princes, Monsieur le Vicomte, in their despair must clutch at straws.'

'That is well said, *pardi!*' swore Narbonne. 'In Puisaye they clutch at straw, indeed: at a man of straw.' He laughed explosively at his own wit, and Monsieur de Bellanger condescended also to be amused.

'Admirable, my dear Count. Yet Monsieur de Morlaix does not even smile.'

'Faith, no,' said Quentin. 'I confess to a failing. I can never perceive wit that has no roots in reason. We cannot hope to change a substance by changing the name of it.'

'I find you obscure, Monsieur Morlaix.'

'Let me help you. It cannot be witty to say that my sword is made of straw when it remains of steel.'

'And the application of that, if you please?'

'Why, that Monsieur de Puisaye, being a man of steel, does not become of straw from being called so.'

The cast with which the eyes of Monsieur de Narbonne were afflicted gave him now a sinister appearance. Bellanger breathed hard.

'A friend of yours, this notorious Count Joseph, I suppose.'

'I have never so much as seen him. But I have heard what he is doing, and I conceive that every gentleman in exile should be grateful.'

'If you were better informed upon the views that become a gentleman, Monsieur de Morlaix,' said Bellanger with his drawling insolence, 'you might hold a different opinion.'

18

'Faith, yes,' Narbonne agreed. 'A fencing-academy is hardly a school of honour.'

'If it were, messieurs,' said mademoiselle sweetly, 'I think that you might both attend it with profit.'

Narbonne gasped. But Bellanger carried it off with his superior laugh. *'Touché, pardi! Touché!'* He dragged Narbonne away.

'You are pert, Germaine'—her aunt's pursed lips reproved her. 'There is no dignity in pertness. Monsieur de Morlaix, I am sure, could answer for himself.'

'Alas, madame,' said Quentin, 'there was but one answer I could return to that, and, again, the disabilities of my profession silenced me.'

'Besides, sir, French swords are required for other ends. What regiment do you join?'

'Regiment?' He was at a loss.

'Of those that Monsieur de Puisaye is to take to France: the Loyal Emigrant, the Royal Louis, and the rest?'

'That is not for me, madame.'

'Not for you? A Frenchman? A man of the sword? Do you mean that you are not going to France?'

'I have not thought of it, madame. I have no interests to defend in France.'

Mademoiselle's eyes lost, he thought, some of the warmth in which they had been regarding him. 'There are nobler things than interest to be fought for. There is a great cause to serve; great wrongs to be set right.'

'That is for those who have been dispossessed; for those who have been driven into exile. In fighting for the cause of monarchy, they fight for the interests bound up with it. I am not of those, mademoiselle.'

'How, not of those?' asked madame. 'Are you not an *émigré* like the rest of us?'

'Oh, no, madame. I have lived in England since I was four years of age.'

He would not have failed to notice how that answer seemed to startle her had not mademoiselle commanded his attention. 'But you are entirely French,' she was insisting.

'In blood, entirely.'

'Then, do you owe that blood no duty? Do you not owe it to France to lend a hand in her regeneration?' Her eyes were challenging, imperious.

'I wish, mademoiselle, that I could answer with the enthusiasm you expect. But I am of a simple, truthful nature. These are matters that have never preoccupied me. You see, I am not politically minded.'

'This, monsieur, is less a question of politics than of ideals. You will not tell me that you are without these?'

'I hope not. But they are not concerned with government or forms of government.'

Madame interposed. 'How long do you say that you have been in England?'

'I came here with my mother, some four and twenty years ago, when my father died.'

'From what part of France do you come?'

'From the district of Angers.'

Madame seemed to have lost colour under her rouge. 'And your father's name?'

'Bertrand de Morlaix,' he answered simply, in surprise.

She nodded in silence, her expression strained.

'Now, that is very odd,' said mademoiselle, and looked at her aunt.

But Madame de Chesnières, paying no heed to her, resumed her questions. 'And madame your mother? She is still alive?'

'Alas, no, madame. She died a year ago.'

'But this is a catechism,' her niece protested.

'Monsieur de Morlaix will pardon me. And we detain him.' Her headdress quivered grotesquely from some agitation that was shaking her. 'Come, Germaine. Let us find Saint-Gilles.'

Under the suasion of her aunt's bony, ring-laden hand, Mademoiselle de Chesnières was borne away, taking with her all Quentin's interest in this gathering.

Lackeys moved through the chattering groups on the gleaming floor, bearing salvers of refreshments. Quentin accepted a glass of Sillery. Whilst he stood sipping it he became aware that across the crowded, brilliantly lighted room Madame de Chesnières' fan was pointing him out to two young men between whom she was standing. His host, the Duc de Lionne, seeing him alone, came to join him at that moment. The interest which made those young men crane their necks to obtain a better view of him led him to question the Duke upon their identity.

'But is it possible that you do not know the brothers Chesnières? Saint-Gilles, the elder, should interest a fencing-master. He is reckoned something of a swordsman. It has been said of him that he is the second blade in France.'

Quentin was amused rather than impressed. 'A daring claim. Rumour could not place him second unless it also named the first. Do you know, Monsieur le Duc, upon whom it has conferred that honour?'

'Upon his own cousin, Boisgelin, the heroic Royalist leader now in Brittany. Oh, but heroic in no other sense. A remorseless devil who has never scrupled to take advantage of his evil, deadly swordsmanship: that is to be an assassin. Boisgelin has already killed four men and made three widows. A bad man, the hero of Brittany. But then'—the Duke raised his slim shoulders —'the House of Chesnières does not produce saints. A tainted family. The last marquis was no better than an imbecile in his old age; the present one is shut up in a madhouse in Paris, and those gentlemen know how to profit by it.' His tone was contemptuous. 'He enjoys the immunity of his condition, and his estates are saved by it from the general confiscation. Those cousins of his live at ease here upon the revenues, and yet do nothing to ease the lot of their less fortunate fellow exiles. I do not commend their acquaintance to you, Morlaix. A tainted family, the family of Chesnières.'

CHAPTER 3

❦

The Brothers

IN THE week that followed, Mademoiselle de Chesnières was too often in Quentin's thoughts, and her cousins not at all. Yet it was these who were presently to force themselves upon his attention. They were brought to him on a Sunday, close upon noon, by the Baron de Fragelet, an habitué of the academy, a flippant, laughter-loving scatterbrain, youthful in all but years.

The day and the hour could not have been better chosen if it was desired to find Morlaix at leisure. Actually he had given some lessons, and, still wearing the high-buttoned white plastron above his black satin smalls, he was idling with O'Kelly, his chief assistant, in the bay of the window that overlooked his little garden, at the end of his main fencing-room.

In this bay, which was abnormally wide and deep, Quentin had fashioned a lounging-place, with deep chairs set about a round mahogany table, cushioned window-seats, and an Eastern rug or two, all in sybaritic contrast to the bare austerity of the fencing-room itself.

His servant Barlow had announced the Baron, and the Baron announced and presented his companions.

'I bring you two compatriots who conceive themselves your kinsmen, my dear Morlaix, and who think, consequently, that you should become acquainted. For myself I do not perceive the consequence, kinsmen being the misfortunes with which we are supplied at birth. I always say that provided I may choose my friends for myself, the Devil may have a kin for which I am not responsible.'

22

Morlaix came forward, leaving O'Kelly in the embrasure.

'I have not your experience, Baron. Fate has been sparing to me in the matter of kinsfolk.'

'Well, here's to supplement it.' And he named them: 'Monsieur Armand de Chesnières, Chevalier de Saint-Gilles, and his brother Constant.'

They were as dissimilar as brothers could be. Saint-Gilles was moderately tall, well-knit, and graceful, his face narrow and of an attractive regularity of feature, something marred by an expression of disdain. His younger brother towered by a half-head above him and was of a heavy, powerful build. He was black-haired and very swarthy, and his wide, coarse mouth was almost as thick in the lips as an Ethiopian's. Both displayed an affluence in their dress which reminded Quentin of Lionne's comment upon their resources, but whereas Saint-Gilles' neat figure was a mirror of elegance in a coat that was striped in two shades of blue, the modishness of Constant but stressed the clumsiness of his shape.

A harsh, domineering manner that went with the younger Chesnières' exterior was advertised as much by his readiness to answer for both as by his choice of terms.

'I'll not suppose the kinship, sir, more than that which is shared by all men of a common name, implying a common tribal origin. A good many Frenchmen bear the name of Morlaix. We, however, are Morlaix de Chesnières.'

'Whilst I, of course, am Morlaix of nowhere. Still, as a Morlaix I bid you welcome, as a compatriot I am at your service.'

He led them down the room to the embayed lounge, presented O'Kelly, proffered chairs, and dispatched Barlow for decanters.

The Chevalier de Saint-Gilles proved gracious. 'You are in great repute, sir, as a fencing-master.'

'You are very good.'

'Under royal patronage, even.'

'I have been fortunate.'

'I cannot forgive myself that I should have been six months in London without making your acquaintance and availing myself of the opportunities your school affords. In a modest way I am, myself, something of a swordsman.'

'Modesty, indeed,' laughed Fragelet, and Constant laughed with him.

'My school is at your disposal. You will meet many *émigrés* here; some who come to fence, and more who come simply to meet one another. You will also meet many Englishmen of birth whose sympathies are warmly enlisted by our exiled fellow-countrymen.'

'And others, I suppose,' said Constant with his sneering air. 'For there are plenty of the school of thought of Mr. Fox.'

Quentin smiled tolerantly. 'It is not for me to discriminate. Besides, I am of those who respect opinions even when I do not share them.'

'A suspiciously Republican sentiment,' said Saint-Gilles.

'Do not, I beg, account me a Republican merely because I seek to cultivate a sense of justice.'

'Acquired, I presume,' countered the younger Chesnières, his sneer now definite, 'from some of the levellers and Jacobins who are active here in England, and hope to set up the Tree of Liberty in Whitehall and the guillotine in Palace Yard.'

'Why, no.' Quentin remained unruffled. 'I do not think that I have been to school to them. Nor do I think that we need take them seriously. The English are of a model calm. It is a virtue that I seek to emulate.' He looked Constant between the eyes and pointed his remark by a little smile. 'Besides, they already possess a constitution.'

'A dishonour to the Crown,' snapped Constant, and then Fragelet cut into the discussion.

'They also possess a Society of the Friends of Man, which is busy spreading here the gospel according to those dirty evangelists, Marat and Robespierre.'

'Perhaps your British phlegm and sense of justice approve of that,' Constant taunted Quentin.

24

Saint-Gilles intervened. 'I am afraid, my dear Monsieur de Morlaix, that we are less than courteous. Forgive it on the score of our unhappy situation. We have unfortunately drifted to the fringe of a subject on which the feelings of all French *émigrés* are very tender; and where feelings are tender, restraint is difficult.'

'Whilst I need take no credit for finding it easy, since I am without politics.'

Barlow approached with the decanters, glasses, and a salver of macaroons.

O'Kelly, who, perched on the arm of a chair, had listened in an astonishment faintly tinged with indignation, jumped up to do the honours for Quentin, glad of the diversion.

'A glass of wine, Chevalier. It settles all arguments, so it does.'

But whilst he was filling the glasses, Constant came back to the subject. 'Is it possible that there should be a man who is without thought for the events in such a time as this?'

'Ah, pardon. I did not refer to events, but to the theories behind them.'

'Do you discriminate?'

'One must, I think. The theories were conceived by great minds, to right wrongs, to make a better world, to bring happiness to unfortunates who knew none. Unfortunately the execution of those theories has fallen into the hands of self-seeking rascals, who have perverted liberty into anarchy.'

'That,' said Saint-Gilles, 'in the circumstances is the best that could have happened. I'll not dispute with you on the quality of the minds that conceived the theories responsible for our ills. What matters to us is that the political scoundrels who have made themselves masters of the State are busily exterminating one another, and by the ineptitude of their misgovernment are hastening the day of reckoning; that is to say, the day of our return.'

'When it comes perhaps it will silence even Mr. Fox,' the Baron hoped. 'He's almost as mischievous here as was in France Mirabeau, whom in other ways he resembles. Mirabeau had the good taste to die before the harvest that he helped to sow. Mr. Fox would be better dead before he inspires any more Horne Tookes and Lord Edward Fitzgeralds.'

'The Government will know when to call a halt to their activities.'

'A wise government,' said the Chevalier, 'resists beginnings. Our Revolution teaches that.' He drained his glass, and rose. 'But we chatter and chatter under the influence of your enhanting hospitality, and I neglect the purpose of this disturbance of you. I came to enrol myself in your academy.'

'I am honoured.' Quentin, too, had risen. The others continued seated. 'We are a little crowded, although I have another fencing floor, beyond the antechamber, and another assistant besides O'Kelly here. But we'll find an hour for you, never fear.'

'That will be kind.' The Chevalier's eyes strayed down the long panelled room, whose only furniture were the benches upholstered in red leather set against the walls, and the trophies of foils and masks, gauntlets and plastrons at intervals above them. 'Shall we make essay now? The first lesson?'

'Now?'

'If not too inconvenient. A fencing-room affects me with longings.'

'Why, to be sure. There's a dressing-room there. O'Kelly, be so good as to find the Chevalier what he needs.'

When Saint-Gilles came back with mask and foil, his blue coat exchanged for a fencing-jacket that set off the compact neatness of him, the assistant's services were again required.

'O'Kelly will give you a bout, Chevalier.'

The Chevalier lost countenance. 'Ah . . . But . . . It is with you that I would measure myself, *cher maître*. I am of some force.'

Quentin laughed. 'So is O'Kelly, I assure you. He would not be my assistant else. He will give you all the work you'll need.'

The Irishman, who had already peeled off his coat, stood arrested. He was a spare, loose-limbed young man of thirty, red of hair and of a lean, pleasant, freckled countenance. His alert eyes were watchful.

'No doubt, no doubt. But it is with the master that I would test myself.' He smiled ingratiatingly. 'Will you not humour me, Monsieur?'

Quentin lounged forward, in scarcely dissembled reluctance.

'If you insist.'

O'Kelly handed him gauntlet, mask, and foil, and they took up their positions. The Baron retained his chair in the embrasure, but Constant de Chesnières came down to find a seat against the wall, whence he could observe the fencers.

In the first passes this man reputed the second blade in France certainly revealed himself for a swordsman of exceptional skill. As the bout proceeded, Constant's thick lips began to curl in a faintly sneering smile.

Soon the Chevalier had scored a hit in tierce following upon a feinte in the low lines, whereupon that ugly mouth of Constant's was stretched in a grin, which drew an answering grin from O'Kelly, who was observing him.

The fencers circled, and the Chevalier, pressing with speed and vigour, planted his button for the second time upon the master's breast, and in exactly the same manner.

'*Touché!*' he cried this time, and paused with a broad smile. 'I am not so rusty, after all.'

'Why, no,' Morlaix agreed pleasantly. 'That was very good. You do not overrate yourself.'

'Shall we try again?'

'By all means. Guard yourself.'

As the blades crossed, Morlaix disengaged and lunged vigorously under the Chevalier's guard. Saint-Gilles swept the blade clear and straightened his arm in a perfectly timed riposte. Morlaix parried it, but a moment later he was hit yet again. They fell apart.

'What do you say to that?' the Chevalier asked, and

to the alert O'Kelly there seemed to be a malicious satisfaction in his smile.

'Excellent,' Morlaix commended him. 'You are of considerable, indeed, of quite exceptional force, Chevalier. Your only real need is practice. There is little that I can teach you.'

Saint-Gilles' smile faded into blank astonishment at words which in the circumstances he accounted presumptuous. But it remained for the harsh contempt of his brother to express it.

'Is there anything you can teach him?'

O'Kelly permitted himself a laugh, that drew the haughty stare of the speaker.

'What amuses you, sir?'

Morlaix answered for him. 'The humour of the question. After all, to teach is my trade.'

Constant got up. 'And you flatter yourself that you could give lessons to my brother?'

'That is not to flatter myself. Monsieur de Saint-Gilles is of great force; yet there are faults I should be happy to correct.'

'In a swordsman who has shown you that he can hit you as he pleases?' Constant's tone could scarcely have been more offensive. But Morlaix's cool urbanity was not touched.

'Oh, no. Not as he pleases. As I please.'

'As you please! Really! Did it please you to be hit thrice without being able to hit him once?'

O'Kelly laughed again. 'Faith, it might be dangerous to take the ability for granted.'

Saint-Gilles spoke at last for himself. 'It seems idle to dispute. You spoke of faults in my fencing, sir. Would you point them out?'

'That is what I am for. I will demonstrate then. On guard! So. Now attack me as before.'

The Chevalier complied. He launched the botte with which he had twice got home. This time, however, the stroke was not only parried, but with a swift counter Morlaix hit the Chevalier vigorously over the heart.

He lowered his blade. 'That should not have happened,' was his quiet comment, to be hotly answered: 'It shall not happen again. On guard!'

The attack was repeated, with an increase of both vigour and speed. Yet once again it was met and answered by that hit in quarte.

The Chevalier fell back and spoke sharply in a manifest annoyance that was shared by his scowling, startled brother. 'But what is this, then? Were you trifling with me before?'

Morlaix was of a perfect amiability. 'You confuse a master-at-arms with an ordinary opponent, Chevalier. That is an effective botte of yours, to which I must suppose that you have given much practice. The fault in its execution lies in that you offer too much body. Keep yourself narrower. Then if you are hit it will be less fatally. On guard again. So. That is better, but not yet good enough. Swing your left shoulder farther back, more in line with your right. Now hold yourself so, whilst making your attack. *Allongez!* Excellent. For whilst I counter-parry it thus, and make my riposte on the binding of the blade, I can touch you only in quinte. Thus.'

The blades were lowered again and Morlaix expounded to the discomfited swordsman. 'That correction of your position to an unaccustomed one will have cramped you a little, so that you lost pace and force, and left it easier for the counter to get home. With practice, however, that will be overcome. When it is corrected, we will come to your other faults,' he promised, and added the cruellest cut of all: 'You display so much aptitude that it should be easy to render you really formidable.'

The Chevalier plucked the mask from his head, and displayed a face dark with chagrin. Formidable he had long been accounted and had accounted himself. It was difficult to preserve his urbanity whilst feeling himself birched like a schoolboy. He contrived to force a laugh.

'You teach me that mastery, after all, is for masters.' He turned, still laughing, to his scowling brother. 'For a moment I think we were in danger of forgetting it.'

'That,' said Constant, without mercy, 'is because

you've deceived the world with the pretence that you are a swordsman.'

They conceived themselves invited to laugh, and did so, whilst Morlaix defended the Chevalier. 'It is no pretence. I have some swordsmen in my academy, but not one against whom I should hesitate to match your brother.'

'What good is that?' was the ill-humoured grumble.

'Good? It is very good. Place yourself in my care, Chevalier; and if in a month I do not make a master of you I'll shut my academy.'

When with many compliments they had taken their departure, 'You'ld be a fool to do that,' said O'Kelly.

'Why so?'

'Sure, now you'ld be teaching him to cut your own throat. What's their quarrel with you, Quentin?'

'Quarrel? I've never seen them till this day.'

'D'ye tell me that? Well, well.' O'Kelly laughed. 'Faith, ye've cut a comb very prettily this morning. It was amusing to see his lordship's arrogance diminished. They're all alike, these French fops, in their vanity. It helps one to understand how necessary they made their Revolution. But—devil take me!—they learn nothing from it, least of all their own empty worthlessness. Anyhow,' he ended, 'I'ld like to know what Messieurs de Chesnières can have against you.'

'What maggot's astir under your red thatch, Ned?'

'A suspicion of what brought them here this morning. Whilst you were busy with the Chevalier, I was watching his blackavisaged brother. His satisfaction at supposing the Chevalier your master was as ferocious as his rage when you demonstrated that he wasn't.'

'That's natural in ruffled vanity.'

'It's natural in disappointment, too. I'm a fool if they didn't come here to take your measure.'

'But to what end?'

'Do I know that now? But I'll be sworn 'twas to no good end.'

Morlaix stared incredulity into the pleasant, freckled face of his assistant, and loosed a laugh.

'Ye can be as merry as ye please, Quentin. But it wasn't a fencing-lesson they came for. I know hate when I see it, and I never saw it plainer than in the eyes of Monsieur Constant. Oh, ye may laugh now. But here's a prophecy for you: You'll not be seeing either of those gentlemen in your school again. It's not lessons they want from you.'

CHAPTER 4

The Heritage

A LETTER worded with portentous obscurity took Monsieur de Morlaix on a blustering morning of May to the dingy office of Messrs. Sharpe, Kellaway and Sharpe in Lincoln's Inn.

He was received by Mr. Edgar Sharpe with a deference such as that worthy man of law had never shown him on any former visit. A clerk was required to dust a chair before Monsieur de Morlaix could be permitted to sit. Mr. Sharpe, himself, remained standing as if in an august presence.

The attorney, a large, rubicund man in a grizzle wig, of a benignity of expression that would have adorned a bishop or a butler, hummed and purred over him as a preliminary.

'It is . . . Let me see, dear sir. It will be fully a year since I last enjoyed the satisfaction of seeing you.'

'It is good of you so to describe it. Myself in your place I shouldn't call it a satisfaction, much less an enjoyment.'

Misunderstanding him, Mr. Sharpe put away his smile. 'But how true, sir! How very true! You do well to reprobate my terms. Most ill-chosen. For the occasion— I should say, the sad occasion—was the lamentable

31

decease of madame your mother, and the settlement of her little estate, in which matter it is a satisfaction to remember that I had the . . . ah . . . honour of being of some service to you.'

So much pronounced by way of funeral oration, Mr. Sharpe permitted the smile to return. 'I'll take the liberty of saying, sir, that you look well; extremely well. It suggests—and I trust it rightly suggests—that you have not found life too . . . ah . . . onerous in the intervening year.'

'My academy prospers.' A smile lengthened the ironic mouth. 'In a quarrelsome world there is always work for men of my profession, as of yours.'

For a moment Mr. Sharpe was in danger of manifesting indignation at an association of professions between which he could perceive no similarity. But he recovered betimes.

'Most gratifying,' he purred. 'Especially in days when so many of your fellow-exiles are suffering want.'

'Faith, sir, as for my exile, I bear it with comfortable unconsciousness. The real exile for me would lie in leaving England.'

'Yet that, sir, is something to which you must have been brought up to be prepared.'

'Having nothing, I was brought up to be prepared for anything.'

Mr. Sharpe sucked in his breath on a whinnying laugh at what he conceived a flash of humour. 'Well, well, sir. I have news for you.' His rubicund countenance became solemn once more. 'News of the greatest consequence. Your brother is dead.'

'Lord, sir! Did I have a brother?'

'Is it possible that you are not aware of it?'

'And not yet persuaded of it, Mr. Sharpe.'

'Dear me! Dear me!'

'There is some error in your information. I know myself to be my mother's only child.'

'Ah! But you had a father, sir.'

'I believe it's usual,' said Quentin.

'And your mother was his second wife. He was the

32

Marquis of Chavaray. Bertrand de Morlaix de Chesnières, Marquis of Chavaray.'

The young man's grey eyes opened wide in stupefaction. Both names had lately been impressed upon him. Words spoken by the Duc de Lionne came floating back into his memory. Then the lawyer claimed his further attention. He was consulting a sheet which he had taken from his writing table.

'His elder son, your brother, Étienne de Morlaix de Chesnières, the last Marquis, died two months ago in a nursing-home in Paris. The nursing-home of a Doctor Bazire, in the rue du Bac.'

Morlaix reflected mechanically that this would be the madhouse to which Lionne had alluded.

'He died without issue,' the attorney concluded; 'therefore I salute you, my lord, as the present Marquis of Chavaray and heir to half a province. And I think that I may say without fear of contradiction that few dukedoms in France are as wealthy as this marquisate of yours. I have a schedule here of your exact possessions.'

There was a long silence, at the end of which Morlaix shrugged and laughed. 'Sir, sir! There is, of course, some grievous error. These Chesnières bear the name of Morlaix. Hence the confusion. It is . . .'

'There is no confusion. No error.' Mr. Sharpe was primly emphatic. 'It amazes me that you should suppose it; that you should not know, at least, that your name, too, is Chesnières.'

'But it cannot be, or I should know it. What purpose . . .'

Again he was interrupted. 'By your leave, sir. By your leave. It is on your baptismal certificate, of which I have here a certified copy, as well as the other documents necessary to establish your identity beyond possibility of doubt. The troubles of the times and the difficulties of communication in view of the war with France are responsible for their delay in reaching me. They come to me with instructions to communicate with you at once if you should still be alive, from a lawyer of Angers named Lesdiguières.'

'Lesdiguières!' Morlaix sat up. 'That was my mother's maiden name.'

'I am aware of it, of course. And the writer is her brother, your lordship's uncle, who is prepared to take all necessary steps to establish you in your heritage.'

Morlaix passed a hand across his brow. 'This . . . I find it all very difficult to believe. If it is correct, my mother would have been Marquise de Chavaray. And that she never was.'

'Pardon. She was, indeed, but did not choose so to call herself. It . . . ah . . . frankly now, it astonishes me to find your lordship so . . . ah . . . uninformed upon your own self. But I think I can throw some light on the matter, although I confess that there is much that I may be unable to explain.

'It is no less than twenty-five years since Madame la Marquise—that is, madame your mother—was brought to me by her distant kinsman and my very good client, the late Joshua Patterson of Esher in the County of Surrey. The Marquis Bertrand de Chavaray had then been dead six months, and, for some reason never disclosed to me, his widow had decided not only to leave France, but to renounce the advantages of fortune, to which as Dowager Marchioness of Chavaray she was entitled. Her maternal grandmother had been English, and in seeking what I may presume to term shelter here with her English kinsfolk, she brought with her no property or means of livelihood beyond her jewels. These, however, were considerable, and they were sold for some six thousand pounds, and on the meagre interest of that sum, this lady, who was as prudent as—if you will permit me to say so—she was beautiful and wise, maintained herself and your lordship, and provided for your education. But I am wandering already into matters that will be known to you.

'My present instructions from Monsieur de Lesdiguières, or Citizen Lesdiguières, as I suppose he will now be termed in the crazy jargon that prevails in France, are, as I have said, to seek you out, and to provide you with all additional documents necessary to you in claiming your heritage.'

'My heritage?' Morlaix was smiling a little scornfully. 'What is this heritage, assuming that the fantastic tale is true? A barren title. London is full of them today. There are *émigrés* marquises who hire themselves out to dress salads, teach dancing, and do needlework. Shall I add to them a marquis who is a fencing-master? I think I shall be less ridiculous as Monsieur de Morlaix.'

Lawyer-like, in answering him Mr. Sharpe ignored all that was irrelevant.

'I have said that the Marquisate of Chavaray is richer than any dukedom in France. You may examine for yourself the schedule of its vast acres, its towns and hamlets, its pasture and arable, its moorlands and forests, its farms, vineyards, châteaux, and mills. It is all here.' He tapped a bulk of papers.

'You mean, of course, if the monarchy is restored?'

'Not so. Not so.'

Mr. Sharpe had recourse to the lengthy communication from the Citizen Lesdiguières. This disclosed a situation very different from Morlaix's reasonable assumption.

The late Marquis, it transpired, being a half-crippled invalid, had lived retired and quiet, aloof from politics, in a province which regarded the excesses of the Revolution with anything but favour. Of a kindly, gentle nature, he had been indulgently regarded by his tenantry. It would also seem that he was of Republican tendencies, and already before the Revolution he had renounced all those harsher feudal rights so largely responsible for that terrible upheaval. In the day of wrath he reaped as he had sown. Whilst the rest of the family of Chesnières had emigrated, he had remained quietly at Chavaray, and had been left undisturbed until after the King's death in '93. Then, when the greedy sanguinocrats took measures to deal with those nobles who by remaining on their estates had avoided sequestration, he was arrested on a trumped-up charge of being in correspondence with his *émigrés* cousins. It did not matter that there was no proof. But it did matter that he disposed of gold and of a faithful steward who knew how to employ it. In the corrupt state of France there was nothing that money could not buy. For a sum of ten thousand livres in gold to the Public Accuser, the steward, one Lafont, obtained that Étienne de Chesnières should be certified insane. It was an easy matter, considering his physical condition; but it would not in any case have been difficult; for there were many instances in which, when money was available, this had been done.

Étienne de Chesnières was transferred from the Prison of the Carmes to the private asylum of Doctor Bazire, where he found others, much the same as he was, who were prolonging their days by the same means. They had to pay handsomely for the privilege. The doctor was exorbitant in his charges, and he would not keep a patient for a day longer than his dues were paid. Lafont continued to provide those demanded for his master, out of the revenues of lands that could not legally be sequestrated until the Marquis had been brought to trial and convicted.

And in the end, untried and unconvicted, he had died in that house in the rue du Bac, and his estates continued free. They were also available to his heir, provided that Quentin were this heir. For, whilst in general all Frenchmen now out of France were considered to be *émigrés* and outlawed, yet by one of the Convention's statutes, quoted in full by Lesdiguières, exception was made in favour of such as were professionally engaged abroad before 1789. Under this statute, Quentin de Morlaix was given six months from the death of his newly discovered brother in which to repatriate himself. Only should he neglect to do so would he, after the lapse of that time, be adjudged an *émigré* and subjected to the penalties of that situation.

Monsieur de Morlaix received this information with a smile.

'Whilst if I return to claim the property I shall

merely have stepped into the shoes of the late Marquis. I shall be arrested on suspicion of correspondence with my *émigrés* kinsmen, convicted, and sent to the guillotine, unless I too get myself certified insane and lodged with Doctor Bazire. Faith, it's an enviable heritage, Mr. Sharpe. I am to be congratulated.'

'But, my dear sir, a great fortune is concerned. We have the word of the Citizen Lesdiguières that the risk in your case is negligible.'

'It exists nevertheless.' He got up. 'You conceive, sir, that all this leaves me a little bewildered. I need to consider; to adjust my mind. You shall hear from me. But I think I shall decide to carry my head safely under a hat rather than see it in Sanson's basket under a coronet.'

CHAPTER 5

❧❀❧

The Acknowledgment

A TAINTED family, the Duc de Lionne had said. How much, wondered Morlaix, had that taint to do with the mystery that enveloped him? How much had it to do with the visit paid him by the brothers Chesnières? Ten days were sped since that visit, and the brothers had not reappeared in Bruton Street. The Chevalier de Saint-Gilles was the next heir to this Marquisate of Chavaray, to which Morlaix had so unexpectedly succeeded. Setting that aside, there was a danger that this succession might make an end of those revenues from Chavaray upon which the Duc de Lionne had informed him that the Chesnières were living. Here was something to colour those suspicions of O'Kelly's, which had seemed so fantastic. Could it be that the Chevalier, already informed of the death of Étienne de Chesnières, had desired to test Morlaix's strength, with a view, perhaps, to picking a quarrel with him and disposing of him in a legitimate manner?

Morlaix cursed the Marquisate of Chavaray and the inheritance which had brought him such odious thoughts and marred the peace of mind upon which he set so high a value. He found it peculiarly ironical that the station he had desired for himself—so vainly, as it then seemed—when announcing his name and quality to Germaine de Chesnières, should prove so disturbing when it was so unexpectedly thrust upon him.

He was fully informed by now touching the family of which he had become the head. His father, Bertrand de Morlaix de Chesnières, at the age of seventy-four had married in second nuptials the girl of eighteen who had been Quentin's mother. Bertrand's only brother, Gaston, had had three children. Of the elder of these, who was also a Gaston de Chesnières, were born Armand, the present Chevalier de Saint-Gilles, and his brother Constant. Germaine was the only child of the second son, Claude de Chesnières, who by marriage had acquired the considerable contiguous property of Grands Chesnes, to which Germaine was now the heiress. She was, therefore, their cousin-german, whilst all three were the second cousins of Quentin himself. The view that he must take of them seemed to hang upon whether they were aware of the relationship in which he stood to them. Meanwhile he must resist the hateful suspicion that if that knowledge was possessed by the brothers it was also shared by Germaine and by her, for the unworthy purposes of her cousins, left unacknowledged to him.

This was something that he hoped that circumstances would disclose to him. In that hope, he kept his counsel, and pursued the normal tenor of his ways.

Some three mornings later, passing, in an interval between lessons, into the antechamber, as was his habit, to greet the company assembled there, he espied to his amazement in that chattering throng Mademoiselle de Chesnières. He made his way to her at once.

'My house is honoured, mademoiselle.'

She sank before him in a curtsey. 'It was inevitable that sooner or later, sir, I should come to do homage to your fame. I have to thank Madame de Liancourt.'

'You mean that I have.' His eyes were upon her with a singular searching gravity.

The little Duchess surged at her elbow, with Bellanger in attendance. 'A shameless intrusion, Monsieur de Morlaix. But naught would content the child but that she must see for herself the most famous rendezvous in London.'

Mademoiselle's cheeks flushed under his steady glance. A little frown flickered between her brows. She was quick to protest. 'Oh, but not all idle curiosity.'

'I should be proud to think that interest had some part in it. But perhaps you come as the deputy of your family.'

'A deputy?' Again her brows were wrinkled, her eyes questioning.

'I have been expecting Monsieur de Saint-Gilles to come again. He was proposing to enter my academy.'

'He has been here?'

'What's to surprise you, mademoiselle?' wondered Bellanger. 'Sooner or later the Académie Morlaix is the Mecca of every *émigré*.'

'But odd that he should not have told us.'

'A matter too insignificant, perhaps.' Morlaix was smiling, yet still she found his eyes disturbingly watchful. 'The only oddness is that he should not have returned, having engaged himself to do so.'

'Perhaps I can explain that. My cousin has received a summons from Holland, from Monsieur de Sombreuil, to join his regiment there. In these last days he has been preparing for departure.'

'All is clear, then,' said Morlaix.

'Save the discourtesy of not informing you.'

'Oh, that!' Morlaix shrugged. 'One does not stand on ceremony with fencing-masters. Monsieur de Saint-Gilles scarcely owes me so much.'

She flushed, in annoyance this time. 'You do yourself injustice, Monsieur de Morlaix. Besides, the question is one of what he owes to himself.'

O'Kelly put his head round the door. 'Will you be coming, Quentin? His Highness is waiting for you.'

'Most apt,' the Duchess laughed, a dimple in each soft, round cheek. 'The Prince to wait upon the prince of fencing-masters. France is honoured in you, Monsieur de Morlaix.'

He was bowing to them. 'Give me leave, ladies. Barlow will supply your needs. Pray command him. You will find friends here.' His hand indicated the little groups of idlers. 'His Highness will not fence for more than twenty minutes. Let me hope to find you here when the lesson is over. I leave them in your care, Vicomte.'

'But who am I,' Bellanger deprecated, with a hint of tartness, 'to serve as deputy for the prince of fencing-masters?'

Morlaix did not stay to answer. With here a bow and there a lift of the hand to answer those who greeted him, he sped to his royal pupil.

When he came back, Mademoiselle de Chesnières was no longer there, and he was left wondering whether he deplored this more for its own sake or because it deprived him of the chance of further probing.

The opportunity to probe, however, was not long to be denied him.

Two days later there came to him a note from Madame de Chesnières.

'Monsieur my cousin,' she wrote, 'we discover that you have been less than frank with us. Pray come and sup with us tomorrow night, so that you may make me your apologies. You may send an answer by my messenger.' Followed her signature and an address in Carlisle Street, and that was all.

It was a communication at once puzzling and enlightening. His hinted lack of frankness explained itself, and from the rest he gathered that the masks were to be off. What he could not surmise was why this particular moment should have been chosen for that revelation. So he went on the morrow to discover.

He found them nobly housed in that still fashionable quarter, and he was amused to think that these haughty cousins maintained at his charges so handsome an establishment, since it was by revenues properly belonging to him and improperly deflected to them that they supported it.

A white-stockinged footman, liveried and powdered, conducted him up the softly carpeted staircase, and throwing wide the doors of the drawing-room startled him by the announcement:

'Monsieur le Marquis de Chavaray.'

He had dressed himself with that care for his appearance which was amongst his qualities, in his black and silver, with a foam of lace at throat and wrists and the light dusting of powder to his hair, and moving with his lithe swordsman's grace, he stepped into the view of the waiting company a figure to fit the announcement.

Madame de Chavaray rustled forward, her sons moving more slowly to follow, whilst mademoiselle remained in the background beside a slight, short young man of a lively, eager countenance.

'Shall I forgive you your deception, Marquis?' Madame was archly simpering.

He bowed over her hand. 'I practised none, madame.'

'Oh, fie! Did you not deny that you were a Chesnières?'

'I merely did not assert it, and that because I was not aware of it.'

'Not aware of it?' Saint-Gilles thrust in. 'But how is that possible?'

'Just as it was possible for you to lie in the same ignorance,' he answered, looking the Chevalier between the eyes.

'Ah, no, no. It is scarcely the same thing. A man must know who he is where others may not.'

'You may accept my word for it that it was not in my knowledge,' said Quentin, without offering to explain, and a touch of hauteur made a barrier to demands for it.

41

'But clearly you know it now,' observed Constant.

'I learnt it within a few days of being honoured by your visit.' And point-blank, he asked: 'How long has it been known to you?'

'Let the Chevalier de Tinténiac answer that,' said Gilles, and with a gesture inviting forward the slight stranger, presented him.

No more than the name was necessary to make him known even to one so aloof from politics as Quentin. Wherever *émigrés* gathered in those days no name was more famous than that of Tinténiac, the dashing, daring gallant Breton Royalist, hero of a dozen battles, who had been the lieutenant of the great Marquis de La Rouërie in the organization of the Royalist forces of Brittany, and was now lieutenant to La Rouërie's successor, the Comte de Puisaye.

Alert and quick of movement as he was neat of figure, Tinténiac came forward with mademoiselle.

'I brought the news of Étienne de Chesnières' death from France two days ago, Monsieur le Marquis.' And he added: 'I have just arrived, and I made haste to felicitate the Chevalier de Saint-Gilles, believing him to be the heir. Instead, monsieur, permit me now to offer these felicitations to you.'

'You are gracious, sir.' They bowed mutually.

For a moment Quentin felt himself shamed for having harboured suspicions so unworthy. Then he remembered that it was now close upon three months since Étienne's death, and thought he understood why Saint-Gilles had chosen to let Tinténiac answer for him. That Tinténiac had brought the news he could well believe. But that it was known long before Tinténiac brought it he must believe also. Saint-Gilles, observing a queer punctilio, would not utter a falsehood which he would not hesitate to leave to be inferred.

'It is almost odd that in close upon three months no word of it should have come to you from Angers.' Quentin was thinking of Lafont, the steward of Chavaray from whom his cousins received supplies. His tone, however, was casually innocent of implications.

'Scarcely odd,' smiled Saint-Gilles, 'when you consider the difficulties of communication between two countries now at war. There are—alas!—few Tinténiacs to brave these dangerous crossings.'

'What I find more odd,' said mademoiselle, 'is that knowing this when I came to your academy, you said no word of it. Indeed, I seem to recall a false humility, an insistence upon the negligible station of a fencing-master.'

'That, mademoiselle, is because such my station must continue. This succession . . .' He waved it away. 'What is it in these days? So nominal as not to be worth proclaiming.'

Madame and her sons all spoke at once.

They were aghast. They did not understand. How could he describe it as nominal, when those vast estates but awaited his claim to them? He answered, laughing, much as he had answered Sharpe.

'You seem to suggest that I should cross to France, so that there I may choose between being guillotined or shut up in a madhouse.'

They were vehement in their protests. They cited the law which so strongly favoured him as one established abroad before '89. Was it possible that because of idle fears, a negligible risk, he would suffer the great estates of Chavaray to pass into the national possession, as must happen if he did not prefer his claim?

'Will you guarantee that they will not so pass if I do prefer it? Is it so difficult in France today to trump up charges against a man of great possessions?' He smiled. 'If there must be a confiscation, I would rather that it be of Chavaray than of my head.'

Tinténiac was amused. Mademoiselle watched Quentin gravely. As for the others, their looks reflected no satisfaction.

'You cannot have considered, my dear cousin,' Saint-Gilles told him in a tone of remonstrance, 'that you owe a duty to the house of which you are now the head.'

'Does that duty include rendering myself a headless head?'

43

'Does a trifle frighten you, then?' wondered Constant, with his ready sneer.

'The guillotine is not a trifle when looked at from the lunette. But frighten is a word I do not like. And I have never reckoned folly to be a part of valour.'

'It is not a folly, sir,' Constant retorted, 'to fulfill the trust that comes to you. For you are no more than a trustee, a life tenant of Chavaray. To take the title and to be afraid to take the estates is to make yourself an object of derision. To be Marquis of nothing is to be a Marquis *pour rire,* a Marquis of . . . of Carabas.'

'That is precisely why I continue to be simply and humbly Morlaix the fencing-master. I had no thought to proclaim myself Marquis of anything. That explains, I hope, my reticence to you, mademoiselle my cousin. I am content with my humble estate.'

'But you no longer have the right to be,' Constant insisted. 'To make no effort to save Chavaray from confiscation, to allow it to pass out of the family, is to be false to the trust imposed upon you, to take no thought for those who are to come after you.'

Quentin's eyes strayed slowly to Saint-Gilles. Under his quiet smile, Saint-Gilles started and reddened.

'I read your thought, sir. It is scarcely worthy. I am on the point of departure for Holland, to join Sombreuil's army, destined to raise in France the royal standard. My brother Constant will go from England with the Loyal Emigrant, of which regiment he is an officer. We go to fight a forlorn hope . . .'

'Faith, not so forlorn,' Tinténiac interjected.

'Brave hearts may not ordinarily admit it. But the moment is not ordinary. We go to offer up our lives upon the altar of the cause to which our birth compels us, as it compels you, Monsieur le Marquis, to offer everything. So that it is unlikely that we shall be of those who come after you.'

'*Morituri te salutant,*' murmured Quentin to that lofty farewell of one about to die.

Anger flashed from the eyes of Constant. But Saint-Gilles merely smiled. 'Regard it so if you choose. It is none so wide, perhaps, of the fact.' And with malice, as

44

it seemed to Quentin, he added: 'Remains our Cousin Germaine.'

At that she protested sharply: 'Nay, nay. Leave me out of your accounts.'

Quentin turned to her. 'Does mademoiselle desire me to make this attempt?'

It was a moment before she answered him, a moment in which she considered him with steady brooding eyes. 'And if I did? Would you go?'

He answered her almost before he knew what he had said. 'Unhesitatingly.'

'Then in God's name bid him,' sneered Constant, 'for the honour of the name.'

Quentin wheeled sharply on the brothers. 'I'll make a bargain with you. For the honour of the name.' There was a sudden queer touch of exaltation in his manner. 'Renounce your rights of succession in favour of Mademoiselle de Chesnières, and I will start for France as soon as it can be arranged.'

They stared at him dumbfounded. Tinténiac, with arms akimbo and eyes mischievously bright, considered them expectantly.

'Well?' Quentin demanded. 'Do you hesitate to forgo chances that you account so slender, for the honour of the name?'

Saint-Gilles made a gesture of impatience, and half-turned from him.

'The proposal is scarcely a sane one.'

'A fantastically mad one,' Constant added.

'It is one that answers you, I think, when you tax me with a lack of courage,' said Quentin. 'On those terms I'll prove my courage to you.'

'Oh, no, no,' madame was interposing. 'No one questions your courage, my dear cousin. It is your . . . your . . .' She struggled for words, her fingers writhing as if in quest of them. 'It is your sense of . . . of the Chesnières tradition that is lacking.'

'I was not reared in it, you see.'

'That's true, *pardi!*' swore Constant, his tone offensive. His temper was on edge, as it had been on that Sunday in the fencing-school when Quentin had demonstrated his mastery, and anger was an emotion that Constant had never learnt to curb or dissemble.

Mademoiselle intervened. She was a trifle disdainful of them all. 'I think this has gone far enough. We have little right to be so importunate with our cousin. It is for him to decide what he will do.'

'And Monsieur le Marquis decides that he will remain a Marquis de Carabas.'

'A fencing-master, Monsieur de Chesnières; a fencing-master,' Quentin corrected him. 'An honourable profession, although it compels a man to labour under disabilities. For instance, it is not for him to meet insult as might another. But then he scarcely needs to heed the insults of any man who, realizing this, still offers them.'

He spoke easily, even sweetly; but his words had the effect of freezing the brothers into a glowering silence. Tinténiac came laughing to the rescue.

'He can always, like the great Danet, choose weapons other than those of his craft. There was a boaster in Paris who took advantage of him too often. One day, Danet, being out of patience, turned upon him. "I may not send you the length of my sword," said he, "but I tell you that you are a fool and a coward, and if you want satisfaction you shall have it with a pack of cards and a single pistol. We'll cut once, and the man who cuts the higher card shall have the pistol. He may then please himself whether and how he shoots the loser." The fellow, being the fool and coward that Danet called him, extricated himself on the pretext that those were not the weapons of a gentleman. "But for the future," said Danet, "let it be known that they are the weapons of a fencing-master." He was given peace from the fellow after that.'

It was a timely turning of the conversation. But the remainder of the evening was scarcely a happy one. A restraint remained; it brooded over the supper table, nor did the flow of the wine appreciably relieve it. Inevitably their talk turned to Tinténiac's Royalist activities, and the little Chevalier was eloquent upon the valour of the Chouans and their skill in the guerrilla warfare they were conducting whilst impatient for the general rising. But even this was productive of some acrid passages. The brothers permitted themselves to voice the disparagement of Puisaye so common then among the *émigrés* nobles. Tinténiac, as Puisaye's lieutenant and close friend, could not let it pass in silence. He insisted with feeling upon the great work of Puisaye, not only underground in the West of France, but with the British Government, whose support he alone had known how to enlist on behalf of the Princes.

Upon this Saint-Gilles was uncompromising. 'I take shame that it should be so, Chevalier, that the cause of the *noblesse* of France should be controlled by an upstart, a Republican, a swindling adventurer, a mountebank.'

Tinténiac smiled patiently. 'You merely repeat the abuse of those who would have done what he has done but that they have not his courage, his energy, or his address.' He sighed. 'It is a poor recompense for such heroic labours. An upstart, you say. But his birth is as good as yours or mine.'

Saint-Gilles raised his brows. His brother laughed coarsely. Tinténiac, however, persisted, unruffled. 'He is called a Republican. A good many gentlemen have been that who have now seen the error of it. You'll not deny that he has atoned.'

'We are not yet at the end,' grumbled Constant. 'His big promises are still to be fulfilled.'

'Be sure he will fulfil them. His plans are too soundly laid for failure. And then, a mountebank, you say. I pray God that I may prove just such a mountebank as he. To the peasants of Brittany, Normandy, and Maine, the Count Joseph, as they call him, is a god. A lift of his hand can raise three hundred thousand men who are ready to follow him into hell. It is given to few of us to accomplish that. And those who hope to see the monarchy restored in France, believe me, will be sadly at fault if they do not take Monsieur de Puisaye seriously, and support him loyally.'

'He possesses a warm advocate,' mademoiselle commended him smiling, and Quentin, observing her, admired her fineness.

'A worshipper, mademoiselle.'

Saint-Gilles laughed. 'It becomes a religious question, then. And those are not for discussion at table.'

But the restraint abode, and Quentin welcomed the evening's end, and the hackney coach that was fetched to take him home. It was only then, when on the point of leaving, that for one brief moment in the drawing-room he found himself alone with Germaine, away from the group into which the other four had fallen.

'I have the misfortune,' he said, 'to be under your disapproval.'

'Shall I disapprove of what I do not understand? I am not by nature rash, I hope, monsieur my cousin.'

The sweetness he discovered in her brought a wistfulness into his glance.

'You find me obscure?'

'Indeed, mysterious.'

He shook his head. 'The mystery is not in me. It is about me.'

'It is as I thought.' She nodded the fair head so admirably poised on her white neck. 'You suspect our intentions. I find that odd, for I cannot conceive the shape of your suspicions. It is not good to be suspicious, Cousin Quentin. The suspicious are seldom happy, for they are seldom at peace. Suspicion creates devils to torment us.'

'It is not in my nature if I know myself. But neither, I hope, am I prone to be credulous, for that is to stumble into pitfalls.'

'There are no pitfalls here,' she answered him.

'Do you assure me of it?'

His tone drew her eyes to his once more. 'Would my assurance satisfy you?'

'In all things,' he answered, with a fervour that visibly startled her.

She was suddenly very grave. A tinge of colour mounted to her cheeks. 'Then . . . then I must go warily. I will answer you that I know of none, and can imagine none.'

She saw a light as of quickened, exultant life, leap to the grey eyes that pondered her. 'That answers for yourself. And it is all I need. The rest are naught.'

It was a reply that left her frowning as her aunt came to join them.

CHAPTER 6

Monsieur de Puisaye

AT PARTING that night with Tinténiac, Quentin expressed the hope of another meeting at which their chance acquaintance might be improved. So cordially was it received by the Chevalier that Quentin counted upon seeing it fulfilled. But hardly as promptly as it occurred. For that was no later than the following evening, just as the academy was about to close.

Tinténiac came accompanied by a man of commanding presence, very tall, loose-limbed, and erect, carrying his handsome head with an air of conscious pride, and moving with a measured grace that was almost histrionic. From his manifest vigour, his age might have been guessed at forty, though in reality he counted some ten years more. His face, tanned by exposure, was long and narrow, lofty of brow and square of chin. The eyes, of so deep a blue as to seem almost black, were set deep under upward slanting eyebrows that rendered sardonic his expression. The mouth was straight and firm, but when the lips parted in a smile, this brought so much gentle charm into his countenance that it seemed to change completely from the disdainful sternness of its repose. He wore his own hair, of a reddish-brown and turning grey at the temples, in a simple queue. His dress, from his wide-brimmed black hat to his Hessian boots, could not have been more

49

simple than it was, yet as worn by him it carried a
suggestion of elaborateness. His riding-coat of a light
blue with silver buttons was very full in the skirt, and
his white nankeens outlined the vigorous muscles of his
long legs.

Morlaix, still in his fencing garments, observed his
stately advance down that long room with an admiring
interest quickened at closer quarters by a something
familiar in the man's face, an elusive likeness to someone he had once known.

Then Tinténiac was presenting him.

'You'll account that I have lost no time in seeking
you. It is due to the insistence of Monsieur le Comte de
Puisaye, who believes that he can serve you.'

'And certainly desires to do so,' said the stranger,
sweeping him a bow.

'Monsieur de Puisaye!' Surprised, Morlaix looked
with deep interest upon this man who might be said to
hold the West of France, and therefore the fortunes of
the monarchy, in his hands; this man who, offering
himself to Pitt, not as a suppliant, but as a valuable
ally in the war with the French Republic, had persuaded the British minister to lend his powerful aid to the
enterprise that was afoot, and who, being appointed by
the Princes Commander-in-Chief of the Royal and
Catholic Army of Brittany, was become an object of
bitter jealousy to the *émigré* nobility. Despite the fact
that the aim of his labours was to end their exile and
restore them to their possessions, they could not forgive
him for achieving what none of them was capable of
achieving, or for being constrained, by the rank bestowed upon him by the Princes, to serve under his
orders.

Whilst Morlaix considered him with the interest his
fame deserved, he became conscious of being himself
the object of a scrutiny more intent and searching than
he could remember ever to have experienced. Then the
smile broke, with all its singular charm, and a lean
hand was holding Quentin's in a grip that proclaimed
the Count's unusual vigour.

'On my soul, Fate is hardly to be forgiven for having

left me unconscious of your existence in all my comings and goings of the past six months. Only by merest chance do I discover it now from Tinténiac.'

Quentin, so schooled in imperturbability that it was wrought into the nature of him, went near, and unaccountably, to embarrassment. It may have been due to the unwavering, insistent stare of those dark eyes.

'You desire to flatter me, monsieur. My obscure existence can scarcely matter to you.'

'Aha! There speaks your ignorance.' His hand was at last relinquished. 'You are to regard me as an old friend, *pardi!* For your mother's people were my friends when I was a lad in garrison at Angers more than a quarter of a century ago. There is nothing for which the child of Margot Lesdiguières may not count upon me. *Voilà!* Now you begin to understand the eagerness with which I seek you, the vexation at not having sought you sooner.' Those smouldering eyes were considering him again. 'Not to have known! Ah, devil take me, but that is unforgivable.' Then he laughed, and clapped Quentin's shoulder with a familiarity that jarred the fencing-master. 'But we'll repair that now. We must become good friends, great friends, is it not?'

'Naturally, monsieur. A friend of my mother's . . . Saving for those she made in England, you are the first I have ever known. I have to thank you, Monsieur de Tinténiac. Our meeting yesterday was more fortunate even than I accounted it.'

Puisaye paced away a little, looking about him. 'You prosper, I learn. You enjoy even royal patronage. I find you well established, oh, and well housed. That is excellent. Excellent!'

Quentin reflected that he would have admired a greater reserve. He cavilled that Monsieur de Puisaye put himself too readily at his ease, presumed a little upon that ancient friendship for Madame de Morlaix. Nevertheless, he summoned Barlow, ordered wine, and conducted his visitors to the lounge above the little garden.

The Count sank with a sigh of satisfaction to a deep

chair, and stretched his long limbs. 'One is very well here, *pardi!* I understand that you should be content, as Tinténiac tells me. But, devil take me, a heritage such as Chavaray is not to be neglected.'

The Chevalier interposed hurriedly, reading resentment in the contraction of Quentin's brows.

'Monsieur le Comte will tell you how you may secure it without incurring the dangers that are making you hesitate. That, in fact, is the real purpose of this visit, Monsieur de Morlaix.'

'Do dangers make him hesitate?' cried Puisaye. 'Ah, bah! I'll not believe it. With that nose and chin, that eagle's glance! That is not the man to shirk a danger, any more than I am.'

To Quentin the flattery seemed gross. He was not being favourably impressed. The flamboyance about this man offended his reticent nature. But he answered civilly.

'You will remember, Chevalier, that last night I discriminated to Saint-Gilles between courage and sheer folly. I do not shrink, I hope, from ordinary risks. But I do not lay a helpless neck under the knife.'

'As they would have you do, no doubt, those people of the family of Chesnières,' said Puisaye. 'I am glad to hear you had the sense not to be taken in their trap.'

'Their trap?' quoth Quentin.

'What else? Is it possible, after all, that you doubt it? They talked, I hear, of the honour of the name, and your duty to it. The honour of the name! Of the name of Chesnières! *Dieu me damne!* There's not much honour to it for anyone to safeguard.'

'It happens to be my name, sir,' Quentin gently reproved him.

But Puisaye was not to be reproved. *'Parbleu!* I paid you the compliment of forgetting it.' He waved the point aside with an eloquent hand, and ran on: 'Those subtle gentlemen would have persuaded you to go to France and get yourself guillotined. A convenient way of murdering you so that Saint-Gilles might succeed to Chavaray.'

Now, whilst this was akin to the very suspicion

Quentin had harboured, yet to hear it bluntly voiced by this stranger was an irritation.

'How would Saint-Gilles succeed if the estates were confiscated to the nation, as they would be on the conviction that must precede my guillotining?'

'How?' Puisaye laughed.

'That,' said Tinténiac, 'is what Monsieur le Comte has come to tell you.'

'But what other can you suppose to have been their purpose?' cried the Count. 'Or did you think they love you, then, these rascals?' A note of mordant scorn and hatred crept now into his voice. 'A vile, degenerate house, the House of Chesnières, my friend. In four generations it has produced only cripples, imbeciles, or scoundrels.'

'It has produced me,' Quentin reminded him.

For an instant Puisaye looked disconcerted. Then his vigorous laugh rang out again. 'Devil take me! I will keep forgetting it.'

'We shall be better friends, monsieur, if you'll remember it,' was the quiet answer.

A swift gleam of anger flashed from the dark eyes, and was gone. Puisaye shrugged, and waved his hand again. He was very free of gesture.

'*Bien!* I'll remember.'

He took up the glass that had been poured for him, held it to the light a moment to judge the colour of the wine, then quaffed it and smacked his lips appreciatively. 'You are well served, too. I should not have guessed there was so well-sunned a wine in England. It grew ten years or more ago on the banks of the Garonne.' As Quentin did not seem to take the hint, he reached for the decanter, and brimmed himself another goblet. 'But to your business. You are not to imagine that you would be safe in France even before you are in possession of the heritage. To announce your claim to it would be to find yourself laid by the heels and in the dead-cart.'

'But the law, then?'

'You conceive that there is law in France. To be sure there is. But who trusts to it walks upon a bog.

The terms of a statute matter nothing when those who administer it are scoundrels. They'll give it any sense they choose. It is just on this that your fine cousins were counting.'

'But,' Quentin objected, 'if I am disposed of, which you assume to be their aim, they, as *émigrés,* cannot inherit. Confiscation must follow.'

'So it must. And the estates would be sold as national property. But your cousins would do just that which I counsel you to do. There are plenty of greedy, corrupt knaves in authority in France who are fattening upon the national calamity; men who are prepared to act secretly as agents of the rightful owners of confiscated property. If it were broken up and dispersed in petty lots, it must be difficult to reassemble it when the time comes and the monarchy is restored. To prevent this, these agents lend their names to the rightful owners, buy in the property for them at prices purely nominal. The incredible depreciation of the paper currency of the Republic makes it easy for anyone with a little gold. Having bought it—for a consideration to themselves, of course—these rascals will hold it against the day when this nightmare is at an end. Your cousins, I fancy, possess a faithful servant in the steward at Chavaray, a rascal whom they will no doubt reward for the supplies he has been furnishing them dishonestly out of the property of the late Étienne. I am well informed, you see. That fellow would, no doubt, discover for them a likely agent and supply the necessary means.'

'Well informed, indeed,' Quentin agreed, and his tone betrayed some of the surprise he felt that a stranger should be so intimately acquainted with the affairs of Chavaray. But his surmise of the intentions of the brothers Chesnières, Quentin accounted shrewdly exact. It supplied a full explanation of all that had puzzled him in their attitude.

Watching Quentin's frowning, thoughtful face, Puisaye asked him: 'Would it not ease your mind to have the matter handled so?'

54

'But who would so handle it for me? Where am I to find a man in France to undertake it?'

'That is perhaps how I can serve you. Believe me, I should be happy to do so. In a few days I shall be returning to Brittany to make sure that all is ready for the general rising. It would be an easy matter for me to pay a visit to Angers, and arrange that the estates be bought for you when through your failure to appear within the time prescribed their confiscation is decreed. It will not be long, I trust, before we shall have swept the sansculottes to hell, and so made it possible for you to enter into possession in your own person. What do you say to that?'

'That you overwhelm me,' Quentin answered frankly, conscious even then that it was an understatement. 'This interest in a stranger, sir . . .'

'I'll beg that you'll not so describe yourself.' Puisaye was emphatic. '*Pardieu!* Is it nothing that I am an old friend of your mother's people, of your mother herself?'

'You know, sir, that my mother is no longer here to thank you.'

'I know. I know. Tinténiac has told me.' His brow was clouded. 'If it had happened that I had come to England during her lifetime I must long since have made your acquaintance. I take it, then, that you agree to let me serve you. You will need, of course, to place funds at my disposal.'

'Funds?' Quentin eyed him sharply. It was as if a gleam of light had suddenly been shed upon the mystification he discovered in a stranger's concern, that was as unsolicited as it appeared exaggerated. After all, Quentin knew his world. He had only Puisaye's own word for that ancient bond of friendship with the Lesdiguières, and as lately as last night he had heard him described as a swindling adventurer. Of Tinténiac, too, he knew nothing, when all was said. The man enjoyed an heroic fame as an active Royalist. But like all men of his class in these days, he would be reduced to neediness, a condition that drives men to queer shifts so as to supply themselves. Even the project which

Puisaye expounded, whilst so plausible, might be no more than a fiction for all that Quentin knew.

'What funds would be needed?' he asked at last.

Puisaye was airy. 'A million or two of livres. Ah, don't let the sound alarm you. So worthless is the currency of the Republic that some two thousand English pounds in gold would more than equal it.'

'Not so much, perhaps. But much for a poor fencing-master.'

Puisaye seemed taken aback. 'Poor?' He laughed. 'My friend, I do not find that you have an air of poverty.'

He could hardly have found words more unfortunate. Quentin remembered the man's interest in the academy's prosperity, the probing half-questions which he had almost resented.

'Believe me, sir, I am touched by your interest in my affairs; but too conscious of having done nothing to deserve it, it is unthinkable that I should take advantage of it.'

He saw the colour rise under the tan of Puisaye's narrow countenance, and then recede again, leaving it of a deathly pallor. The anger that momentarily glared from his eyes gave way to a look of pain and wonder. The smooth suavity of Quentin's tone had not deceived him.

'By God! He takes me for an *escroc*.' He got up as he spoke.

Tinténiac laughed uncomfortably. 'You suffer the fate of those who offer unsolicited assistance.'

'To have my face slapped by . . . by Margot's child! That is . . . Oh, but no matter what it is. The fault is mine, for being importunate.'

'Sir,' Quentin begged him, 'do not regard it so. I am sensible of your excellent intentions. It is only, as I have said, that I cannot bring myself to trespass upon your good nature.'

As if he felt himself mocked by the urbanity of that emotionless voice, Puisaye yielded suddenly to anger. 'Suspicion is among the meanest traits. I am sorry to discover it in you.'

Quentin inclined his head a little. 'I am pained to deserve your disapproval, Monsieur le Comte. If you have affairs elsewhere, pray do not stand on ceremony.'

Puisaye's lips twitched oddly in his white face. He advanced, clenching his hands, and for a moment Quentin thought that a blow was coming. Then Puisaye recovered. He bowed from the hips, theatrically, with an arm outflung.

'I take my leave, Monsieur le Marquis. Pray forgive the intrusion. Come, Tinténiac.'

Tinténiac made a leg. '*Serviteur*,' he murmured with a curling lip, and marched off in the wake of the tall, swaggering Count.

Quentin remained by the table in the embrasure, and as they passed down the long room, Puisaye's voice floated back to him, laden with indignation.

'I could have forgiven the cub if he had but had the manners to say that he could not find the money!'

CHAPTER 7

The Safe-Conduct

THAT night Quentin de Morlaix made an examination of conscience. 'Suspicion,' Puisaye had said, 'is among the meanest traits. I am sorry to discover it in you.' It was impressive because it followed upon Germaine de Chesnières' more veiled reproach: 'The suspicious are seldom happy, for they are seldom at peace.'

It was because he agreed so cordially that unwarranted suspicion is the fruit of a mean imagination that he now searched his soul. Of the suspicion with which Mademoiselle de Chesnières had reproached him he found ample justification in the irresistible explanation which Puisaye had given not only of their aims, but of the manner in which they might fulfil them. If he accepted this, he must accept the fact that such things as Puisaye suggested could be done. But that Puisaye, with such mighty interests to serve, moving in France at great risk and with a price upon his head, should volunteer to increase his jeopardy for the sake of a stranger became more and more incredible the more he considered it. Therefore he might acquit himself, he thought, of the odious charge of being too lightly moved to suspicion.

From pondering all this in detail, he came to reflect that what Puisaye had proposed to do for him, he could do for himself, if only he could be sure of immunity in France whilst doing it. That, of course, was the difficulty, if it were true, as Puisaye said, that the bloody-minded scoundrels who governed France did violence to their own laws. A month's brooding on this begot at last an inspiration. He remembered the English Jacobins, the Society of the Friends of Man, whose aim was to establish the Tree of Liberty on English soil, the Lord Edward Fitzgeralds, the Horne Tookes, the Tom Paines. There were in England, as there had been in France before '89, many men of birth who had been seduced by those philosophies for the regeneration of mankind, which, so philanthropic in theory, had proved in practice so abominable.

One of them, a young baronet, Sir George Lilburn, frequented Quentin's academy, finding it expedient, no doubt, to advertise a practised suppleness of wrist, so as to keep at bay the insults which his political creed might provoke among his peers.

With him Quentin took counsel, mentioned, without specifying it, that he had inherited a property in France and that so as to enter into possession, it was expedient that he should go to Angers. England being at war with France, there were obvious passport difficulties. Yet Quentin knew that members of the Society of the Friends of Man came and went in spite of them.

The young baronet needed no more spurring. He was willing and glad to be of assistance. The passport difficulty was easily overcome now that Prussia had left the coalition and made a separate peace with France. Monsieur de Morlaix must travel on a Prussian passport, readily obtainable from the Prussian Embassy. For his greater protection whilst in France, however— where, Sir George euphemistically admitted, officialdom could be of a vexatious zeal—it would be desirable to procure him a safe-conduct, a *laissez-passer,* from the Committee of Public Safety. This was a service that Sir George could easily render him. He would give it his immediate attention.

By an odd coincidence this undertaking of Sir George's was given on July 27, which in Paris, by the Calendar of Liberty, was the 9th Thermidor, the date of Robespierre's abrupt fall and extinction.

The news of it reached London a few days later, to be followed soon by reports of a reaction from the Terror that had brooded over France. To Quentin it seemed that this sudden turn of events must enormously simplify the course upon which he had decided. And not only to Quentin; for scarcely was the matter known in London than Saint-Gilles came seeking him.

He was suavely cousinly. He explained that his departure for Holland had been repeatedly postponed. But he was glad, since it afforded him this opportunity of offering his felicitations. 'Your apprehensions will have been removed with the removal of that monster Robespierre. There should be nothing to deter you now from claiming your possessions.'

'I am considering it,' Quentin told him, and saw the eyes of his cousin brighten with satisfaction.

'Decide it, my dear cousin. Lose no time. Although the law of suspects is suspended and the Terror has passed, still delays may be dangerous, and where so much is at stake you would do well to hasten to France. Already the time allowed by law for your repatriation has grown dangerously short.'

'Your anxiety for my interests touches me,' said Quentin in that cold, emotionless voice of his.

'It is not only for your interests that I am anxious,

but for those of the House of Chavaray, for which, next to yourself, it is my duty to care.'

To be rid of him Quentin let him known that arrangements to enable him to cross to France were already afoot.

'You relieve me,' Saint-Gilles confessed. 'Myself, on the eve of departure for Holland, at the call of duty to the King, I am glad to take with me the assurance that duty to our family will not be neglected. My farewells, dear cousin, and my good wishes.'

He departed, leaving his dear cousin to smile over that final impertinence, and over the thought that Saint-Gilles might have been less satisfied had he known of the safe-conduct upon which Quentin was depending.

There were now delays in procuring it, since the Jacobin agents in London were left in uneasy doubt as to the consequences of the Thermidorian upheaval, and delays were not lightly to be borne, with little more than a month remaining for repatriation so as to avoid being listed as an *émigré;* for in this legal respect the extinction of the Terror had brought as yet no change.

At last, towards the middle of August, he found himself, thanks to Sir George's good offices, in possession of a Prussian passport and a safe-conduct from the Committee of Public Safety, describing him and the purpose for which he re-entered France, and bearing the signatures of Barras, Tallien, and Carnot. In addition he had armed himself, through Mr. Sharpe, with properly attested copies of all documents necessary fully to establish his birth and parentage.

The academy he placed in the care of O'Kelly, with authority at need to engage another assistant and to provide otherwise according to his judgment.

'Why will you be going at all?' wondered O'Kelly, who was imperfectly informed in the matter of the heritage. 'Things being as they are in France, d'ye suppose now ye've inherited anything worth the risk of collecting, considering what you're leaving here?'

O'Kelly was by no means the only one to ask him

that question, for news of his imminent departure was spreading from the school through the *émigré* colony. But the only one that he took seriously was one who reached him at the eleventh hour.

On the very morning of his departure, when the travelling chaise that was to bear him to Southampton stood already at the door, his luggage in the boot, Barlow brought him word that Mademoiselle de Chesnières desired to see him.

He was in the white-panelled dining-room above stairs in which he had just breakfasted, saying a last word to O'Kelly and Ramel. He dismissed them, so that he might receive her, a sudden tumult in his pulses.

It startled her to see him already booted for the journey. She betrayed it in her parted lips and widened eyes.

'I am no more than in time, it seems,' she cried.

'To bid me Godspeed. I take it very kindly, mademoiselle, that you should . . .'

'Oh, no, no!' she cried, interrupting him, and stood before him for a moment twisting her gloves in agitated hands. 'You'll account me of a monstrous presumption, Cousin Quentin. I've come . . . I've come to attempt even now, at this last moment, to dissuade you from this journey.'

'To dissuade me?' It took his breath away. Yet he so controlled himself that she should not suspect it. 'To dissuade me? But I thought you so fully in accord with your cousins that the honour of the name—was not that the phrase?—demands it.'

'Never that. I was never in accord with them on that. And now less than ever.'

'You reproached me, I thought, with suspicions of their disinterestedness in urging this course upon me.'

'That is another matter. I could understand your hesitation, and see nothing cowardly in it, and yet deplore that you should harbour your suspicions. But now . . .' She broke off, to recommence: 'You are deceived in your hopes that the death of Robespierre has brought changes which make it safe for you to go.

The Terror may be diminishing; but the Republican laws remain, the hatred of our class remains, and between one and the other you will find yourself in great danger.'

'Since I owe this sweet concern to it, I cannot but take satisfaction in it.'

Her lovely eyes, of a deep gentian blue, dilated as she looked at him. Her face matched now in whiteness the graceful neck and almost the muslin fichu that crossed the gentle swell of her young breast. 'Be this mockery or gallantry, monsieur my cousin, both are out of season. I have come only to warn you of the dangers into which you will be going.'

He smiled. 'Dare I ask what is the source of your information, of your knowledge of what is happening in France?'

'I have it from Saint-Gilles.'

'You will not say that he has sent you here to tell me this?'

'If I told you that, you would not believe me?' she asked.

'I hope that I should never disbelieve whatever you might say.'

'You never would have cause.' She was recovering her imperious air. 'Saint-Gilles did not send me. He did not even tell me these things. But if you must know my authority, I heard him saying them yesterday to Constant.'

'I see. I see. And how did he say it? Something like this, I think: "The fool will discover when he reaches France and they lay him by the heels the blindness of trusting to the rumours of this change of spirit among the sansculottes." It was so, was it not, mademoiselle?'

She eyed him in a stupefaction that was blended with annoyance.

'And if it were? Oh, but don't trouble to answer that. It was just as you say. I will admit it.'

'You see, I begin to know these cousins. And it would be said with a chuckle, not a doubt.'

'Since you are so well informed, you will know, of course, just what that chuckle meant.'

'It is not difficult to imagine.'

'Not when one is by nature suspicious; then one imagines chuckles, too, and every conceivable kind of malice.'

'Whereas, of course, you would have me understand that Saint-Gilles is regretful that I should put my neck in danger.'

'Why should you not imagine it? It is as easy to imagine as the opposite.'

'Not in a man who some few days ago was here urging me to go because this change of spirit in France would make it safe for me.'

The scorn which had been deepening about her was all suddenly cast aside. Impetuously she came close, and laid a hand upon his arm.

'Saint-Giles did that?'

He smiled. 'That it surprises you shows how little you understand your cousins' aims for me.'

'Oh, I see what you think. But it is impossible, revolting, something of which it is impossible to suspect them. After all, I know them, and you do not, and I know Saint-Gilles incapable of any baseness. If he came here to urge you as you say, it can only have been because he believed at the time what everyone believed. He had not yet learnt that the change of spirit was not so great, after all.'

'Then why does he not come again, to warn me?'

She considered a moment, candidly eyeing him, a little frown between her eyes. 'Was your last reception of him such as to encourage him?' she asked. 'Or did you display again that offensive suspicion of his motives?'

'Faith, it's not impossible,' he admitted, a little shaken in his convictions.

'And I take it that you did not even consent to go. For what I overheard from him was: "*If* the fool goes. . ." You begin to see, I hope, the snares that too ready a suspiciousness can make for you. But let us leave that. You have my warning. You'll heed it?' The question came on a pleading note that thrilled him.

'I'll treasure it. But it comes too late. My plans are laid. My chaise is at the door. I must follow my destiny.'

She was very grave. 'It is not for me to be importunate. I tell you only this, that if you go I shall never look to see you again.'

He was very close to her. He lowered his head, and sank his voice to a murmur. 'Would that matter to you, Germaine?'

She drew away as if in sudden panic. Then recovering, she answered with admirable dignity: 'It must naturally matter that any member of my family should put himself in peril.'

'And that is all?' He spoke in infinite regret, then, too, recovered. 'Of course. Of course. But let me reassure you. I go armed against the peril that you foresee. I shall travel in France under a safe-conduct from the Committee of Public Safety.'

She showed him not relief, but blank surprise. 'How can you have contrived it?'

He laughed. 'I have good friends of every political colour.'

'I see. And you look to your Republican friends to protect you.' Once again her mood was scornful. 'Why, then, of course, I have foolishly wasted my time and yours. Forgive these importunities. *Adieu et bon voyage, monsieur mon cousin.*' She sank to the very ground in an exaggerated curtsey, and with a swirl of petticoats was at the door.

He sprang after her. 'But what is this, Germaine? In what have I offended now?'

'Offended? How can you suppose it? You are free to choose your friends, sir. I trust they will prove all you hope.'

He understood that he had wounded the fierce royalism in which she had been reared, a royalism so intolerant that only under the stress of bitter necessity would it consent to link hands even with constitutional monarchists. To move in Republican favour was fantastically to these pure ones the unpardonable offence.

'You judge me harshly.' he complained.

'Judge you, sir! I?' Her brows were raised. 'I have neither right nor wish to judge you. Again, good-bye.'

It was a command not to detain her. He yielded, a little out of temper; and if his soul ached as he followed her down the stairs and handed her into her coach, yet his lips displayed a chill, formal smile to match her own.

CHAPTER 8

The Claim

AT ANY time the crossing of the narrow sea between England and France must have seemed to the traveller as the passage from one world to another, so different were the aspect, manners, language, customs, garments, architecture, food, and almost every other detail of the life of the country entered from that of the country left. But in the year '94—year II of the Republic One and Indivisible—the difference was intensified by the traces of the violent political whirlwind that had swept over France.

Quentin had crossed by the ordinary packet from Southampton to Jersey, and thence in a French fishing-boat had been conveyed to Saint-Malo, or Port Malo as it was termed in the new vocabulary of Freedom, which excluded heavenly hierarchies as rigorously as earthly ones.

Once Port Malo was left behind, desolation spread an aspect of rugged misery upon the land. As he travelled in his chaise from posting-house to posting-

65

house, along the highroad to Rennes, neglected parklands and weed-choked gardens about more than one
untenanted château were grim reminders of how it had
fared with the lordly class from which he had so lately
discovered that he sprang. Grimmer still were here and
there the blackened ruins of a mansion once stately; for
by a curious irony this Brittany, now to be regarded as
amongst the last strongholds of loyalty to Throne and
Altar, had been amongst the first and most violent of
the provinces to rise against the old order. It was here,
where the distinction was most marked between noble
and simple, where feudal practices weighed most harshly upon the common people, that the earliest out-
breaks of revolt had taken place. And just as violent
had been the reaction when the new order interfered
with the Bretons' freedom of worship, driving forth
their priests and attempting to replace them by renegade constitutional strangers, and when conscription
was introduced and a levy of men decreed.

To the peasants of the West, shedding in hunger the
illusions of ease and abundance so glibly promised
them in the name of Liberty, Equality, and Fraternity,
this was the last intolerable affront. They would levy
the men demanded of them by the Republic, but they
would levy them, not to be sent to slaughter on distant
battlefields, but to defend the only liberty left them by
the new Age of Reason, the liberty to keep their lives
and save their souls.

In that hour of their need they turned again to their
natural overlords, from whose rule they had earlier
revolted and of whom so few remained.

The great Royalist rising of the West against the
Republic was not, at least in its beginnings, promoted
by the nobles so as to re-establish the order in which
they throve; it was a rising of peasants who marched in
bands of thousands to implore, and in some cases—as
in that of the famous Monsieur de Charette in Vendée—
even to compel with menaces the nobles to take command of them.

These were the bands of which the Marquis de La
Rouërie had been the organizer-in-chief, holding them

selves now at the orders of the Comte de Puisaye, who had carried on and perfected La Rouërie's organization.

At the moment of Quentin's arrival in Brittany many of them, temporarily dispersed, were back at the cultivation of their fields pending the summons to action. Others, however, continued under arms, lurking in the dense forests of the West, where no Republican troops dared to hunt them, and sallying forth upon occasion to fall upon Republican convoys, in order to victual themselves and improve their equipment. The cry of the owl—the *chat huant*—was their rallying signal, whence was derived their designation of Chouans.

Quentin's acquaintance with them, however, was not to come until later. He saw nothing of them as he drove his hundred miles or so from Port Malo to Angers, by roads which, thanks to the forced labour of the old *corvées,* were better far than any in England. That, however, was the only comparison he could make to the advantage of France. Everywhere in that province he beheld stark misery, uncultivated or half-cultivated acres, with squalid villages in which the houses were hovels built of mud, their windows unglazed, inhabited by ragged starvelings who stood to stare with animal dullness at the chaise that swayed and rattled over their broken pavements.

Midway between Port Malo and Rennes he drove through miles of empty desert moorland, where gorse was the only thing that blossomed, with an occasional menhir or cromlech standing gaunt against the sky. After that, as he approached Rennes, there was some improvement, with signs of intermittent cultivation. The toilers in the fields were mainly women, and even those who were still young in years presented the weathered, wrinkled aspect of age, in which all feminine softness was extinct.

He lay in Rennes at a fine inn, where the food was execrable, for scarcity and want were the only visible fruits so far borne by the Tree of Liberty. There, too, he had his first glimpse of a guillotine, standing red and menacing, but idle, in the great square that once had

been styled of Louis XV. There, too, he was pestered
by cockaded and sash-girt officials, in a state of ner-
vousness resulting from their bewilderment at the
changed state of things which the fall of Robespierre
had produced. They seemed relieved when Quentin
presented papers which disposed of any possible doubts
concerning him.

At last, and without accident, he came to Angers, a
substantial town of stone houses with slate roofs, some
open spaces, and a fine promenade flanked by Lombardy poplars along the river Sarthe.

He put up at the Inn of the Three Pigeons, which
was also the posting-house, and acting upon the advice
received from Mr. Edgar Sharpe, he began by seeking
that Pierre Lesdiguières who was his mother's
brother.

On the threshold of one of the more modest houses
in the square to which he had been directed he was
checked by a slatternly housekeeper, and informed
that the Citizen Lesdiguières had gone two days ago to
Nantes. The housekeeper did not know when he would
return. These were days in which no one could venture
a guess as to what might happen on the morrow. The
Citizen Lesdiguières had much business to transact in
Nantes. He had gone there with two commissioners
who had arrived from Paris to look into the conduct of
public affairs. It was known that in Nantes there had
been many abuses by a representative named Carrier,
a creature of that monster Robespierre. All was in
confusion, and the Citizen Lesdiguières was to assist
the commissioners in restoring order. That might take
some time.

The garrulous flood fell at last to a trickle, which
Quentin was able to stem by handing her a leaf torn
from his tablets, on which he had scribbled his name
and the name of his inn, requesting her to let the
Citizen Lesdiguières have it on his return.

With more time at his disposal, he would have been
content to await the return of Lesdiguières before taking any action. As it was, though disconcerted by this

68

absence of one upon whose assistance he had counted, he boldly decided to seek at once the prefecture.

Past the portals, guarded by a couple of slouching National Guards in striped trousers and blue coats, he was ushered into a dingy room and there received with cold civility by the underprefect. That august functionary, young and not overclean, remained seated at his writing-table and covered by a conical hat on the front of which a tricolour cockade was plastered. He assumed judicial airs as he listened to Quentin's statement, and waved away the papers Quentin offered in support of it.

If he was peremptory, he was considerably less so than Quentin would have found him a month earlier. Then he would have overwhelmed any *ci-devant* marquis with minatory official thunders. Less sure of himself in these days of sudden moderation, which he deplored, and with no other aim but that of avoiding responsibility as far as possible, he coldly informed the Citizen Morlaix that his case was one for the Revolutionary Committee of Angers, which would be sitting tomorrow at the town hall from ten to twelve.

Thither on the morrow Quentin repaired. He found a committee similarly shorn of the truculence with which for many months it had terrorized the public, and similarly anxious to practise inactivity, since in these days of transition it knew not what activities might ultimately be accounted incriminating.

After examining his papers, and after long deliberation, the President concluded that the decision of such matters really fell within the duties of the Public Accuser of Angers, to whom Quentin was now referred.

The Public Accuser being also lodged in the town hall, and as Quentin could think of no other official to whom he might be passed on, he imagined that satisfaction would now be prompt. But never was he more mistaken. The Public Accuser, he was informed by a clerk, was too deeply engaged to receive him that day or the next.

Nor was that the end of the delay. Day followed day, and still that high functionary continued to deny himself on the same plea. Quentin curbed his impatience only by the reflection that, after all, the date of his entering France made him safe from any chicanery that should classify him as an *émigré*, and so imperil his possessions. He was to realize his error when, at last, the Public Accuser consented to receive him. He afterwards blamed himself for his dullness in not perceiving a coincidence in the fact that the date of this was the 12th September, the day after the expiry of the six months' grace accorded to a justifiable expatriate.

He found the Public Accuser, the Citizen Besné, installed in a lofty chamber, furnished with the plunder of some nobleman's mansion. Cabinets richly inlaid and adorned by exquisitely painted panels contained his archives; armchairs of gilded wood with brocade coverings were set for the great man's visitors, and the great man himself, very correct in black with a formally clubbed wig and the airs of a *petit maître,* sat at a bow-legged writing-table of mahogany and gilt bronze that might have come from the Palace of Versailles.

The Citizen Besné was of those, as Quentin was soon to discover, to whom Puisaye had alluded as having grown rich out of the national misfortune. Not only had he assembled for himself a great estate out of confiscated *émigré* property sold at vile prices, but he had driven a great trade as the nominee of others who could afford, or whom he could constrain, to pay his extortionate fees for purchasing on their behalf. He was a wizened, pockmarked little man, with a thin tip-tilted nose, an almost lipless slit of a mouth, and a pair of gimlet eyes that twinkled craftily.

His reception of Quentin was smoothly genial. He heard his statement, and glanced at his papers cursorily, whilst admitting that he had knowledge of his case.

'It is unfortunate, however,' he said, 'that you arrive just a day too late. The law is as precise and clear as it is generous to persons in your position; but it can tolerate no abuse of the benign consideration for which it provides.'

Quentin protested that he had been in France two

weeks and in Angers ten days, as he could prove. The Citizen Besné's mouth was stretched in a smile.

'Two weeks! You have been in France two weeks, and it is six months since the death of the *ci-devant* Marquis de Chavaray. Such tardiness, permit me to say, hardly argues a patriotic zeal or a love for the country of your birth and that eagerness to return to it at the first opportunity, such as should inflame the breast of every true Frenchman. The Republic, my friend, is patient with her erring children, and clement in these fortunate days of equality in justice as in all else. But there are limits beyond which clemency becomes mere weakness, and of weakness the Republic never can be guilty.'

Quentin dissembled his nausea at this turgid rhetoric sonorously delivered; for the Citizen Besné possessed a voice that was startlingly big in so small a man.

'With submission, citizen, may I indicate that we are to be governed by the letter of the law, and not by sentimental assumptions. The letter of the law has been fulfilled by me. I was in France within the time prescribed.'

'That,' he was smoothly answered, 'has a specious sound. But let me tell you that he is a bad man of law who concerns himself only with the letter of it and ignores the spirit. However, I will waive the fact that but for the excessive leniency of the Republic the estates of Chavaray would have been sequestered long ago, and that the death of the *ci-devant* Marquis before conviction was merely an accident by which the Nation was cheated of her dues. I will keep to the letter of the law which you invoke. By that the estates, for lack of a claimant, became yesterday the property of the Nation. You make your claim a day too late.'

'Only because I was denied admittance to you earlier. The Revolutionary Committee will confirm my statement that I first applied ten days ago.'

'And the Committee informed you that application must be made to me. Do me the justice,' rejoined the booming voice, 'to believe that mine is an exacting office. I am overburdened with work and with petitions of every kind. I must receive them in the order in which they are preferred, and the only date of which I can have cognizance is the date on which they come before me. You should have taken this into account instead of remaining out of France until the eleventh hour. Let me add, citizen, that you are fortunate in not being impeached as an *émigré*.'

Inwardly convulsed with anger, yet perceiving that nothing could be gained by exploding it against this sleek rascal whom the Revolution had clothed in local omnipotence, Quentin set himself calmly to plead against the assumption of lukewarmness which he insisted was being permitted to weigh against him. It was to be remembered that a state of war existed between England and France, which created enormous difficulties in passing from one country to the other. The time lost had been lost in seeking to overcome them, and even when he had overcome them the events of Thermidor, and the changes resulting from the fall of the party of the Mountain, had created fresh delays.

The Public Accuser heard him out with patience; even, if that crafty face was to be read at all, with satisfaction.

'The events of Thermidor certainly favour you,' he admitted. 'They ensure for you a leniency which a few weeks ago would have been denied you. Yet the facts—the legal facts—are as I have stated them. The sequestration of Chavaray became due yesterday. In that matter I can do nothing. It is beyond my power to put back the clock. But the explanation you supply is one that certainly deserves my sympathy. To cancel the sequestration is not possible. The estates are now national property, and for sale. Strictly, they should be put up to auction. But that, after all, is a matter within my discretion, and I am prepared to stretch a point in your favour so as to right a wrong which you make me understand has happened automatically.'

He cleared his throat, and leaned forward across his writing-table. 'I will offer no opposition to—in fact, I will facilitate in every way—your private purchase of the estates.'

'Purchase them!' Quentin was aghast at the rascally impudence of a proposal that he should purchase that which belonged to him. He began to understand fully the delay in giving him audience and the trick of extortion of which he was being made the victim. The times, after all, had not changed to the extent that he had so confidently supposed.

Besné smiled amiably into his staring eyes. 'After all, and between ourselves, my dear citizen, the price need not be a high one. Indeed, prices of confiscated lands have been ruling ridiculously low, largely as a result of the depreciation of the paper currency of the Republic. Then, again, patriots are not rich. So that the levels established are little more than nominal.' The boom of the voice was muted to a confidential key. 'In strict confidence I may tell you that I have acted as nominee in one or two cases similar to your own, for *ci-devants* whose offences, of course, were merely technical. I am, I hope, too good a Republican to act for any others. In those cases I have naturally been allowed a commission for my pains: a commission of one third of the purchase price.'

He paused there a moment, his crafty eyes seeking to read the impassive countenance of the young man before him. Then he moistened his lips with a pale tongue, and softly expressed an opinion that drew a gasp from Quentin.

'Five million livres would be a reasonable price for Chavaray.' He paused again to smile upon the other's manifest dismay. 'Since that would be the value of it in normal times, it cannot be complained that we keep to it now, whilst disregarding a depreciation of the assignat of which we are under no obligation to take cognizance. You take my point. When that depreciation is reckoned, the gold equivalent of five million livres is little more than a paltry three thousand louis; a bagatelle; far less than the yearly yield of the estates in ordinary times.'

Quentin passed from dismay to amazement at a guile that could so dissemble an outrageous transaction, and name a price that in itself was speciously reasonable if one ignored, as Besné claimed to be entitled to ignore, the shrinkage in the value of the Republican currency.

'Even so,' he said at last. 'Where shall I find three thousand louis?' Either he did not choose to remember that he could procure it in England, or else he assumed that the matter could not lie in suspense whilst he crossed the sea again to seek it.

'It offers difficulties, eh?' Besné stroked his chin reflectively. 'Ah! That, now, is unfortunate.' He considered further, quietly humming through pursed lips. 'I wonder. I wonder.' He became effusive. 'Account me anxious to serve you, recognizing the unfortunate situation in which you are placed. I stand not only for law, but also for justice. Yet it would not be just—would it?—that I should forgo a commission to which I think I am entitled. Look, now, citizen, here is a friendly proposal for you; entirely between ourselves, you understand. Pay me the thousand louis which would come to me as my commission on the extraordinarily low price I have fixed, and I will offer no opposition to your claim to the heritage; I will even recommend that it be admitted. Considering how that will simplify matters for you, you will hardly grudge me that fee for such a service, eh?'

Dissembling his contempt, Quentin made answer smoothly: 'I should not. But, faith, it's no easier for me to find a thousand than three thousand.'

The Citizen Besné screwed up his eyes. 'Are you so sure?'

'I am sure.'

'It is possible that you are mistaken. I was lately informed that the family of Chesnières, the cousins of the late *ci-devant* and yours, are in London, living in luxury and wanting for nothing. I was about to order an investigation of this mystery of the source of their supplies, when the events of Thermidor, whilst nowise altering the laws relating to the property of *émigrés*, yet seem to palliate, at least for the present, their evasion. I have every reason to suppose that the revenues of Chavaray, whilst diminished, are by no means extinct. Out of these revenues the steward of Chavaray has been supplying what was necessary for the maintenance in Paris of the late *ci-devant,* and at the same time remitting moneys to the family in England. It's an abuse that could not have continued but for the sudden wave of moderation by which the country is flooded.

'I advise you, then, to pay a visit to your steward at Chavaray. He should be able to supply what you require from the funds in his possession. Go and see him, my friend. In the meantime I will stay my hand.'

Quentin passed from amazement to amazement as he heard this rascally official instructing him in the very course which it was his intention to pursue.

Besné stood up, intimating that the interview was at an end.

'Of course you understand that all this is in strictest confidence between us. To a man of sense I need not add that an indiscretion on your part must compel me to repudiate the entire transaction. I could not expose myself to a misunderstanding of the motives out of which I act.' He smiled. 'I shall hope to see you soon again.'

With a formal echo of the hope, Quentin bowed himself out of that scoundrel's presence, not without a sense of shame at being the conscious victim of so impudent a robber.

CHAPTER 9

The Home-Coming

ON THE morrow, having ascertained that Lesdiguières, whose guidance became more and more necessary to him, was still absent, Quentin hired a chaise and was driven to his ancestral domain by a post-boy who claimed to know the country as well as he knew his own pocket.

They left Angers, and headed north along a level road through a well-wooded country that followed the course of the river Mayenne. Some five miles out the boy informed him that they had now entered the Chavaray lands, and when yet another five miles were behind them the chaise swung to the right into a lane that ascended gently between fields of stubble from which the harvest had been gathered, until at last on an eminence above the river the Château de Chavaray stood revealed in the August sunshine, an imposing mansion of grey stone of the time of Louis XIII, with projecting pavilions under extinguisher roofs at either end.

The chaise rolled between the massive stone piers of a wide gate, and went rocking and swaying down a long avenue in need of repair, set between two rows of tall Lombardy poplars. On either hand the comparatively open undulating parkland, where the grass stood tall and rank, fell away to woods of oak and beech that gradually increased in density.

The post-boy wound his horn as the chaise swept to a standstill before tall iron gates set in the grey wall which, with the flanking pavilions, enclosed the grass-grown forecourt.

Quentin alighted, and standing before the gates, looked through with interest at this home of his fathers, chilled by the air of desolation that overhung its stateliness. With its shuttered windows and the faded blistered paint on the great doors at the head of the perron, it looked like a house that was dead.

The post-boy, seeing that the flourish of his horn had aroused no response, tore at the handle of a chain that hung beside one of the piers, and a bell clanged mournfully upon the silence.

Presently a low door in the pavilion on the left was opened. A man's ill-kempt head appeared, and a pair of bovine eyes dully regarded these intruders. Then slowly there shambled out a fellow in short and baggy breeches with naked legs that ended in a pair of wooden shoes. He clanked slowly over the grass-grown cobbles, and came to observe them at closer quarters, always with that dull, animal stare.

'What do you want?' he asked at last, in a deep, guttural voice.

Quentin's instinct was to announce himself for the Marquis de Chavaray, and demand the instant opening of the gate. But remembering that there were no longer any marquises in France, he preferred to ask for the Citizen Lafont.

'What do you want with him?'

'That I shall tell him when you fetch him. Open me this gate.'

Whilst the fellow stood without making shift to obey, a second man emerged from the pavilion. Like the first he was stockily built, and wore the same pattern of enormous peasant breeches. His legs, however, were gaitered, and he boasted a short jacket of green velvet and a broad black hat. His face was tanned and strongly featured and his eyes were light and clear as those of a hawk.

'What is it, Jacquot?'

'Strangers asking for you, master.'

The newcomer reached the gate, and surveyed them sternly. 'Who are you? What do you want?' he asked, as curtly and rudely as his man before him.

'You will be Lafont, I think. My name is Morlaix de Chesnières. Open the gate.'

The man eyed him suspiciously. 'If your name were Chesnières I must know you. But I don't.'

Nevertheless he drew the bolt. The gate swung open, and Quentin stepped into the forecourt.

'A nice, friendly welcome home,' he said. There was an asperity in his smile. 'But, of course, you were not to know me.'

The steward, on wide-planted feet, considered this rather military figure, sparely elegant in long dark riding-coat, buckskin breeches, and boots reversed at the top.

'Who do you say you are?'

'The present master of Chavaray.'

The pale eyes flashed contempt. 'A purchaser of national property, are you? I hadn't heard of the sequestration of Chavaray; though, of course, it was to be expected. But didn't you say that your name is Chesnières?'

'That is what I said. It should tell you that I am master of Chavaray by inheritance; not by purchase.'

The rugged countenance became forbidding. 'Will this be a trick or a jest? The inheritor of Chavaray is Monsieur Armand de Chesnières.'

'The present inheritor, yes. But I am the owner, Quentin Morlaix de Chesnières, the late Marquis's brother.'

'His brother? What tale is that? The late Marquis had no brother. You're not even a good imposter, my lad, or you'd have informed yourself that the late Marquis was old enough to be your grandfather.'

Quentin began to lose patience. 'Look you, my man. I haven't come to argue with you. I . . .'

'I know very well what you're here for.' Lafont's voice was harshly raised of a sudden. 'And I've had enough of you. Out of this!'

'A moment!' Quentin was peremptory. 'I do not ask you to take my word for my identity. I bring papers to establish it. Conduct me indoors, if you please.'

He was met by a grin of malicious understanding. 'Indoors, eh? Oh, very likely. Now be off before I make you sorry that you came.'

As he spoke, a young man in hunting-dress, booted to the middle of his thighs, came briskly out of the pavilion. He was followed by three knaves in goatskin jackets, baggy breeches of white linen, and wooden shoes, their weathered faces shaded by broad-brimmed hats worn over knitted caps, each carrying a fowling-piece.

'What is it, Lafont?' The young man's air and accent proclaimed the gentleman.

'A joker who has the impudence to tell me that he is the Marquis of Chavaray.'

As if taken aback, the gentleman checked in his stride, and there was a sudden quickening of his glance. Then slowly he resumed his advance. He was bareheaded, and his fair hair hung in a thick mane about a thin-featured countenance that was arrogant and masterful.

'The imposture is too gross,' he said contemptuously, and he addressed himself to Quentin. 'Better be off, of your own accord, my lad.'

'It does not happen that I am your lad,' said Quentin. 'Nor do I know your right here. As to mine, I have the means to satisfy you if you will step indoors.'

'Indoors, Monsieur de Boisgelin!' said Lafont significantly, with a grin and a wink.

'Enough!' The gentleman's peremptoriness increased. 'Will you go, or shall my men throw you out? It's yours to choose.'

Still Quentin suppressed his anger. From the breast of his riding-coat he pulled a sheaf of papers, and proffered them. 'Look at these.'

'What are they?'

'My papers. They will prove my identity.'

'That needs no proving. Do you think I don't know a Republican spy when I see one? Be off!'

He made a sign to Lafont, who at once began a truculent advance, whilst the other three moved forward to support him.

Quentin's eyes hardened in a face that anger had made white. 'Very well,' he said. 'I'll go. But I shall remember your name, Monsieur de Boisgelin, whilst awaiting the opportunity to call you to account for a violence offered to me upon my own doorstep.'

'By God, you *mouchard,* if you linger another moment I'll have my men drive a charge of lead through your carrion.'

Quentin stepped out of the forecourt, and Lafont slammed the iron gate so closely upon him that one of his heels was bruised by it.

The post-boy, already mounted, watched his approach with scared eyes. He was barely in the chaise when it was whirled away at a speed that argued panic. Not until they had rattled down the avenue between the poplars and regained the open road did the pace slacken. Then Quentin put his head out, and ordered the boy to stop.

'You boast your knowledge of the country, my lad. Do you happen to know who is this Monsieur de Boisgelin who appears to be in possession of Chavaray?'

'Do I know Boisgelin de Chesnières? Ah, name of a name! A bad subject. He doesn't shrink from murder, that one. I was mightily afraid for you, citizen, when you stayed to brave him.'

And then Quentin remembered where he had heard the name of Boisgelin before, and much in the same terms. The Duc de Lionne it was who had spoken of him as the first blade in France, a duellist of fame, and cousin to the brothers Chesnières.

Meanwhile the post-boy ran on: 'Those rascals with him are Chouans. He's a Chouan himself, and not a doubt there'll be more of those wolves behind the shutters of the château. Sacred name! When I saw you obstinate there was a moment when I wouldn't have given ten sous for your life. They're murderous brigands.'

'Chouans, eh? And what do you suppose Chouans may be doing at Chavaray?'

'Just lurking. You never know where they'll appear. Likely they'll be there in strength. And that rascal Lafont has always passed for a good sansculotte, which is how the two-faced scoundrel comes to have been left in peace at Chavaray. Next time you go there, citizen, you should take a regiment of the Blues with you, and burn out that nest of brigands. God of God!' he ended, 'but it's lucky we weren't murdered.'

He cracked his whip, and baffled and angry the Marquis de Chavaray was rattled back to Angers.

There, however, a message awaited him that went some way to raise his spirits from their dejection. Lesdiguières had returned from Nantes, and had left word at Quentin's inn that he awaited him at home.

Quentin went off in quest of him without even waiting to dine, and was instantly admitted by the slatternly housekeeper.

In a dingy, dusty room, severely furnished as an office, he was received by an untidy man of fifty of an incipient portliness, whose shrewd, kindly countenance, however, was prepossessing. His garments were rusty, his wig ill-kempt, and there was an ounce of snuff on his soiled neckcloth. He thrust a pair of horn-rimmed spectacles up onto his forehead, and rose with alacrity to receive his visitor.

'You are Maître Lesdiguières?' Quentin inquired.

The shrewd, kindly eyes smiled as they subjected him to a searching consideration. 'And you are Margot's child! Faith, you have her eyes and the same proud look, and you'll have papers to prove you, no doubt.' Lesdiguières advanced upon him, and embraced him. 'For her sake I am glad to see you, nephew. For years I have wondered whether she and you were alive or dead. It was a little hard to be so utterly without news of her. Tell me, is she still living?'

'Alas! She died a year ago.'

'Ah!' He sighed, and his round face was troubled. 'I hope her days in England were happy, peaceful.'

'Peaceful they certainly were, and I believe them to have been happy.'

Lesdiguières nodded gravely. He sighed again. 'Here we have been through evil times, so evil that often it needed all a man's wit and prudence merely to keep a head upon his shoulders. But that is now happily overpast, though prudence is still advisable. Great prudence.' Quentin was thrust into a chair. 'And so, Étienne de Chavaray being dead, you've come to claim your heritage. God knows it has been hard-earned, and it's a miracle that it should have escaped confiscation.'

Quentin proffered his papers.

'What are these?' Lesdiguières asked. 'Let them lie for the present.' He dropped them onto his table, resumed his seat, and tapped his snuffbox. 'Now render me your accounts. You'll not have been idle since you came.'

81

Quentin was commendably succinct, and his uncle listened without comment beyond a grim smile over the interview with Besné and a deepening frown over that day's indignities at Chavaray.

'Boisgelin, eh?' said Lesdiguières when the tale was done. 'A cousin of yours. A Chouan leader, as ardently sought by the authorities as his other cousin, Boishardi, also a Chouan leader, but a man of very different stamp. Boisgelin is a graceless scamp. An evil devil, a duellist. There was a young man I knew in Rennes, a lawyer, a good lad, whom this bully swordsman insulted and killed on the eve of his wedding-day. And he's sheltered by Lafont at Chavaray, eh? Between them they gave you a pleasant welcome home. Anyway, it was a wasted journey. Lafont I know to be a rogue, probably a thief, and entirely in the interest of Armand and Constant de Chesnières. It's certain that he has been supplying them with funds from the revenues of the estate. He'll have helped himself, too, not a doubt. No wonder he wouldn't look at your papers. He'll want no master at Chavaray. Perhaps not even Armand. Though, as things are, he is capable of coming to terms with Armand so as to ensure his succession.' His eyes widened on the thought that assailed him. 'Thousand devils! Perhaps it was lucky for you that he did not believe you today, or Boisgelin's Chouans might have done your business for you.' He wagged his head with solemnity. 'You may have more than the Republic to contend with before you enter upon your heritage. Meanwhile, there's this money to be found for Besné.'

'Must we indeed submit to this extortion?'

'And smilingly.' Lesdiguières was emphatic. 'That robber may be less dangerous than he was a month ago, now that terror is no longer the order of the day. But he is still dangerous enough, for he is still in control of the legal machinery which the terrorists perfected and which no one has yet ventured to destroy. Besné goes more carefully in his abuses. That is all. A couple of months ago he would have demanded ten times as much for his rascally services. There is nothing to do but pay his bribe if the estates are not to become national property.'

'But where am I to find a thousand louis? Actually I dispose of less than two hundred. I was depending upon Lafont for what might be necessary.'

Lesdiguières laughed outright. 'Beware of optimism, nephew.' Then he made a wry face. 'If I possessed the money I'ld never begrudge you the loan of it. I'ld gladly spend my last sou to bring success to the plans my father formed when he married poor Margot to the old Marquis.' He sighed as if the memory saddened him. 'But perhaps we can contrive.'

His manner of contriving depended upon a wealthy Marquise du Grégo, who with her daughter, the Vicomtesse de Bellanger, was deeply in the debt of Étienne de Chavaray. They had been arrested under the law of suspects, and at a moment when imprisonment made their own wealth inaccessible to them, Étienne had advanced great sums—some three or four thousand louis—as bribes for their deliverance. As a result of his own arrest occurring almost at the moment of their release, the debt had remained undischarged. The present should be their opportunity. It happened that business of the Republic was compelling him to visit Port Malo at once. He would go by way of Coëtlegon, taking Quentin with him so as to present him to the Marquise. As it was Lesdiguières himself who had acted for the Marquise du Grégo in the matter of the money supplied by Étienne de Chesnières, Quentin need have no doubt of their reception.

CHAPTER 10

❧❧❧❧

Madame de Bellanger

THEY set out, Quentin and his new-found uncle, very early on the following morning, and so that the lawyer might make the better speed on a journey to Port Malo which he represented as urgent, they travelled on horseback. Thus Quentin was under the necessity of leaving the greater part of his belongings at his uncle's house, taking with him no more than he could pack into a small valise, strapped to the saddle behind him. Never a marquis who was owner of half a province travelled in more modest fashion.

Elsewhere in France the display of a tricolour cockade would have been a prudent measure; but here, in a country infested by Chouans, the tricolour would be as dangerous on the one hand as the white cockade on the other. So they eschewed devices of political significance, leaving themselves free, according to Lesdiguières, to cry either *'Vive la République!'* or *'Vive le Roi!'* according to their challengers.

By riding hard they reached and lay that night at Châteaubriant, and on the next at Ploermel. Here they put up at the Inn of the Cicogne, whose tubby little landlord, Cauchart, welcomed Lesdiguières as an old friend.

They were visited there by two members of the local Revolutionary Committee who came to demand their papers. When the demand had been satisfied, they practised a civility which in the past two years had been unknown in such functionaries. Almost they excused themselves for troubling these travellers, explaining that the brigands—by which term they designated

84

the Chouans—had of late been of an increasing activity.

On the morrow they set out to cover the dozen miles or so to Coëtlegon. The September day was overcast and cooled by a strong westerly wind, and in the grey light the empty moorlands looked bleak and desolate. Across these they made their way by tracks that grew ever steeper and less defined. Over the summit, however, they descended into a district of forests of an ever-increasing density. They met no travellers other than occasional peasants, men and women, who called a greeting to them in a tongue unknown to Quentin.

Towards noon they emerged from these woodlands, through which they had wound their way as through a maze, into a wide valley that was sparsely planted, dominated by a massive flat-fronted mansion, grey, four-square, and severe, which seemed to take that wide valley for its park.

At the foot of the balustraded terrace upon which it stood they dismounted, left their nags to the care of a stable-boy who came to meet them, and went up a broad flight of lichened steps.

Crossing the terrace, Quentin had a fleeting impression of a face at one of the tall windows, hastily withdrawn as he raised his glance. An elderly manservant out of livery stood to receive them on the wide threshold, and conducted them to a lofty spacious salon of faded glories, where presently they were joined by the ladies of Coëtlegon.

For Lesdiguières there was a greeting of a warmth that seemed to annihilate all barriers of rank. It was followed by an amazement that bordered on incredulity when the old lawyer presented his companion as the new Marquis de Chavaray, and the amazement endured even when incredulity had been conquered by explanations and an insistent display of the young man's credentials.

They studied him with an interest equal to that with which in his turn he considered them. In the Marquise du Bot du Grégo he beheld a tall, faded beauty, angular and shrivelled, but gentle-mannered and kindly.

Her daughter, the Vicomtesse de Bellanger, as tall as her mother, was of a beauty neither faded nor shrivelled, but of an almost startling opulence. A coil of her luxuriant hair, black and glossy as velvet, lay alluringly on her neck as if to stress its warm, ivory whiteness. Against that same warm pallor of her face her full, sensuous lips were vividly red. Her eyes were large and dark and languorous, and all her features of a miraculous regularity. The clinging lines of her riding-habit, of iron-grey velvet laced with gold, revealed a beauty of shape to match her splendid countenance.

In returning the papers the Marquise spoke in a voice as faded as her person, a voice gentle to the point of plaintiveness.

'I recall that the old Marquis Bertrand made a *mésalliance* late in life.' There was no shade of malice in her melancholy utterance of the ill-chosen words.

'He married my sister, madame,' Lesdiguières answered without embarrassment. 'Hence my interest in her son.'

'Your sister? To be sure. I remember now. Her name was Lesdiguières, and she was accounted a great beauty; beautiful enough, I suppose, to make amends in a man's eyes for her humble birth. That was before you were born, Louise. But I did not know that the union had borne fruit.'

The fruit of it submitted himself impassively to her scrutiny. In the lithe upright carriage, the elegance of the riding-coat, with the sword worn through the pocket, the proud poise of the head, and the masterfulness of the long, lean countenance under the queued chestnut hair, her myopic old eyes may have found something to admire.

'Not much of the Chesnières in you,' she commented. 'You'll favour your mother, I suppose.' Softly she invited him to sit. 'Is Armand de Chesnières aware of your existence?'

'Oh, yes, madame. And of my succession. We met in London.'

'In London!' exclaimed the daughter, with an increase of interest in him, which Quentin perfectly understood. 'So you come from England.'

But it was her mother who pinned his attention. 'And what had Armand to say to it?' she was inquiring.

'It was his advice that I should come to France to make good my claim.' He explained at length the situation in which he found himself towards the law, going on to acquaint them briefly with his general circumstances.

They heard him out with every sign of friendly interest, blent in Madame de Bellanger with a certain amusement, of which she made it clear that the Chevalier de Saint-Gilles was the object.

Then Lesdiguières took up the tale, to inform them of Besné's proposal. 'Whether,' he said in conclusion, 'you can supply the sum, as a repayment of your debt to the late Marquis or simply as a loan, would be, madame, of your own determining. But in either case Monsieur de Chavaray, as he will tell you, will be profoundly obliged.'

Quentin fancied that the warmth of their attitude was a little diminished. Madame du Grégo looked slightly more wistful. 'I should wish it to be towards the repayment of the debt, of course. Should we not, Louise?'

'Naturally.' The Vicomtesse was definite. 'We must see what we can do. I will consult our steward at once.'

'At the same time, sir,' the mother added, 'you will understand that in these unhappy days, with revenues not merely shrunken but so difficult to collect at all, it is no easy matter to lay hands upon so large a sum.'

'My mother means,' explained the Vicomtesse, 'that we may require a little time, a few days. But you may depend upon us not to keep you waiting longer than we must. Meanwhile, of course, you will do us the honour to remain the guests of Coëtlegon.'

Quentin looked to Lesdiguières for direction. It was promptly given.

'You relieve me of concern for Monsieur le Marquis, mesdames. Myself, I am on my way to Saint-Malo, and in haste to reach it. I shall be happy to think of Monsieur de Chavaray in such hospitable hands meanwhile.'

Nevertheless the lawyer allowed them to persuade him to stay to dine, and at the well-served table the conversation soon became political, as was inevitable in those days. It resolved itself mainly into a dialogue between Lesdiguières, who in that aristocratic household did not scruple to reveal his strongly monarchical sentiments, and the Vicomtesse, who almost shocked Quentin by the opposition which she offered them. She argued strongly that the Terror being now overpast and succeeded by a spirit of moderation, which, developing as was to be expected, held out the promise of sane government under which all might live at peace, one must deplore the renewed activities of the *chouannerie,* which were provoking in Brittany a state of civil war under which all must suffer.

They had endured enough at the hands of the Terrorists, she insisted. She and her mother had been gaoled, had suffered unutterable indignities, and had stood in imminent peril of the guillotine. To stifle by futile revolt the present spirit of moderation might well be to bring back those evil days.

Less, as it seemed to Quentin, from conviction than from deference, Lesdiguières allowed her to have the last word, whereupon, conscious of the silence in which Quentin had followed the debate, she turned to challenge him.

'Do you not agree with me, Monsieur le Marquis?'

Had he answered truthfully, he must have expressed amazement that the wife of an *émigré,* who in his London exile was preparing to take his place in the Royalist army about to invade the West, should utter sentiments so Republican. He wondered what that pure Royalist, the pompous Bellanger—for news of whom she had not yet troubled to seek—would say if he could hear her.

'Madame,' he replied, 'I am hardly in case to hold an opinion.'

'By which I suppose you mean that gallantry prevents you from uttering one that is in disagreement with a lady's.'

'Indeed, madame, all that I mean is that I am too indifferently informed in these matters. It happens that I am not politically minded.'

Her magnificent eyes glowed upon him in a smile. 'It shall be my privilege to instruct you, sir, during the time you are to honour us here.'

Lesdiguières seems to have found that promise suspect. For at parting he had a word to say to Quentin about it.

'There are, no doubt, many matters in which Madame la Vicomtesse would find amusement in instructing you. But I doubt if you will discover politics to be amongst them. Keep a guard on yourself, my lad. Women sometimes have their own way of paying debts, and your need at the moment is a thousand louis. Once you have the money make haste back to Angers, and should I not have returned before you get there, await me before seeing Besné again. God prosper you, my lad.'

He rode away, leaving Quentin to make the discovery that the shrewdness of Lesdiguières' countenance was the faithful mirror of his mind.

Madame du Grégo, as aimless and ineffective as her plaintive exterior suggested, left all matters of consequence to her daughter, and it was Louise who that very evening sent for the steward and shut herself up with him to consider—as she afterwards told Quentin—measures for raising the money required.

She told him of this on the following morning. It broke fair after a night of rain, and sky and earth, sparkling with a new-washed air, drew them out-of-doors as soon as breakfast was done.

She did not think that after two long days in the saddle Quentin would care to ride, and in the vast park it was too wet underfoot for walking. But they could take the morning air on the terrace, and there she lingered with him almost until the hour of dinner.

The matter of the money was soon dismissed. It was

entrusted to the steward, and he was to exert himself
to collect it. Almost as soon did she dismiss the matter
of her husband when Quentin brought it up.

'The Vicomte de Bellanger happens to be known to
me, madame.'

She tossed her head. 'Then you know a good-for-
naught,' she shocked him by replying. 'I am told that
Englishwomen are notorious for their frailty. Monsieur
de Bellanger should be happy amongst them.'

'At present I think he is more concerned with the
Royalist army that is forming.'

'Then he's greatly changed since last I saw him.
Shall we find a less dreary topic?'

She plunged headlong into those politics upon which
she had promised to instruct him, and poured scorn
upon the petty jealousies among the leaders of the
chouannerie which made impossible that cohesion
which alone could ensure any success against the arms
of the Republic. She spoke of the Vendée, where it had
been the same, and where the great forces serving
under Stofflet and Charette were being destroyed
piecemeal by the Blues simply because their jealousy
of one another prevented them from combining. Hence
her conviction that no good could come of the present
Chouan activities, and that all that would result from
them would be to distress the country with civil strife,
in which the greatest sufferers must be those who occupied the land. There might even be a repetition in
Brittany of the horrors seen in the Vendée, when, so as
to stamp out the ill-conducted rebellion, the land was
systematically laid bare by the fire and sword of the
'Infernal Bands,' as the Republican troops detailed for
that work of extermination by incendiarism and
wholesale massacre had been designated.

Quentin listened with interest to the information all
this contained for him. But neither the rich, musical
voice nor the superb muliebrity of his companion could
dull his perception of the fundamental egotism that
shaped her views. The cause in which her birth should
have enlisted all her sympathies, even at some sacrifice

of reason, was of little account when weighed against apprehensions for her personal well-being.

She sought next to draw him to talk of himself and his life in London and in particular of the *émigrés* he had known there, and thus there came again a mention of her husband. This time she did not dismiss it as summarily as before. She sighed, fell into thought, then sighed again, and unburdened herself.

'Ah, my dear marquis, you behold in me a woman to be commiserated.'

'Say a woman to be admired, envied, desired even; but never to be commiserated.'

She smiled upon him wistfully. 'You do not know. Married as a child, without any voice in the matter, a marriage of convenience, arranged for me in the usual way, I am neither wife nor maid, and have been so for years.' With increasing frankness she ran on: 'I am a woman made for love; a woman in whom loving is a need; life's greatest need. And I am tied to a name, fettered to a worthless man whom I have not seen in years, and whom it would be a pleasure never to see again.'

Quentin shrank a little. These were confidences that he did not desire. Mechanically he answered, 'The times, no doubt, are to blame for that.' And he thought that courtesy demanded the addition: 'Only the force of cruel circumstances could keep a husband from your side, madame.'

Mockery trilled in her laugh. 'Not such a husband as mine. And then the different conditions in which we live. He is at large, moving freely amongst the men and women of his class, and finding consolation in abundant measure, whilst I am wasting here in solitude and even in danger. Do not despise me, Marquis, for pitying myself a little.'

He could only repeat himself. 'The times, madame! The times are to blame for all.'

'Neither the times nor his emigration. Bellanger married my fortune, not me.'

They had come to lean upon the granite balustrade. Quentin turned his head to consider her: her splendid height, her noble shape, and the beauty and vitality of her countenance.

'That is not to be believed, madame, when one beholds you.'

The languorous eyes smiled wistfully into his. Her fine hand fell caressingly upon his arm. 'I thank you for that, my friend. Almost you restore me some self-respect. For a woman neglected by her husband is in danger of despising herself. Do you know that he desired me to share his emigration as little as I desired to accompany him?'

'Of what do you complain, then? It seems to me that you are quits.'

A sort of horror filled her glance. 'You laugh at me,' she reproached him. 'Perhaps I deserve it for inviting your pity. But you deceived me.'

'I, madame?'

'You seemed sympathetic. Your eyes are kind. I thought you would understand, or I should not have ranted so. Forgive me.'

Contritely he abased himself, comforting her with assurances of liveliest feeling for so sad a case. But as if his attitude had chilled her, she gave him no more of her confidences that day.

Neither, however, did she deny him her company. Assiduous in her attentions and solicitous for his entertainment, she seemed in the days that followed to have no other thought or care. She rode with him mornings, now through the woodlands beyond the immense meadows of Coëtlegon, now farther afield, over the wide moorland of Menez, empty of all save gorse and broom, reaching it by way of a country wasting for lack of cultivation and through villages of mud huts with unglazed windows, tenanted by grim-faced men and women.

He was drawn to perceive in this squalor the justification of the Revolution against a system that permitted it. Unconvincingly she would answer him that much of the present indigence was a result of the *chouannerie*. Fields remained indifferently cultivated because the peasantry under arms abandoned them at the first summons to the brigandage composing the warfare they conducted.

Daily, after dinner, she would take him to the *étang* of Coëtlegon, a pleasant little artificial lake contrived for irrigation purposes and fed by waters of the Liè, to fish for the monster carp that inhabited it; and in the evenings she taught him backgammon, whilst her melancholy, self-effacing mother sat eternally knitting.

She was not only of a superb, alluring beauty, but gay and witty when not concerned to parade her unfortunate circumstances; and even when engaged in this, she seemed to employ the subtlest arts of seduction, as if inviting Quentin to make free with treasures neglected by their lawful lord. She was not to suspect that the eyes of his mind setting beside her the chaste image of Germaine de Chesnières, found the rich muliebrity of Louise du Grégo excessive and almost repellent. Assigning to timidity his reticences, she displayed herself with an increasing boldness, which still had no power to move him from his restrained and formal courtliness. Under cover of this she grew impatient of the delay, and ventured at last, on the evening of the fifth day of his visit, gently to approach the subject of his purpose there.

They were alone in the library of the château, a chamber which owed its existence and equipment to the late Marquis du Bot du Grégo, who had been a man of studious habits. She had brought him there to show him the illuminated missals and the incunabula which her father had taken pride in collecting, and which in value represented so considerable a fortune that she had more than ordinary cause for thankfulness that Coëtlegon had not shared the fate of so many Breton châteaux during the days of revolutionary incendiarism.

He turned from the last of the missals she had displayed. 'Madame, I begin to grow conscious of my monstrous abuse of your hospitality.'

'Have you not every claim upon it? Do you forget the great debt we owe you? But perhaps you grow impatient here. You find us dull.' She confronted him wistfully, at close quarters, beside the heavy oaken table on which the ponderous volumes lay.

'How can you suppose it? I grow impatient only of my own encroachments.'

'That you may certainly dismiss. Our steward is proving dilatory, I know. Can you blame me if I am not distressed by it? It is ordinarily so lonely for me here. I have been so . . . so happy in your companionship. Why should I conceal it? I have hardly given a thought to the matter of the money. I avoid unpleasant thoughts, having had too many of them. And that thought is unpleasant because bound up with the thought of your departure.'

She had drawn nearer still as she spoke, and the rich swell of her breast was within an inch of his own. Her moist, red lips were parted in a gentle smile.

'Madame, you are too good.'

'Too good? Too good for what?' She turned aside with a sigh. 'Caradec has gone to Ploermel, to endeavour to collect what is still needed of the money for you. But rents in these days are difficult to obtain. Hence a delay, which I say that I cannot deplore. Content you, however, that no effort will be spared to satisfying you.' She lowered her voice to a gentle murmur, her eyes played over him with an increasing languor. 'To satisfy you must always be our aim. We owe so much to the late Marquis. Oh, and for your own sake as well. You are a man to whom a woman could deny nothing.'

He drew back a step, out of the enveloping aura of her seductiveness, and parried so direct a thrust by a jest and a laugh. 'Madame, you give me news of myself.' Then, turning aside, and moving slowly towards the window he added: 'I recognize in it another proof of your great goodness towards me.'

Hungrily her dark eyes followed the lithe, graceful figure.

'You might recognize more than that,' she breathed.

'Only if were a coxcomb.'

She was silent for a long moment. When next she

spoke there was a hint of hoarseness in her voice. 'How terrible is your self-restraint.'

He thought it well that one of them should practise it. 'How terrible,' he evaded, 'is the necessity that imposes it.'

She caught her breath. 'Ah! What necessity is that?'

Because he did not know, himself, he answered darkly: 'Madame, there are things of which I cannot speak.'

That hint of a mystery raised a barrier for a moment. In the next her feminine wit and persistence were overcoming it. She rustled to his side again, and stood with him looking out upon a sweep of lawn to the tall yew hedge that enclosed a garden. The lawn was unkempt, almost a field, and the hedge was ragged; for Coëtlegon, which in normal times had maintained a dozen gardeners, now employed but one. The Revolution had served to prove that if you destroy the rich, you render destitute those who live upon them.

'My friend, what is it that oppresses you?' Her voice was rich in sympathy. 'Confide in me. A burden shared is a burden halved. Let me help you. Regard me as a friend who would spare herself nothing where she might serve you.'

The caressing hoarseness of her muted voice, her touch upon him, the consciousness of her warm, palpitating, sensuous loveliness, the very perfume that hung about her, a subtle distillation as of lilac, began to trouble his senses. He fought sternly against these impalpable tentacles that were laying hold of him, yet ever with a chivalrous reluctance to bruise her feelings.

'Madame, I have no words in which to mark my sense of the honour that you do me.'

'No words are needed.' It was almost a whisper. She leaned against him. He had but to turn, and she would be in his arms. And it was only by doing violence to himself that he succeeded in drawing away from that alluring contact.

'You are right, madame. Words will not serve. It is

by deeds that I must prove my gratitude, my awareness of the debt in which your friendship places me. And when occasion offers you shall not find me wanting.'

He scarcely knew what he was saying. But whilst he spoke mechanically, he obeyed the need again to be widening the distance between them. As he ceased, there was a silence in which she stood curiously regarding him. There was a flush on her normally pallid cheeks, and her quickened breathing showed itself in the heave of the lovely breast, so generously displayed by the low square cut of her corsage. Then she laughed a little, softly, on a rather jangled note.

'I wonder what it is that makes you afraid of me?'

'Perhaps it is the fear of myself,' he answered just as boldly, and added quickly: 'By your gracious leave, madame, I think I will take the air before we sup.'

On that, and in the best order that he could command, he made his retreat.

An hour later, Lazare Hoche, the general commanding the Republican Army of Cherbourg, arrived unexpectedly at Coëtlegon, to crave its hospitality and to create a diversion and procure Quentin the relief which had become an urgent necessity.

CHAPTER 11

Lazare Hoche

THIS Lazare Hoche, but for his untimely death, might well have played in France the rôle that was to be filled by Bonaparte. Already the fear that he might play it had all but brought him to the guillotine. His swift rise from the ranks to generalship, such as only the revolutionary conditions could make possible, and the victorious campaign of the Vosges, so brilliantly conducted by this general in the middle twenties, with the power accruing to him from his consequent popularity, had alarmed the jealous masters of the Revolution. Robespierre and his fierce acolyte, Saint-Just, perceived what opportunities were offered to a resolute soldier who had won the affection of his troops and the esteem of the people. They may even have felt that the increasing anarchy could ultimately be resolved—as, indeed, ultimately it came to be—by a military dictatorship, and in Hoche, with his high courage, his talents, his engaging personality, and his popularity, they may have suspected a potential dictator. So they trumped up an impeachment of treason, and cast him into gaol. Fortunately for him, whilst he awaited the trial that would undoubtedly have furnished him with a passport to the scaffold, the events of Thermidor supervened, and the prison doors that opened to receive Saint-Just and the half-dead Robespierre opened at the same time to deliver the young general.

Not only released, but restored to the confidence of the present masters of the State, Hoche was presently given command of the Army of Cherbourg, and dispatched into the West with the mission of stamping out the smouldering insurrection.

It was on his way now to take over that command, and accompanied by a half-dozen members of his staff and a little troop of fifty horse as escort, that General Hoche came to solicit for the night the hospitality of Coëtlegon.

A man of the people—in his early youth he had been a groom in the stables of Versailles—Lazare Hoche in his twenty-seventh year presented every mark and attribute of nobility. Commandingly tall and admirably proportioned, elegant in his appointments, graceful in his movements, he was of a grave, lofty beauty of countenance, with calm, intelligent eyes and a generous, mobile mouth. His gentle voice and his speech singularly cultured—for, of studious habits, he had been at pains to repair the omissions in the education with which he had started life—went to complete the mirror of courtliness presented by this child of the gutter.

Even the old Marquise's fierce pride of birth succumbed in graciousness before his natural nobility, whilst her daughter received him as if he had been royal.

His brigadier, Humbert, who accompanied him, a man of his own age, and like himself a son of the soil, was also of an exterior to take the eye. Shorter and more lightly built, he was quick and graceful and of a lively countenance. If Hoche wore the airs of a prince, Humbert presented the appearance of a typical soldier of fortune, gaily bold and swaggeringly gallant. Whilst his military talents were considerable, he had remained illiterate, and whilst Hoche, in his present surroundings, disdained the terminology of the Republic, and gave the ladies of Coëtlegon their proper titles, Humbert advertised his republicanism by scrupulously respecting the revolutionary dictionary. He rendered it evident, too, that he was of a greater enterprise in gallantry, and his bold and open wooing of the lovely Vicomtesse, next to whom he was seated at supper, was not confined to an ardour of glances.

The Vicomtesse, however, as blind to the fire in Humbert's eyes as she was deaf to the inner meaning of his phrases, had attentions only for the handsome Hoche, seated opposite to her, beside her mother.

Martin, the old *maître d'hôtel,* with a lad in plain livery to assist him, waited upon them at a table that was reasonably well supplied. Wine was abundant and good, and liberal indulgence in it did not improve the manners of the half-dozen officers at the table's lower end. Towards the end of the meal they grew boisterous, shatteringly loud in their laughter, and of rather too coarse a jocularity. Two of them brought forth their pipes and lighted them at the candles, and calling for more wine were disposing themselves for a carousal. But observing the Marquise's sudden trouble, the General was prompt to make an end.

He raised his gentle voice. 'Citizen-officers, Madame du Grégo gives you leave to withdraw to the quarters she will assign to you, where you may take your ease. You will, of course, practise that circumspection becoming Republican officers who are guests in a lady's house.'

There were no murmurs, and if in their rising the members of his staff were still noisy, nevertheless they were promptly obedient, and allowed themselves to be led forth by Martin to the quarters Hoche had suggested.

Louise du Grégo leaned forward to thank him. 'So much considerateness does you honour, General. My mother and I are deeply grateful.'

That was all that she said in words. But a deal was added to them by the ardour of her magnificent eyes, and the warm smile on her red lips.

Humbert at her side made bold to set a hand upon her arm. 'Eh, but we are not boors, citoyenne, we soldiers of the Republic. In our duty to the ladies we are nothing behind the men of the old régime.'

'I do not doubt it, my General,' she answered him, but her eyes were ever upon Hoche.

They moved to the salon, and almost at once the Marquise bade them good night, with plaintive, formally expressed hopes that they would find the quarters assigned to them all that they could desire. Hoche returned gravely courteous assurances of his confidence in this; Humbert laughingly protested that he possessed the soldier's faculty for bivouacking anywhere.

'So that I may dig a hole for my hip-bone I can sleep comfortably on the bosom of mother earth; which is not to say,' he added with a grin for the Vicomtesse, 'that there are not other bosoms I should prefer.'

Quentin wondered would she have frowned with the same displeasure at a similar brutality from Hoche.

'My friend,' his General told him, 'I am sure that madame will excuse you if you wish to join the others.'

But Humbert ignored the hint. 'Madame might excuse me. But I could never excuse myself,' he answered, and flung himself into a chair.

Madame du Grégo was moving towards the door.

Hoche went to open for her. As he returned Humbert was saying: 'The citoyenne promised that she would sing for us.'

'I promised,' she corrected him, with an arch look at his superior, 'that I would sing for General Hoche.'

She moved to meet him, and halting very close to him, looked up into his face. 'What shall I sing for you, my General?'

Hoche, tall and dominant in his close-fitting blue coat with red facings, the tricolour sash to his waist, and a high black military stock sharpening the line of his strong jaw, looked down into the siren's eyes with a glance in which the disdainfully watchful Quentin perceived a kindly responsive warmth. Humbert from his chair grunted a laugh that went unheeded.

'So that you sing, madame,' said Hoche, 'it will matter little what you sing.'

They moved together to the clavichord. She sighed aloud. 'It shall be something to express myself, my loneliness and my repining.'

'You were not made for loneliness, madame.'

'I have, none the less, been doomed to it. Thus Fate abuses me.'

'Fate is to be constrained.'

She sighed. 'Alas! I have never learnt the art of it.'

'For one so endowed there is nothing to be learnt. To desire is to possess.'

She flashed him an upward timid glance from under fluttering eyelids. 'For such as you, my General, I can well believe it.'

She sank to the seat at the instrument, and her fingers trembled for a moment over the keys. Then she began to sing, a heart-broken little song that was all tears and thwarted passion, and ever and anon as she sang her eyes would be raised to the commanding figure standing over her as if she addressed to him the song-maker's palpitating words.

Humbert, huddled in his chair, looked on and scowled. Quentin, observing all with secret amusement, regretted only that the man who so completely engrossed the lady's attention should be departing again in the morning.

Very soon, however, he thought that he perceived evidence that the lady, sharing his regret, did not mean to leave the course of things unchanged. When, the song being ended, she broke the spell of silence that marked its close, it was to comment upon the General's going.

'Is it inevitable that you continue your journey to-morrow, sir?'

So much had she gone to his head already that he answered gallantly: 'Be sure, madame, that I should not continue it otherwise.'

She was still seated at the clavichord, he standing beside her. She frowned throughtfully awhile, with bowed head; then suddenly looked up and swung to face him. 'I conceive you, of course, a man indifferent to danger. Yet I ask myself are you really aware of how much danger threatens you between here and Cherbourg.'

He raised his shoulders. 'Naturally, I am not unaware of the unrest, since I am sent into the West to quell it. But it's in my trade to face whatever dangers may present themselves.'

'Is it not also in your trade to see that you are in case to overcome them? Is not that a soldier's elementary duty?'

'I think I am in such case.'

'Oh, no. That is your error. Strong bands of Chouans are operating between here and Rennes. It is only two days since one of them attacked and seized a strongly escorted convoy.'

'What's that?' rasped Humbert, coming to his feet.

She stared at him, and then at Hoche. 'But is it possible that you have not heard of it?'

Both denied all knowledge of it, whilst Quentin wondered how it came that she had made no earlier allusion to so startling a fact. Humbert pressed her with questions as to the exact whereabouts of the attack, the substance of the convoy, and the strength of the escort. She was vague in her replies. She had the information from one of the peasants of Coëtlegon, who had not been precise in the matter of details. All that she knew for certain was that the Chouans were in strength and that their eyes were everywhere. She dwelt upon their methods, moving unseen through the woods, assembling in force to strike terribly from their ambushes, and dispersing again as soon as the blow was struck, ever an elusive, impalpable menace. She stressed the triumph it would be for them to seize the general sent to suppress them. If they had not yet fallen upon his flimsy escort, it could only be because he had not yet reached the particular ambush they were sure to have laid for him. It was impossible that they did not know of his presence now at Coëtlegon. He could be sure that his every movement would be known to them and watched.

'You mean,' cried Humbert, 'that they may descend upon us here?'

She shook her head so vigorously that momentarily she displaced a heavy black ringlet that fell across her white bosom. 'Oh, no. They will not attack you here, lest that should bring reprisals upon us. At Coëtlegon you are safe. I will answer for it. And you would do well, my General, to take advantage of it.'

'What advantage does it afford?'

'Shelter, until you can reinforce your inadequate escort. I will send one of my own men to Rennes or Saint-Brieuc or Saint-Malo, or wherever there is a garrison to supply your need.'

Seeing Hoche grow thoughtful, Humbert protested inevitably: 'But the delay!'

'It is better,' said madame, 'to arrive late than not to arrive at all. And that, be sure, is what will happen if you go on. Indeed, General, knowing the unrest of the country, I don't know whether to marvel more at your temerity in venturing into it so indifferently guarded, or at your good fortune in being still alive.' She stood up. 'Write two lines to the commander of the nearest garrison, and one of my men shall set out with it at once.'

'But the monstrous encroachment upon you,' Hoche protested.

She smiled alluringly into his eyes. 'The burden, my General, will be heavier for you than for us.'

'Never say that. For I know of no burden I would carry with greater delight.'

'It is settled, then.' She laughed like a pleased child.

He looked at Humbert. He spoke slowly. 'I think that we should add madame's generosity to the heavy debt in which her timely warning leaves us.'

Humbert, who had watched her with suspicious eyes, took a turn before answering. 'I should like to know more of this attacked convoy,' he grumbled. 'I find it odd that there should have been no word of it at Vannes this morning.'

'The Chouans may have seen to that,' madame informed him. 'They are ever vigilant to intercept couriers.'

He shrugged, and spread his hands. 'Very well. But if we are to send for a further escort, I should prefer that one of my own men carry the message.'

She raised her brows. 'By all means, if you think that one of your dragoons could ride a dozen miles unmolested through this country.'

'He need not ride as a Blue. We can dress him as a peasant.'

'As you please. My own man would travel more quickly and be more certain to arrive. But as you please.'

'He would also,' said Humbert, with a crooked smile, 'be more likely to have friends among the brigands.'

'Name of Heaven, Humbert! What do you imply?' Hoche disapproved him.

Madame, however, remained serene. 'He is right to take no risks.'

Humbert looked at his chief. 'You have decided, then, my General?'

'I think so. Yes. Don't you agree it would be prudent in view of what we have learnt?'

Humbert's glance, growing humorously insolent, moved from Hoche to the Vicomtesse. A smile of understanding flickered on his firm lips.

'We make holiday, then. Very well.' He shrugged, and turned on his heel. 'I go to give the order,' he said, and marched out.

CHAPTER 12

Departure

BRIGADIER HUMBERT paced the terrace of Coëtlegon on the following morning before breakfast, in company with Captain Champeaux of General Hoche's staff.

Looking up at one of the windows of the first floor, the Captain had indicated it by a jerk of the thumb, a laugh, and a coarse jest. Humbert's angry rejoinder greeted Quentin, emerging at that moment from the château.

'God of God! It's no subject for jests. With Hoche playing Samson to Madame's Delilah, there's every chance of all our throats being cut. Ah, *sacré bleu!* Who will assure me that this talk of brigand activity is not a trick to keep us here whilst brigands are being assembled in strength to exterminate us? Before I'd dally with a damned aristocrat, I'ld make sure that the door was safely barred. Those cursed woods on every side would mask an approach until the enemy is upon us. Post your pickets with care, and well advanced. At least let us provide against surprise. If we're attacked, we must entrench ourselves in the château and turn it into a fort.'

The Captain went off to the stables, where the men were quartered and the horses stalled. Humbert turned, and came face to face with Quentin. He uttered

a surly good morning, which was pleasantly returned.

'You are early abroad, sir,' said Quentin.

'I lack the General's inducement to lie abed,' was
the ill-humoured answer. Then, with Republican di-
rectness, he brusquely questioned Quentin. 'What exactly is your place in this household, citizen? Are you
of the family?'

'Oh, no. A guest, like yourselves.'

'But less richly entertained, perhaps, than some of
us,' grumbled the handsome brigadier.

'If it were not so I might quarrel with you for that
sneer.'

'I am fortunate,' was the sneering rejoinder, on
which Humbert stalked away.

Quentin was left thoughtful. Persuaded that the story
of the raided convoy was a fiction, he wondered whether Humbert's suspicions of treachery might be justified.
But he dismissed the notion almost instantly. Not only
did he call to mind the opinions she had so freely
expressed to him, but he accounted her the last woman
in the world to invite the cruel vengeance that would
fall upon Coëtlegon afterwards. If she desired to betray
Hoche, there were safer ways of accomplishing it.

So he reached the settled conviction that the trap she
had laid for Hoche was no more than a trap for his
senses, so as to hold him there as a consoler of that
loneliness of which she had made such bitter lament to
Quentin.

For his past ungallant indifference he found himself
punished now by a neglect that could scarcely have
been more discourteous to a guest in his position. All
those attentions she had lavished upon him were lavished now upon Hoche, and Quentin was left to solace
himself by amusement at the jealous furies of Humbert.

There was a display of them on that first morning
after breakfast, when the Vicomtesse was setting out
with Hoche on one of those rides in which hitherto
Quentin had been her companion. To Hoche, already
mounted beside his lovely mistress, Humbert had come

storming down the terrace steps with jingle of spurs and clatter of sabre.

'Whither do you ride, my General?'

'Why, through the lands of Coëtlegon, to take the morning air.'

'You may take more than that. I'll beg you to remember, my General, that your life is of importance to the Republic.'

'Oh, and to me.' Hoche laughed. 'Be tranquil. I am not likely to imperil it.'

'It may be imperilled for you.'

'By whom, sir?' the Vicomtesse fiercely challenged him.

'What do I know by whom? On your own word the brigands infest the woods of the countryside, and you don't want for woods hereabouts. You'll take an escort, my General?'

'I think Madame la Vicomtesse will be my sufficient escort. I am sure that she will answer for my safety. Come, madame.' He touched his horse with the spur, and they were off, leaving a blasphemous Humbert to fume until their return. Nor thereafter, disgruntled though he remained, did he renew the scene on any of the abundant occasions they offered him for it. For in the succeeding days Hoche and the Vicomtesse became more and more inseparable, and their manner towards each other quite shamelessly proclaimed the relationship into which they had come. Whilst Humbert scowled and writhed, and Quentin was scornfully amused, Madame du Grégo appeared plaintively unconscious that a low-born Republican soldier had become the accepted lover of her noble daughter.

With Quentin's amusement, however, there was mingled a growing irritation at the delay in the fulfillment of his purpose, and four days after the coming of Hoche he ventured at last to break through the neglect to which the Vicomtesse had doomed him.

'Madame, my consciousness of this continued trespass upon your hospitality compels me to trouble you with a reminder of my purpose here.'

Her countenance became overcast. 'My friend, you

can't imagine that I should wantonly detain you. Your affair has not been neglected. But alas!—all Caradec's efforts have so far failed; and in the present state of things I see little chance of their succeeding. He has contrived to collect only a few hundred louis, which you may have if you will. But it is still less than half the sum required.'

It was borne in upon him that she was not being sincere; that the will to serve him was no longer present. If his heart sank at this failure, his pride urged him to accept it stoically.

'Since you tell me that there is no chance of succeeding, nothing can justify my continuing here.'

'Alas!' she sighed. 'We have been honoured by your visit. We are desolated that it should prove fruitless to you.'

He met these polite insincerities with insincerities equally polite, and passed to his preparations for departure on the morrow.

That evening the messenger sent out by Humbert returned, bringing an escort of two hundred and fifty dragoons. Thus Hoche, too, was deprived of all pretext for lingering another day in the seductive company of Louise du Grégo.

The only persons in good spirits at supper that night were the Marquise, whose pride had been secretly outraged by her daughter's attachment to a sansculotte, however gallant of bearing, and Humbert, whose mixed disgust over the affair had been dominated by uneasiness lest, with or without the contrivance of the person he had come to call Madame la Sirène, Coëtlegon, in the very heart of the Chouan country, should come to prove their death-trap. He marked his relief by a noisy humour that jarred upon the silence of the others.

Next morning the last farewells were spoken on the terrace, whilst the troop paraded immediately below. The Marquise did not appear. She left to her daughter the task of speeding the guests.

For Quentin, who had begged Hoche's leave to ride with the troop as far as their ways lay together, the

Vicomtesse had little to say in answer to his renewed thanks for the sterile hospitality dispensed him. All her thoughts were visibly for Hoche.

She wore upon her all the signs of a sleepless night, with dark stains about eyes that had manifestly wept. At the last moment, when Quentin was already in the saddle, she delayed the departing general, and drew him away along the terrace, out of earshot.

Side by side they paced to the terrace's end, and paused there a long while in earnest talk, during which she seemed to sway towards him. At last they came slowly back. At the head of the steps, Hoche, bareheaded, his plumed hat tucked under his arm, bowed down from his stately height over her hands both of which he was grasping, and both of which he kissed. Then briskly he came down to the horse that a trooper held for him, mounted, and made a sign to the officer commanding the dragoons.

There were sharp orders, a wheeling movement of horses, with clink and clank of accoutrements and stamping hooves, and they were in march, which almost immediately quickened to a trot.

The General, in the rear with his staff about him, turned again and yet again to raise his hat and to receive the last waved salutation of the white figure that remained at the balustrade until distance made an end.

Quentin conceived this to be the definite close of a love story, not only because he remembered the Vicomte de Bellanger in London, but also because Hoche had lately married a young wife, to whom Humbert accounted him deeply attached. If the wanton aristocrat, so hungry for consolation in her semi-widowed loneliness, had seduced the young Republican from his married loyalty, at least, thought Quentin, it was an aberration no more than temporary, to which there could be no sequel.

He was to discover before a year was out how egregiously rash was this conclusion, and how unpredictably his own destiny was to be shaped by the sequel when it came.

Hoche rode in silence, aloof, sunk in thought from which he scarcely roused himself when somewhere about midway between Josselin and Ploermel there was an alarm.

Their road skirted a wood at the time, and a considerable body of men moving carelessly within it betrayed its presence to an experienced under-officer from Port Malo, who passed word of it to the commandant.

The troop was halted, and wheeled to face a possible attack. Carbines were unslung, and held at the ready. Thus they waited, whilst within the wood all became still again.

Humbert spurred forward, along the front of the line, indifferent to the fire that he might draw. He went to urge the commandant to send in half his troop to clear the wood. But the commandant, with experience of Chouan methods, urged sound reasons against any such blind adventure. Let the brigands, if they so chose, first betray their exact whereabouts by opening fire. Since to do so they must approach the wood's edge, they would then be at the mercy of a swift charge before they could retreat into the depths again. There it would be highly imprudent to follow them.

Hoche roused himself, and with contemptuous impatience gave the order to ride on, and thus, without incident, they came into Ploermel.

Here Quentin, with courteous words of leave-taking to Hoche and the members of his staff, detached himself from the troop, which rode on through the town without pausing.

CHAPTER 13

Boisgelin

QUENTIN drew up at the Inn of the Cigogne, where he had lain the night with Lesdiguières when on his way to Coëtlegon. Recognized by the tubby Cauchart, he was made welcome.

It was already past noon, and when refreshed here, and with a fresh horse, Quentin hoped to reach Rédon, thirty miles away, before nightfall. Lesdiguières, he learnt, had passed that way two days ago on his return journey, imagining no doubt that his nephew would already have returned to Angers.

Cauchart set before him a pot of cider, deploring that he had no wine worthy of his guest, and Quentin was awaiting the food he had ordered when he became aware of the rhythmic tramp of a very considerable marching body. His idle conclusion was that a company of infantry was passing through Ploermel; and even when the march ceased before the inn this conclusion still abode.

He raised his eyes as a quick step rang upon the threshold. Into the common-room, in the middle of which Cauchart stood at gaze, came a brisk man in hunting dress with gaitered legs, whose appearance was familiar. He looked sharply about him, espied Quentin, said, 'Ah!' and whistled shrilly.

At once there was a stir beyond the door, and a dozen men of fairly uniform appearance surged into the room. They all wore the baggy Breton breeches, mostly of linen, but some of fustian, short jackets, which in many cases were of goatskin, and broad, round hats; all looked villainous, and each was armed with a musket.

110

The man in the hunting dress swung upon the land-lord, whose eyes had grown uneasy. 'Whom do you house here, Cauchart?' The offensive, masterful tone stimulated Quentin's memory. This was that Monsieur de Boisgelin who had ruffled it at Chavaray, denying him access to his own house.

'Monsieur le Chevalier,' Cauchart answered hurried-ly, 'all's well. This is the new Marquis of Chavaray.'

Boisgelin started at that, turned his head sharply, advanced a pace or two, and looked more closely at Quentin.

'Marquis of Chavaray!' he echoed derisorily. 'Of Carabas, perhaps. I know him now. Were you fooled by that impudent lie, Cauchart?'

'Monsieur! Monsieur!' Cauchart was scandalized. 'It is no lie. I have Maître Lesdiguières' word for it.'

'Lesdiguières!' jeered Boisgelin. 'Lesdiguières! He answers for him, does he?' Yet there was clearly some-thing here that gave him pause. 'Now, what's the truth of this?' He walked boldly up to Quentin's table, and confronted him across it. 'You are the man that rode with Hoche just now. Are you not?'

Quentin, with a sense of peril strong upon him, liked this man even less than when he had seen him at Chavaray. He had been jarred, too, by the use of the name 'Carabas.' He remembered Constant's applica-tion of it, and it seemed to him beyond mere coinci-dence that it should now be repeated by this cousin of Constant's. Nevertheless he contrived that his answer should be quietly civil.

'Why, yes. I am.'

'Useless to deny it, anyway.' Boisgelin made a sign to his men, and at once their sabots clattered across the stone floor towards Quentin.

Cauchart flung himself forward in a panic. 'Mon-sieur! In God's name!'

'Quiet, Cauchart. Don't interfere. We've a short way with *pataud* spies in this country. The nearest tree will do his affair.'

'You take me for a spy?' said Quentin. He kept cool.

'And for no better reason than that I rode with General Hoche? Permit me to find you ridiculous.'

'You forget that we've met before. At Chavaray. You were very eager to enter the château.'

'As was my right. You have been told who I am.'

'I am more concerned with what you are. We waste time.'

The words were as a signal. He was seized under the arms and pulled to his feet.

Again Cauchart, in liveliest distress, attempted to intervene, only to be brutally repressed by Boisgelin.

Under no delusion, now, appalled by the perception that he was facing death at the hands of these ruffians, Quentin's wits worked at desperate speed. He heard the vintner's wailing voice: 'Monsieur le Chevalier, you must be in a mistake. I tell you again that I have Maître Lesdiguières' word for it that this is the new Marquis de Chavaray.'

'There'll be no mistake,' was the astounding answer, 'whether he's that or the common *pataud* spy that I suppose him. Very likely he is both.'

To Quentin, it was as if in his angry, cruel haste Boisgelin had said more than he intended. It confirmed the suspicion begotten by that contemptuous 'Carabas' which the man had flung at him, and with it came the thought that whilst this might be a chance encounter, yet it presented an opportunity that was sought. In Boisgelin he began to see an agent of that movement to suppress him of which glimpses had already been afforded him.

Already his aggressors were thrusting him away from the table, when his desperately questing wits recalled Lionne's description of Boisgelin as the best blade in France, 'a remorseless devil who never scruples to take advantage of his evil, deadly swordsmanship.'

The recollection brought inspiration. Such a man, swollen in pride and self-confidence by the easy successes his sword had won, would probably be of a vanity easily provoked. Besides, as a gentleman born, he would be imbued with a gentleman's notions of how to defend his personal honour, the more certainly because of his confidence in a skill that he believed matchless. It remained to see what calculated insult might wring from that evil confidence.

Boisgelin was already striding towards the door, and Quentin was being impelled after him by his captors when he spoke, throwing into his voice all the contempt of which he was capable.

'You may act, sir, in spite of a doubt of what I really am. But you leave me in no doubt of what you are.'

Boisgelin, arrested as much by the tone as by the words, swung round to face him. The movement halted the Chouans.

'What I am?'

Quentin laughed in his face. 'One sees it at a glance. You may play the bully with a dozen of your ruffians at your heels, as you would never dare to play it without them. For it's written plainly on your vile face that you are by nature a poltroon.'

Boisgelin lost some colour. 'Leave this to me,' he sharply silenced his men. He stood staring at Quentin, and slowly a cruel smile took shape on his lips. 'By God, sir, whoever and whatever you are, I shall have the pleasure of proving you wrong before you die.'

The *spadassin* had gulped the bait. His insulted vanity had snatched at this invitation to display his prowess before his followers. But Quentin betrayed no relief. He merely raised a languid brow, his glance a fresh insult.

'Is it really possible? Could I be mistaken, after all? Or is this mere play-acting?'

'You'll find it of a deadly earnest. You wear a sword. I suppose you can use it?'

'I could try, if you dared to supply the occasion.'

'Outside, then. Here behind the inn.'

Cauchart flung forward and caught his arm. 'Monsieur! You cannot do this. It would be murder.'

'It will be.' Boisgelin flung him off. 'Peace, fool. Come on, sir.'

Quentin, however, now chose to manifest hesitation; for the whole of his purpose was not yet fulfilled. 'All this is so irregular,' he complained.

'You begin to find it so.'

'What I find is that the dice are cogged against me. It is what I should have seen.' He looked at the lowering faces about him as if he indicated them. 'I am hardly among friends, and I should like some definite assurance of what's to happen afterwards.'

'Afterwards? After what?'

'After I shall have killed you,' said Quentin coolly.

Boisgelin's mouth fell open in astonishment. Then a laugh came from it and found an echo among his men. 'You make very sure.'

'In this life,' said Quentin, 'the only thing of which we can be very sure is death. And you may be sure of it this afternoon, Monsieur de Boisgelin.'

'Don't keep me waiting, then.'

'But I must until I know what is to happen afterwards. If I am to have my throat cut by your men here, I need not be at the trouble of killing you first."

To Boisgelin this was as yet another blow in the face. He turned in fury to the door, and called. 'Grosjean!'

A burly Chouan, whose accoutrements announced a leader, appeared almost at once in answer. He wore a grey coat over a red waistcoat, and the cockade in his hat was of silk. He was armed with a sword, and a brace of pistols were displayed in his belt, whilst his legs, like Boisgelin's, were gaitered.

'This cockerel and I,' Boisgelin informed him, with a grin, 'are about to take a turn in the garden. After that, should he still be alive, you will see that no obstacle is placed to his departure.'

'By Saint John, if he's still alive, he should deserve his liberty,' grinned Grosjean.

'I require your word for that.'

'*Bien.*' Grosjean solemnly stretched out his hand. 'It is sworn.'

Boisgelin looked at Quentin. 'Does that satisfy you, *fanfaron?*'

Quentin inclined his bare head. 'Perfectly. Let us go.'

Beyond a vegetable patch at the back of the inn there was a stretch of well-cropped, even turf where Cauchart grazed his goats. The shadow cast across it by a belt of pines mellowed the strong light of that September afternoon. To this they came, followed not only by the Chouans who had invaded the inn, but by those who had remained outside, making in all a company some forty or fifty strong.

Their light chatter and little bursts of laughter bore witness to their confidence in the invincible swordsmanship of their leader.

Once, however, the two men were face to face, an orderly silence fell and the Chouan ranks became rigidly immobile.

Quentin had removed his riding-coat, and had rolled the right sleeve of his shirt above the elbow. Boisgelin disdained to do even so much, contenting himself with casting aside his hat and sword-belt.

'You may put off your boots as well if you please,' he sneered.

'Only if you will put off yours, sir,' was the grave answer.

'I do not account it worth the trouble.'

'As you please. No doubt it is written that you are to die in your boots.'

'No doubt. But it will not be today. On guard!'

On the word he attacked.

That he looked to make short work of it is certain. Just as it is certain that when he fell back baffled and paused at the end of a half-dozen disengages, some of the contemptuous confidence went out of him. He had discovered in the opposing blade a quality that had not been present in any of those of his past easy victims.

Quentin in his time, if only on the fencing floor, had met some famous swordsmen since his discomfiture of the very competent Rédas. But he could not remember to have met a better blade than this. It was little wonder, he thought, that Boisgelin had been so ready to take in hand the punishment of his insults and to engage his followers to let his opponent go free should he survive. Not on that account was he perturbed.

Formidable Boisgelin might be to the ordinary swordsman, but hardly formidable to the practised master. Beyond realizing that the engagement was on a level that would permit him to take no chances, Quentin was at ease.

At a distance of three paces Boisgelin addressed him provocatively in that pause.

'Well, sir? You are something slow to perform as you promised.'

'But sure, I trust. I must not disappoint you. I await your convenience.'

Boisgelin bounded forward, feinted and lunged with admirable suppleness. Quentin encircled the blade, swept it clear, and drove his opponent back by a thrust that presented the point at his throat. As if exasperated at being so easily foiled, Boisgelin attacked again at once, and displayed now a speed and force that, coolly met, was dangerous only to himself. For a spell the blades flashed and circled, making arcs of light for the amazed spectators. Then, at last, for the second time, and breathing hard now as a result of his fury, Boisgelin fell back and lowered his point.

But having winded him by his strictly defensive tactics, Quentin would not allow him a second's leisure for recovery. He went in, in his turn, and the lowered point must be raised again at once to meet him. As he fenced, Quentin was moved to a savage mockery of this murderous duellist.

'You begin perhaps to feel as you have made lesser swordsmen feel. Think, for instance, of that young lover of Rennes whom you butchered a year ago, and how he faced you, as sure of his doom as you should be by now of yours.'

Deliberately, then, he exposed his low lines to invite a lunge. He wheeled aside as it came, desperately driven to spend itself unresisted on the empty air, whilst now, inside the other's guard, he drove his blade to transfix him from side to side.

It was so swiftly done that Quentin had recovered before the spectators fully realized that their leader had been hit.

For a moment Boisgelin remained erect, taut, his eyes suddenly wide as if in astonishment. Then a shudder ran through him, a moan broke from his lips, and he collapsed and sank grotesquely into a heap, snapping the sword that was thrust out as if to stay his fall.

Instantly there was a clatter of tongues, swelling to a roar, from the Chouans and the beginning of an angry forward surge. But Grosjean, loyal to his oath, flung himself before Quentin, to face them, shouting sternly, a pistol in either hand. He used the Breton tongue; but his tone and action left little doubt of what he said.

The uproar fell to a mutter. Then at last it was stilled, and in a heavy silence those wild men came across the grass to the spot where the vanquished lay, with the victor standing above him.

Quentin swayed a little as he stood there and looked down at the crumpled heap that so lately had swaggered threateningly in the full pride of life. To physical nausea in him was added a deep spiritual disgust. It was the first man that he had killed, and for all that they had fought and he had dealt this death in self-defense, he felt himself a murderer, conceived that this crumpled heap, those staring eyes, those grinning lips, flecked with blood and froth, must ever hereafter abide hauntingly in his sight.

His arm was roughly clutched by Grosjean. The Chouan did not need to look twice so as to realize that the man at their feet was dead.

'We keep faith,' he growled. 'Get you gone!'

Quentin felt the need to say something, yet was at a loss to know what might fit the occasion. So, in silence, under the lowering glances of the band, he turned to go back to the inn. Again there were the beginnings of a threatening mutter, but again their leader quelled it.

He was met in the vegetable patch by Cauchart, who had stood there to watch the events. The taverner hurried him away, found him a horse, and urged him to profit by the miracle that permitted his departure and make the best speed he could out of the district.

CHAPTER 14

Boishardi

CAUCHART judged shrewdly that the present lull could not endure.

Very soon the Chouans were in mutiny against Grosjean, abusing him for having restrained them when they would have avenged their chief. To his reminder of the word pledged, one of them, in whom a lawyer was lost, raised a question.

'The pledge was that the *pataud* should be allowed to depart. That pledge is now fulfilled. But what if any of us should ever meet him again? What then?'

Grosjean delivered judgment. 'That would be another matter.'

'Very well, then. We'll contrive to meet him again. Today. We've only to find out what road he took. Who is with me?'

Saving Grosjean, who had a clearer sense of the engagement made, and who perceived in this no more than a fraudulent evasion, all were on the side of that tricky casuist.

And so it came to pass that some three hours later, when Quentin had come down from the moorland heights of Ploermel and was ambling quietly along the flat road in the neighbourhood of Paillac, he found himself suddenly surrounded by a score of Chouans on shaggy Breton ponies, in whom he thought that he recognized some of the followers of Boisgelin.

Presently the sight of Grosjean amongst them made a certainty of the assumption. He guessed then that, using that intimate knowledge of the country which rendered them so mobile, they had cut straight across it

118

to intercept him and correct the error of having allowed him to depart.

'Is this the faith you keep?' he asked them.

For answer they pulled him from his horse, deprived him of his sword, and tied his hands behind him. They went to work in comparative silence, ignoring alike the questions and the abuse which he permitted himself, Grosjean close beside him throughout.

He could not guess that Grosjean's presence was protective, and that Grosjean, in yielding where he had lacked power entirely to oppose, had at least been able to enforce the condition that the slayer of Boisgelin should not be put to death until their chief commander, Monsieur de Boishardi, with all the facts before him, should pronounce judgment.

Having bound his wrists, they searched him and removed from him the effects they found, the chief of which were his safe-conduct from the Committee of Public Safety and a money-belt, containing the best part of two hundred guineas in English gold.

Then, after an altercation which he was unable to follow, his wrists were again unbound so as to enable him to ride. He was ordered to mount, and was led swiftly away.

Almost at once they quitted the highroad, and by narrow byways, sometimes by mere bridle-paths through wild tracts of country, through woods and once through the ford of a river, but always moving at speed, they brought him towards the close of that autumn day into the gloom of a great forest.

On the edge of it, uttered by one of them, he heard for the first time the note of the screech-owl, the *chat huant* from which they derived their appellation. From a distance within the forest an answering cry floated back to them. They advanced more slowly now, but no less surely towards the heart of that labyrinth of mingling oak and elm and beech, and they emerged at last into a clearing vast as a cathedral square, on the farther side of which the outlines of a mean building were just visible in the dusk. In the middle of the clearing a fire flamed about a huge cooking-pot borne on an iron tripod, and bivouacked about it were some five or six score men, whose garb and accoutrements proclaimed them of the same brotherhood as Quentin's captors. Several rose, and came to meet the newcomers. At the news imparted, always in that Breton tongue unknown to Quentin, their cries brought others from the fire.

Quentin was now dismounted and again pinioned before being led forward by four of the Chouans, following in the wake of Grosjean.

They came to the hut across the clearing, and the leader, having rapped upon the door, then opened it and passed in, the others following.

Quentin found himself in a small chamber, brightly lighted by a lamp on a big trestle table that carried the remains of a meal at one end and a litter of papers and writing materials at the other. Over these sat a man of perhaps thirty, darkly aristocratic of face, and of a certain richness of dress incongruous in these mean surroundings. His coat was of grey velvet with silver buttons, and on the breast of it he wore as a badge a flaming heart. His dark, glossy hair was carefully dressed, a diamond gleamed in the rich lace of his cravat, another on the fine hand that held the pen.

A Breton bed, presenting the appearance of a cupboard, was set against the wall on the right, and a couple of wooden stools completed the furniture of that chamber of blackened mud walls, earthen floor, and shuttered windows.

The man at the table, who was Boishardi, one of the most famous and elusive of the Royalist leaders in the West, had paused in his writing to see who came. At sight of the prisoner he threw up his head with a quickening of interest in his dark eyes. 'What's this, Grosjean?'

Grosjean's brisk account was interrupted by corrections and amplifications from the other Chouans, delivered in a French so slurred and imperfect that to follow it was a strain upon the prisoner's attention. At moments all of them talked at once, as when they came to the death of Boisgelin. The mention of it brought

Boishardi suddenly to his feet, so terrible of aspect that their clamours were instantly extinguished in awe.

After a pause he spoke, in a dull, concentrated voice. 'Dead! Boisgelin dead!' He sank into his chair again, as if overcome, a hand to his brow.

Grosjean went forward, and placed upon the table those effects which had been taken from Quentin, the safe-conduct on top. It was some time before Boishardi paid any attention to these. His voice tortured almost to a moan kept repeating monotonously: 'Boisgelin dead! Murdered!'

At last Quentin spoke. 'Not murdered. I killed him in fair fight. He chose to challenge me.'

Boishardi looked up. His wild glance questioned the Chouans, and Grosjean answered: 'So much is true. The fight was fair enough. We all saw it.'

'But it is not possible. Fair! How could it be?' He leaned heavily upon the table, glaring at Quentin. 'You say he challenged you. Why?'

'Because he liked the unpleasant truth as little as another. Because I told him that he was a poltroon to bring a score of brigands at his heels to attack a single man.'

'You do not tell me why he attacked you.'

The others answered for him. He was a spy of the Blues. Let Monsieur de Boishardi look at the safe-conduct found on him. Monsieur de Boisgelin knew him of old. He had attempted to force his way into Chavaray when Monsieur de Boisgelin was there with a band of followers. He had been at Coëtlegon with Hoche, and with Hoche had travelled as far as Ploermel, where the Republican general had left him, so that he might pursue his filthy trade in the country-side.

'Then why do you bring him to me?' demanded Boishardi. 'Why didn't you hang him from the first tree by the roadside?'

Grosjean told him of the pledge, and of how having obeyed the letter of it they subsequently recaptured the man. 'Because I wasn't easy about it; because it seems

121

to me a point of honour for a gentleman's deciding, I bring him before you, monsieur.'

'A waste of time.' Boishardi's handsome face was white and wicked with grief and rage. 'A waste of time. It is all beside the point. The dog is a spy, and that is all that matters. We do not keep faith with spies. They are outside the pale of honour.' The diamond flashed in the lamplight, as peremptorily he waved his hand. 'Take him out and finish it.'

'Wait, sir!' cried Quentin with the brigands' hands already upon him. 'There is a monstrous error in all this. I am not a spy.'

Boishardi looked at the safe-conduct. He took it up, and waved it, his mouth curved in scorn. 'I take it that it was because you could not persuade Monsieur de Boisgelin of that, that you found it necessary to murder him.'

'That, too, is false. I did not murder him. Even these men have told you that we fought fair and clean.'

'I do not choose to believe it. There was no better blade in France.'

In the face of death, Quentin actually laughed. 'And that's as much a lie as the rest, as I've proved today.'

He could have said nothing more incautiously exasperating. Boishardi's fist crashed upon the table. 'Take him out, I say, and finish it.'

Quentin found himself struggling wildly in their grip. 'Are you all murderers, then? Do you care nothing for the truth that you will not even listen to it? I was at Coëtlegon as the guest of the Marquise du Grégo before Hoche arrived there. Send word to her. She will answer for me. I had nothing to do with Hoche. I had a right to be at Chavaray, as you've been told. Because . . .'

Boishardi interrupted him. 'Enough!' he thundered. 'You should have urged your reasons to Boisgelin, who was in case to judge them. That you preferred to kill him is proof enough for me. That you have killed him is more than enough, whatever and whoever you may be. Away, Grosjean! Get it over.'

'But in God's name, sir,' cried Quentin as they were

dragging him away. 'Do you not even care to know who I am? At least let me account for myself.'

'I care not if you are a prince of the blood. I care only for what you have done,' was the implacable answer. 'And for that you shall pay.'

They had dragged him to within a yard of the door, when it was thrust open from without, and two figures surging on the threshold blocked the way.

The Chouans pulled their prisoner aside so as to give passage to these arrivals, one of whom was tall and spare, with an aspect of command in every line of him, the other plump and stocky.

They came forward staring, the tall man slightly in advance of the other. 'What is happening here?' he asked incuriously, and then caught his breath as his lively eyes came to rest upon Quentin. 'You, here, sir? And a prisoner!' His excitement mounted. 'What is this?'

Quentin raised his drooping head, and to his amazement and the revival of his fainting spirit, beheld the Comte de Puisaye, whom he had so cavalierly dismissed in London. Without cause to suppose that here was one who might be interested in his fate, yet undying hope leapt up in him.

He heard dimly Boishardi's answer: 'It is a scoundrel upon whom justice is to be done.'

'Justice? What manner of justice?'

'The only kind we keep for spies, and murderers. Away with him, Grosjean.'

But if the command was peremptory, so peremptory was the gesture of the Count's uplifted hand that the Chouan did not move. Puisaye stepped forward past Quentin, moving with that confident swaggering peculiar to him. 'I'll know more of this, if you please.'

Boishardi looked up in a surprise that changed to angry impatience. His tone was almost curt. 'The matter is judged and finished. Take him away.'

'Wait!' Puisaye's manner swelled in authority. 'You did not hear me, I think. I said that I require to know more of this. Justice that is in haste is ever suspect. Untie his hands, Grosjean.'

More than by the order was Quentin astonished by the promptitude with which that voice of quiet authority was obeyed.

Boishardi, on his feet again, was raging. 'What does this mean, Puisaye? Do you interfere with me?'

'You make it necessary. It happens that I know something of this gentleman, something which you, who have sat in judgment on him, can have been at no pains to discover. That does not please me.'

'I care nothing for any of that. What I know, and you do not, is that he has killed Bosgelin. And for that I'll have him hanged whatever you may know about him, and whatever you may say.'

'I see.' Puisaye's tone was sardonic. 'You've a nice sense of justice. You make yourself the instrument of a private vengeance. I arrive no more than in time.'

'In time for what, if you please?' Boishardi was not all truculence.

'To prevent a crime for which I must have called you terribly to account.'

'Call me to account!'

'That is what I said. As a beginning, let me present you to the Marquis de Chavaray.'

Boishardi stared, his white face distorted by passion. 'What lie is that?'

'Let us be clear, Monsieur de Boishardi. Do I understand you to give me the lie?'

'Ah, bah!' There was a gesture of fierce impatience. 'I mean, how do you come to credit such a thing?'

'I happen to know it. Of sure knowledge. Monsieur de Chavaray and I have met before. In London.'

'But the creature is a spy.'

'Somebody has told you that. It is merely foolish.'

'But here's the evidence.' And in a shaking hand Boishardi held out the safe-conduct. 'And if you want more, question Grosjean there.'

Puisaye would not even look at the paper. 'There is no evidence at all. There cannot be evidence of what is not. You've fastened upon some contemptible nonsense not worth sifting. What's this of his killing Boisgelin? Or is that in the same class?'

'Tell him, Grosjean!' cried the exasperated Boishardi.

When the tale was told, Puisaye turned quietly to Quentin. 'Do you agree with all that?'

'I do, sir. These men set upon me. At Boisgelin's orders they were about to hang me. He would listen to no reason.'

'Of course not.' And now Puisaye laughed. 'Of course not. A dear friend and kinsman of your cousins of Chesnières, that Monsieur de Boisgelin. Quite possibly their agent. And then?'

'I remembered his fame as a duellist. I took advantage of it. I insulted him grossly in the hope that such a swordsman would make a personal matter of it. When that succeeded, I exacted a pledge of immunity from his men before I would meet him.'

'And the pledge was violated. Perfect.' He turned again to Boishardi. 'And you would have made yourself a party to that dishonour by murdering Monsieur de Chavaray. Do you begin to see from what I save you?'

Boishardi was unmoved. 'Monsieur de Puisaye, I will not tolerate your interference. It is well to be frank. For what that man has done he shall certainly hang, whatever you may say.'

'You should pay attention. You cannot have heeded my allusion to Boisgelin as a dear friend and kinsman of Saint-Gilles and his brother.'

'What shall that mean?'

'Boisgelin's repute was none so sweet as to place him above suspicion of serving his kinsmen and friends in his own fashion.'

'By God, sir! Are there no limits to the lengths to which your interest in this person will carry you?'

'None. None. So now that you understand that you may dismiss these lads. There will be no hanging tonight.'

Tense and white, Boishardi leaned heavily upon the table.

'Is that a challenge, Monsieur le Comte?'

'No. It's an order. You'll submit or else . . . But

there! You'ld never be fool enough to drive me to deal with you for insubordination. You'll still remember, I hope, that here I represent the Princes.'

A flush of anger welled up to stain Boishardi's pallor. He came stalking round the table to confront Puisaye at close quarters. 'I am your subordinate only for so long as I choose to be. My followers are my own, and their obedience is to me.'

'That is brave, Monsieur de Boishardi.'

And now for the first time Puisaye's plump companion spoke. 'So brave as to be almost treason.'

'You are new to Brittany, Monsieur le Baron,' he was pointedly answered. 'Breton loyalties are not perhaps as those of others.'

'Faith!' the plump gentleman retorted. 'You make it evident, if what you offer is a sample of it. The great cause we serve is by your lights to yield to petty personal differences.'

'This difference is not a petty one, Monsieur de Cormatin. A dear friend and one of our most gallant leaders has been done to death by a rascal who travels under a safe-conduct from the Committee of Public Safety. Judge if that condemns him. But judge as you please, I will not be baulked of justice upon the slayer.'

'If we are still to talk of justice, I'll use plainer terms,' said Puisaye. 'This gallant leader, this dear friend, has met at last the fate which he has long been inviting. And that, if you please, is the end of the matter.'

It proved also the end of what little patience Boishardi still possessed. 'Grosjean,' he commanded, 'you will take that man and deal with him as I ordered.'

'Grosjean!' said Puisaye, and the sternness of his voice and aspect rooted the Chouan where he stood. Then Puisaye took Boishardi by the shoulders and span him round, so that they faced each other again.

'Listen to me, madman. I should break you for this if I were not your friend. If you think to prevail against me because you have your lads at hand, dismiss the thought. I am not alone. I have a thousand men with me, for work that's to be done. They outnumber your band by five to one. So let me invite you to bow to force since you will not bow to reason.'

Abruptly Puisaye cast off his sternness, laughed, and held out his hand.

'Come, my friend. Let this end peaceably. We've work to do together. It is not for us to quarrel among ourselves.'

Boishardi ignored the hand. He continued stiff and hostile, breathing hard. 'The quarrel is not of my making. You come hectoring it here to assert yourself against me in defence of a man who is of no account to you.'

'It happens that he is. Honour, too, is of some account to me. Yours as well as mine. Tomorrow you will thank me for this intervention.' And again he held out his hand.

Still ignoring it, Boishardi turned and paced away to put the table between them.

'There is no more to be said.' His tone was bitter.

'I hoped there might be,' Puisaye answered. 'But I will not urge it. I regret to say that you do not impress me favourably, Monsieur de Boishardi.'

'That desolates me, of course,' was the insolent answer. 'Must we continue this interview?'

'Not upon personal matters. But there is something else. The fact not only that I arrive, but that I come in force might suggest it. I have a word of a convoy of arms, ammunition, and equipment for the Army of Cherbourg, which should pass this way, on the road to Rennes, by noon tomorrow. It travels under the strong guard of a whole regiment of Blues, also on its way to reinforce that army. Therefore, we must be in strength if we are to deal with it. I require your co-operation, and I have to ask you to see that your men are under arms soon after daybreak and ready to be moved to the post I shall assign you.'

He had employed a hardening tone of authority as if to beat down any opposition that might spring from Boishardi's resentful, mutinous state of mind. As

127

Boishardi remained silent, his handsome face darkened by his angry thoughts. Puisaye added after a pause: 'You have heard me, Monsieur de Boishardi?'

The other inclined his head. 'I have heard,' he coldly acknowledged.

'Then, if you please, you will report to me at daybreak.' He turned without waiting for an answer. 'You will come with me, Monsieur de Chavaray, and you, Baron.'

He passed out, and none now dared to hinder Quentin as he followed the stately figure from the hut in which he had looked upon the awful face of death.

CHAPTER 15

The Chouans

IN THE little time that Puisaye had spent with Boishardi, a three-sided log cabin, a dozen feet square, as if by magic had sprung into existence on the far side of the clearing. A company of the Count's followers, a score of them perhaps, who had gone about the task of construction with the energy of ants, were now, by the light of lanterns, completing its roof of ramage.

Within, when Puisaye had brought Quentin and the Baron to it, they found a table and some stools, of short, round timbers, that had been swiftly knocked together. For bedding there were piles of leaves and ferns, over which cloaks might be spread. A couple of lanterns slung from side poles adequately lighted that interior.

It was a method of construction in which the Chouans were expert, offering an alternative to the trenches built for the shelter of the main bodies in their forest fastnesses. These, dug to a considerable depth and solidly roofed by branches under a dissembling cover of turf and leaves, would defy detection by any soldiers rash enough to carry pursuit into the depths of a forest. They help to explain the mystery of Chouan movements in the guerrilla warfare they conducted, their sudden appearances where least suspected, and their equally sudden and complete disappearances once their work was done. Reports that they vanished as if the earth had swallowed them were often nearer the literal truth than the reporters suspected.

A young man in Chouan dress, of little more than middle height, but of a massive breadth and corpulence suggestive of great power, stood forward with a grin of welcome. It was Georges Cadoudal, a Chouan leader from the Morbihan, already famous, and destined to still greater fame.

'Behold your quarters, my General. A wave of my fairy wand, and it springs from the ground. Another wave and the commissariat will arrive, though I doubt if it be equal to our appetites.' Light, prominent eyes stared at Quentin out of a round red face. 'A newcomer?'

Puisaye named them to each other, describing Quentin as his friend the Marquis de Chavaray, a description that checked further questions, whereafter Cadoudal went off to quicken the sluggards in charge of supper.

Then, at last, Quentin came to the matter of returning thanks. 'I owe you my life, Monsieur le Comte.'

'Faith, that's the sort of truth one doesn't hear every day,' was the answer, delivered with a grim humour that rendered it surprising. 'It was fortunate for both of us that I arrived when I did. I begin to believe I have the gift of timeliness.'

'I perceive the good fortune to you, sir, as little as I am overwhelmed by the good fortune to myself. It was a nasty situation.'

'From which you would not have extricated yourself as readily as you did from the toils of Boisgelin.' He set a hand familiarly upon Quentin's shoulder and smiled gravely into his face, and the memory of their parting

129

in London rose to shame Quentin, perhaps the more bitterly because Puisaye appeared to have forgotten it. 'I admire your wit in that affair. And on my soul I believe that you performed better than you suspect. I would wager that Boisgelin—a rascal at heart, who has met his deserts—was aware that in extinguishing you he was serving the interests of his dear cousins. You'll realize before all is done that you have to fight more than the Republic for your patrimony.'

'Be that as it may, it does not explain the luck to you in arriving when you did.'

It was Cormatin who supplied unexpectedly the answer. 'It has enabled the General to form an accurate judgment of the man whom he intended for his deputy in his absence.'

'That is your assumption, Baron. It was never more than a passing thought with me to appoint any of these acknowledged leaders to the supreme command whilst I am gone. Their pestilent jealousies make them untrustworthy. To appoint any one of them is to risk the anger and defection of all the others. That's how the Vendée was lost. Fused into one, those armies must have prevailed against the Blues and made an end of the Republic. But because Lescure would not be subject to Charette, and Stofflet would not take the orders of either, the Blues had easy work to defeat them piecemeal. It must not happen again, and it shall not, if it lies in my power, as I believe it does, to prevent it. But here comes Georges with supper.'

Cadoudal reappeared, boisterously ushering a couple of peasants, one of them bearing on a wooden platter a goose that had been roasted in the forest, the other with a basket on either arm, into which had been packed some loaves of rye bread and a half-dozen bottles of wine.

'A goose as heavy as a swan and juicy as a suckling, and enough wine of Anjou for it to swim in!' roared Cadoudal's big voice. 'The General is served. To table, sirs.'

They drew up the rude stools, and Cadoudal sat down with them. He had sent Boishardi an invitation to join them. But his messenger returned with word that Monsieur de Boishardi begged to be excused.

Puisaye shrugged. 'Let the fool sulk in his tent if he will.'

'A whiff of that goose would lift the sulks from a prouder stomach,' vowed Cadoudal. 'But his loss will be our gain. And, after all, what would be one goose among five?'

A prodigy of a trencherman, he gauged the appetites of his companions by his own.

When of the goose no more than the bones remained, a cheese of goats' milk and some figs were discovered in the bread basket, and after that, with a second bottle of wine to each of them, Cadoudal and Cormatin loaded their pipes.

Through the open front of their cabin they would see in the clearing the glow of the bivouac fire, which had now been banked, and the shadows of men lying or moving quietly about it.

The talk was mainly political. Cormatin was in correspondence with the secret Royalist agency in Paris, an organization which Puisaye distrusted, denouncing it as in the hands of self-sufficient mischief-makers. The Baron was informed by it of the state of things in the capital, the new government's total lack of orientation, and the rumours that many of those now in power, Barras amongst them, favoured the return of the monarchy. Hoche himself was said to entertain Royalist sympathies since his imprisonment by the Convention, and they would find that his mission in the West would prove to be one of pacification rather than repression.

Puisaye poured scorn on it all. 'Thus the windy Abbé Brottier, who imagines himself the axis on which monarchism now revolves. Let him chatter his fill, and send his gossipy reports to the Princes. Our task is to work, and the West will be pacified when this task is done and the King is back in the Tuileries.'

'Amen and amen,' said Cadoudal. 'Bring over your English reinforcements, and our lads will sweep the putrid remains of this Republic to hell.'

From what followed Quentin gathered that Puisaye's final mission of preparation in Brittany was now complete, and in the assurance that his army, computed at three hundred thousand men, would rise at a word, he was about to return to England to report to Pitt and claim the powerful aid he had been promised. Within three months he counted upon being ready to strike. His Royal Highness, the Comte d'Artois, as Lieutenant-General of the Kingdom, had engaged himself to take the supreme command; and so, with one of the Princes at their head, jealousies would be extinguished and all rival Royalist bands be fused into a single solid army.

From that Puisaye came to matters personally concerned with Quentin, and drew from him an account in detail of how he had fared in France.

'And so,' Quentin ended, 'lacking the means to satisfy the Republican needs of Monsieur Besné, my marquisate passes into national property, and I remain a Marquis *pour rire;* or, in the words of Monsieur Constant de Chesnières—since repeated, by the way, by Monsieur de Boisgelin—a Marquis of Carabas.'

Cormatin was amused. *'Chapeau bas!'* he quoted with a laugh, which earned him a sardonic reproof from Puisaye.

'You are too fat for Puss-in-Boots, Baron.'

'I wonder where I shall find me one,' said Quentin. 'At the moment it seems the only thing I lack so as to complete me.'

'We'll find you one, never doubt it,' Puisaye assured him. 'Your only need is patience. Meanwhile, you should have had enough of France. A little more of it, and—name of a name!—your bones would have remained here permanently. You invite danger from both sides.'

'Yet to retreat defeated!' He sighed.

'A strategic retreat is not a defeat, child. You draw back so that you may leap the better. I start for the coast tomorrow night. You'ld be well advised to travel with me back to England.'

Again Quentin was shamed by this fresh display of a

kindly solicitude from a man who would have been justified in the very opposite. Puisaye overbore in his high-handed way the young man's hesitations, and before he slept that night Quentin had penned a letter to Lesdiguières to inform him that failure at Coëtlegon left him no alternative but to return whence he had come, and await events.

Whilst he was doing it, Puisaye was concluding with his two companions the disposition still to be made before he departed; the appointment of a lieutenant to represent him in the West during his absence. He was settled in the determination to appoint none of those gentlemen who headed bands raised in their own districts.

'I perceive the folly of it as clearly as I perceive that had I been a Breton with an immediate following of my own peasantry, not even my appointment by the Princes to the supreme command would have induced these gentlemen to submit to me.'

'Jealous as Spaniards, these Bretons,' Cormatin agreed with him.

'Oh, as to that, Baron, don't imagine that Bretons are the only Frenchmen cursed with that disease.' He was bitter on the subject of the obstacles jealousy had insensately raised for him in England, seeking in reckless malice to destroy his credit with the British Government, without which nothing would be accomplished.

'The only possible nobleman here,' Puisaye continued, 'is one whose influence, gallantry, and repute inspire an almost superstitious dread in the Republicans. I mean Boishardi.'

'A mistake, Monsieur le Comte,' Cadoudal condemned it. 'I know his worth, and I'ld willingly serve under him with my lads. But the others . . . *Parbleu*, not one of them would recognize Monsieur de Boishardi as better than himself.'

'That is why I have brought Monsieur de Cormatin.'

The Baron looked up, his prominent eyes widening in his florid face.

'You are not proposing . . .'

'I am. It must be settled tonight. And there is no other way but by bringing in a man from outside, since no Breton will be served by these Bretons. Just as they accepted my nomination by the Princes because I am not a Breton, so they will accept my nomination of you as my Major-General, paying attention only to your military qualifications, which my proclamation will not fail to stress. *Parbleu,* you may laugh if you please. It deserves that you should.'

Cormatin, shrinking visibly from the responsibility, was all protests. But Puisaye masterfully swept them aside. 'Men's deference goes more readily to the unknown than to the known,' was his crowning, sardonic argument. 'What do you say to it, Georges?'

'It's the solution,' said Cadoudal.

'That, Baron, is the voice of the rank and file of the army you'll control.'

'But the duties!' cried Cormatin. 'What do I know of them?'

'They are soon summed up: to preserve the cohesion of this great secret army that awaits the call; to avoid any dissipation of its strength in minor encounters and inconclusive skirmishes; and to maintain its monarchical spirit, its high resolve, and readiness to strike for Throne and Altar when the moment arrives. There are your duties. They are simple, and in the discharge of them you will have the support of the chiefs, with whom you will work in consultation. In honour you cannot refuse the charge.'

'Monsieur le Baron can depend upon me; and I count for something hereabouts.'

'Both with the men and with the chiefs,' Puisaye added. 'With Georges beside you, you may make your mind easy. And so, I'll draw up my proclamation before I sleep.'

At once reassured and overborne, Cormatin dismissed what reluctance lingered in him, and went to dispose himself on one of the rude beds the forest yielded.

They were astir again at peep of day, and after a

crust and a draught of wine they were following an army that moved forward scarcely visible and with little more than a rustle through the forest twilight. Every man—and there were fully a thousand moving to that ambuscade—bore the white cockade in his hat, the emblem of the Sacred Heart on his breast, and his gun slung from his shoulders. Boishardi was not visible; but he marched at the head of his own contingent, and when the sally into the open came it was he who led it.

That sally followed upon a massacring fusillade poured from the forest's edge upon the convoy as it moved, unsuspecting, along the road to Rennes.

The Blues were some four hundred strong, and in two detachments, one ahead of the long line of wagons, the other following it. The attack was made simultaneously upon front and rear, and when the rolling volleys had accounted for more than a quarter of each detachment, the Chouans poured forth from their cover in two parties, one led by Boishardi, the other by Cadoudal, and fell upon the remainder before they could recover from the confusion into which they had been flung.

Vainly did the surviving officers seek to rally them; vainly did a mounted major seek to curse them into standing firm. They were youngsters mostly newly conscripted, until this moment unbaptized by fire, and appalled by the wild aspect of the fierce men who now assailed them. Once broken it was beyond their power to form their ranks anew, and as the major was brought to earth by a shot that killed his horse, the lads, flinging away their muskets so that they might travel lighter, fled the field of battle, some sweeping along the road towards Rennes, others taking to the woods opposite to those from which the attack had come.

All happened at such speed that within a half-hour of the attack, no evidence remained of it but the plundered and shattered forage wagons. The wounded and the dead had been borne into the woods, and the Chouan horde, having struck its blow, had vanished again completely. Only the tale of it remained to be borne by the fugitives to the garrison at Rennes, which, recognizing its impotence to seek out so elusive an enemy, would merely race and curse and indite a report, for the exasperation of the Convention in Paris, of the rich haul of arms, ammunition, accoutrements, and provender by which the Chouans were supplied towards a continuance of their brigand warfare.

BOOK II

CHAPTER 1

Germaine

ON A COOL but sunny October afternoon, Quentin de Morlaix, newly arrived in London, walked down Bruton Street towards the academy that bore his name.

His return to England in Puisaye's company had been rendered possible without adventure by the secret Royalist lines of communication whose network was spread over the face of Brittany, and the perfection of which in the district he had traversed had moved Quentin to amazement, as well as to respect for, and confidence in, the man who had established and maintained them.

Travelling by night and sleeping by day, they had made their first stage at a house to the north of Lamballe belonging to a Madame de Kerverso, in the loft of which a secret hiding-place received them; their second had been at Villegourio, where they were well received in a peasant homestead; and their third at Nantois, whence word was sent on to Puisaye's agent at Saint-Brieuc to hold his fishing-boat in readiness for the following night. This agent had met them in the outskirts of Saint-Brieuc, and had conducted them safe and unchallenged through the cordon of coast guards and excisemen that barred the passage to the coast. Bribes, Puisaye explained, played a part in dulling the vigilance of those custodians of the shores.

From the water's edge a little boat had taken them a couple of miles out to sea to the waiting fishing-smack. In this they had crossed to Jersey, and thence, by the regular packet, to Dover. So smoothly had they fared from start to finish that it was scarcely conceivable that the journey could have been accomplished more easily in times of peace.

And now Quentin was going up his own steps, entering his own house again, and stalking unannounced into the long fencing-room.

At sight of him the grizzled Ramel, engaged at the moment with a pupil, uttered a cry that brought O'Kelly from the far window-bay, where he was idling.

'Glory be, now! Is it yourself, Quentin, or will it be the ghost of you?'

Before he could answer, O'Kelly was upon him, holding him by the arms and chuckling into his face, whilst Ramel, his pupil unceremoniously neglected, hovered exclamatory about him, and old Barlow, who had suddenly appeared, quivered in dumb excitement in the background.

'And us thinking we'd never be seeing you again this side of hell!' cried O'Kelly, a hand on Quentin's shoulder, a glow of affection in his eyes.

'That was to be wanting in faith.'

'It was not. It was from putting faith in a lie that was told us. Wasn't Mademoiselle de Chesnières here, nigh on a month since, to tell us you were murdered?'

'Her tale,' said Ramel, 'was that you'd been killed by Chouans, somewhere in Brittany.'

'Mademoiselle de Chesnières told you that?'

'She did so. And with the tears in her sweet eyes that I'ld be glad to earn by dying. They had word of it, she said, from . . . What would his name be, Ramel?'

'From the steward of Chavaray, she said. I don't recall his name. The news had come in a letter from him to Monsieur de Saint-Gilles.'

'I see,' said Quentin. A bitter little smile broke on his lips. 'It explains a lot. A rash anticipation on the part of that rascal.'

Then the thought of the tears that O'Kelly had mentioned swept all else from his mind. He desired more particular information upon those tears. Yet he dared not ask for them. He would seek them at the hands of the lady who was alleged to have shed them.

'There's an error to be corrected without delay. I'll be paying a visit to Carlisle Street at once.'

'Ye'll do nothing of the kind if it's Mademoiselle de Chesnières you'ld be seeking. They've moved to Percy Street, off the Tottenham Court Road. I've written down the exact address. There's been a change in their fortunes, I'm thinking.'

After that Quentin did not tarry long. Supplied with the address of a glover in Percy Street, he went off in quest of it. Directed by the glover to the second floor, he climbed the creaking, gloomy, narrow staircase of that mean house, and rapped on the door that led to the rooms at the back.

When the door opened, to his surprise it was Mademoiselle de Chesnières herself who appeared, contrasting sharply in her shimmering grey gown and neatly coifed head with the background of a frowsty living-room.

She stood before him with dilating eyes, the colour slowly draining from her cheeks. Then there was an inarticulate cry, followed at last by coherent speech.

'Is it really you, Monsieur de Morlaix?' The question was almost whispered.

'I've startled you. Forgive me. If I could have suspected that you would yourself answer my knock . . .'

'That is nothing,' she interrupted him. 'We have believed you dead, Cousin Quentin, and . . . and . . .'

'I know. O'Kelly told me. You had word of it from Lafont.'

'Lafont wrote that he was informed of it by the Public Accuser of Angers, and that as a result Chavaray has now been sequestrated.'

'I understand.' He smiled apologetically. 'If I might come in?'

But the suggestion awakened alarm in her. 'Ah, no. No. I . . . I prefer that you do not. I am alone here. My aunt and Constant are out. And it is fortunate. It is perhaps better that they should not know of your return. I don't know. I must have time to think.' She panted and trembled as she spoke.

'I would not for the world embarrass you.'

'Then, go, please. Go at once. I would not have Constant find you here. I dread what might happen. Living, he will never forgive you.'

'He's to forgive me, is he? Pray for what?'

'For murdering our cousin, Boisgelin. We know, you see.'

'So! That's the tale now!' Quentin laughed his scorn. 'I killed him. But I shouldn't call it murder. The only murderer in the affair was Boisgelin himself.'

She was staring at him, with sorrowful inquiring eyes, when a sound below revived her alarms. 'Ah, *mon Dieu!* If it should be they! Go, monsieur, please, please go.'

'When there's so much to say,' he sighed. He was thinking of the tears of which O'Kelly had told him.

'Go now, and you shall have the opportunity. I'll provide it. I will come to you.'

She was gasping over the words, and Quentin understood that it was to get rid of him that she uttered them.

'When will you come?'

'When you will. Today. This evening. Oh, please go.'

'I shall have the honour to await you.'

'Do so. Yes. Yes.'

The door closed whilst he was bowing, and he departed wondering whether she would keep her word.

He went home to wait, and at six o'clock that evening, Barlow ushered her cloaked and hooded into the panelled room above-stairs where she had come to him on the morning of his departure, less than three months ago.

When she had suffered him to take her cloak, he saw that sternness now replaced the earlier panic in which she had repulsed him.

'I keep my word,' she said. 'I was forced to give it because of my fears of what might happen.'

'And for no other reason?' he gently asked.

'It . . . it seemed proper to give you an opportunity to explain.'

142

He advanced a chair. 'I'll make a plain tale of it,' he said, 'and leave the inferences to you.'

She sat, whilst he, pacing the room under her grave eyes, made of it the plain tale he promised, beginning with his visit to Chavaray, and ending at Puisaye's intervention to save him.

'One understands the report of my death. Once the Chouans had carried me off no more will have been heard of me. One understands, too, some other things. One understands that Boisgelin should address me as Marquis of Carabas, remembering that it was Constant who first applied the name to me. You perceive the coincidence?'

'It is none so remarkable.' Her manner, which had softened during his narrative, grew stiff again. 'Nor do I perceive what inference you draw.'

'Then I will draw none.'

'If you imply some conspiracy between my cousins and Monsieur de Boisgelin, the thought is unworthy. Are you not too prone to suspicion, to drawing harsh conclusions? Was it not enough to justify Monsieur de Boisgelin's assumptions that he should have found you travelling with a safe-conduct from the sansculottes?'

'He did not. I was not searched until after his death.' This startled her, he saw. 'I hope, mademoiselle, that you'll judge me leniently for the course I took to save my neck from the noose he offered me. It was the only way.'

'That I can understand.' She had softened again. 'It is a wretched affair. You have made a determined enemy of Constant. He must not know of your return.'

'I think he must. I do not mean to hide myself. Inevitably he will hear that I am back in London.'

'It is possible that he may not, for we are about to return to France. In two or three days we shall be gone. Saint-Gilles is already in Holland with Sombreuil.'

'You are returning to France? Now?' He was horror-stricken. 'But the danger of it!'

There was a further softening of her glance as if she

143

were touched by this fear on her account. She even smiled a little, and shook her golden head.

'We have no choice. You have seen how we are lodged. My aunt cannot endure it.'

'Name of Heaven! It is still better than a French prison.'

She paid no heed. 'The confiscation of Chavaray has put an end to our means. They were all remitted to us by Lafont, who regarded Saint-Gilles as the next heir. My aunt cannot face this destitution. All her life she has been pampered in the luxury of her position. And now that the Terror is at an end, the risks are negligible. The decrees against the *émigrés* continue in force, but they are being disregarded. So we are assured.'

'But where will you go?'

'That offers no difficulty.' Her smile broadened. 'You are not the only one who has thought of using the Citizen Besné as a nominee. By Lafont's contriving, and for a fat bribe, with moneys from the revenues of Chavaray, he purchased for us Grands Chesnes when it was sold as national property two years ago, after our emigration. We are assured that if we return we shall be left undisturbed in possession of it in these days of tolerance.'

'It is a risk,' he said, and his eyes pondered her in almost sorrowful gravity.

She shrugged. 'All life is that. What can I do? My aunt will face the risk rather than continue in this intolerable poverty. And so, we are making our packages, and in a couple of days we shall be gone. At least,' she ended, 'if for no other reason, I can be glad because it removes the chance of a clash between you and Constant.'

'Do you fear so much for him?' he asked her.

'For him!' Her voice soared on the exclamation. 'For him? It is for you that I fear. I know his remorseless, vindictive nature.'

'For me! Oh, the happiness to hear you say that! To believe that you should know concern for me!'

He saw that he had startled her. 'It . . . It is natural. Is it not?'

'I have hoped—how I have hoped!—that some day it might be.' He came to stand near her. 'Measure by it my concern for you. My dread of the thought of your going to France. If you go, it may be that I shall never see you again.'

She looked down at her hands that were folded in her lap. 'It is what I said to you when I came here to warn you against going.'

'But with a difference. I fear. Or could it have mattered to you if I had not returned?' Then he remembered the tears reported by O'Kelly, and let them wash away the last of his hesitation. 'Do you conceive how it matters to me? Germaine!' He sank down on one knee beside her chair, and his arm went round her. She stiffened a little in the clasp of it, but made no shift to disengage herself. 'You are not to go to France.'

She looked at him suddenly in surprise. She laughed, but her eyes were very tender.

'Let Madame de Chesnières and her son go if they will into this danger.'

'And I? How do I avoid going with them?'

With eyes gazing deep into hers he answered softly: 'You have guessed, haven't you? You see, it becomes necessary to be brusque; there is no longer time for timid approaches. You may avoid it if you will marry me, although I remain no better than a fencing-master, and Marquis only of Carabas.'

'If you were less than that, you would still be Quentin,' was her soft answer, and leaning forward, she kissed him.

'Dear heart,' he cried, when he recovered breath. 'It is settled, then.'

'Ah, no. You forget, my dear, or, rather, you do not know my age. For another year I shall not be mistress of myself. Meanwhile, Madame de Chesnières is my legal guardian, and the law is on her side. It would be so easy,' she ended on a sigh, 'if it were otherwise.'

'But if she consented . . .'

'It would be madness even to ask her. No, no, my Quentin. That happiness is not yet for us.'

'And for me not even the happiness this hour has brought me, since it must be lost in dread for you.'

She stroked his bronze-hued hair. 'That dread is so easily exaggerated, my dear. Already the *émigrés* are beginning to return, and so long as they are prudent, we are assured that they are in no danger of being molested, particularly in the West, which the Government is anxious to pacify.'

'And I am to be content with that assurance?'

'What other do you need? The assurance that I shall be waiting for you? That I give you, my dear, if you still require it.'

'Waiting until when?' he asked her, gloomily.

'Until Fate shall so have shaped things that you may come for me, or else until having attained full age and become mistress of myself I may come to you. And that is less than a year ahead.' Seeing him still sunk in gloom, she ran on: 'Dear Quentin, it will not be long, and in the meantime there is the joy of knowing that we are travelling steadily towards each other, that every day is a step along that blessed road.'

His arms were round her, and he held her close. 'Let me draw from you some of your fine courage.'

'Take freely,' she urged him, smiling into his eyes. 'That and my love. Know always that it is yours, Quentin.'

And then the knell of their ecstasy sounded from the little ormolu timepiece on the overmantel. Its striking came to remind her of the need to depart, lest an account should be asked of her absence. Whatever the obstacles, she would see him again before she left for France.

With that assurance, given in a farewell embrace, she swirled away, leaving him in a state approaching frenzy, between alternating exaltation and despondency.

The Warning

peasants will descend upon you, to drag you from your
château and murder you. That is how Constant

CHAPTER 2

The Trust

FOR four months thereafter Quentin, who had resumed
the conduct of his academy, exasperated O'Kelly by
the grim face and absent mind with which he performed his daily tasks. Yet from all that Quentin could
glean from the French nobles who frequented his
school, the dangers to returning *émigrés* were as negligible in these days of pacification as Germaine had
represented them, and if so many of them still abode in
England, it was because they waited to form the regiments that under the British aegis should presently be
landed in the West of France for the purpose of making an end of the Republic.

From the lofty heights of his scorn for all the world,
the Vicomte de Bellanger derided one day the notion
that Constant de Chesnières would have taken chances
in the matter of his return to France.

'We may be very sure that Constant's native caution
would never permit him to set foot there until his
advisers in France assured him that he might do so
without fear of being called to account for his emigration. Faith, I would go back myself, and await in
France the coming of the Royalist army, if I did not
find life so pleasant here in London.' It was notorious
by then that he had not gone because Madame de
Laitonges would not permit him to leave her side until
the last moment.

Further, Quentin was reassured by letters—some
three or four—which Germaine had contrived to send
him, but to which he was denied the satisfaction of
replying.

Nevertheless, dejection sat heavily upon him. Paradoxically it was increased, perhaps, by what had passed at his last meeting with Germaine; for he was left in the position of one who has won something which Fate denies him the ability to grasp.

He was in a particularly black mood when, on a morning of February, Monsieur be Puisaye surprised him by swaggering into his academy. He had not seen the Count since that morning when they had reached London together four months ago, a circumstance explained to him by the gossip of the *émigrés* who frequented Bruton Street. According to this, Puisaye had returned almost at once to France in the pursuit of the will-o'-the-wisp by which he was to restore the monarchy.

'Behold me returned, my dear Quentin,' was his airy announcement, 'to the chagrin, no doubt, of your friends our compatriots. No friends of mine, these fribbles. Sometimes I think they would rather continue to starve here than be restored to their possessions by anything that I may accomplish. I am not pure enough for the high stomachs of these gentlemen.'

His tone was carelessly loud considering that several of those to whom he so scornfully alluded were present in the fencing-room. Count d'Hervilly, who had become of considerable authority among his fellow exiles, was of these. He had just been at practice, and he was in the act of readjusting his cravat before a mirror on the wall. A tall, rather long-bodied man, stern-faced, with hard blue eyes and a domineering manner, he turned.

'Not pure enough for what?' he asked, as he sauntered towards them.

'To lead you to victory over the infernal Republic.'

'We recall that you served it once.'

'Then you are pleased to recall a lie. I led an army of Girondins, in the hope of smashing the Terrorists.'

'You distinguish between them! That is too subtle for the minds of Monarchists or honest men.'

His manner was superciliously insolent, and his tone was drawing others about them into the window embrasure. Puisaye was unabashed by their general air of hostility. He laughed at D' Hervilly.

'You should not assume that all Monarchists and honest men are half-wits. The percipient ones will see that to lead one half of a faction against the other is to destroy the whole.'

'If successfully led, it might be so. But I have not heard that you were successful.'

Puisaye shrugged. 'Because I led a pack of cowards, who fled at the first discharge. Besides, your quarrel, I think, is with the act itself, not with the result.'

'By what else do you judge an act?'

Quentin was finding d'Hervilly's insolence distasteful. He ventured to interpose. 'Sometimes, surely, by its intention.'

'I thank you, sir,' said Puisaye with a flourish, and turned again to d'Hervilly. 'So it has been judged by your betters.'

D'Hervilly threw up his head. 'My betters!'

'You'll suffer me so to describe the Princes, I suppose. In statecraft you might even suffer me so to describe Mr. Pitt.'

The old Duc d'Harcourt interjected: 'Do you say, sir, that they honour you with their confidence?'

Puisaye raised his brows. 'God save us! Your Grace has been asleep in these last months, I must suppose. It is their confidence, Monsieur le Duc, that enables me to bear with equanimity the lack of it in lesser folk. Though you may question my purity, it is freely accepted by the purest of the pure, by my dear friend, Monseigneur d'Artois.'

That brought a gasp from some of them. The old Duke angrily stabbed the ground with his cane.

'Unsurpassable effrontery! My God, I choke! To call His Royal Highness your dear friend!'

Puisaye's suave insolence was untroubled. 'The term is His Highness's own.' He brought a letter from his bosom. 'See for yourself, Duke, how His Highness addresses me. "My dear friend," is it not? Read on, if you will. You will find that he commends my labours, speaks of his impatience to co-operate with me and to take command of the army I have raised.'

Before his magnificent amused contempt there was a general, shocked, resentful silence in that courtly group.

'I hope Monseigneur's trust will not prove misplaced,' was the Duke's sour comment.

'You may hope it confidently,' Puisaye assured him. 'In fact you may believe it, like Mr. Pitt.'

'Mr. Pitt's beliefs will hardly help us,' sneered one.

'I think they will when translated into material assistance: ships and men, besides equipment and munitions for the army that awaits me in Brittany.'

'You have persuaded Mr. Pitt that an army awaits you! *Pardieu!* I felicitate you on your persuasiveness.'

'I thank you. I deserve no less. That army will rally to my standard when I raise it.' He looked at them, almost seeming to flaunt his splendid height, his magnificent head thrown back. 'Ah, messieurs, I could make myself Duke of Brittany if I would,' he boasted.

'I suppose,' cackled d'Harcourt, 'that Mr. Pitt believes that, too. An ingenuous gentleman, this Mr. Pitt.' He turned contemptuously away, and it was as a signal for the others to depart.

'You will believe it when you are invited to enrol,' Puisaye flung after them. 'A chance for you all, messieurs, to bleed instead of merely talking.'

Disgruntled they melted away, and very soon there was not a Frenchman remaining in the academy.

Barlow came with his decanters, and in the window-bay overlooking a garden now sodden with the February rains Quentin made shift to entertain his guest.

'I wonder you think it worth while to bait them with your boasts.'

'Boasts? Did I boast?' Puisaye settled himself in a chair. 'If I did, I boasted only of what I can perform. And it amuses me to see those numskulls squirm and squirt their futile venom. There's not a man amongst them but would rather not see the monarchy restored than that I should be the leader of that restoration. Don't begrudge me the amusement of crowing in their silly faces now that at last I've brought the British Government to support my enterprise.'

'Is that really assured?'

'*Pardieu!* Will you, too, be offensive? Ships, men, arms, clothes, provisions, and the rest. I have Pitt's definite promise. And in Brittany my army is ready. It awaits my signal.'

Quentin stood facing him, suddenly inspired. 'When do we sail?'

'*We?* What have you to do with it?'

'You'll not suppose I would not wish to be of the expedition. I have something to fight for, I believe.'

Puisaye looked doubtful. 'There's not the need. You'ld do better to remain here until the business is finished. Trust me then to see you settled in your marquisate. It will set a crown to my work.'

Quentin stared at him. 'You want to laugh,' he said.

'How so?'

'A little more, and you'll imply that the British ships and your Breton army are to be applied to the restoration of the Marquis of Carabas.'

'Of Chavaray,' Puisaye gravely corrected. Then increased Quentin's amazement by adding with a careless laugh, 'Faith, it may be nearer the truth than you suspect.'

'It could not be farther from it. Let us be serious. When you go, I go. And it cannot be too soon for me.'

'You'll have some reason for this. What is it?'

'My own.'

'Devil take you. Keep your confidence, then. But if it's the thought of Chavaray that's troubling you, I can tell you that Chavaray is safe. I took care to inform myself on my last journey. It has been sequestered, and is for sale. It could be bought for next to nothing. But lack of faith in the present order of things makes a sale impossible. There are no fools to buy lands from which they may be expelled tomorrow by a restoration. It was, in fact, to assure you of this that I came here today.'

'I am more grateful than I can say.' Indeed, Puisaye's interest in him was a source of ever-increasing wonder to Quentin. 'But my anxiety to return to France is on quite other grounds.'

'Of which you have told me that you do not wish to speak. Well, well. We shall see.' Puisaye drained his glass, and stood up to take his leave. 'You shall hear from me when I'm ready to sail.'

Bruton Street did not see him again for a full month. But Quentin heard of him, and what he heard was little to the Count's credit; for the *émigrés* were the reporters.

At first they were seeking to discover the link between Quentin and one whom they never scrupled to describe as an upstart adventurer.

'He is my friend,' Quentin had coldly discouraged more than one of them. 'In France he saved my life. That is a sufficient debt, I think.'

At first, and at least in part, it curbed their slanderous tendencies. Soon, however, news spreading to confirm Puisaye's boast that he had won the support of Pitt and the confidence of the Princes, the festering bitterness could no longer be repressed. It was remembered and repeated that he had been elected to the States General in '89 as a representative of the nobles, and had treacherously voted with the Third Estate. He was a Republican at heart, and because even revolutionaries had rejected him he now made war upon the Republic. He had won the confidence of the Princes by a trick. By a trick he had imposed himself upon the Chouans, seizing the chance afforded by the death of La Rouërie, who had organized them.

This, and much more, Quentin heard and scorned, assigning it rightly to a mean jealousy of the man's extraordinary ascendancy. He even made some enemies by defending Puisaye's name; and a few *émigrés* there were, such as Bellanger and d'Hervilly, who ceased to frequent the academy on that account.

O'Kelly took these defections to heart, and was acid on the score of Puisaye and Quentin's growing regard for him. Quentin, however, had other matters on his mind. His hunger to return to France so that he might be near Germaine had been at once sharpened and its satisfaction revealed as possible by Puisaye's account of the growing spirit of toleration and the difficulty of selling national property that was the fruit of confiscation.

The seed thus sown had germinated to such purpose in Quentin's mind that, taking advantage of the fact that Sir Francis Burdett, who had lately married the youngest daughter of Mr. Coutts, often came to fence in Bruton Street, he procured from him a letter of introduction to his father-in-law. Armed with this, he went off to the City, to seek that famous banker's guidance and assistance. To such purpose were they accorded him that presently it was reported in the academy that Monsieur de Morlaix was preparing to pay a second visit to France.

Hard upon the spreading of that report, on a wild night towards the end of March, Puisaye descended upon him to annoy him by a reproach of the intention.

'You have me spied upon, it seems,' Quentin complained.

'That's an ugly description of my interest in you, child.'

'Faith! You're cursedly paternal sometimes.'

Puisaye's mouth fell open in astonishment. Then he laughed, and slapped Quentin's shoulder with his vigorous hand. 'To the devil with your impudence! Have I not the right to be? Can't I boast that you owe your life to me? What more can a father boast?'

'I am not likely to forget it.'

'Tush! It may be a meanness to remind you of it. But you drive me to it by your resentment of my concern. And that's a meanness, too. What is this haste to return to France?'

'To regain possession of Chavaray, of course. My arrangements are made. It's for sale. I propose to purchase it.'

'A silly waste of money. Our guns will buy it back for you, as I've told you. But if you're too cursedly impatient—*peste!*—I'll not argue with you.'

'You would lose your time.'

'Curse your inflexibility.' Puisaye laughed. Then his manner changed. He became serious. 'To dissuade you now might actually be against my own interests. For if you're set on going, there's a service you can render me.'

Suddenly conscious that an indefinable resentment had been rendering him churlish, Quentin leapt impulsively at the chance of repaying something of his heavy debt towards this man. 'You have but to ask.'

'That's good of you. My need is of a certain urgency, and peculiar. It's this. I have a message for Cormatin, but I must have a messenger who is personally known to Cormatin as well as to Tinténiac, who is now with him. The matter is one that I dare not commit to writing. I cannot risk at this stage that a letter should fall into Republican hands. Will you bear this message for me?'

'But very gladly. Where do I find Cormatin?'

Instead of answering, Puisaye asked him: 'How do you propose to enter France?'

'I have my safe-conduct still.'

'Too dangerous. It may be considered out of date. There have been changes again. You will go to Jersey. Thence one of my agents, whose name I will give you, will put your ashore in the neighbourhood of Saint-Brieuc. From there you will travel along my lines of communication from one to another of the houses of confidence I'll indicate. Now, please attend carefully.'

Followed the substance of the message he was to bear. Puisaye's arrangements with Mr. Pitt were now complete and final. A fleet under Sir John Warren was already being equipped for the expedition. It should be ready to sail by early June, and the determined landing-place in France was the Bay of Quiberon. After this came details of arms, munitions, and equipment for the Chouan army which the British ships would

carry. Of these he supplied a written note, so couched
as to be unintelligible to any who did not possess the
key, and another, similarly framed, detailing the forces
that would be landed to supplement the Chouans.
There would be some four thousand British troops
besides the regiments made up of the *émigrés* in England, amounting to some three thousand men. There
would be a further contingent of some two thousand
émigrés now in Holland with Sombreuil, and yet to be
brought over. In addition there would be an enrolment
from among the French prisoners of war now in England of such as would be willing to earn deliverance
estimated at a thousand.

Acting upon this information, Cormatin was at once
to make such dispositions as would ensure that the
three hundred thousand Chouans upon whom they
counted would be held in readiness to rise in June as
soon as the British ships reached Quiberon.

'It is all so important,' Puisaye ended, 'that I would
go myself if my presence here were less urgently needed. There is not a single one of these pestilential
émigrés I could trust to be my deputy in England. I
have the less scruple to ask this service of you because
of your determination to go in any case. And I reflect
that if I ask you to serve me, I can repay you by
helping you on your way. Along my lines of communication you can be certain of travelling in safety, and of
obtaining assistance and protection at every stage.'

'Thus,' said Quentin graciously, 'we shall be quits.'

'Not until I see you safe at Chavaray in a land
restored to monarchical rule. Believe me, my lad, the
one is as important to me as the other.'

CHAPTER 3

The Return

ABOARD a Breton fishing-smack that in these days fished only so as to dissemble its real activities, Quentin de Morlaix came in the dead of an uneasy night of March to the Bay of Saint-Brieuc. If the foul weather deliberately chosen brought peril of shipwreck on the one hand, on the other it lessened the other lurking perils, no less deadly, that awaited a clandestine landing.

Rémisol, the master of the smack, an old smuggler by trade, who, with a man and a boy for crew, plied now a form of smuggling more dangerous far than the old running of contraband cargoes to England, had picked his weather for the trip from Jersey, and was grateful for the blustering westerly wind that blew them into the gulf, and the driving rain that hung a veil about them.

Within a couple of hundred yards of the beach of Erquy, greatly daring, Rémisol, having lowered the rag of canvas, no more than had been needed to keep the smack handy, swung her beam across the wind, and whilst she rocked from gunwale to gunwale on the long rollers, he drew under her lee the boat she towed. To descend into her was not the least of the perils Quentin was called upon to face. Stumbling and sliding across the vessel's slippery deck, clutching for support at whatever came under his hand, he reached the gunwale. Guided by Rémisol he climbed upon it, clinging desperately to a ratline, and peering through the gloom for the dark patch upon the oily sheen of the sea that marked the boat. Then came the fearsome leap, to be caught in the arms of the seaman, who had preceded him, and to crouch with him, lest they be flung out of that wildly tossing shell.

He came to rest in the stern, whilst his companion thrust out an oar. The boat was swung into the wind, and her antics became less fearful. Soon her keel was grating on the shingle, and the spray was breaking over her, to add to the drenching bestowed by the rain.

'Look alive, sir,' the seaman admonished Quentin.

He clutched him, and at closest quarters pointed, his outstretched arm barely visible in the gloom. 'Yonder is Erquy. See that glimmer of light? That'll be a house in the village. The road to Nantois lies to the right of it.'

'Thanks. I know. I've been this way before. With Erquy before me I cannot go astray.'

'Have a care how you cross the line of coast guards. There's not above a hundred yards between their tents. Give thanks for the rain. It should keep them under cover while it lasts, and as they show no lights they're likely asleep. But we never can tell for sure. So go cautious. You'll find them at the top of the beach. God be with you, sir. Give me a shove.'

With the waves breaking about his thighs, Quentin thrust the boat off. In a moment it had vanished into the darkness, and the creak of rowlocks was lost in the boom and rattle of the waves upon the shingle.

For a moment Quentin thought less of the difficulties awaiting him than of those the seaman must be facing in regaining the smack, which, daring to show no light, remained invisible. Before he turned, he caught faintly above the noise of wind and sea a hail that was answered and repeated, and he understood the device by which boat and smack would find each other again.

Cautiously, his sodden cloak wrapped about him, he began the ascent of the beach towards the danger-line of the coast-guard tents. The downpour was lessening, but the blackness of the night continued almost impenetrable, so that he might be said to be constrained to steer his course by the sound of the sea behind him.

Suddenly, very faintly grey, a vague shape loomed before him and brought him sharply to a halt. He had all but walked into one of the tents, one of the links drawn wherever a landing was possible along the Brittany and Normandy coasts. He was sidling away to the right when the blackness in that direction was abruptly cleft by a glowing cone. Startled by that sudden, silent, luminous explosion, he checked again, his eyes on the tent that had abruptly become visible by the kindling of a light within it.

Shadows moved against the glowing canvas, the shadows of two men, one of them topped by a monstrous distortion of a three-cornered hat, which at once suggested to Quentin that its wearer was about to come forth. Instinctively he dropped to the ground, and instinctively his hand sought the butt of the pistol within the breast of his coat.

A shaft of light from that conical glow cut athwart the night, to be darkened almost at once by the human bulk that appeared in the opening of the raised flap. Immovable it stood there for some seconds, and Quentin began to realize that the man was doing no more than taking stock of the weather. Prone upon the sand, thankful to be beyond the range of the light, he waited. Voices reached him faintly, the words indistinguishable. Then came a snatch of song to reassure him. The black silhouette was withdrawn from the opening; the flap was allowed to fall again, cutting off the shaft of light. But because the tent remained aglow, Quentin, having risen, edged away in the opposite direction, nor began to move forward again until he judged himself to be somewhere midway between the next two tents, which remained in darkness.

He was through at last, and at the foot of the dunes that made an irregular wall at the head of the beach. He climbed these on hands and knees, not daring in the darkness to trust his feet over surfaces so irregular. From their summit, venturing at last to stand, he sought the light of Erquy, and was thankful when he perceived it, now straight ahead. In the dark he had swerved unduly to the left. This, however, was easily corrected now that he possessed anew that orientation. With that beacon in view, he went stumbling over the dunes, through the driving rain which had increased again, and was beating upon his back and shoulders.

Thus he came at last upon a road. The light of Erquy was behind by now, and no longer visible. But he knew the road. This way he had come with Puisaye. Along that firm surface he made better progress, and the day was breaking when he reached the outskirts of Nantois. He got his bearings from a gaunt ruin that reared itself from a belt of pines on an eminence, a little way back from the highway, the Castle of Gué-madec, raggedly silhouetted in the vivid light of dawn. Leaving the highway, he skirted the eminence until he struck a path that led through a screening spinney to the homestead.

Recognized there as the sometime companion of the Comte Joseph, he was readily sheltered by the farmer. He spent the day abed and asleep, whilst his garments were being dried. Soon after nightfall he resumed his journey, accompanied by a vigorous peasant girl to serve him as guide to Villegourio, where the next stage was established. After that, traveling by night and resting by day, he found friendly shelter, first at Villeneuve, north of Lamballe, in the attic of the house of Madame de Kerverso, then at Quesnoy, in the humble abode of the sisters du Gage, and at last at Ville Louët, a dangerous neighbourhood because near Boishardi's abandoned manor, upon which the Blues kept a close watch.

Thence on the fifth day after landing, and without waiting for the night, because not safe to linger, he set out alone on a borrowed horse, to make for the uplands and the Ridge of the Anguille, where his journey was to end.

Avoiding Moncontour, he followed a track that led through fertile, well-cultivated lands, to the slopes of Menez. As he climbed these, the signs of life and cultivation vanished, until from the heights, looking south towards the Morbihan, was spread an empty moorland landscape, broken only by scattered copses, to a far horizon of forests, dark and solid.

Thus through a country ever more forlorn, whose

increasing visible expanse displayed never a hamlet or
other sign of human habitation, he plodded upwards.
Heather and gorse became the only vegetation of this
arid soil, broken at intervals by surging blocks of granite.

At last, towards sunset, as he gained the empty
heights of Bel Air, a solitary dark grey building showed
on the Ridge of the Anguille above him, which he
knew for the dwelling of Jean Villeneuve, or Jean of
the Ridge, as he was generally known. He bore in the
district an unsavoury cut-throat reputation, which may
have been due to no more than the desolate situation
of his tavern dwelling. It was a little frequented house
of call for travellers crossing the Menez on the way to
Ménéac.

Goats grazed on the slope by which a winding path
led Quentin to the summit. Fowls scattered noisily and
a dog barked threateningly as he came to a halt before
the two long, low, one-storeyed buildings, one of which
was the inn, the other the barn and stable.

A slatternly girl in a red petticoat, bare of foot,
unkempt and black as a gipsy, showed herself on the
threshold. Bright black eyes scanned him from that
grimy countenance. A raucous voice challenged rather
than invited him. 'Do you stop here?'

'By your leave.' Quentin came to the ground. 'Supper and a bed. Can you provide them?'

She turned to send a harsh call through the house. It
brought forth a big loose-limbed man in a goatskin
jacket, above grey breeches so wide that as he stood
they took the form of a skirt. His naked legs were so
hairy as to seem stockinged, and his feet were thrust
into wooden shoes and packed with straw. His flat,
weathered face, showing between curtains of grizzled
hair, was sinister from sheer vacuity.

'Ohè! Supper? Aye. There's a kid new-killed, and
maybe Francine can fry you an omelette. Come you
in.' He spoke on a dull, uninterested monotone, in an
accent not easily followed. 'Take Monsieur's horse,
Francine.'

Within the gloomy, narrow, unclean, and evil-smelling common-room, on the floor of which some fowls were scratching themselves dust baths, the host took stock again of his guest.

'Where'll you be coming from?'

Deliberately Quentin mentioned the last house of communication at which he had stayed.

'Oh! Ah!' The flat face gave no sign of intelligence. 'And where may you be going?'

'That will depend upon whom I meet here.'

'Here? Whom should you meet here? This be a lonely house. Few comes this way.'

'Baron Cormatin might come if you were to let him know that I am asking for him.'

'Baron what? Na, na.' He shook his head and grinned. 'We've no barons here, citizen. 'Tis a lonely house. Travellers this way be scarce. And barons? Name of a pipe! I've never seen a baron.'

Quentin paid no heed. 'I am from Count Joseph,' he announced.

'Who? Count. . . ? You're in a mistake, my master. You're come to the wrong house. Supper you may have and a bed, and welcome. But don't believe you'll meet any of your fine friends here. Not in Jean de la Butte's house.'

By insistence Quentin succeeded only in arousing the wrath of this dullard and of the comely but unclean Francine who had slouched in.

'You must be cracked, my lad,' she told him, with the freedom that annoyance breeds. 'We're poor folk, and this is no house for the nobility, even if there were any left. Where do you come from at all with your talk of counts and barons? By faith, Jean, I believe it's a traveller from the moon.'

'I've told you that I come from . . .'

'Aye, aye,' Jean interrupted him. 'That's enough! We want no more of it. You break our heads.' He shambled off, a man whose patience was exhausted.

Now, this had not been one of the houses of confidence at which he had called when journeying with Puisaye, and Quentin began to fear that he had blundered. He was less annoyed than disconcerted. Night

was falling and he was exhausted. Even if he knew
how to repair the error of which he was by now convinced, he could do nothing until tomorrow.

So, in a disgruntled mood he ate a supper that
almost turned his stomach, and thereafter went to
throw himself half-dressed upon the rude pallet
provided.

He awakened with a glare of light upon his face in a
room that seemed full of men, as indeed it was; for
although there were only four of them, they sufficed to
crowd the narrow little chamber. The first he recognized was Jean de la Butte, who at the foot of the bed
held aloft a lantern. Beside him stood a bulky man,
whose face was lost in the shadow of his hat's wide
brim, and who carried a musket slung from his shoulders. Two others standing by the bedside were similarly
masked by the shadow of their round hats.

Quentin jerked himself up. 'What's this? What do
you want?'

A hand fell lightly on his shoulder. 'All's well, Monsieur de Morlaix.' There was a hint of laughter in the
brisk voice. 'I am Tinténiac. And here is Cormatin, for
whom you've been asking.'

'In effect,' came the Baron's deeper tones, 'prompt to
your summons, as you see. You may go, Jean.'

Quentin recovered his breath. 'The promptitude is a
little disconcerting. I was not so impatient for the pleasure of your visit that I could not have waited until
morning.'

' I was not to know who asked for me until I had seen
you.'

'And,' said Tinténiac, 'we have good reason at
present to move only by night. The Ridge is under
surveillance.'

'So if you'll forgive the disturbance, we'll be glad of
your news,' the Baron added.

Sitting up on his pallet Quentin came to it at once,
and by the light of the lantern Jean had left, he read
details and figures from the cryptogram he had
prepared.

Tinténiac was moved to a glad excitement, which

the Baron was slow to share. 'Can we be really sure,' he asked, 'that the Count is not taking British support too much for granted?'

'It is not Puisaye's way to take things for granted,' exclaimed the Chevalier, with a touch of indignation.

'That is not my judgment of him,' the Baron answered. 'Is it yours, Monsieur de Morlaix?'

Quentin hesitated. Had he been entirely frank, he would have said that Puisaye's swaggering ways suggested an oversanguine temperament. 'My acquaintance with him,' he evaded, 'does not permit me to pronounce.'

'Mine does,' said Tinténiac. 'And I very definitely hold you mistaken, Baron.'

'That the Count is of those who are prone to believe what they hope? Well, well. And then the British Government . . . I do not choose to trust implicitly to British promises, even if they are as definite as Monsieur de Puisaye asserts.'

'You may be sure that they are or he would not assert it,' Tinténiac retorted.

'Need you wrangle over it?' wondered Quentin. 'You are committeed to nothing definite until the British ships actually arrive.'

'There is the preparation of the ground,' the Baron objected on a grumbling tone.

'What then? What else are you doing here? The information I bring is to encourage you in zeal, so that you see to it that the men are ready when the hour strikes. You'll hardly permit yourself to be deterred by fancied misgivings on the score of British help.'

Cormatin shrugged. 'Easy, of course. Yet I do not choose to believe in it, because I do not believe that it is in the policy of Mr. Pitt to see the monarchy restored in France.'

'To the devil with what you believe, Baron,' was Tinténiac's testy answer. 'You've said yourself that a man believes what he hopes. How if we apply that to yourself?'

'My dear Chevalier!'

'How are you competent here in Brittany to judge of

163

what is happening in England, as against Puisaye who
is at work there?'

Cormatin spread his hands in a pacifying gesture. 'I
may be wrong. I hope I am, and that Monsieur de
Puisaye's buds will bloom.'

'It is for you, Baron, to labour so that they may,'
Quentin told him.

The Chevalier agreed impatiently. 'We have our
orders, and nothing remains but to obey.'

'Oh, agreed! Agreed! I merely sound a warning
against the delusion of false hopes. You may carry my
assurances to the Count, Monsieur de Morlaix, that I
shall dispose as he commands.'

'There is not the need. He has no doubt of it. And I
am not returning.'

He spoke of his reasons. The Baron displayed little
interest. He seemed bemused. But Tinténiac expressed
the view that as things now were, with the spirit of
conciliation abroad, Quentin should have little difficulty in obtaining possession of his estates and in being
left in peaceful enjoyment of them.

'And at need,' he added, 'I can lend you a dozen
stout, trusty lads for a bodyguard. You can distribute
them as servants, and depend upon them to bring you
off in case of trouble.'

They were still discussing it when Cormatin roused
himself to interrupt them.

'It wants little more than an hour to daybreak, and
we've all of a dozen miles to ride. We should be
moving.'

Quentin went with them, needing their guidance in a
country now entirely strange to him. Outside the inn a
dozen men awaited them, mounted on Breton ponies,
and in the wake of this bodyguard they began to
descent in the dark towards Saint-Uran. Once the
steepness of the ground diminished the pace was quickened. With sure knowledge of the ground they pushed
briskly through that harsh, wild country, thickly wood-
ed as it was and broken by ravines. As the pallors of
dawn were lightening the east on their left, they

reached the borders of the vast, sombre forest of La
Noué, which was their destination.

Within the heart of that dense labyrinth Cormatin and
Tinténiac had their present refuge, in the quarters set
up there by the Chouan leader Saint-Regent, commonly known as Pierrot, who was one of the most active
and resolute enemies of the Republic. His immediate
following, numbering a couple of hundred men, were
for the most part old contrabandists, who under the
monarchy had been engaged in the smuggling of salt
from Brittany, where it was free, into the neighbouring
provinces, where in those days it had been heavily
taxed. Rude, vigorous men, enured to danger by the
risky trade they had followed, they were amongst the
most formidable of those who conducted the guerrilla
warfare against the forces of government. Saint-Regent
himself, undersized and frail, with a keen weasel face
and lively, piercing brown eyes, exercised over them
the authority that only a skilful, proved leader can
command.

A charcoal-burner's hut served him for quarters,
whilst the men were lodged underground in the entrenchments which they had dug, roofed with turf and
leaves over a stout framework of branches, so that they
would defy discovery to any but the most minute
search. Amongst them several refractory priests found
shelter, ready to go forth when needed to perform their
offices, men the interdict upon whom had been so
heavy a factor in the revolt of the pious peasantry.

On the Sunday morning of Quentin's arrival amongst
them, he attended the Mass, celebrated in a great
clearing, at which the entire band was present. The
deference shown him, as Puisaye's emissary, by Saint-
Regent and every man of his following, was an evidence to him of the esteem in which the Count Joseph
was held and the powerful influence of his name.

'It is the same throughout the entire West,' Tinténiac
assured him. 'Puisaye is their messiah, and when he
gives the signal such an army will spring from the soil
that the scoundrels in Paris will believe that the Day of
Judgment is upon them.'

'Yet Cormatin seems lukewarm,' Quentin observed. Tinténiac became grave. 'A doubter by nature. And he has been badly shaken by a near escape of capture by the Blues. He was not the man to leave here as Puisaye's Major-General. Still, I do what I can to buttress his crumbling spirit pending the arrival of Puisaye himself. We shall continue to prepare the ground, which, for that matter, is well prepared already. We could rise tomorrow if the word came. The Republicans are aware of it, aware of this fire smouldering under the ashes, which it cannot locate, and which it has tried in vain to stamp out. An unexpected flare-up at this point or at that; a bold attack upon a convoy; a sudden raid upon an arsenal, for arms and powder; a seizure of corn or cattle intended for the troops; all this by bands that melt away and vanish when the stroke has been delivered. These things shake the confidence and nerves of our Republican friends. Having tried in vain the brutal plan of wholesale devastation, they now betray their fears by conciliatory measures, the cessation of persecutions, the abolition of the trees of liberty, even toleration in matters of religion. As things are you'll have little difficulty at Chavaray. Your cousin, Constant de Chesnières, with more to answer for than you can have, is left to dwell in peace at Grands Chesnes.'

This was news that Quentin hardly welcomed. 'I thought that he would have gone to join his brother in Holland.'

'He is an officer of the Loyal Emigrant, which has been assembled in England. Seeing the condition of things in the West, he has been persuaded to await it here, supplying meanwhile a rallying-point for the peasantry of his district. It will be pleasant for you to have your cousins for neighbours at Chavaray.'

'It will certainly be interesting,' was the extent of Quentin's agreement.

CHAPTER 4

In Possession

ON A BRIGHT day of spring, Monsieur de Morlaix can-
tered up the long avenue of Lombardy poplars, about
the roots of which the crocuses gleamed golden, to the
gates of Chavaray. Three men who had the air of
grooms rode with him; Chouans these, of that dozen of
the bodyguard with which Tinténiac had provided
him.

Monsieur de Morlaix had fared reasonably well, all
things considered, at the hands of the Public Accuser
of Angers. He had presented himself boldly three days
ago at the office of that important public functionary,
and had been paid the compliment of immediate recognition.

'Behold me, if I am not mistaken, the Citizen Morlaix returned at last. Name of a name! But where have
you tarried this long while?'

'I have been to England.'

'To England!' The Citizen Besné made a wry face.
'That's no place for a true Frenchman. A land of
perfidy. Our natural enemies, the English, from im-
memorial time. I thank God for it. I would not have
them for our friends. In the name of reason what took
you there?'

'A matter of twenty-four thousand livres in gold.'

'That is some excuse.' The lean, livid, pockmarked
face was split by a grin. 'A man might go even to
England for that.'

'The friends in France upon whom I counted could
not help me, so I had no choice. I bring you a draft on
a bank in Amsterdam for that amount.'

167

A lively flicker in Besné's little eyes resolved itself into a cold stare. 'For twenty-four thousand livres?'

'In gold. Was not that the sum agreed?'

Besné displayed indignation. 'But that, my friend, was a solatium to me for offering no opposition to your inheriting. Since then the situation has changed. The sequestration has been effected and registered. Chavaray is now definitely national property, and for sale.'

'It was already national property then: so you informed me. But you were prepared to rescind the sequestration. What was possible then should be possible now.'

'Indeed, it is not. Since then you have placed yourself definitely outside the law, by emigrating again.'

'To leave the country for the express purpose of obtaining the money necessary to satisfy legal requirements is not to emigrate.'

Besné's full face was puckered into a grin. He made little humming noises. 'You should have been a lawyer. You certainly know how a hair should be split. Nor can I say that your argument is really unsound. Indeed, considering it, I could hardly be held guilty of a grave dereliction of duty if I yielded to the temptation of serving you.'

'I have it here.'

'You have what?'

'The temptation.' From a wallet of oiled silk, Quentin drew one of the bills of exchange on Amsterdam which had resulted from his visits to Mr. Thomas Coutts. He thought it well to add: 'It is worthless until I endorse it to your order. But that is quickly done. As quickly as your signing the admission of my claim.'

With the figure '1000 guineas' dancing before his eyes, the Public Accuser pursed his lips. 'Vexatious!' he muttered. 'Most vexatious. The sequestration, I repeat, is registered. Only by actual purchase can you now become possessor of the place. But that would have the advantage of making it doubly yours: by purchase and by inheritance.' Amiably the Citizen Besné proffered his open snuffbox.

Quentin waved it impatiently away. 'And the price?'

'Oh, but at a nominal price, of course. I might say, as before, five million livres. In that case you would be well served by the further depreciation of the national currency. In gold today that is not more than two thousand English guineas. A bagatelle. A farce of a price. I may come to be bitterly reproved for it. But there!' He shrugged his shoulders. 'There are no buyers in these days, and the nation must take what it can. Look you, citizen: you shall have the estates for five million livres, or two thousand English guineas. I'll have the deed of sale ready for you by tomorrow. And, of course, there will be the little commission of a thousand guineas that we agreed.'

So in exchange for his bills, two of them endorsed to the National Treasury, the other to the Citizen Besné, Quentin received his deed of ownership, and with it came once more to those tall iron gates from which on his former visit he had been ignominiously driven.

The clang of the bell was answered by the barking of a dog, and presently from that same low doorway in the left wing emerged as before the steward Lafont, this time with a growling liver-coloured mastiff at his heels.

He stared through the bars at Quentin, who sat his horse. 'Who are you? What do you want?'

'The owner of Chavaray. Unbar the gate.'

Recognition gleamed in the fellow's glance. 'So it's you again!'

'Your memory is better than your manners. Unbar the gate, I say.'

'Ah, bah! The nation is the present owner of Chavaray, and it's in my charge.'

'That is at an end. I have this for you.' He leaned from the saddle, and passed a paper through the bars.

Scowling over it, Lafont read it aloud. 'The bearer of these, the Citizen Quentin Morlaix, having acquired by purchase the property of . . .' The steward broke off, and looked up with a malevolent sneer. 'I see. A buyer of national property.' He laughed with sour malice. 'I hope you may enjoy it longer than is usual in these days.'

'Meanwhile, the gate.'

'To be sure. The gate.' He turned the key in the lock, and opened one of the wings, driving his dog to heel with an oath.

In the forecourt Quentin left his Chouans to stable the horses, and with Lafont for reluctant and surly guide, went to acquaint himself with the house.

Whilst the architecture was that of the days of Louis XIII, the decoration of the spacious rooms was mainly in the baroque style of Louis XV. Exceptions were the wide hall with its elegant pilasters, the black and white chequers of its marble pavement and the vast fireplace, its cowl adorned by the shield of the Chesnières with its oak-tree device. At either end of the hall a wide marble staircase, carpeted in faded red, led to the gallery that surrounded it on three sides above. The dining-room, too, of dark oak wainscoting and massive furniture, was contemporary with the house. But all the rest was of the style of more frivolous days. Quentin passed through a succession of rooms on the ground floor, panelled in silks and tapestries within frames of ornately contorted escutcheon shapes: a green room, a pink room, a room known as the peacock room from designs on the satin panels, another known as the room of the monkeys, from the old tapestries of arboreal designs upon which monkeys sported. In some, the furniture and the lustres overhead were conserved in linen shrouds; in others their glories were bare to the dust that overlaid everything within that neglected mansion and matched the cracked mirrors, the broken picture frames and tattered tapestries, some of which disfigured almost every one of those splendid rooms.

It was to be Quentin's task in the days that followed to restore some order, and to this he set the peasant lads that Tinténiac had supplied him. They had been chosen from among those who, rendered homeless by the troubles, were willing and even glad to exchange the comforts of life under a roof for a roving forest existence. They were under the direction of an elderly Chouan named Charlot, who had been a sort of seneschal-intendant at the Château de Plougast, burnt by the Blues in '93. He possessed a wife and a daughter, with whom employment at Chavaray permitted reunion, and because of this, Quentin received from the three of them devoted service.

Restoration of order in the château was followed by attention to the estates. It was necessary to make the acquaintance of the *métayers* and other tenants, and to seek the guidance of Lesdiguières for the appointment of a steward to succeed Lafont, whom he had instantly dismissed. Of no less urgency was it to pay a visit to Grands Chesnes, a matter reluctantly postponed from misgivings of the reception that might await him there. To continue the postponement, however, seemed to him a frustration of the real purpose of his coming to France. Resolved, therefore, for the sake of seeing Germaine de Chesnières, to face at once whatever hostility there might be, he ordered a horse to be saddled for him one fine April morning, and set out.

He rode alone, and his way ran through level lands dotted with coverts, which grew denser and more frequent as he approached the banks of the Mayenne. The meadows were green and lush with herbage left too abundant by the scarce cattle set to graze; of the tillage, some stood fallow and empty, other was so rank with weeds that it advertised its neglect even to such inexpert agrarian eyes as Quentin's. The few isolated rustics whom he met eyed him from under lowering brows, and it was rarely that any returned his greeting. An old man of whom he inquired if he were on the right way to the ford, jabbered for answer in a langauge Quentin did not understand, but the tone and manner of which did not lead him to suppose himself the object of civilities.

By following a path through a fringe of woodland, he came at last to the shrunken river, singing and sparkling in the sunshine as it rippled and frothed over a broad gravel shallow. He urged his horse to the water, through the tall rushes and golden king-cups that fringed the bank; and splashed his way across. Thence a well-defined pathway led him a straight two miles or so to a sober grey manor, flanked by a single tower with an extinguisher roof, which he rightly supposed to be Grands Chesnes.

To the elderly man in peasant dress, without pretence of livery, by whom he was received, he accounted it prudent to announce himself in the Republican style, as the Citizen Morlaix, and after a waiting pause in a gloomy hall, he was brought to a lofty room of a sombre dignity, where Constant de Chesnières stood cool and sardonic to receive him.

'I am honoured, Monsieur de Morlaix.' It was thus that Constant now elected to address him. 'I had heard of your arrival at Chavaray. Permit me to say that I admire your courage.'

Quentin bowed. 'I shall study always to deserve that admiration.'

'Too gracious. In what may I serve you?'

'In nothing of which I am aware. Rather am I here to offer my services to you.'

'Again, too gracious. We hear reports that you have purchased Chavaray from the nation.'

'It appeared to be the simplest course, all things considered.'

'Simple, perhaps. But fraught with risks. You'll recall the old warning maxim, *Caveat emptor.*'

'It is scarcely applicable to me.'

'By your leave, sir, it is applicable to any man who buys stolen goods.'

'But not if they were stolen from himself.'

'I see.' Constant's eyes were insolently raised. 'You take that view?'

'What view do you take, monsieur?'

'That is of little consequence. What should be, is that purchasers of national property have fared none too happily of late. In your own case, too, the Chouans many recall that a Monsieur de Boisgelin, a cousin of ours, who was of some esteem amongst them, met his death at your hands. They are of a tenacious memory, these Chouans, and not without vindictiveness. I do not wish to alarm you,' he added, with his sneering smile. 'And, as I have said already, it is impossible not to admire your courage.'

'And just as impossible to shake it,' Quentin answered him amiably. 'As for Boisgelin, it will be known that I killed him in a fair engagement.'

'A fair engagement!' For a moment Constant's voice was charged with anger. It was instantly controlled. 'I should deplore to intrude a harsh note upon so amiable an occasion by reminding you that you are a fencing-master.'

'I am not on my defence. But I may remind you in my turn that Boisgelin was a practiced duellist.'

'You knew that of him. But he was not so well informed concerning yourself.'

'That I can believe. His friends were oddly negligent, or else unduly confident.'

'His friends?' Constant questioned, his glance sharpening.

But already Quentin was turning from him. He had heard the door open behind him, and he was brought face to face with Mademoiselle de Chesnières.

For a moment there was a breathless pause, then she sped impulsively forward.

'Quentin . . . Cousin Quentin!'

He bent over her hand, bearing it to his lips, whilst ahead, Madame de Chesnières advanced into the room with solemn dignity, and behind him, Constant remained sternly at gaze.

'Germaine!' Madame's utterance expressed disapproval and commanded restraint. Then, with a manner that might have been modelled upon her son's, and employing the same mode of address, 'Monsieur de Morlaix, is it not?' she said.

'Your servant, madame.'

'I was told that you were here. I am wondering what may be the occasion.'

It was discouraging. But he continued coolly urbane. 'No more than the natural desire to express my duty.'

Germaine stood beside him, apprehension in the

173

watchful glance that moved from her aunt to her cousin. 'You do us honour,' she declared with an air that seemed to defy them both.

Constant laughed. 'Why, so I was telling Monsieur de Morlaix. I must take an early occasion of returning the civility.'

'We have not been in the house,' said madame, 'since your Republican friends removed the late Marquis.'

'My Republican friends! Oh, madame!' He smiled his astonishment. 'I was not aware that I had earned the Republic's friendship.'

'But since it has placed you in possession of Chavaray . . .'

'No, no,' Constant intervened. 'You forget, madame. Monsieur de Morlaix is there by right of purchase. I was explaining to him the dangers of purchasing national property when you came in.'

'It is possible,' said Germaine, 'that Cousin Quentin's right to it is still better founded.'

'Can there,' wondered Quentin, to annoy them, 'be a better right to anything than that conferred by a deed of sale?'

'Always provided,' Constant reminded him, 'that the vendor himself possesses a sound title. That is what renders Monsieur de Morlaix's position delicate.'

'You repeat yourself, Constant,' Germaine coldly reproved him.

'A cardinal truth cannot be too often repeated.'

'Nor a cardinal lie, it seems.'

'Germaine!' Her aunt was scandalized. She directed upon Quentin her deliberately false smile. 'You will excuse the child, Monsieur de Morlaix. The very young will always be dogmatic in matters they do not understand.'

'But I assure you that I regard mademoiselle's understanding of this matter as complete and perfect.'

'A dangerous chivalry, sir.'

He chose to be sententious. 'Where there is no danger there can be no chivalry.'

174

'Since you perceive both,' said Constant, 'we need say no more on that score.'

There fell a pause, and it was impossible for Quentin longer to ignore that they kept him standing, even could he have ignored the hostile eyes in the smiling masks assumed by mother and son. If he did not regret that he had come, at least he perceived that it became impossible to protract the visit.

'I will remove the inconvenience of my presence.'

They murmured protests in tones calculated to mark their insincerity, and anger flashed from Germaine's eyes.

'You may look for me soon at Chavaray,' Constant assured him at parting, with a mockery that was but too apparent, and the echo of which rang in Quentin's ears until he was home again.

CHAPTER 5

The Warning

OUT of a gloomy absorption in which he sat plunged at the breakfast table on the following morning, Charlot startled him with the announcement that Mademoiselle de Chesnières was at Chavaray to see him.

She came in trimly vigorous in a long drag riding-coat *à l'anglaise,* a three-cornered hat jauntily surmounting her tight-coiled golden tresses.

Today, there being no witnesses, he did not content himself with bending over her finger-tips, but folded her into an embrace to which she went with a tenderly laughing eagerness.

'How dear in you to seek me, Germaine! And so soon. How very dear!'

175

'It was so necessary, Quentin.' Gently she disengaged herself from his arms.

His invitation to the hospitality of his table she waved aside. Perched on the arm of a chair, her riding-whip tucked under her arm, she began to peel off her gloves. 'Why did you come yesterday to Grands Chesnes?'

'You'll suppose, of course, it was to see Madame de Chesnières and the dear, good Constant.'

'It was so unwise. Had you forgotten the warning I gave you in London?'

'But I had to see you. It is for that I came to France. And as for danger . . .' He raised a shoulder. 'If Constant means me mischief, I am here to be assailed. My visit to Grands Chesnes neither helps nor hinders that.'

She smiled wistfully. 'Yet it might have been wiser to have practised patience.' And then she asked a curious question. 'Do you set great store by Chavaray, Quentin?'

He looked at her in surprise. 'It is to be your domain, Germaine.'

'I do not covet it. Grands Chesnes is mine, and is enough for me. Whilst Chavaray . . . Quentin, it is not lucky to you. Your life has been in danger ever since you had a claim to this heritage. It terrifies me.' She flung hat and whip on the table, and came to him. 'Let it go, Quentin. Let them have it who covet it, who will do murder to possess it. Go back to England, to your academy. Do this if you love me, Quentin; for I can know no peace whilst you are here. Your calling is an honourable one and yields you abundance for your wants. Go back to it. Wait for me there in confidence, as I shall be content to wait until I can come to you.'

He was aghast. 'Abandon Chavaray? Surrender my rights because I am threatened? That is to advise me to play the coward,' he expostulated. 'Should you really respect me if I bowed before evil rather than stand to defend what is mine? What counsel is that, sweetheart?'

'The counsel of the woman who wants you spared to be her life's companion.'

'You would account a coward a fit companion? Quiet your fears. The menace of our cousins leaves me calm. I shall know how to deal with it. If my existence is proving inopportune to Messieurs de Chesnières, it is an inopportuneness I shall study to maintain, and they'll attempt to overcome it at their peril.'

'You consider only yourself and your pride, Quentin,' she complained, 'and me not at all.'

'Is it merely pride to refuse to turn tail before a criminal greed?'

'It is not only criminal greed, as you call it, Quentin. There is something else.' She hesitated, averting her glance.

'Well?' he demanded.

'They . . . they do not believe that your title is sound. Oh, they are sincere in that. I know.'

'Not believe it!' There was anger in his laugh. 'Not believe it, when it is established by every document that completes the chain!'

'Legally, yes. But . . .'

'But what?'

'It is because they have no hope to prevail at law, because they cannot legally destroy your claim, that they will end by destroying you.'

'That I can understand. But. . . ?' His puzzled glance was questioning her.

'Must I be plainer?' She was almost in anguish. 'They do not believe that you are your father's son.'

'That's to explain one riddle by another. Whose son else can a man be?' But the question was scarcely asked when the answer came to him. 'God of Heaven!' he cried out.

'Ah, forgive me, Quentin. It hurts, I know. But I had to tell you.'

'And I am grateful.' Passion shook his voice. He swung with a wild gesture to the tall portrait of Bertrand de Morlaix de Chesnières, Marquis of Chavaray, that hung above a carved oak serving table. It had been painted by Boucher when Bertrand was little more than Quentin's present age. 'They dare in the face of that! The same hooked nose, the same grey

177

eyes, the same glint of red in the hair.' He laughed fiercely, 'Don't you see, Germaine?'

There was no such ready agreement as he invited. She met his look with a steady round-eyed stare, her face expressionless. Then, 'Don't, my dear,' she begged. 'There is not the need for this.'

'But there is, if my mother's sweet fame is to be smirched by these rascals so as to justify their thieving covetousness.' He swung away from her to the window and back again, in long strides, his manner wild. 'You could give me no better reason for standing firm against these villains, for dealing mercilessly with them and thwarting them in the end. It becomes a sacred duty. Let them beware the mistake that was made by their cut-throat Boisgelin. I am not so helpless as they may suppose, to their undoing.'

Germaine, pale and scared before his passion, had sunk into a chair. When his ranting ceased, 'God forgive me,' she exclaimed. 'I have only made matters worse. Yet, listen, Quentin. I have not told you all. You do not know to what you are exposed. Saint-Gilles might choose to fight you openly. But Constant never. He is sly and treacherous, and the more vindictive since I have allowed him to perceive my regard for you. His mother and he have hoped that I would one day marry him. There are all the lands of Grands Chesnes that will be mine one day, if ever order and justice are restored. They would make a fine property for the younger Chesnières when the elder is in possession of Chavaray. Constant will no more suffer you to interfere with that than with Saint-Gilles' succession. For you to remain here is to deliver yourself into his hands.'

'So Boisgelin thought when he went out to measure swords with me behind the inn at Ploermel.'

This merely increased her agitation. 'Constant will never measure swords with you. He has other methods. It needs little to raise the peasantry against a buyer of national property. And that is what Constant is doing already, with the assistance of Lafont. One night soon, any night now, if you remain here, a mob of furious peasants will descend upon you, to drag you from your château and murder you. That is how Constant works.'

She looked up piteously into his face and gathered hope from its startled expression. 'What could you do against that?' she cried.

His lips grew set, the grey eyes were bright and hard as steel. 'That they shall discover when they come. I shall know how to make them welcome.'

She sprang up and came to clutch his arms. 'Do not deceive yourself, my dear. For pity's sake!'

'Let Constant remember Boisgelin. He, too, accounted me a lamb to be led to the shambles.'

'There is no parallel.'

'You shall find that there is. Now that I am forewarned, let them come.' On a quieter tone he strove to reassure her. 'Had they taken me by surprise, it might have gone ill with me. But now, the surprise will be theirs. Thank you for warning me, Germaine.'

'Do you want to mock me with your thanks? I come to persuade you to go. And I still beg you, for my sake . . .'

Abruptly she ceased, and started away from him, her eyes upon the door. From beyond it came a jingling ring of spurred steps on the marble of the hall and a sound of voices, one of which shouted, 'Out of my way, my good man. I'll announce myself.'

Her eyes dilated as she glanced at Quentin. 'Constant!' she breathed.

Then the door opened, and Constant appeared upon the threshold. Pallor turned his olive skin of a greenish hue, and his eyes were evil. Then a smile came like a mask to cover his countenance.

'You'll forgive the intrusion, Monsieur de Morlaix.'

'Not readily,' said Quentin, cool and haughty. His glance went beyond Constant, to Charlot, who stood flushed and angry behind him. 'The times do not permit, perhaps, of great ceremony. Yet I am not so destitute of service that my visitors need come to me unannounced.'

Constant advanced slowly, ever with that hateful smile on his thick lips, which Quentin promised himself that his glove should one day wipe off. 'Ascribe it,' he begged, 'to my eagerness to return your so courteous visit. An eagerness which I am ashamed to see has been exceeded by my cousin Germaine.' He turned to her, his manner blending mockery with deference. 'My dear, in a censorious world this was scarcely prudent. Had you told me of the intention I should have been happy to accompany you. I have repaired matters by following at the earliest.'

'To spy upon me?'

He laughed. 'But no. To guard you.'

'You are not required to be my guardian.'

'I think so. Always. And the need is suggested at the present moment. Monsieur de Morlaix, I am sure, will agree. As a man of honour it must have distressed you that a lady should expose herself to criticism by a thoughtless intrusion here alone.'

Quentin looked coldly upon that sardonic affability.

'You exaggerate. You forget that there is a degree of kinship to screen Mademoiselle de Chesnières.'

'Degrees of kinship, even when they exist, are not adequate for so much.'

'You say, "even when they exist." What does that mean?'

Constant affected surprise. 'Just that.' And then, as if becoming for the first time aware of the laden table, he turned the subject. 'My faith! I perceive how inconvenient is the moment. You were at table. Then it must be *Ave atque vale*. Let me beg you to forgive us an intrusion at so unreasonable an hour. We rustics have a notion of time that is different from that of you city-dwellers. We must choose some later occasion. Come, Germaine.' He held the door for her.

'Willingly,' she coldly answered him. 'I have said what I came to say.' She looked steadily at Quentin. 'You will give it thought, my cousin.'

He took her hand. 'Be easy on that score.' He bowed

180

to kiss her fingers, whilst Constant watched them narrowly. 'I shall provide.'

When they had gone he sat lost in thought. Preoccupations on the score of Germaine alternated with shivers of anger at the thought of Constant. He was being too nice, he told himself, to stand upon a fencing-master's punctilio with a scoundrel who traded upon his trust in it. Let him strike Constant across his sneering face, and so compel him to come out and be killed before he wreaked his evil, treacherous will. Ah, but would Constant come? Even if Quentin could descend to that?

He shook off the thought, and turned to the portrait of that father whose tenderness was Quentin's earliest dim memory. 'Faith, old gentleman, you may have been none too fortunate in your sons. But I can make you my compliments on your nephews.'

After that, he took thought for the danger of which Germaine had warned him. He summoned Charlot, and told him that, regarded as an intruder by the peasantry, he had cause to fear a raid on Chavaray.

'A treacherous lot of dastards, these hinds of Anjou,' the Breton pronounced them. 'As for their raid, we've a dozen good Brittany lads here, our gates are strong, the walls are stout, and we're well armed. You may sleep in peace, Monsieur le Marquis.'

But Monsieur le Marquis, if heartened, was not tranquillized. 'They may overwhelm us with numbers. I must have reinforcements, and the nearest to whom I can appeal are the Chevalier de Tinténiac and Saint-Regent.'

Charlot scratched his grizzled head, his seamy old face thoughtful.

'It's a long way to La Noué.'

'A hundred miles, and we haven't a messenger to spare.'

'There's my girl. Marianne's as strong as a man and she can travel as fast. But there's the time it'll take.'

'Four days, at least, before her message would bring anyone. I've even thought of sending to Angers for a detachment.'

'Of Blues!' cried Charlot in horror. 'Mother of Heaven! That would set the countryside on fire against us. I doubt if even our lads would stand by you. Don't think of it, Monsieur le Marquis.'

So in the end, Marianne was sent to La Noué, and they remained to hope that no attack would come before her return. In the meantime, they fortified the house, and set a watch at night.

CHAPTER 6

❦

The Assault

THE candles had just been lighted and the curtains drawn that evening when Quentin, who sat at work upon the account books of Chavaray, in the Chinese salon, which he particularly affected, became aware of a hum, as of a hive at swarming time.

Scarcely had it drawn his attention from the riddle in which Lafont' had left the accounts when Charlot, agitated and of a pallor that seemed to have spread to his bald skull, broke in upon him.

'Monsieur le Marquis, they are coming. They are coming.'

Quentin was in no doubt as to whom was meant. 'Ah!' He set down his pen. 'And I had looked forward to a quiet evening. Well, well! Are the shutters fast?'

'Marton is closing them now. I have sent for the lads. We are ready, monsieur. But it's an army.'

'We must do what we can.' His calm had the effect of quieting Charlot's alarms. 'Assemble the men in the hall. I will post them myself!'

The windows of the ground floor were equipped with stout external shutters, and in a dozen of these, those of the hall, the dining-room on one side, and the salon of the monkeys on the other, they had that afternoon opened loopholes for their muskets. It was through those in the hall shutters that they now observed the approach of a noisy peasant horde, lighted by torches, whose flames were reflected from the pikes and scythe-blades with which they were armed.

Quentin's Chouans, men who in two years of their fierce guerrilla warfare had been broken to every danger and to every kind of engagement, whether offensive in raids or ambuscades, or defensive in withstanding siege and assault by Republican troops, displayed no alarm at the prospect of attack by a disorderly mob. Had the advancing peasants been Bretons like themselves, a strain might have been placed upon their loyalty. For the men of Brittany are a race apart. Their language and customs set up a barrier between themselves and all other people of the earth. It mattered nothing that this assailing mob was made up of peasants like themselves, of Royalists like themselves; it remained that they were Angevins, and therefore of an alien breed, whilst the Bretons served one in whom they had been told to behold a representative of their Comte Joseph, who was the very messiah of the restoration of Throne and Altar.

The stout iron gates of the forecourt stemmed the onslaught, as a dam stems the rushing waters of a river. Unlike a dam, however, it was not to be overflowed. The gates stood tall, and whilst the high wall in which they were set might, notwithstanding the spikes that guarded the summit, have been easily scaled, the assailants had lacked the foresight to bring ladders. They hung now, angrily clamant, upon the scrollwork of the gates, and a musket shot or two were loosed, so as to stress their menace.

Quentin crossed the hall to the vestibule, where Charlot was on guard with a double-barrelled gun, a second one, ready loaded, leaning in the angle of the door. He had opened the little shutter in the grille and was observing the demoniac antics outside.

'Unbar the door. Let me out,' said Quentin.

'Monsieur le Marquis!' It was a horrified protest. But

Quentin was very much the Marquis at that moment. 'This *canaille* shall not suppose that I am afraid. My chance to speak to them is whilst the gates hold. They may not hold long.'

'They have firearms. They may shoot.'

'If they do I must hope that their markmanship is bad. The light will not help them. Open.'

He was so resolute that Charlot, muttering, complied.

It was in Quentin's mind that to wait unseen behind these walls was to wait for an assault which, when it came, must in the end be overwhelming. Something might be achieved by a display of dauntlessness. Men are to be impressed and dominated by a bold, contemptuous front.

As the massive door swung open, he showed himself bare-headed on the summit of the steps which ran down on either hand, guarded by a parapet which came to the height of his breast.

His appearance produced an instant silence of astonishment. For a moment, silhouetted in black against the light from the open door behind him, he was unrecognizable. But as the door closed again, and some of the light from the flaming torches beat upon his face, they identified him, and loosed their yells of execration.

'*Pataud!* Sansculotte! Thief! Purchaser of national property! We'll show you whose property it is. You shall vomit your Republican banquet!'

They had been stirred up against him in just the manner he supposed.

He held up his hand for silence, but the outcries continued. He saw a musket-barrel being poked through the scrollwork of the gate, and by the light of a lantern he recognized Lafont for the man who wielded it. But he continued to hold up his hand.

The musket cracked, and some splinters of stone rattled down behind him. He had not moved, and his cool courage, creating the impression for which he hoped, earned him at last a silence. On that his voice rang clear and firm.

'Men of Chavaray! I do not parley with you out of

any fear. We are well armed and ready to resist you at the cost of much of your blood until the help arrives for which—expecting this—I have already sent out an appeal. I parley with you because you are brought here by the lies of those who labour for ignoble ends.

'It is not true that I am a buyer of national property. I may have had to pay so as to enter into possession of Chavaray; but it remains that Chavaray is mine by right of birth and inheritance, as is well known to those who send you against me. I am the Marquis of Chavaray, as I will show proof to any half-dozen whom you may depute to come and seek it.'

His confident almost disdainful tone had not failed of its effect. It was recognized for the tone of the exalted class to which he claimed to belong. And this tone was matched by his erect, virile figure, his air of scornful indifference to threats. This could be no *pataud*, no misbegotten upstart. Only the gentleman born could present a front of such stiff-necked intrepidity.

And so there was an amazed silence when he ceased, which endured until broken by the jeers of Lafont.

'Will you heed that mountebank? A marquis, he? Oh, to be sure, a marquis: Marquis of Carabas.' And he lifted up his voice to a singsong declamation:

Chapeau bas! Chapeau bas!
Gloire au Marquis de Carabas!

Thus, by the use of that term, he betrayed himself to Quentin, as Boisgelin had done, for the agent of Constant.

He had swung to face the gates again, and again thrust the barrel of his musket through the scroll-work.

'Here's to give him glory. A *feu de joie* for Monsieur le Marquis de Carabas.'

He fired, and missed again. Quentin, who had not flinched, let them hear his laugh.

'Your aim is as false as your tongue, Lafont.'

There was the crack of another shot. It was fired

185

from the château, and this time by a marksman; for
Lafont staggered back and crumpled screaming into
the arms of the man behind him.

Quentin swore under his breath, conceiving that this
shot must undo all that he had striven to accomplish.
Confirmed in this when the mob loosed again the fury
that he had been bridling, he turned and quitted the
perron.

Once he was within, Charlot made haste to close
and bar the door.

'To expose yourself so! God be praised that that
murdering ape did not hit you.'

'Who fired that shot?'

'Does it matter, monsieur, who fired it? The animal
is well served. I hope he got it through his dirty
heart.'

'It was ill done. The trouble is now certain.' But he
did not pursue the inquiry. It was not the moment to
discourage his lads by reproaches.

From outside, above the uproar, came the clang of
metal on metal. 'They are using sledgehammers to the
gate,' he said, and turned to peer through the grille.

One of the Chouans from the dining-room approached the vestibule.

'Are you there, Monsieur le Marquis? They are
smashing the lock of the gates. Will you order us to
fire?'

'Is it you, Jacques?' He continued at the grille.

Saving where a space had been cleared to allow a
man to swing his great sledgehammer, the assailants
were tight-packed against the gates. A volley into them
would be of murderous effect.

'We burn our boats if we do,' said Quentin calmly.
'We shall be committed to a fight that will end in
massacre.'

'Perhaps a volley would make them run, like the
cowards they are,' said Charlot.

'It might. But . . . What now?'

The clamour which had risen momentarily in a fresh
excitement fell suddenly to a mutter, and the hammer-
blows ceased.

As an undertone to the angry murmurs of the horde, they could hear now the beat of hooves rolling rapidly nearer.

'A troop of horse, and of some numbers by the sound. Who are these?'

'Could it be the Blues?' wondered Charlot.

'Who else could it be?'

'Faith, then, we pass from purgatory into hell,' muttered Jacques.

Quentin returned no answer. His whole attention was upon the happenings outside.

The tumult had risen again, but, as it seemed to him, on a fresh note of execration, in which rage and fear were blending. The torchlight showed him that their backs were now to the château. Soon they were falling away from the gates. The thunder of the hooves was close upon them, and at last, beyond and over the heads of the mob, Quentin beheld leather helmets decked with tails of red horsehair and the flash of sabres that were being swung like flails.

'Dragoons,' he announced. 'Though by what miracle they arrive so timely I'll not dare to guess.'

The gates were now clear of the last of the peasants. Scattered in flight before the Republican cavalry, they took their lights with them, so that the gates and all about them for a moment were lost in darkness. But the night was clear, and very soon Quentin's eyes adjusted to the gloom could make out the shadowy figures of horsemen, whilst the jingle of accoutrements dominated now the receding sound of the yelling peasantry.

Quentin laughed in relief. 'We're delivered,' it seems.'

'Delivered?' cried Jacques, who had never met a Blue save as an enemy.

'Of course. We are not outlaws here at Chavaray, but decent pacific folk. At least, so we'll appear. To your fellows, Jacques. Bid them vanish with their muskets. Let only three or four of you remain to lend Charlot a hand in peaceful service.'

187

There was a rattling at the gates, and shouts of: '*Olà! Olà!* Open! Open!'

'Be off, Jacques.' Quentin threw wide the door, and let the light stream forth, to quiet those who demanded admission. 'Go down and open, Charlot.'

'You know what you are doing, Monsieur le Marquis?'

'I don't. Neither do you. But we'll hope for the best.'

Charlot went out to find the lock of the gate so beaten out of shape that only by drawing the vertical bolts from their stone sockets in the ground, and drawing both wings inwards together, was it possible to open.

The dragoons, however, did not advance. They remained ranged in two files on either side of the avenue. Between these a little group of horsemen came up at a brisk, jingling trot. Behind them, at a little distance, could be seen the swaying lamps of a carriage that followed.

The riders came on into the courtyard. There were five, and one of them, cloaked and wearing a high two-cornered hat heavily plumed in red, white, and blue, rode a little in advance of the others.

He pulled up, and came instantly from the saddle with athletic ease, to confront Charlot. 'What house is this?' His tone whilst authoritative was courteously attuned.

'The Château de Chavaray.'

'Chavaray? Chavaray? I know the name. Who tenants it?'

'Monsieur le . . .' Charlot caught himself up, remembering that he addressed a cursed sansculotte.

But the soldier laughed. 'Monsieur le . . . Go on, man.'

Defiantly Charlot obeyed. 'Monsieur le Marquis is in residence.'

'Conduct me to him, if you please.'

With the airs of a *maître d'hôtel* of the old order, Charlot inquired: 'Whom shall I have the honour of announcing?'

'General Hoche, commanding the Army of Cherbourg.'

Charlot inclined himself. 'Give yourself the trouble of following me, my General.'

Into the light of the hall, where Quentin waited, the General strode in the wake of that house steward, his four plumed officers following close.

Quentin's recognition of that splendid figure was immediate.

'General Hoche!' He stepped forward with a courteous smile. And he added quickly: 'You arrive too opportunely to be in doubt of your welcome.'

'Chavaray! *Parbleu!* I knew that I knew the name. We rejoice to have been, it seems, of service. And your words relieve me. For we are here to impose upon the hospitality of your house. Not my escort. Let me hasten to remove alarm. My troops will bivouac in the grounds. The commissariat wagons follow them. The hospitality I come to beg, without suspecting that I should beg it of an old friend, is for myself and these officers of my staff, and for a lady whom we are escorting to Rennes. Her carriage is entering your courtyard now. In her, too, you will meet an old friend; older, indeed, than I am. Madame du Grégo de Bellanger.' Perhaps it was the look in Quentin's eyes made him add the explanation: 'It happens that she is travelling in the same direction as ourselves.'

Quentin bowed. 'Such hospitality as my house affords at such short notice would always have been yours, my General. But tonight I am to hail you as my deliverer.'

'But from what, if you please, have I delivered you? Ah! I hear madame's carriage. Give me leave.' He was gone again in a swirl of blue cloak.

His officers remained, to exchange knowing, smiling glances, whilst one of them, detaching from the group, came forward, his sabre trailing. It was Humbert.

'I hope you do me the honour to remember me, Monsieur de Chavaray.' His peasant accent was oddly at variance with his courtly words and elegant air.

'Most agreeably, my General. Welcome to Chavaray.'

'My thanks. Let me present my comrades.'

By the time he had accomplished the ceremony with a grace worthy of an officer of the Maison du Roi, Hoche was re-entering with the Vicomtesse de Bellanger.

She came forward, thrusting back the hood of her cloak from her intensely black and lustrous hair, an eagerness in her stride and in her lovely face.

'Monsieur de Chavaray! The happiness not only of finding you, but of finding you in your own château! It lifts a burden from my spirit, eases my daily self-reproach that I could not help you to it. I envy the worthier friends who were able to do what circumstances denied me the satisfaction of doing.'

He bore her long jewelled fingers to his lips. 'Madame, if you did not bestow my house upon me, your coming tonight has preserved it for me; and that is fully as great a service.'

'Ah, no. For that your thanks are due to General Hoche.'

'But from what have we delivered you, my friend?' the General asked again. 'There's a tale to be told.'

'Not an amusing one.' Standing in the circle they made about him, Quentin told it briefly and with restrictions. Believing him to have purchased Chavaray, the peasantry had come to deal with him as buyers of national property were usually dealt with.

'If they are to recommence when we are gone,' said Hoche, 'our scattering them tonight will be a very transient gain for you.'

'Unless they should suppose that it was not by chance that the troops of the Republic rode to my protection.'

'The lesson was a sharp one,' Humbert laughed. 'We broke some heads with the flat of our sabres.'

'Sabres,' said Hoche, 'which God be thanked are no longer to be used in a fratricidal war.'

It was an obscure utterance, the explanation of which was not to come until after they had supped, and supped better than might be expected considering how Chavaray had been taken unawares, and also what was the political faith of Quentin's household.

Their restricted resources had been strained to prepare quarters for these officers and for the lady who travelled under their escort. Marton, with Charlot and one of the Breton lads to help her, had been at pains to table a supper that if homely was savoury and abundant, and to grace it Quentin had produced from the cellar some bottle of Spanish wine which had found its way there no man knew whence.

When the meal was done, and under the influence of that heady Spanish wine the veneer of good manners began to wear thin and crack on the rude Republicans of Hoche's staff, the Vicomtesse begged leave to retire, and Quentin sprang to wait upon her. Hoche, who was no bibber of wine, and who had a care for his dignity, rose with them.

So, leaving the others at table, with Charlot to see their wants supplied, the three passed into the peacock salon, where candles had been lighted and logs were blazing on the hearth.

The Vicomtesse, tall and lithe, in a rather masculine spencer of a golden brown, moved admiringly about the handsome room, with the tones of green and blue and gold of its tapestried walls repeated in the curtains of brocade that masked the tall windows and in the soft Aubusson carpet underfoot.

'Like a chamber at Versailles,' she declared.

Hoche, who knew of Versailles no more than the stables, smilingly concurred.

'It is an irony,' he said, 'that a populace which a little time ago would have burnt this château because a nobleman dwelt in it, would have burnt it tonight because of an assumption that its tenant is not a nobleman. But, then, who would look for consistency in the populace?'

'Does a Republican ask the question?' the Vicomtesse rallied him.

'A Republican who left his illusions in the prison of the Conciergerie, when the mean democrats he had served would have had his head because they feared his popularity. Nor do I love their successors, who sent me here to pacify the country by massacring Frenchmen.'

'Let your rancour slumber,' she bade him, 'since you are now relieved of that odious task.'

'It was never one for a man who had gathered his laurels in battle against the enemies of France. That is what I do not easily forget. Even now, it is only expediency that dictates conciliatoriness.'

'Since it does, why so bitter? Think less of what you might have had to do, and more of what you are to do.'

Hoche turned to Quentin with an indulgent smile. 'A rare woman that, Monsieur de Chavaray. One whose eyes perceive only the cardinal point.'

'The cardinal point? What is that?'

'Why, that I am going to Rennes to make peace with a pen instead of with the sword, to spill a little ink instead of a deal of blood.'

'But with whom do you make this peace?' Quentin asked him, puzzled.

'With whom? With whom have we been at war? With the Royalists, of course. Are you so aloof here at Chavaray that you do not know what is happening in the world?'

Quentin's countenance was blank. 'With the Royalists? I am wondering whom you mean by that.'

'I mean the Royalists of Brittany, Normandy, Maine, and Anjou. Are there any others?'

'And the Republic hopes to make peace with these?'

'Hopes?' Hoche laughed easily. 'Rather more than that. The truce is called; the conference is summoned. The citizen-representatives of the Republic are on their way to meet the Royalist leaders, to be embraced by them as brothers, tricolour and white cockade in fraternal confrontation.'

Quentin smiled his disbelief. 'My attitude towards the miraculous is much like that of Saint Thomas.'

'Yet this miracle has happened. The peace treaty awaits our signatures.'

'Oh! A peace treaty! And the terms?'

'A general amnesty, liberty of religious cult, and the renunciation of levies, for our part; acknowledgment of and submission to the government of the Republic, for theirs. Thus an end to brigandage and civil war and a restoration of tranquillity to the land.'

To Quentin it seemed in that moment that the room, with its peacock tapestries, the graceful female figure in golden brown on the blue-green settle, the erect and virile soldier in his tight blue frock with his shoulders to the overmantel, were all phantasmal; like Hoche's words, the projections of a dream. Puisaye in London, and Cormatin, his representative in Brittany, were the realities that would shatter it.

Then, as if to answer that unannounced impression, Hoche spoke again. 'I am just from Nantes, where Charette has signed the peace. Stofflet, who commands the Catholic Army of Anjou, is still obstinate; but Boishardi has been sent to convert him.' This was incredible enough. But something far more incredible was now to follow. 'As for the Royal and Catholic Army of Brittany, I have already discussed the peace preliminaries with Monsieur de Cormatin, its Major-General, as he calls himself. He is bringing all the chiefs of the *chouannerie*—some two hundred of them —to meet us at Rennes.'

'Monsieur de Cormatin! It is with him that you have discussed the peace preliminaries?'

Hoche laughed at his face of consternation. 'My dear Monsieur de Chavaray, I seem to carry you from amazement to amazement.'

'You do. That Monsieur de Cormatin should consent to treat with the Republic . . .'

'Consent!' Hoche interrupted him. 'It was he who sought us with proposals. He has proved himself a good Frenchman, labouring hard for peace. It was he who was the chief agent of Charette's pacification, and since then he has worked unceasingly to accomplish the same on the right bank of the Loire.'

'Cormatin! Cormatin has done that! But it is incredible.'

'Incredible as much as you please. You may credit it, nevertheless.'

'I must, since you assure me of it so positively.'

'And you rejoice with us, I am sure,' the Vicomtesse interposed, 'to know that there is an end to bloodshed.'

'Naturally. Oh, naturally,' Quentin agreed, aghast.

Hoche and the Vicomtesse fell into talk. Quentin never heeded them. His mind was on his last meeting with Cormatin and Tinténiac at La Noué, and he recalled the Baron's pessimism on the score of Puisaye's labours, which at the time he had thought so oddly obstinate. He understood now. The man must already have committed himself to his cursed treachery. The havoc to come from his betrayal of his trust was at present incalculable. Whilst Puisaye in London was preparing the expedition that was to join the Army of Brittany, Cormatin, his agent in France, was actively labouring to dissolve this army.

Quentin's frowning, pensive glance fell upon the Vicomtesse. Her head thrown back, languidly smiling, she was gazing up into the face of Hoche, who had come to lean over the back of the settle she occupied. As he jested with her, his air possessive, he fingered a ringlet of her lustrous black hair. Quentin thought of Bellanger, who would be joining in England one of the *émigré* regiments that was coming to meet the ruin and treachery preparing, and pondered the indifference to him of this high-born lady in her infatuation for the handsome, plebeian soldier, so utter that she warmly approved the projects that were to encompass that ruin.

Observing his cold stare, she moved uncomfortably. 'Monsieur le Marquis, you seem bemused.'

'Forgive me, madame. Aware as I am of what were once Cormatin's professions, I find it difficult to imagine the impulse that can so completely have changed them.'

Hoche laughed curiously. 'I have told you what the Royalists demand and what the Republicans are prepared to concede. There is an additional trivial matter of indemnities. Under that title Cormatin will pocket a matter of a million livres when the pacification treaty is signed.'

'I see. The impulse of Judas.'

Hoche shrugged. 'It's a point of view.'

'And the Republic consents to pay him a million for his services.'

'After all those now in power are concerned to efface the work of the Terrorists, so that they may establish themselves securely. And the means at their command are exiguous. Surrounded as we are by enemies abroad, internal peace is a first necessity. The possibility of a rising of the Chouans became a nightmare to the gentlemen of the Convention. That was Cormatin's opportunity; and like an opportunist he seized it and turned it to account. Let us be grateful. But the Vicomtesse is yawning.'

'It is that the tale has not the same novelty for me as for our host.'

'Nor the power to disgust you,' Quentin complained.

'That is because you have not yet perceived your own profit in all this,' Hoche told him. 'It is not impossible that you might come to be placed outside the law as an *émigré.* That danger is removed by the amnesty for all returned *émigrés,* which is amongst the terms we are to concede.'

The tragic disillusion that awaited Puisaye in this, the cruel frustration of all that he was accomplishing, were the only considerations that weighed now with Quentin. Only because of the imprudence of opening his mind to his guests did he set a curb upon the anger stirring in him.

That anger kept him awake far into the night. He had come to France as the bearer of Puisaye's orders to Cormatin, and he took the view that this traitorous contravention of those orders called for action on his part. What the action should be was the problem that kept him wakeful. The impulse to return to England, so as to warn Puisaye, he dismissed as futile. Already it was too late for that. Long before he could reach London, the

pacification conference to which Hoche now rode
would have been held, and the mischief would be
complete. If Puisaye and all those committed with him
in England to the gallant adventure, trusting to be
received by the great Chouan army he had recruited,
should arrive unwarned in France, they would face
irrevocable ruin. Impossible for Quentin to sit still at
Chavaray whilst this treachery was being consummated. The only course that suggested itself before he
wearily fell asleep was to hunt out Tinténiac at once,
and take counsel with him.

CHAPTER 7

Inferences

HOCHE took himself off betimes on the following morning, with his staff, his Vicomtesse, and his escort, after
leave-takings that were patterns of courtesy and cordi-
ality. 'Symbolical,' the Vicomtesse laughed, 'of the embrace of the old order and the new.'

When he had handed her into her travelling carriage,
Hoche still lingered.

'You should take measures for your protection,' he
recommended Quentin, and his eyes were gravely
friendly.

'They are taken. Give yourself no concern, my General. I am disposing so as to leave Chavaray for the
present.'

'That is prudent. Once the pacification is proclaimed
another spirit will come to reign over the land, and you
will have no more to fear. Forgive the disturbance we
have caused you, and fare you well.'

He mounted and rode away in the wake of the

carriage, his staff about him. At the gateway he turned
in the saddle to wave his hat with its tricolour plumes.

From the steps of the perron Quentin watched them
ride down the avenue between the files of dragoons,
which closed up to follow. Then he went to give Charlot his last instructions before, himself, departing to
make his way to the Chouan cantonments in the forest
of La Noué.

He was still at this when a clatter of hooves in the
courtyard announced another visitor, and to his joyous
surprise he beheld Germaine in the act of tossing her
reins to one of his lads.

Her appearance checked his gladness. She was not
only pale, but coldly stern.

'You are disturbed,' he said, when he had kissed her
hand.

'Deeply. I have come to talk to you. In here?' She
pointed with her whip to the dining-room, from which
he had just emerged.

'If you will forgive the confusion in which you find
it.'

'Ah! The legacy of your Republican guests.'

Her tone prompted him to reply: 'And my very
timely saviours.'

He closed the door, whilst she went forward to the
table from which all traces of his guests' breakfast had
not yet been cleared. There was a significance in the
glance this perfervid, ultra-royalist lady bestowed upon
it. Then she was steadily regarding him.

'You must be on singularly intimate terms with the
sansculottes to be able to summon a troop of
dragoons to your assistance. It lends colour to what has
been said of you, to the very beliefs that led to last
night's affair.'

'You mean, to what Constant has said of me. He
shall unsay it presently when he follows you hither, as
no doubt he will again.'

She shook her head. 'Constant will not follow today.
He has been dangerously wounded. He was cut over the
head by one of your dragoons.'

'God's Heart! I supposed that he inspired the raid.

But I should never have supposed that he actually led it. That is not in his usual methods.'

'What Constant may have done matters less to me than what you did. You have not answered my question: Will you tell me the truth of your relations with this *canaille* that at one time you travel under its safe-conduct, and at another you can summon its troops to protect you?'

Upon his amazement followed laughter. 'Is that how it looks? But I summoned no troops. Hoche happened to halt here, demanding quarters for the night, on his way to Rennes.'

'Why should Hoche seek quarters at Chavaray?'

'Faith, it's the way of these gentlemen, to requisition what they lack. For the rest, he did not even know that Chavaray was the château to which he came.'

'And so, it was all just chance—miraculously timely chance?'

He met her incredulous, faintly scornful smile with a smile of patient gentleness. 'As you say.'

'And I am to believe it?'

His manner stiffened a little. 'Since I tell you so.'

At a loss, she toyed a moment with her whip, her eyes on the ground. Then she raised them again to meet his patient gaze. 'Listen, Quentin. It is true, is it not, that last night when the peasants came, you went out and spoke to them?'

'And was twice fired upon by Constant's friend, Lafont. That is a detail worth adding.'

This she ignored. 'And is it true, as several have reported, that you warned them that help was on its way to you?'

He considered for a moment. 'It is almost true. What I actually said was that, expecting the attack, I had already sent out an appeal for help.'

'To whom, if not to General Hoche?'

'To the Chevalier de Tinténiac. My messenger left for La Noué yesterday morning, immediately after I received your warning.'

'But La Noué is a hundred miles away. How could

198

you say yesterday evening that help was on its way to you?'

He shrugged. 'Isn't it plain that I must say something to intimidate them into abandoning the attack?'

'And then the help arrived. A really fortunate coincidence.'

'Most fortunate. Unless you would prefer that I had been massacred. It is your grievance, Germaine, that I have survived?'

The half-humorous question turned her hostility to distress.

'It is because you are not being frank with me; because of things that seem to confirm what is being said of you: that you are at heart a sansculotte. I am ever being reminded, first that you came to France on a safe-conduct from the sansculottes; then that by favour of the same you were permitted to enter into possession of Chavaray; and now, when you are attacked here because of just these things, Republican soldiers hasten to protect you.'

'It seems to hang together,' he admitted. 'But for each of those counts, you have my explanation. Although, even without that, I do not see that I should deserve your censure.'

'Should you not? You claim to be Marquis of Chavaray. Where is your place, if it is not beside the throne?'

'Agreed, so long as there is a throne to stand by. But where is the throne of France?'

'In the dust, I know. But it will be raised again, as surely as will the altars which have been defiled and overthrown.'

He sighed, remembering what he had learnt from Hoche. 'I would I could share your faith. But at least I can deny this calumny of Republican sympathies.'

'What are denials when set against the deeds themselves?'

'Deeds! Well, well. You shall have some. I am leaving now to perform them. Let me hope that they will not be misrepresented.'

'What do you mean? You are leaving?' She was peremptory. 'Where are you going?'

He possessed an answer to crush all her suspicions. On the point of delivering it he checked. He saw her, in her turn, confounding Constant with the tale of it, and he conceived that Constant, in his muderous hostility, might not hesitate to use against him the knowledge thus obtained, even at the price of contributing to the threatened ruin of the Royalist cause. A word of warning from Constant to Cormatin, and the odds were that Quentin would be destroyed by the betrayers of Puisaye before he could make the proposed attempt to thwart them.

Whatever the cost, then, he must conceal his intentions until he had contrived to reach Tinténiac.

'Where I am going is no matter. You would not expect me to wait at Chavaray for a renewal of last night's attack.'

'But you spoke of deeds.'

'Naturally. I shall not be idle. I must labour to the end that I may enjoy quiet possession of what is mine. They are labours that may come to improve your opinion of me.'

'If you hesitate to tell me what they are, there is no more to be said until they are done.' She gathered up her whip and gloves.

'Unless you should wish to felicitate me upon my preservation last night.'

'There are things that do not need to be spoken, Quentin.' She was grave, almost sorrowful. 'I shall look to hear from you again . . . soon.' She extended her hand.

Abruptly, impulsively, he brushed it aside and took her in his arms.

'A little faith, Germaine,' he begged. 'A little faith! What is love without it?'

Within the grip of his embrace she looked up at him with her solemn eyes. 'Nothing, Quentin, I know. You must inspire it.'

'Very well.' He let her go. He sighed, his brow

clouded again. 'I shall hope to supply an antidote to this poison.'

On that, as she was moving to the door, he went to hold it for her. He was helping her to mount before she spoke again, and then it was only to repeat herself. 'I shall hope—I shall pray—to hear from you soon.'

He stood watching her until the poplars of the avenue hid her from his sight, then gloomily went within to make his preparations for departure.

CHAPTER 8

La Prevalaye

IT WAS on the afternoon of the second day after that when, having covered over a hundred miles, he rode, a weary man, into the forest of La Noué, to be instantly held up by two armed Chouans, who seemed to rise out of the ground.

He announced himself an emissary of the Comte Joseph in quest of the Chevalier de Tinténiac.

'He is not here.'

'Where is he?'

'We will conduct you to someone who will tell you.' The tone made a threat of the promise. 'Dismount!'

They blindfolded him, and one of them led him forward on foot for a considerable distance; the other followed with his horse, and thrice as they went forward he heard echoing through the forest the owl cry.

When at last sight was restored to him, he was in that vast clearing whither he had first been brought by Cormatin and Tinténiac. He beheld there an assembly of some three or four hundred men, some seated at meat, others at work upon their arms or accoutrements, others merely idling. Farther off, on the clearing's edge, some scores of hobbled, shaggy Breton ponies were cropping the meagre herbage.

In the low doorway of the charcoal-burner's hut stood a slight little man in a hussar jacket with white facings, whose brilliant dark eyes observed the approach keenly and questioningly until recognition dawned in them. Then he moved forward nimbly to meet Quentin, peremptorily waving back his conductors. It was Saint-Regent.

'Monsieur de Chavaray! God save you!'

'Well found!' was Quentin's answering greeting. 'I am seeking the Chevalier de Tinténiac.'

The dark eyes twinkled in the brown, roguish face that was wrinkled like a withered apple. 'Faith, sir, to find him you'll need to cross the sea. The Chevalier is in England with the Comte Joseph.'

'When did he go?'

'A month since.'

The answer dashed the hope in which the question had been asked. 'Then he went too soon.' And in a few swift words, Quentin told him of the treachery preparing in Rennes by Cormatin.

The humour died out of the Chouan's face. Unceremoniously he took Quentin by the arm, and drew him towards the hut. 'Georges had better hear this tale.'

Within the dingy little chamber the corpulent Cadoudal lay wrapped in slumber. Startled out of it by Saint-Regent's shout, he sat up grunting, instinctively reaching for his musket. 'What the devil now?'

'A friend. Monsieur de Chavaray.'

'Peste! Why will you yell so? I thought it was the Blues.' He heaved himself to his feet.

'Well met, Cadoudal. I am a bearer of ill tidings. But let me wet my throat before I begin. Have you anything to drink?'

'Cider.' Saint-Regent went to fill a can at a barrel in the corner. 'Good, honest Breton cider of last autumn, with an edge to it.'

Quentin gratefully drained the can, wearily lowered himself to a stool by the plain deal table, stretched his booted legs, and told the tale that he had learnt from Hoche.

Their amazement culminated in a boisterous refusal from Cadoudal to believe it. 'They're Republican lies,' he concluded.

'Hoche does not suggest a liar to me,' said Quentin.

'Then he's a madman.'

'He does not suggest that either.'

Saint-Regent intervened, a thoughtful frown on his wizened face. 'The meeting at Rennes for next Wednesday is, at least, a fact.'

'But not the purpose of it,' Cadoudal stormed back. 'God of God! The armistice, too, is a fact. But who sought it?'

'Cormatin, says Hoche.'

'He lies. Are they not liars all, these foul democrats? The facts refute them. Wasn't it they who begged for the armistice? Theirs is the desperate need. The Republic is crumbling, and driven to make terms. The poor Republican troops which the Convention can spare for the West move through it at their peril. And they're so well aware of it that they move only when they must. The rest of the time they're huddled together, a flock of panic-stricken sheep that smell the wolves. Is it for the wolves to go bleating to them of peace?'

'No. But a wolf who saw profit in it for himself might do so. According to Hoche, Cormatin is to earn a million livres by this.'

Cadoudal's rejection of this was even more indignant. 'Are we to believe that of a man appointed by the Comte Joseph to represent him? Do you think that a man whose talents have built up this great organization would commit the childish error of appointing such a Major-General?'

Saint-Regent, however, was less confident: 'All traitors owe their opportunity to the trust reposed in them. And in these days . . . Bah! Who would believe that Charette, the most knightly of the Royalist generals, would have made submission to the Republic?'

'What is not yet so well known,' Quentin told them, 'is that that, too, is the work of Monsieur de Cormatin.'

'Hoche will have told you that,' scoffed Cadoudal.

'We might dispute like this forever,' said Saint-Regent. 'Let us go and see for ourselves what's happening.'

'Why, so we shall, at Rennes, on Wednesday, when we come to hear what the *patauds* have to propose. If it should be that we are to recognize their obscene Republic, then—God of my life!—they'll discover that they waste their time. Are the Chouans in defeat, that they should submit to the enemy? Haven't we sworn to fight the battle of Throne and Altar to triumph or to death? Are we to betray that oath at the very hour in which the Republic is agonizing, and the exhausted people, from one end of France to the other, pray only for the restoration of the monarchy? When the English help arrives with Monsieur de Puisaye, such an army will rise out of the ground as the world has never seen.'

'It is not necessary to talk so much, Georges,' said Saint-Regent. 'We are going to Rennes.'

To the fair city of Rennes they came on the eve of that Wednesday of late April, with a bodyguard of a hundred Chouans, openly displaying the white cockade in their round hats and the emblem of the Sacred Heart on the breast of their jackets.

They found the city crowded, and a festive exhilaration everywhere, at the prospect of a cessation of hostilities and a restoration of peace of the distracted countryside.

Saint-Regent found amusement in the spectacle of Chouans, in goatskins or iron-grey jackets, drinking with blue-coated Republicans, and of the white cockade in such friendly cheek-by-jowl with the tricolour, and he laughed to hear the new version of an emasculated *Marseillaise* being sung in the streets. Cadoudal, who lacked his comrade's humorous outlook, glowered upon this ubiquitous fraternizing of Royalist and Republican. It filled him with foreboding. Most ferocious was his glance when Republican officers saluted them as they passed. It was, he complained, no sort of spirit in which to prepare to cut each other's throats.

They moved hither and thither in quest of Cormatin, who was nowhere to be found. They learnt at last that he was at La Prevalaye, a château on the banks of the Vilaine, some three or four miles out of the town, where they would also find the Royalist chiefs summoned for the morrow's conference.

They slept that night at their inn in Rennes, and betimes on the morrow they made their way to La Prevalaye. There they found some hundreds of Chouans encamped, under their white standards, in the grounds of the château, in tents supplied by the Republic, and lavishly entertained at the Republic's charges. Drawn from the ends of the Morbihan, from the moorlands of Paimpont and Lavin, from the depths of the forests of Camors, of Vernet, and the like these men, who from the distant days of La Rouërie had scarcely ever left their burrows and fastnesses but so as to deliver battle, were a little dazed and intoxicated by the honours paid them now that they moved openly and without furtiveness.

Within the lordly manor of La Prevalaye, that once had housed Henri IV, the chiefs had been assembling for some days: gentlemen of family, many of whom had been schooled in arms in the King's regiments or in the Royal Navy. Here they were received and entertained by Hoche's staff and Republican officers of the Army of Cherbourg, and feasted on a scale that spared no expenditure of public funds.

Between Royalists and Republicans, La Prevalaye was housing close upon four hundred men, all displaying that fraternal spirit which Cormatin on the one side, and Hoche on the other, had laboured to inspire. Hoche himself was present with his staff, the gay, debonair Humbert conspicuously solicitous of the comfort of their Royalist guests.

Cormatin, aglow with satisfaction at the excellent prospects of his pacificatory schemes, moved smiling and genial, his portliness tight in a grey frock, with a high stiff collar about his white cravat, a white sash girding his middle, white plumes to his hat, the Sacred Heart on his breast, and a chaplet threaded through his buttonhole.

Nor were ladies lacking to complete the social amenities, although in this respect there was no Republican contribution, unless the Vicomtesse de Bellanger were so to be considered from her now playfully open attachment to the splendid Hoche. A score of other noble ladies, wives or sisters of some of the Royalist chiefs, who hitherto had wooed security in obscurity, rejoiced in this occasion of recapturing something of the gay days of the old departed order.

A glimpse of all this, when on his way to the summoned conference, went far towards dispelling Cadoudal's obstinate disbelief in the mischief that was planned. Hence the scowl on his round, red face, when he came, with his rolling gait, to be deafened in the great conference chamber by the clatter of conversation from more than a hundred tongues. Known to most, he was familiarly greeted on every hand. Saint-Regent, too, numbered many acquaintances. Quentin, completely unknown, attracted little attention. He remained aloof, observant, whilst others continued to arrive, until the gathering in that spacious, bare, and rather dilapidated hall must have numbered fully a hundred and fifty.

A score or so were of the agrarian type, like Cadoudal, loudspoken, rude of dress and manner. The remainder were gentlemen, many of whom revealed in their carriage their military antecedents; some displayed it even in their dress, the close-fitting frocks, high collars, and wide cravats. Many who like Cormatin flitted hither and thither among the groups wore the steel-grey with black facings that was the recognized Royalist uniform, and were girt with the white Royalist sash. Others affected the short Chouan jacket over gaily coloured waistcoats of red or green, and some wore the wide Breton breeches above leather gaiters.

Beyond the white cockade on his sugar-loaf hat, Quentin displayed none of the Royalist insignia, and in his fawn riding-coat, buckskins, and boots, with his chestnut hair severely tied, he had a sense of being on that account conspicuous. Saint-Regent, however, seemed to supply, by his presence beside him, a sufficient answer to inquisitive glances.

Cadoudal could be seen striving to cleave a way through the press to Cormatin, but being ever detained by those whom he sought to pass. He had not succeeded in reaching him when the Baron moved briskly and purposefully to the long table ranged at the hall's end. With him went a group of a half-dozen officers composing his staff, in one of whom Quentin recognized Boishardi, to confirm the tale that this Royalist, famed the most gallant of them all, was in alliance with the pacifists.

Cormatin reached the middle chair of those set beyond the table, and with the butt of a pistol rapped sharply for silence. Then, waving the members of his staff, right and left, to their seats, he himself remained standing.

The chatter died down, the general movement was arrested, and Quentin found Cadoudal once more beside him.

In that attentive stillness Cormatin began to speak, his manner confident, his voice strong and pleasantly modulated. 'Messieurs the officers of the Royal and Catholic Army, we assemble today for what should be our final conference, and at the conclusion it will be the duty of this assembly to appoint ten of its members to convey, tomorrow at La Mabilais, the result of our deliberations to the ten representatives who have been sent by the National Convention to conclude with us the terms of this pacification.'

He paused a moment before proceeding. 'The desire for peace must be present in the hearts of all. For three years now we have seen this fair land of the West, this Brittany, Maine, Normandy, and Anjou, ravaged by fratricidal war. We have seen entire hamlets, villages, and even townships put to the sword and then razed to the ground. We have seen the cattle driven from the land and the fields laid waste, and famine added to the other horrors by which it was hoped to bend us into surrender. All failed. We were not suppressed, because we are unsuppressable.'

A sudden explosion of applause instead of encouraging seemed to disconcert him. Nevertheless, recovering, he continued.

'But if it has not suppressed us, it has brought, is still bringing and will continue to bring, desolation to the land; and we should not be worthy of the name of Frenchmen if we could look on this with indifference. We may perhaps have to admit that the Republicans have set us an example by proposing the armistice which enables us to meet them in a brotherly spirit . . .'

Here Cadoudal, who for some moments had been restive at Quentin's side, harshly interupted him. 'We are brothers to no regicides.'

Upon that followed a scene that showed how divided were the opinions. Yet if many applauded the interruption, there were more to resent it and to call for silence from its supporters.

Cormatin waited patiently until order was restored.

'Suffer me, sirs, to have done without interruption. Then let frank discussion follow. I was saying that the Republicans, weary of this bloodshed and this havoc, have called this armistice in the hope of an accommodation that will lift the horrors of civil strife from the land. They meet us in a spirit, which to me, as Major-General of the Royal and Catholic Army, seems generous.

'Monsieur de Boishardi, whom you see at my side, and in whom you all recognize Brittany's stoutest and most gallant champion of the Royalist cause, is newly returned from the Vendée, whither he went in an endeavour to induce Stofflet to attend this conference. He will not leave his army. But, at least, he has not refused to be bound by the treaty we are to make.'

'Has he consented?' someone asked.

'Presently Monsieur de Boishardi himself will tell you of Stofflet's attitude. I have no cause to doubt that he will be ready to lay down his arms on my recommendation, uttered as it is with the authority of the Princes, whose representative I am.'

'That is false!'

The interjection, sharp and loud, came from Quentin.

There was a startled movement through the assembly. Chairs scraped and ground at Cormatin's table. His aides-de-camp were on their feet, their glances angrily searching the quarter whence the words had come. Upon a silence almost of awe rang the challenging voice of Cormatin.

'Who said that?'

'I did.' There happened to be a chair near Quentin. He reached for it and mounted it, so that he might be seen by all. Muttered inquiries into his identity rippled through the room.

'Do you give me the lie, sir?' Cormatin demanded, his face empurpled.

'Directly and categorically.'

'And there you are,' said Cadoudal below him.

'By God . . .' Cormatin was beginning. Then he checked. 'Who are you, sir?'

It was the question in the eyes of a hundred faces turned towards Quentin.

'I am plain to behold. I trust that you recognize me, for then you will recognize my right to speak as I have spoken. You were the representative of Monsieur de Puisaye. I say "you were," because from the moment that you disobey his orders and betray his trust as you are doing, you cease to represent him.'

Now Cormatin recognized him. Pale with anger, mastering himself by an effort, he named him. 'You are Chavaray.'

'Puisaye's emissary to you, who last brought you his orders from England. To those orders your present activities prove you false. And you magnify the offence when you let it be understood that you act with the authority of the Princes. It was Monsieur de Puisaye who, acting with that authority, sent you orders which precluded any accommodation with the regicides.'

He could add no more because of the sudden turmoil about him.

The secret resentment of the proceedings in the hearts of the majority, lulled hitherto by the guile with which Cormatin or his aides had worked upon them separately, now exploded.

The Baron, his staff standing with him and seeking to calm the hubbub, banged the table again and again with his pistol-butt. Above the din his voice, grown shrill with anger, rang out. 'Hear me, messieurs! Hear me!'

When at last they consented to be silenced, he spoke with assumed calm and dignity, suppressing his distress.

'What there is of personal between Monsieur de Chavaray and me can wait for the moment. The occasion is too grave, my responsibility too heavy, to suffer interruption by any personal insult. I am accused of being false to my orders from Monsieur de Puisaye. So rash is this accusation that it comes before I have even announced the terms of the proposed accommodation. Before I announce them, let me add that even at the risk of being charged with neglect of Monsieur de Puisaye's instructions from England, I, as the fully empowered Major-General here on the spot, must claim to be the judge of what is profitable and expedient to the cause we serve.'

'The good man perorates too much,' grumbled Saint-Regent.

It was evidently a fairly general opinion, for from every side rose the cry: 'The terms! The terms!'

'I am coming to them. The Convention offers a general amnesty to all who have been in arms against the Republic. It will likewise accord an amnesty to all *émigrés* who have returned in defiance of their proscription. Freedom of worship is to be restored, and the ban to be lifted from those priests who have not taken the constitutional oath. The Republican troops are to be withdrawn from the West, the indemnities on a generous scale are to be paid to those whose property has suffered in the course of the civil war.

'That is what the Republic offers us for the peace that all honest men must ardently desire, and they are terms which it is my considered opinion we should best serve the country by accepting.'

He paused there, and the silence was such as to encourage him that the generosity of the terms had impressed the audience. Then a voice asked for something more.

'You have told us what the sansculottes offer. You have not said what they demand in return.'

'That follows logically. That we lay down our arms, recognizing the Republican government.'

'Is that what you urge this meeting to accept?' asked the same voice.

'It is, and that after very careful consideration. If you agree, as I hope you will, it only remains to elect the deputation that is to wait upon the Conventionals at La Mabilais tomorrow, to sign the treaty.'

Quentin looked for another explosion. It did not come. Although downcast by the proposal, which hardly took them by surprise, seeing that they had been privately wrought upon beforehand, yet there was no angry opposition. Already the assembly was breaking into groups, and the hum of discussion growing louder; already Cormatin had resumed his seat when again Quentin raised his voice.

'Have you the authority of the Comte de Puisaye for the recommendation?'

In the stir that followed, he perceived that some there were who resented this reopening of a question which they accounted that the Baron had already answered. Of this, the Baron in his reply coldly reminded him.

'You have answered, sir,' Quentin rejoined, 'that you have no such authority. Then let me ask by what right you make it.'

'By the right of my own judgment. For the rest, sir, the decision lies with this assembly, as it still must if Monsieur de Puisaye himself were in my place.'

'But you seek to guide that decision against all that

211

Monsieur de Puisaye could wish. You betray your trust.'

'I shall be happy to discuss that privately with you afterwards.'

'You shall discuss publicly now.'

Quentin perceived from the hostile, impatient murmurs that the assembly was not in sympathy with him. Impulsively he climbed his chair again, to address not Cormatin, but the entire gathering.

'Messieurs! Whilst Monsieur de Cormatin is here urging you to make a treaty of peace with the regicides, to lay down your arms and recognize the Republic, in England Monsieur de Puisaye, in whose place he claims to speak, is raising reinforcements for the Royalist cause. Any moment now may see the sailing of the ships which Monsieur de Puisaye has induced the British Government to dispatch to Brittany with arms, munitions of war, the regiments composed of *émigrés,* reinforced by British troops and commanded by one of the Princes of the Blood.

'Has Monsieur de Cormatin informed you of this before urging you to enter into this treaty of peace, which I here denounce as a betrayal?'

Cormatin, on his feet again, was again banging the table.

'Silence me that Rhodomont,' he clamoured, 'who out of his ignorance would have us drench the land in blood again.'

But now it was Cormatin himself who was silenced by the angry demands that Monsieur de Puisaye's emissary be heard.

Vehemently Quentin resumed. 'That expedition counts upon finding here an army of three hundred thousand Chouans, likewise raised by the fervent loyalty of Monsieur de Puisaye. Ask yourselves, gentlemen of Brittany, of Normandy, of Maine, of Anjou, is this the moment in which to disband that army, which Monsieur de Cormatin has been instructed through me to hold in readiness?

'Monsieur de Charette may have laid down his arms, seduced by just such a recommendation as is

urged upon you, and in the assumption of an authority
behind it which does not exist. But Stofflet, as you have
heard, has rejected these blandishments. He is still in
the Vendée, ready to unite with the troops that are coming from overseas led by Monsieur d'Artois in person.
Thus reinforced, can you doubt your power to account
for the Republican battalions, whose leaders listened to
Monsieur de Cormatin's peace proposals only because
too conscious of their weakness? Will you betray King
Louis XVII, still a prisoner in the Temple, to whose
cause you have vowed yourselves? Ask yourselves
these questions, gentlemen, and when you have found
the answer, deliver it to Monsieur de Cormatin.'

He climbed down, leaving the room in uproar.

Cadoudal clutched his arm. 'You've driven him
against the wall. He'll need Satan's own guile to answer
all that.'

Saint-Regent was grinning into his face. 'That's a
sour draught you've poured him. And, God help him,
he needs must drink it.'

But they reckoned without Cormatin's ingenuity and
effrontery, and the despair that drove him recklessly to
exercise them. Erect, almost contemptuously master of
himself, save for a pallor so excessive that his eyes
looked black against it, he waited for the clamour to
die down.

'You do me wrong,' he complained, when at last he
could make himself heard, 'if you suppose that I have
no answer.'

'Answer, then,' someone shouted to him. 'Answer,
and be done. What were your orders from the Comte
de Puisaye?'

Cormatin raised a shaking hand. 'Give me leave!
Let me answer in my own fashion.'

A tall, swarthy man, authoritative of manner, Poirer
de Beauvais, an officer who had distinguished himself
in the Vendée, interrupted him again. 'The King?
What of the King in your fine schemes? Did you leave
His Majesty out of your accounts?'

'You insult me by the question!' Cormatin thundered
back, and in an excitement that made him slur his

213

words, delivered his reply. 'There is an understanding that the King shall be restored to liberty as soon after signing the treaty as may reasonably be contrived.'

'Why did you not mention it before?' Beauvais demanded. 'And what is that understanding worth? What is the nature of it? Be more precise.'

'To what end?' Cadoudal stormed in. 'To hell with his understandings! I, for one, have heard enough. He has admitted that he speaks without the authority of the Comte Joseph. Of what importance, then, is anything that he says? Remain who will. I am going.'

That was to set a match to a train that Quentin had laid. There was such an immediate and general movement to depart that Cormatin saw the conference wrecked. In frenzy, beating the table, shouting himself hoarse, he again demanded to be heard. Mocked at first, he ended by prevailing. Then, having entirely lost his wits before the danger of shipwreck to his plans, he begged them excitedly to preserve their own.

'A little calm! A little calm, messieurs!' he implored.

He paused to bend his elegant head towards Boishardi, who, pallid and distressed, was whispering to him under cover of his hand. Then he cleared his throat, and resumed.

'Your mistrust, your prejudices, your readiness to listen to every voice that would discredit me, forces me to reveal that which I had hoped for the present to withhold, because it is dangerous to utter it even among ourselves.'

He gesticulated nervously, holding his hands clumsily before him, clenching and unclenching them as he spoke. 'I have said that we must recognize the Republic. But . . . that is a mere formality. No more. We fulfil it with the mental reservations justifiable wherever there is duress.'

This sounded so much like empty nonsense that questions, excited, angry, derisive, bombarded him from every side.

With his handkerchief he mopped his brow and dabbed his lips alternately, in distraction, until some quiet being restored he was able to plunge desperately on.

'Is my meaning not plain? Must I add that such an undertaking will give the Royalist Party time to organize itself and to prepare for a victorious struggle?' In a foaming rage he added, his voice cracking on the words: 'Now you have forced me fully into the open. You perceive, perhaps, how far I am from betraying Monsieur de Puisaye's trust.'

'More than ever would you be betraying him if that were true,' cried Quentin. 'For that is something which he could never sanction.'

'And why not? Expediency, after all . . .'

He got no farther. Cadoudal, raising a clenched fist and shaking it menacingly, cut him short with a roar of anger and disgust.

'Sir, in the name of every man of honour, in the name of the Royalists of Brittany and Vendée, I forbid you to continue.'

With that he swung on his heel, clove angrily through the press of those about him, and stormed out of the room, leaving a fresh uproar behind him.

Cormatin, fulminated by the apostrophe of that simple husbandman, sank in limp anguish to his seat, whilst others went trooping noisily from the room in the wake of Cadoudal. It was curious and notable that the first to go were men of his comparatively humble class, setting an example to the nobles to abandon a conference over which honour had been shamelessly declared no longer to preside.

Saint-Regent was detained by Quentin, who would have detained Cadoudal as well had he been given time. For he perceived that if many were disposed to go, many were disposed to linger, and to these he accounted that he had yet a word to say, lest Cormatin should win them back under the treacherous spell of his pacificatory intentions.

'Messieurs, hear yet a word,' he called, and Cormatin, in his dejection, made no attempt to check him. 'Peace is the common desire of all. But not peace purchased by cowardice and treachery. Could we recognize the Republic with our lips and deny it in our hearts? Could we enter into such a treaty, with the intention to violate it? Such falsity must be repugnant to every gentleman of France, whose boast it is to be a model to the nations of the world in all that concerns honour.'

Here at last Cormatin, brought to his feet again, would have arrested him had he not been howled down and ordered to be silent.

Quentin proceeded. 'I invite you to reflect that the action requested of you must close the doors of France forever to the Princes on whose behalf you have taken up arms, and this at the very moment when one of them is preparing to place himself at your head with the resources supplied by England.'

That rendered the confusion final and complete. Beyond the table the members of Cormatin's staff, led by Boishardi, broke into invective that aroused answering invective from the assembly. A little more, and swords would have been drawn had not Quentin contrived to make himself heard about the tumult.

'Monsieur de Cormatin has the honour to command in Brittany by virtue of a commission from our General-in-Chief, Monsieur de Puisaye. Whatever he may pretend, he cannot pretend that this commission was given to him in the name of the Princes in order that he should recognize the Republic.'

His utterance was smothered by applause, and few indeed by now were those who did not join in it. At the table Cormatin's officers exchanged despairing glances.

'I summon you, gentlemen, in the name of your General, Monsieur de Puisaye, to suspend Monsieur de Cormatin from his command until fresh order can be taken.'

The affirmative answer to that demand thundered from a hundred throats, and made an end of the conference.

Men pressed about Quentin, addressing him by the name which he had suddenly made famous amongst them, praising what he had done, and felicitating him upon the manner in which he had done it.

He did not win free until more than half the assembly had melted away.

'You've given them a passport back to their burrows,' said Saint-Regent. 'They'll all be on their way before nightfall, and Cormatin will be left to explain himself to the gentlemen of the Convention he had brought from Paris to settle the peace terms. He's in luck that the guillotine has suddenly become so unpopular.'

CHAPTER 9

The Rescue

THE reality exceeded Saint-Regent's prognostication. The Chouan chiefs did not wait for nightfall to lead the men back to their fastnesses.

Already a score of indignant gentlemen were at Quentin's heels as he left the hall. They formed the vanguard of the departure. They trooped noisily out into the gardens, where some ladies took the sunlit air, with a few Republican officers in attendance. Hoche was not of these; but his handsome brigadier was moving as his merry deputy in attendance upon the responsive Vicomtesse de Bellanger.

They stared askance at the excitement of the Royalists, who, with scarcely a salutation, passed on, some to call for their horses, others to summon from their tents and lead away such following as they had brought.

Quentin and Saint-Regent were confronted by Cadoudal, who had been morosely waiting for them. 'I wondered how much longer you would stay once that energumen had shown his hand. For what did you wait?'

'To break his eggs for him,' said Quentin.

'And the stench their rottenness has raised,' added Saint-Regent, 'should drive everyone away.' In a dozen picturesque words he gave a sketch of what had happened.

Cadoudal's glance lost some of its gloom. 'We'd better be going. Faith, it's not safe now to linger. And for you least of all, Monsieur le Marquis. When the explosion comes it'll blow this peace conference back to hell, where it was invented.'

'And messieurs the *patauds* will want to know who fired the train,' Saint-Regent agreed.

Quentin shrugged indifferently. But he was to learn at once that the *patauds* did not provide the only danger for him. Cormatin in his pride of white plumes had appeared in the doorway with some members of his staff. From this group Colonel Dufour detached himself and came in long strides to tap Quentin on the shoulder.

Quentin turned to be met by the bow of a tall, lean man, who was severely formal. 'On behalf of Monsieur le Baron de Cormatin,' he introduced himself.

'*Serviteur!*' Quentin bowed in his turn.

'It will not astonish you that Monsieur le Baron considers himself affronted by certain terms you had the temerity to apply to him.'

'It does not.'

'So much the better. You will the more readily apprehend my purpose.'

'To the devil with that . . .' began Cadoudal.

There Quentin's raised hand checked him. 'I cannot refuse to meet the Baron if he insists. Considering, however, the occasion and all that hangs upon it, you would serve him better by persuading him that he is ill-advised.'

'You will permit me, sir, to be the judge of how best to serve him.'

'In that case there is no more to be said.'

Cadoudal, nevertheless, had a deal to say, and

would have said a deal more had Quentin permitted it.

Thus, since Dufour reported the Baron in haste to have done, they met ten minutes later, behind the château, in an enclosure formed by tall yew hedges, where the turf was springy and the light soft.

Colonel Dufour and a Monsieur de Nantois seconded the Baron, whilst the two anxious and indignant Chouans stood by Quentin.

It was one of Monsieur de Cormatin's many illusions that he was a swordsman, and he came to the meeting in a temper and with the avowed intention to kill Monsieur de Chavaray. Fear of interruption rendered him of an impatience which was conveyed to his opponent by the Colonel.

In the act of binding back his luxuriant hair, Quentin politely smiled. 'Assure Monsieur le Baron that since he is in haste I will make the engagement as short as possible. He shall have no cause to complain of delays.'

'Rhodomontades are out of fashion among gentlemen,' Dufour coldly reproved him.

'You misunderstand me, I think. As you shall see. I am ready, monsieur.'

By the fury of his countenance and in his onslaught the Baron looked dangerous. But Quentin could scarcely better have kept his promise to make the engagement a brief one. He met the Baron's opening thrust on a deflecting forte, and with the riposte ran him through the sword-arm. Thus the witnesses had no sooner realized that battle was engaged than they beheld the Baron disarmed, his sword on the ground, and his right arm in the grip of his left hand, through the fingers of which the blood was oozing.

Quentin flourished his blade in a salute. *'Ave atque vale,'* he murmured, and looked at Dufour. 'Do me now the justice to confess that you misunderstood me.'

Cormatin spoke through his teeth. Not even this prompt disposal of him had dispelled his illusion that he plied a deadly blade. 'You've had the luck today,

Monsieur le Marquis. But we shall meet again. This does not end here.'

'I think it does,' said Cadoudal. 'For we're not to wait for more.' He took Quentin by the arm. 'We'll be going, Monsieur le Marquis. The Baron has too many cursed friends among the sansculottes, and what you've done may annoy them.'

They found their horses and their men, and they were trotting briskly away from La Prevalaye, where the tents of the Chouans were being rapidly deserted, before either of his companions paid any attention to Quentin's repeated question.

'Where are we going?' echoed Saint-Regent at last. 'Why, back to La Noué, that land of luxury and plenty. And you're coming with us. After the work you've done today there's only the forest for you until we've regenerated this unhappy country.'

He demurred, announcing the intention of returning to Chavaray.

'You're tired of life, then,' said Cadoudal. 'How long do you think it will be before they seek you there?'

'A day or two, perhaps,' Saint-Regent assured him. 'They'll want to present an account to you for wrecking their joyous peace plans.'

Cadoudal elaborated. 'Cormatin will make you his scapegoat, so as to turn the Republic's wrath from his own head. It may not suffice, and God knows I pray that it may not. But that will not help you. The sansculottes will show you their own particular kind of mercy if they lay hands on you.'

It was too clear to admit of discussion. So Quentin rode south with his companions. On the morrow, however, Cadoudal left them, announcing the intention of doubling back to Rennes, so as to ascertain the end of this peace-making business.

Saint-Regent pursued his way to the Forest of La Noué, and Quentin went with him, there to make his home for the next two months. Thence he sent a message to Charlot to inform him of the situation, and bidding him, should trouble come, to quit the château with his family and the lads, and fend for themselves.

After that there would be nothing to do but sit still and wait for the coming of Puisaye. His impulse was to take up the duties to which Cormatin had been false, and go forth as the forerunner of the Comte Joseph to stimulate the Royalists into holding themselves in readiness. He was restrained, however, by his lack of the necessary knowledge of the country and of acquaintance—despite the fame acquired at La Prevalaye—with the actual Royalists. Nor was there really the necessity, for Cadoudal, who paid them a visit a fortnight after the *débâcle* at La Prevalaye, had himself shouldered the task.

He brought news of Cormatin. In spite of what had happened, clinging obstinately to a purpose already shattered, the Baron, with his arm in a sling, had presented himself on the morrow of the revolt to the ten Republican deputies who awaited the decision of the conference. Out of the members of his staff and a few Royalist leaders whom he had deluded into adhering to him after the general defection, he had made up the number necessary for the deputation that was to sign the treaty in the name of all the insurgents north of the Loire.

Of the two hundred Royalist leaders summoned to La Prevalaye and the hundred and fifty who had responded, not more than twenty attended the Baron to La Mabilais, where the treaty was to be signed.

With an impudence of which history offers few parallels, he brought his white-cockaded band into the pavilion where they were awaited by the citizen-representatives, a raffish group of play-acting, Jacobin gutterlings, tricked out in tricolour plumes and sashes, and trailing sabres which they had never learnt to handle.

The proceedings were brief. Cormatin announced that he and his companions were empowered to sign the treaty as the representatives of all the Royalists north of the Loire, saving only some odd recalcitrant ones, who would inevitably lay down their arms when they found themselves forsaken. He delivered even an address of some magniloquence and of that histrionic flavour so dear to the sansculottes.

'Our inspiration springs from the love of all Frenchmen for their native land, the desire to extinguish civil discord, the oblivion of the past, the glory common to both parties, the common regard for all that may ensure the safety and happiness of France.'

His conclusion lay in a solemn declaration to submit to the French Republic, One and Indivisible, to recognize its laws, and to engage never to bear arms against it.

To the citizen-representatives it was most satisfactory. They would be able now to announce to the Convention this triumph of their diplomatic measures where force of arms had failed, and the thanks of a grateful nation would be theirs. In return they readily accorded freedom of worship, the withdrawal of Republican troops from the West, the amnesty to returned *émigrés,* and the indemnities that had been stipulated.

They signed. The peace was concluded. Guns were fired; flags were unfurled; military bands filled the air with their music to announce to the world these joyous tidings.

Cormatin, adding a laurel crown to the white plumes that bedecked his hat, rode into Rennes like a conqueror at the head of his faithful twenty and their bewildered white-cockaded following. After them, in their carriages, came the citizen-representatives, whilst Hoche and his dragoons formed a glittering rearguard to the triumphal procession. National Guards lined the streets of Rennes; the drums rolled; the trumpets blared, and the populace shouted: 'Long Live the Peace! Long Live the Union! Long Live France!'

Royalist and Republican passed to a fraternal banquet offered by the nation, to celebrate the occasion. There Cormatin perorated at length in self-glorification, and the citizen-representatives responded with a prolixity that increased in a measure as they became more drunk, and ended only when the wine had robbed them of the faculty of speech. All very touching and impressive.

But on the sober morrow there were unpleasant rumours. These increased as the days passed. Not all the Royalists who had departed in disgust from La Prevalaye had accounted it necessary to practise discretion. The name of the *ci-devant* Marquis de Chavaray began to be heard. What he had said began to be quoted, and at last it became widely known that he had smashed the conference, and that the adherents of Cormatin were only a negligible few.

Paris heard the tale, and the Convention quivered with anger at the imposture of which its representatives had been the victims. Orders went out to the West, and whilst Cormatin still swaggered in his bravery of white plumes, waiting to pocket the agreed indemnity before making his exit from the scene which he had so gloriously adorned, a thunderbolt fell from apparently clear skies.

At the very moment when a proclamation setting forth the peace terms was being pasted on the walls of the Brittany townships, announcing among other things the freedom of worship now accorded, the Convention decreed—on the first of May—the penalty of death against all refractory priests found on the territory of the Republic. Upon this followed an order for the arrest of all men known to have been leaders of the *chouannerie*.

It brought Boishardi to perceive the error of his ways. He waited for no more. In a mood of savage penitence, he called his Chouans about him, fell upon a Republican convoy, and with the arms and ammunition of which he plundered it, went to earth once more in his district of Moncontour.

Cormatin, less clear-sighted, and reluctant to depart without his hard-earned million, allowed himself to be caught, and was flung into prison, to make the discovery that it was easier to fool the Royalists than the Republicans.

Such was the tale that Cadoudal brought back to La Noué. He related it with cynical humour, until at the end he came to add that the name of Quentin de Morlaix de Chavaray was first upon the list of those upon whose heads a price had been set. Republican troops had gone to Chavaray with orders to take him dead or alive, and at the same time to clean up what was described as the *émigré* nest of Grands Chesnes. Apart from the fact that the Chenières were related to the arch-rebel Chavaray, not only had the amnesty to *émigrés* been cancelled by the events, but also the toleration with which since the Thermidorian reaction their return had been regarded.

This was news that wiped from Quentin's lips the smile with which he had listened to the epopee of Cormatin.

Cadoudal was quick to reassure him. 'I've taken order about it. That is one reason why I am here, with three hundred of my lads at my heels. The Blues are conveying the prisoners to Saint-Brieuc.'

'What prisoners?'

'Constant de Chesnières, his mother, and Mademoiselle de Chesnières. The escort, a company of the National Guards on foot, are travelling slowly. They come by way of Châteaubriant. My scouts are observing them, and I shall have word as soon as they reach Ploermel. The time of their arrival there will decide the rest. The *patauds* are not to imagine that they can make arrests with impunity in this country.'

It was not until the following evening that word came of the troops' arrival at Ploermel. It was brought by a mounted Chouan, the condition of whose horse showed the speed he had made. He had gleaned that the Blues would lie the night at Josselin, and proceed by way of Pontivy on the morrow.

Cadoudal required no map by which to plan his operations. He knew the countryside as he knew his pocket. Between Pontivy and the village of Pont Havion, a dozen miles of highway ran through country that was chiefly moorland, as wild and empty as any in France. At a point some four miles beyond Pont Havion the road skirted a wood that clothed the rising ground to the north. It was there that Cadoudal would deliver battle.

'I shall be in it,' Quentin announced.

The Chouan looked dubious. 'It's a peculiar form of warfare, ours. Unlike any you'll ever have seen.'

'I've seen none. So it won't seem peculiar to me. I can ply a blade or handle a musket.'

Cadoudal was relieved. 'I was afraid you'ld want a command. If it's just sport you seek, come by all means.'

Sport was by no means Quentin's object. But he did not argue the point.

Some time before this, Hoche, in writing of his difficulties to the Convention, had complained: "I am engaged with an unseizable enemy. These Chouans seem to materialize suddenly out of the ground to deliver battle, and when it is over they melt away and vanish again in the same mysterious manner, so that even when we repel them it is impossible to render definite their defeat.'

Of these Chouan methods Quentin was now to make acquaintance.

The little army, marshalled at evening in the clearing in the heart of La Noué, knelt in prayer before an oak that bore a great brass crucifix. A proscribed, refractory priest in a white surplice, over which he wore a stole of red, the colour of blood and symbolical of martyrdom, which is love's highest expression, pronounced a brief benedictory address. He assured them that there was remission of sins and assurance of salvation for those who fell in the cause of God's Altars.

Thus fortified, they set out in the dusk, and in a manner alien to all military conceptions. There were no banners, no drums, no trumpets, no marching formations swinging spiritedly shoulder to shoulder along the highway. They went off in the manner of a spreading fan, in little groups of threes and fours which vanished from the sight of one another through the woods.

Cadoudal kept a position somewhere in the middle of that invisible line. Three of his men were with him besides Quentin. Saint-Regent, who had insisted upon being of the party, was on the extreme left, commanding the detachment that in action should form a rearguard, whilst a skilled Chouan leader named Guillemot was on the extreme right and in command of the section intended for the van.

Night, moonless but clear and bright with stars, had completely closed down when Cadoudal's little party emerged from the forest, and to Quentin it might have seemed that these five men were the only ones astir. Of the remaining four hundred there was neither sight nor sound.

They crossed the highroad and a meadow beyond it that was sparsely planted with fruit trees, and emerged into a lane between ditches, skirted a hamlet, and breasted slopes of a diminishing vegetation that brought them to a moorland plateau, arid and empty. At the end of an hour's steady trudging they came to a group of massive monoliths, the menhirs of a druidical cromlech. A little beyond it the track dropped again, to levels of increasing fertility; and then, moving in the dark with the unhesitating certainty of men to whom every yard of the ground is known, they turned aside and lowered themselves through the larches of a sharp declivity to a ravine at the bottom of which Quentin could hear the tinkle and rattle of a brook. By this cleft they continued their descent, until they found themselves once more upon level ground, with the outbuildings of a farmstead looming dimly ahead.

Here Cadoudal halted them, and uttered the thrice-repeated cry of an owl. After a waiting pause in which a man might count to twenty, he loosed the triple cry again.

Presently, ahead of them, a window revealed itself in a yellow flash, and vanished. Twice more in quick succession it sprang into light, and after that remained steadily glowing.

They went forward, across a cobbled yard, to a door which opened as they reached it. A lantern was thrust forward to reveal them to the bulky man who held it.

'And is it you, Georges! Come in.'

It was already after midnight, and for three hours they rested in this farmstead, which was one of the established points in the Chouans' network of lines of communication. They supped on bread and cheese and ham and cider, and slept after that until within an hour of daybreak, when the farmer roused them.

Cadoudal kept horses here, and when they left he and Quentin were mounted. They had not far to go. Beyond the farmlands, which lay in a fold of the shallow hills, they climbed a heather-grown slope as day was breaking in a rosy glow. Once over the crown of it, they entered a belt of woodland that fell gently away to the Pontivy road at a point where it dipped into a hollow. As they advanced through this, the owl's cry greeted them repeatedly, to inform them that the band, which had scattered from a point a dozen miles away, was here reassembling as concerted. Soon the men were revealed in groups, taking their ease until required for the raid.

With Saint-Regent and Guillemot, Cadoudal left the wood for the highway at the bottom of the hollow, to survey the ground which his dispositions were to turn into a death-trap for the Blues. He was short and sharp in his instructions. Guillemot was ordered to marshal his men under cover in line with the summit ahead, so as to close the way to the advance of the Republicans; Saint-Regent was posted similarly at the other summit, whence he could deploy upon their rear. The ambush between, at the foot of the hollow, would be Cadoudal's own care.

They posted sentries, and then the men broke their fast on such provisions as they had brought with them.

Not until close upon noon did the head of the Republican column, six men well in advance of the main body, acting as scouts, come into view on the brow of the hill. Next followed a couple of drummer lads, with their drums slung from their shoulders. There was no need to beat step at present, and the men marched in no sort of orderly formation; rather they trudged along in the relaxed fashion so common to the troops that fought the battles of Liberty, Equality, and Fraternity.

In all they amounted to a hundred men, and they were seen not to be National Guards, as had been reported, but infantry of the line in blue coats with white facings and black-gaitered legs. A two-horse chaise conveying the prisoners was in the middle of the contingent, the commandant on horseback beside it on the left.

They came on without suspicion, for the eyes of the scouts could detect no movement in the stillness of the wood. The leading half of them came abreast of Cadoudal's invisible muskets when the crack of his pistol gave the signal for a volley.

As the thunder of its echoes rolled away, men reeled or sank, some to rise again staggering, others to lie where they fell. Those who were unhurt halted and wheeled about, their muskets levelled, their voices raised in a babel of imprecations.

Instinctively, if disorderly, without awaiting any word of command, they answered the volley of the Chouans by a futile, ragged fire. Yet one bullet sent thus blindly through the trees found Cadoudal, who with Quentin was screened by no more than a tangle of brambles. He span half round with a groan and an oath, and would have fallen but that Quentin caught him in his arms. Gently he lowered him to the ground, so that he sat with his shoulders supported by a tree.

'Leave me,' Cadoudal ordered him. 'Take charge in my stead. You know what's to do. This is nothing. I need a blood-letting. I'm too plethoric. So Father Jacques says, and he's a doctor as well as a priest.'

He had laid bare the wound. It was high in the right breast, and bleeding freely. 'Send me Lazare. He understands these things. Don't waste time here. Take charge of the men.'

Meanwhile the Republican commandant had ridden forth in frenzy from the shelter the chaise afforded him, shouting orders to go about, with no thought but to extricate his company from this ambuscade.

It was as a signal for the Chouans to disclose themselves.

Saint-Regent's men poured across the road to close the way of retreat, whilst Guillemot placed a solid phalanx ahead. The Chouans in the front rank of each detachment lowered themselves in genuflection, with muskets at the shoulder, whilst the file behind took aim over their heads.

The effect upon the soldiers of finding themselves thus covered front and rear was paralyzing. Their commandant, however, though rendered frantic by lack of perception of how to meet such a situation, was far from intimidated. He perceived at least and instantly that to attack either of the disclosed bodies he would have to charge uphill, and would probably see the whole of his company mown down before they could come to grips. And since if they remained in the open this might happen in any case, he decided to attack the party in the wood. Once within the timber he would be on equal terms with those in ambush, and would be at an advantage over those in the open.

So he swung his men to face the trees. 'Charge!' he roared, waving them on with his sword.

He was obeyed with eagerness by men who understood the chances such tactics might afford them. But the beginning of that forward movement was stemmed by a volley from fifty muskets. A dozen Blues rolled in the dust.

'On! On!' the commandant urged the wavering ranks. 'Forward!'

Then a single musket cracked, and his horse went down under him. He leapt clear, and sprang forward. 'Follow me, my children!'

The answer was an enfilading fire on both his flanks, which accounted for another score of Republicans and broke the officer's spirit.

Trapped, helplessly held by superior numbers, nearly half his men out of action, his muskets might account for a few of the Chouans, but only at the price of the annihilation of the remainder of his company.

'Hold!' he yelled, in despair.

He stood forth, alone, facing the invisible enemy, and uncovering held up his hat. 'This is a massacre. Quarter! I ask for quarter.'

Quentin's neat figure, with nothing of the Chouan about it save the white cockade in his conical hat, slid round the bole of a tree on the very edge of the wood, and came fully and fearlessly into view.

From the little that he had seen of Chouans in action he trusted to the mercy of neither Saint-Regent nor Guillemot. Therefore, as Cadoudal's deputy, he decided to take matters into his own hands.

'We shed no more French blood than our safety demands. Throw down your muskets and your pouches.'

For a moment the commandant, a tough, grizzled man of forty, who looked the professional soldier and might under the old regime have been a petty officer, seemed to hesitate, pain and anger in his grey face. Then ill-humouredly he shrugged.

'Ah, sacred name of a name, it's to make one die of rage!' He swung to his men. 'You have heard, my children. The brigands are too many for us. Useless to the nation to get ourselves butchered. So down with your arms.'

Conscripts, young and raw, they were glad enough to hear such a command.

The Chouans swarmed out to collect the abandoned weapons and ammunition. There were odd jesters amongst them, with gibes for the conquered, but in the main they went about the business in grim silence.

Quentin, who had come forward among the first, thrust his way to the chaise.

From its window round eyes stared at him: stark fear in those of Madame de Chesnières; a glad amazement in Germaine's; and an affected irony in Constant's.

'God save us!' he cried, with a laugh. 'If it isn't Monsieur de Carabas!'

'To serve you,' said Quentin, his tone grim. He pulled open the door. 'Pray give yourselves the trouble to alight.'

CHAPTER 10

The Thanks

NOT until the morrow, when they were back in the cantonments of La Noué, did Mademoiselle de Chesnières find an opportunity to express a confusion that had found its climax when she beheld Quentin in the rescue party.

The return of the Chouans to their fastness had been similar to their departure from it. Leaving the disarmed Republicans to care for their wounded and bury their dead, they had dispersed into small groups, and so melted away.

On a stretcher, hurriedly improvised from branches, Cadoudal had been conveyed by a party of his Morbihannais lads back to the farm at which they had that morning rested, there to be put to bed, whilst one of their own surgeons was summoned to tend a wound that was fortunately not dangerous.

The journey to La Noué was one that taxed the endurance not only of Madame de Chesnières but also of Constant, who was still in a state of convalescence. Pauses were necessary, and by the time they came in deadly weariness to the Chouan cantonments, all those who had been in the affair near Pontivy were already back there in their quarters.

The ladies found the charcoal-burner's hut made ready to receive them. Under Saint-Regent's directions fresh rushes had been laid on the earthen floor, and fresh bracken had replaced the old under the cloaks to form their beds.

Constant, who reached La Noué in a state of exhaustion, was housed in one of the log cabins.

Of the three, Mademoiselle de Chesnières, whose

231

lithe vigour had suffered least, was the first to be astir
upon the morrow. Refreshed by some hours of sleep,
she emerged from the hut, active in a trim riding-gown
of bottle green and a plain three-cornered hat, her fair
hair stiffly dressed in a fashion almost mannish.

She came forth to survey in daylight her odd surroundings, to acquaint herself with one of those Chouan encampments of which she had heard the fabulous
accounts that were current. But she found little to be
seen beyond the three log cabins, the great brass
crucifix aloft on its oak, and a cluster of Chouans,
wild-looking men, most of whom, at their ease, were
now in shirt and breeches about a fire of logs over
which a great cooking-pot was suspended from an iron
tripod. The steam of it, borne to her nostrils on the
morning breeze, was appetizing.

The men scrambled respectfully to their feet at her
approach. Not for them, savages though they might
appear, to remain seated in the presence of a gentle-
woman, whatever new doctrines might govern conduct
and manners in Republican France.

She returned their greetings with the gracious dignity
that made most men her willing servants. For some
moments she stood in talk with them upon their
cookery and their general mode of life, following with
difficulty the answers from those amongst them who
prided themselves upon speaking French. Then, with
an eye on the log huts on the edge of that two-acre
clearing, she asked for Monsieur de Chavaray. He had
gone walking, she was told, some time since in the
forest, with his gun, perhaps looking for his breakfast.
Ah, but there he came, returning, and, faith, it looked
as if he would have to be content with the stew of kid
in the cauldron, like the rest of them.

Fowling-piece on shoulder he came sauntering into
the open, and she went eagerly to meet him.

'Do you know my greatest joy in this deliverance,
Quentin? It is in the thought that I owe it to you.'

'Oh, no. Not to me. The design to rescue you was
Cadoudal's.'

His almost too courteous tone troubled her glance.

'You are angry with me. Perhaps you have cause to be. I was not generous with you at Chavaray.'

'There is nothing in this to prove that your judgment was at fault.'

'And in what you did at La Prevalaye? Do you imagine that we have not heard of it?'

'That was no great matter.'

'No great matter? It was matter enough to cover me with shame for heeding lying tales and for having drawn unhappy conclusions.'

'They were quite logical, given the appearances.'

She stood in sweet humility before him. 'There was your word, as you reminded me. That should have outweighed appearances. It should not have needed the proofs you have since given, and at such cost to yourself. You must have known that you would be proscribed and hunted for what you did. You were setting out to do it, and yet you would not tell me. In your pride, you left me in my unjust doubts of you.'

He was melted by her frank, sweet penitence. 'Not in my pride. No. In my prudence. I dared not announce the intention even to you.'

'You did not trust me! Perhaps I have no right to complain of that. I earned it by my own mistrust. That is what shames me.'

He smiled. 'In forming our opinions, the evidence is all, unless . . . But there! That is another matter.'

'Unless . . . Unless what?'

'Unless an intuitive faith—shall we call it?—should override the evidence, repelling inimical conclusions. You see, you had said that you loved me.'

She hung her head. 'Yes,' she softly answered him. 'You have the right to say that. My faith should have lent me a better vision.' She raised her eyes again, and they were magnified by sudden tears. 'Can I say more, Quentin?'

He was completely conquered. If he did not take her in his arms, standing as they did within sight of those men about the cauldron, yet his tone almost supplied the place of the embrace.

'I should not have driven you to say so much. But I

233

desired you to realize for yourself the errors by which you made me suffer.'

'Quentin!'

'That is no matter now. You have seen how mendacious evidence can be. Another time you will mistrust it. For all that I told you was true as truth itself: of the safe-conduct, of the death of Boisgelin, of my possession of Chavaray, of the fortuitous coming of Hoche. As for what I did at La Prevalaye, if I am to continue truthful, I acted rather from a sense of duty to the Comte de Puisaye than from any political feeling. I desire to be honest with you in this, as I have been in all else.'

She held out her hands. 'Is our peace made?'

He took them, his eyes glowing. 'For all time, I hope.'

Then, as if the very expression reminded him of the perils that might shorten time for them, he spoke of the need to conduct them to the coast, and to ship them back to England until strife should be at an end in France.

She shook her head, but without concern. 'It would not be possible. Madame de Chesnières could never face the dangers and hardships of that journey. It requires all the resource and vigour of a man. Besides, our plans are made. When we were arrested we were already packing up to go to Coëtlegon. Madame de Bellanger must have been aware of the orders for our arrest. She sent us word of it, urging us to go to her, and assuring us that at Coëtlegon we should find a sanctuary where we would be secure from violence. But for my aunt's hesitations, due to a personal hostility to the Vicomtesse, we should never have delayed departure.'

Quentin thought he understood both Madame de Chesnières' hostility to the Vicomtesse and the inviolability of Coëtlegon. A common source supplied one and the other. For once he approved Madame de Chesnières. But not to the extent of scorning the aegis provided by General Hoche.

'The arrest,' Germaine concluded, 'has put an end to

any lingering hesitations in my aunt. She is very human, after all.'

'I confess I had not found her angelic.'

Germaine smiled and sighed. They had begun to move side by side across the clearing. 'There is little that is angelic about any Chesnières, nor do they attract angelic mates. A queer, turbulent, unhappy family it has always been, tortured by internal hatreds that more than once have led to fratricide.'

'Then all that happens to me is explained. It is in the Chesnières tradition.'

Constant came to interrupt them. He approached, leaning heavily upon a cane. Pallor lent a greenish cast to his swarthiness. He greeted them with his sardonic grin.

'Ah, Germaine. You seize opportunity to return thanks to your saviour. Very proper.'

'Is he not your saviour, too, Constant?'

'Do not make me laugh, child. I am still too weak from the wound his friends dealt me. And that is the answer.'

It was Quentin who laughed. 'With what comic tenacity you cling to a cherished conceit.'

'To be sure, you've changed your company since then. That, I suppose, would be to suit your convenience. You may run with the hare and hunt with the hounds until the hounds discover it and tear you down. It usually ends like that.'

'Have you enlightened Saint-Regent?'

'Oh, sir! It is not my way to return good for evil.'

'Ah, no,' Germaine told him. 'Evil for good is your way. You're proving it now.'

With his sneering smile, Constant looked at Quentin. 'You've a stout champion, sir, in Mademoiselle de Chesnières. I felicitate you.'

'I thank you. A woman is my sufficient champion in this instance.'

'Ah? I am dull. Be so amiable as to explain that to me.'

'It's plain enough,' said Germaine. 'It means that he

despises you too much to quarrel with you. And with reason. You're contemptible.'

Constant still smiled. 'If beauty dwells in the eye of the beholder, why, so must ugliness. You see me according to your vision. I must deplore the deception it practises upon you.'

'He means,' said Quentin, 'that he's impervious to insult. A lofty state of mind.'

'Oh, I hardly claim so much. It must depend upon whence the insult comes. A woman's tongue, now, does no dishonour; a man's only if he is honourable himself.'

With an exclamation of disgust Germaine turned her shoulders upon him. Quentin, however, chose to enter into Constant's humour. 'A nice point; a nice discrimination. I ask myself should you stay to practise it if a man were so hasty as to box your ears.'

'A coarse suggestion,' said disdainful Constant.

Germaine broke in with heat: 'Oh, why do you trouble to answer his empty, offensive chatter, Quentin?'

'Oh, feminine inconsequence!' Constant mocked her. 'If I am empty I cannot be offensive.'

'Of course not,' Quentin agreed indulgently.

'Ah?'

'Merely empty.'

'You relieve me. But of course I had not supposed that it was possible to offend you.'

'That is rarely a safe assumption, Monsieur de Chesnières.'

'I had not paused to think of safety, Monsieur . . . Monsieur de Carabas.'

Quentin stepped forward so quickly and moved to such obvious sudden anger that the leer perished on Constant's lips. He may well have asked himself had he not perhaps pushed insolence incautiously far. He may have been relieved to find Germaine slipping between them, to lash him with the controlled scorn of her quiet voice.

'What a poor, paltry, insolent coward you are, Constant! You lean on your cane, a sick, feeble man, spitting venom from the shelter of your sickness, abusing a patience that you suppose inexhaustible, and this against a man who rescued you only yesterday from the peril of death.'

He interrupted her. 'Ah, that, no. All the rest, if you please. They are merely opinions; a girl's negligible opinions. But that Monsieur de Morlaix was moved by any thought of rescuing me is more, I think, than even he will pretend.'

'A fair statement,' Quentin agreed. 'I should have been as unlikely to go to your assistance as you are to acknowledge it.'

'I am obliged to you for your frankness, monsieur,' said Constant.

Saint-Regent, slight and agile in his hussar jacket, came to bid them to breakfast, and led the way to the hut with Monsieur de Chesnières.

Germaine, following at leisure with Quentin, set a hand on his arm.

'You possess a brave man's forbearance,' she commended him.

'My dear,' he answered her, 'my wrath is not required. Monsieur Constant is a man who will dig himself a grave with his tongue before he is much older. To that fate I am content to leave him.'

BOOK III

CHAPTER 1

D'Hervilly's Command

FOR a full month Quentin abode at La Noué, whilst Cadoudal, restored to vigour, assumed in Brittany and Normandy the task abandoned by Cormatin, and in the discharge of it grew daily in authority among the Royalists.

It was a month of much activity on both sides. There were surprise attacks upon townships held by the Blues and raids upon their convoys, and there were counter-raids and massacres by Republicans more or less at bay in that hostile countryside. It was in the course of one of these that Boishardi met his death, on the very eve of his intended marriage.

Meanwhile in England the tireless, indomitable Puisaye, generously supported by Pitt and Wyndham, prepared the expedition which was to set the West in movement that was to sweep like a tidal wave across France and overwhelm the gutterlings that dominated her.

At his summons French *émigrés* from the depths of Germany and bands of old soldiers who had emigrated with their officers in '92 or who had deserted Dumouriez in '93 hastened to reinforce the French regiments recruited in England: the Royal Louis, of four hundred gunners who had escaped from Toulon; the Royal Marine, of five hundred *émigrés* under the Comte de Hector, composed almost entirely of former naval officers; the Loyal Emigrant, raised by the Duc de la Châtre, seven hundred strong; the regiment of the Marquis du Dresnay, of the same strength; the regiment of the Comte d'Hervilly, of twelve hundred Breton conscripts, who had come to England as prisoners of war, and a hundred volunteers. In all they made up four brigades. To these were to be added five regiments assembling in Holland under Sombreuil, and some eight thousand British troops that Pitt had undertaken to add to the lavish war material he was providing.

Monsieur d'Artois displayed in his letters a quivering eagerness to lead them, and his presence alone should be worth an army corps. The Prince, a visible, tangible incarnation of the ideal for which they fought, should rally every able-bodied man of the West to the banner of Throne and Altar.

At Portsmouth a fleet under Sir John Warren was rapidly fitting out, and the supply ships were loading the material, which comprised twenty-four thousand muskets, clothing and footgear for sixty thousand men, and a vast store of food and ammunition.

Puisaye might flatter himself that all this was the miracle wrought by his energy, vision, intelligence, and persuasive powers. His satisfaction, however, was darkened by the jealousies and intrigues that seldom fail to poison any Gallic enterprise. At every step these came to create obstacles for him and to add to the difficulties inseparable from so Herculean a labour as his.

The vain and pompous d'Hervilly perceived here his chance to magnify himself. Endowed with few talents save the talent of intrigue, and endowed with this one to excess, he so shrewdly exercised it as to obtain, despite the fact that he held only a colonel's rank, the chief command of the actual *émigré* contingent.

In view of the support he had won, the four generals commanding the four brigades made no protest beyond relinquishing their commands, since it was impossible that they should serve under a man of inferior rank. Of those nobles who had raised the other regiments, La Châtre, Dresnay, and Hector adopted the same course for the same reason. Nor did it end there. Every colonel in the service retired rather than submit to one whose rank was not superior to their own, with the result that the regiments were left under the command of lieutenant-colonels, who were not of the same authority over either officers or men.

If Puisaye did not interfere it was because he realized that this must lead to a trial of strength between himself and d'Hervilly; and whilst he could not doubt that he must prevail, yet he perceived that a worse state of things might result, such was the influence d'Hervilly had won by his intriguing over the nobles who filled the lesser ranks. He imposed himself by assertiveness and obstinacy, which were mistaken for strength of mind, and by a veiled jactancy that conveyed an impression of high military gifts acquired in the war of American independence, in which he had served as an aide-de-camp to the Comte d'Estaing.

Had not Puisaye underrated the man's assertiveness, he would now have perceived a greater matter for alarm in the continued absence of Monsieur d'Artois.

'It is in the field of honour,' the Prince had written to Puisaye, 'that I hope soon to be able to give you in person the proofs of my esteem and confidence.'

Puisaye cared less about these proofs than about the actual presence of the Prince, so passionately awaited by the devout and simple Chouans. Yet ready as they were to set out for that field of honour of His Highness's letters, Monsieur d'Artois continued abroad. He would not, however, go the length of delaying the expedition. So it weighed anchor, a fleet of close upon a hundred sail, and steered for Brittany.

A French fleet, which disputed its passage, was put to flight after the capture of three of its ships, and driven into the harbour of Lorient, where it was blockaded.

On the evening of the twenty-fifth of June the British ships sailed into the Bay of Quiberon, and then the real trouble began. With immediate assumptions of paramount authority, d'Hervilly refused to disembark until the twenty-seventh, by when his constant use of the telescope had assured him that no enemy was in sight to dispute the landing.

Wondering how long he would be able to maintain a contemptuous patience with this creature of routine, this martinet of the parade ground, Puisaye allowed him to have his way, but only because the delay was giving the Bretons time to come to meet them.

When at last the expedition landed on the shore of the great bay, at the foot of the mournful dunes and tumuli of Carnac, the sands were black with the Chouans who had hastened thither as soon as the news had reached them that the sails were in sight. Fifteen thousand of them waited to greet the *émigrés* regiments. They had not travelled furtively, as was their habit, gliding invisible through herbage, stealing through woodland and by ravines, taking advantage of the concealment offered by every fold of the ground; they had marched boldly and openly by the highways in their thousands, conceiving that the time of skulking was at an end.

They came dashing waist-deep into the water, to drag the boats ashore: they harnessed themselves to the guns when these were landed, so as to haul them up the beach. On the sand of Quiberon they leapt and danced in joy about the arriving *émigrés*, with mighty shouts of *'Vive le Roi!' 'Vive la Religion!'* and *'Vive le Comte Joseph!'* which was the extent of the French that many of them knew. They were like great shaggy dogs capering in welcome, and as dogs from the outset were they scornfully regarded by the *émigrés* to whom they came to supply the necessary strength. Their very friendliness and the familiarities that sprang from it served only to arouse in the gentlemen from England all the old arrogance of caste.

Their transports were momentarily quelled by reverence when the Bishop of Dol, in his mitre and carrying the pastoral crooks, set foot ashore followed by forty attendant priests. In sudden awe the wild peasant horde knelt on the sands with bowed heads to receive the episcopal blessing.

After the landing of the men came the landing of the stores. First the fine muskets and the ammunition, which were at once distributed and went to swell the enthusiasm of the Chouans. So as to express it, they lost no time in biting cartridges, and the sounds of firing were added to the hilarious din.

With a frown at the root of his great nose d'Hervilly surveyed that peasant multitude. Men who appeared to be without notion of military formations, who had no uniforms beyond the white cockade and the chaplet through the buttonhole, could not be soldiers in his eyes.

'Are these your troops, Monsieur de Puisaye?'

Puisaye quietly smiled. 'A small sample of them, a mere vanguard.'

'I shall not know what to do with them.'

'I shall have the satisfaction of showing you.'

He took ten thousand of them to form three army corps, the commands of which he gave to Tinténiac, Vauban, and Boisberthelot, gentlemen who had led and were trusted by them, and sent them forward at once to seize and hold Auray in the East and Landévan in the West, thus placing the Royalist army within a quadrilateral as a beginning.

Because relieved to be rid of two thirds of that savage horde, d'Hervilly raised no objections. But on the morrow the brewing storm broke at last between them.

Some further contingents arrived, brought in by Cadoudal, with whom came Saint-Regent and Quentin, all of them very cordially received by Puisaye in the kitchen of the farmhouse at Carnac where he had taken up his quarters.

For Quentin he had a welcome of particular warmth. Retaining his grip of the young man's hand, he placed his left on his shoulder, and the keen eyes were softened by affection.

'By your action at La Prevalaye you saved my credit. It is beyond thanks, beyond anything I had the right to expect from you.'

'God's thunder!' swore Cadoudal, 'I envied him a performance that should have been mine. But I lacked the wit. All I could think of was to march out, slamming the door after me.'

'And it was done,' Puisaye continued, patting the shoulder under his hand, 'at great danger and discomfort, as I gather. That was brave.' His deep-set eyes glowed. 'I shall hope before long to hear the King thank you in person.'

Quentin laughed a little, to dissemble his embarrassment. 'I was the bearer of your orders to the Baron de Cormatin. I could hardly stand silent when I saw him frustrating them.'

There he was relieved by the abrupt arrival of d'Hervilly, with four of his officers in attendance. The Colonel clanked into the kitchen with his swaggering gait, an incarnation of importance.

'Ah, Monsieur le Comte, I have to complain of these undisciplined savages of yours. They seem to be without any sense of respect for their betters, or, indeed, sense of any kind. I warn you that unless you can control them we shall have trouble. My gentlemen are not disposed to suffer the insolences of these animals.'

Cadoudal took a step forward, his face flushed, his great bulk seeming to swell. He flung out a huge hand. 'God's thunder! Who may this be?' he demanded in a roar.

Puisaye, a figure of elegant authority in his gold-laced coat of madder red, the grey in his queued reddish hair giving it the appearance of being lightly powdered, standing a half-head taller than the long-bodied d'Hervilly, dominated the little gathering by his suave urbanity. He made the presentation.

'The Colonel Comte d'Hervilly, who commands the *émigré* contingent,' was his short announcement on the one hand. On the other he was deliberately more elaborate. 'This is the Marquis de Chavaray, in whom you discover an old acquaintance. He leaves us all in his debt by his exposure of the treachery of Cormatin. And these are Georges Cadoudal and Pierre Saint-Regent, two of the great heroes of Brittany, who have carried the white cockade victoriously into a hundred encounters.'

D'Hervilly stared in surprise at his sometime fencing-master, and paused to exchange civilities with him. Then his glance swept on, and in his cold, hard eyes there was only contempt for the portly, frowning

Cadoudal, in his grey coat and baggy breeches, and the grinning Saint-Regent, with his mobile, wide-mouthed, comedian face and his ridiculous hussar jacket. His nod was scarcely perceptible.

'Messieurs!' was all that he could find to say to them, and with that he swung again to Puisaye. 'I am to request you to take order so that I may not again have to complain of your Chouans.'

Still Puisaye ignored an arrogance that amused Saint-Regent and enraged Cadoudal. He answered quietly: 'As we shall be going forward almost at once, these trifles need no longer preoccupy you. I was coming to inform you, Colonel, that we march tomorrow at dawn.'

D'Hervilly's glance was haughty. 'What you suggest is quite impossible.'

'It must be made possible. And I do not suggest it. I command it. You will be good enough to see that all are ready.'

The haughtiness became more marked. 'To march whither, if you please?'

'Forward. To Ploermel. That is our first objective.' He turned aside to the long kitchen table on which a large-scale map was spread. 'I will show you . . .'

'A moment, Monsieur le Comte. A moment! You cannot be proposing that we leave the coast before the arrival of the further forces under Sombreuil, which the transports have returned to Plymouth to embark.'

For a moment Puisaye's urbanity was ruffled. But he was content to vent his impatience in a sigh. He looked over his shoulder at the Colonel. 'You must allow me to be the judge of that.'

'I cannot.'

Puisaye wheeled round. 'You cannot? Name of a name! I begin not to understand you. God give me patience! I should not need to tell you that speed is here of paramount importance. A swift, bold advance, to take the Army of the West by surprise before it can concentrate, and to stimulate the general rising that is to yield us the army with which to march on Paris.'

Coldly, his lip curling, d'Hervilly shook his head. 'You do not persuade me, monsieur.'

'Good God!' said Cadoudal.

Puisaye was smiling again. 'The events will do that by the time we reach Ploermel. By then our fifteen thousand Chouans will have become not less than fifty thousand, and will, more likely, be a hundred thousand. These numbers will be more than doubled by the men from Normandy and Anjou before we reach Laval, where we shall be joined by the Maine contingent.'

D'Hervilly shrugged ill-humouredly. 'Your Chouans, from what I have seen of them, inspire me with little confidence; with none unless they are leavened by seasoned troops, such as we await.'

Puisaye's patience began to ooze away. 'My Colonel, I do not admit your competence to judge the fighting qualities of the Chouans, of whom you have no experience.'

'I have experience to know soldiers when I see them. But we will not argue. I should regard it as a folly to go forward until the second expedition arrives. And I know what I am saying. Military prudence, of which I also know something, dictates that we remain here in touch with the sea, so as to ensure their landing.'

'Shall we ensure it any the less if all Brittany is in our possession? And I promise you that it will be by the time Sombreuil arrives.'

'Unless,' Quentin ventured to put it, 'you delay in seizing it.' Disregarding d'Hervilly's glance, which was such as he might turn upon an impertinent lackey, Quentin prodded Cadoudal. 'Why don't you tell them what you know?'

'About Hoche? Faith, listening to monsieur upon the art of war takes my breath away. He knows it all. Still, here's the situation: Hoche is at Vannes with not more than five hundred men, the remainder of his Army of the West being scattered about Brittany. Your landing and the rising have taken the *patauds* by surprise, and I don't suppose Hoche has enjoyed much sleep since he heard of it. He'll be haunted by the nightmare of his scattered detachments, expecting them to be cut to pieces before he can concentrate them again. But he is losing no time, and his recalled troops are already hastening to Vannes. By tonight he should have a couple of thousand men; by the end of the week if we do nothing to prevent it he will have thirteen or fourteen thousand, and his couriers are on the way to Paris at the gallop, with demands for reinforcements to meet the emergency. It will put such a panic into messieurs the sansculottes that within ten days Hoche will have received every musket and every sabre they can muster.'

D'Hervilly considered him for a moment in silence, his glance veiled and sullen. 'What,' he demanded at last, 'is the source of your information?'

Quentin looked at Puisaye in frank amazement. 'He asks for sources!'

'Oh, a meticulous gentleman,' sneered Puisaye.

'Our Lady of Auray!' Cadoudal was gasping. 'Is it possible, sir, that what I have told you does not leap to the eye? How else does this military experience of yours tell you that Hoche would be acting?'

'And that,' said Puisaye, 'is just why it is of such importance to move swiftly; at a bound make ourselves masters of Brittany and rally its loyal sons to us before a Republican concentration can either hinder or discourage it.'

D'Hervilly's face was set. He would waste no breath on their pertness. 'I say again, monsieur, that I am not persuaded.'

Puisaye shrugged. 'To the devil with persuasion, then. You have my orders. Let that suffice.'

'I am not to take your orders.'

'Monsieur!' Puisaye was suddenly stern and formidable. 'I do not think I understand.'

'You understand, I suppose, that your authority is confined to your Chouans. The command of this expedition has been entrusted to me.'

'By whom?'

'By the British Cabinet.'

Puisaye had need of a moment in which to master himself before replying. 'If that were so, which I take leave to assert it is not, it cannot override my commission from the King. It should not be necessary to say this, and I resent that you compel me to say it. It is within your knowledge that His Majesty, whilst still Regent, appointed me General-in-Chief of the Royal and Catholic Army.'

'Why do you stop there?' snapped d'Hervilly. 'Complete the title so as to remove misunderstanding: General-in-Chief of the Royal and Catholic Army of Brittany. Of Brittany. The army I have landed does not come within that narrow designation. Your command, as I have said, is confined to your Bretons, to your Chouans. You . . .'

'Listen, sir. I hold in addition the office of Lieutenant-General of the Kingdom, and I shall continue to hold it until Monsieur d'Artois arrives to assume it himself.'

'I have no knowledge of that. All that I know, all that concerns me, is that, as my commission proves, I have been placed in command of this expedition by the British Government, which organized it, and I will permit no other to dictate courses of action in an enterprise of which the responsibility is mine. Do I make myself clear?'

'Clear! A thousand devils! Can rubbish be clear? The organization was mine; the inspiration was mine; the preparation of the soil was mine; the persuasion of the British Government to support us was mine. Are you drunk? Is it likely that the command of the expedition could be entrusted to another?'

'If that other were of military experience and ability to warrant it.'

'Good God!' muttered Cadoudal again.

'And you possess them? God save us! Acquired, I suppose, in America, as an aide-de-camp. That warrants your authority over a man who has commanded an army in the field, who has created the army that is now to be led! You want to laugh, Monsieur le Comte. Your commission may be vaguely worded. It must be or you would not dare to take this tone. But you must be entirely crazy if you suppose that your command extends beyond the *émigré* contingent from England.'

Purple with anger, the veins in d'Hervilly's forehead stood in bold relief. 'I find you singularly offensive, sir. And singularly foolish. The *émigré* contingent, as you call it, is the army. Your untrained, undrilled, undisciplined Chouans are merely auxiliaries.'

Cadoudal exploded into angry laughter. 'An army of four thousand men! You'll storm Paris with it? Name of a name!'

D'Hervilly ignored him. 'I waste no more words, sir. The army does not move from Quiberon until Sombreuil arrives with his reinforcements.'

'You'll be in hell by then if you remain,' said Cadoudal. 'Hoche will see to that.'

At last d'Hervilly condescended to notice him. 'I am not to be spoken to in that manner,' he rasped. 'Monsieur de Puisaye, I have to require that you instruct your followers.' He swung on his heel, beckoning the members of his staff. 'Come, messieurs.' And he clanked out with tremendous dignity.

The four who remained looked at one another. Puisaye laughed, wry-mouthed. 'And now?'

Cadoudal bounded forward. 'Do you ask? Arrest that Polichinelle. Let a court-martial deal with him.'

Puisaye stared at him as if he did not understand. All the swagger and flamboyance seemed to have perished in him. He was a man suddenly bowed under a load of weariness. He dropped heavily into a chair. 'The consequences,' he said. 'I should split the camp into two parties. The *émigrés*—and the weight of authority is with them—will range themselves, almost to a man, on the side of that intriguer. They don't love me. They mistrust me as one who is not quite a pure. In the States General I voted with the constitutionalists; I once commanded a Republican army. D'Hervilly will have worked upon all that.' He rested his head on his hand, his countenance dark with trouble. 'If we fall to quarrelling among ourselves, there's an end to the expedition, a ruin to all that I've worked for.'

'There's an end to it, anyway, if this colonel is left in command,' said Saint-Regent, and Cadoudal swore agreement with him.

Puisaye sighed wearily. 'Almost it was to have been foreseen. From the beginning this man has been a source of trouble, a problem with which I should long since have grappled had I not believed that Monsieur d'Artois would embark with us and solve it for me by taking the supreme command.'

'You must grapple with it now,' swore Cadoudal.

'We're in a deadlock.'

'Never! If you can't have him shot without provoking mutiny, if he insists that the *émigrés* are not to march with us, we'll march without them. To delay would be fatal.'

'Don't I perceive it? But we promised the Bretons a Prince of the Blood. They look for him as for a messiah. He has not come. But at least we have these martial *émigrés*, these nobles, these officers of the King's army and navy, to lend a glamour to our advance and rally the peasants in their thousands. If we march without them, who will believe in this army of saviours from overseas? Our peasants will not quit their fields. Do you suppose that I should have laboured and schemed these months in England if I had not perceived all this?' He rose, and stamped tempestuously across the stone floor, in momentary surrender to his feelings. 'Ah, God of God! To have the fruits of all my labours, of all my striving, jeopardized by the vanity of this cursed popinjay!' He broke off, and looking at Quentin, before whom he had halted, he laughed as if in self-mockery. 'I have never yet failed to dominate Fortune by insistence and tenacity of purpose. But now it seems that Fortune takes her revenge.'

Cadoudal had nothing more to contribute to the discussion. He sat down to curse d'Hervilly with fluent ferocity. Saint-Regent swore that for his part he had never set great store by these pimps and dancing-masters of the Court. Quentin, in silence, watched Puisaye, pervaded by a deep sympathy for him and a dull anger against those incompetents who were frustrating him in the very moment of his triumph.

He was pacing to and fro, in thought, his hands behind him, his fine head bowed, his chin on his neckcloth.

'A deadlock it is,' he said at last. 'Argument is futile. Force, still worse. The English must resolve it.'

'The English?'

'This expedition is theirs, and the British Cabinet must remove d'Hervilly's misconception on the score of the command. Mr. Pitt shall amend the Colonel's commission, so that it leaves him no room for presumptuous doubts.'

'But the time this will take!' Cadoudal protested in dismay. 'When instant, swift action is demanded.'

'I know. I know. But there is nothing else to be done. We must hope for the best; hope that delay in taking the field will not too ruinously prejudice us. I will write to Mr. Pitt at once. Sir John Warren shall dispatch a cutter with my letter. In ten days—a fortnight at most—we shall have the answer.'

'A fortnight!' Cadoudal showed a face of horror. 'And what will Hoche be doing in that fortnight?'

'All that Monsieur d'Hervilly is making possible. You should see that I cannot help it.'

CHAPTER 2

The Rat-Trap

MONSIEUR DE PUISAYE waited upon d'Hervilly, to inform him of the letter he had written.

'I tell you this so that you, too, may write if you so wish, Colonel.' He seemed to stress the title.

'I shall certainly take the opportunity to let Mr. Pitt

know that I have occasion to complain of you, and on what grounds.' D'Hervilly was white with passion and perhaps with fear of a humbling loss of the authority he usurped.

Puisaye bowed coldly, and withdrew; and they did not meet again until two days later, when Puisaye sought him with a message from Auray. Vauban sent word that Hoche had assembled thirteen thousand men at Vannes, and was about to march on Auray, which could not be held unless Vauban were supported.

The Loyal Emigrant Regiment, in red coats, white breeches, and three-cornered hats, was parading on the sands for inspection by d'Hervilly when Puisaye came up with him and penetrated the group of white-plumed officers.

'You perceive the first fruits of our inactivity. Thirteen thousand men, who in their scattered detachments might easily have been suppressed, are now concentrated into an army.'

D'Hervilly's curt answer ignored the criticism. 'You must recall your Chouans.'

'Unless we can support them.'

'I have said that they must be recalled. You force me to repeat myself.'

'In that case we must also recall Tinténiac from Landévan. For Vauban's withdrawal will leave his flank exposed.'

'Of course.' D'Hervilly was contemptuous. 'You merely state the obvious.'

'Let me continue to do so,' said Puisaye dryly. He pointed across the dunes to the Fort Penthièvre, the massive stronghold that bestrode the narrowest part of the Isthmus of Quiberon, on their right. The Republicans had renamed it Fort Sansculotte. 'Once we have withdrawn our outposts from Auray and Landévan, we shall not only have Hoche before us here, but when that happens our flank will be threatened by that fortress. The position becomes untenable.'

There was a stir and mutter in the group of officers as the peril was realized. The blood darkened d'Hervilly's countenance. Too hastily he answered: 'At need we can re-embark.'

Puisaye laughed, to annoy him further. 'That will be encouraging to our Breton friends. And after that? You will return to England, I suppose.'

'Monsieur de Puisaye, I begin to find you intolerable.' The man swelled with rage. 'Let us hear, pray, how you would deal with the situation.'

'There is only one way to deal with it. The fort must be taken.'

'Really! Really! It would be difficult to better the ineptitude of that suggestion.' He was smiling now, conceiving that he was about to expose Puisaye's military ineptitude. 'And how, pray, does one take a fort without siege artillery? Or perhaps you are not aware that I have none.'

'I am not.'

'How?'

Puisaye turned, again to point, this time to the tall British ships riding at anchor in the bay. 'There it is. Sir John Warren's guns will provide all the bombardment the sansculottes will need.'

'Ah!' Meditatively d'Hervilly stroked his chin, so as to cover his confusion. 'It is a thought,' he admitted after a moment.

'Not one to exhaust the intellect.'

'So I perceive. Yet artillery alone will hardly accomplish it. Storm troops will be needed, and I should be reluctant to expose my regiments to the fire of men behind stone walls.'

'Cadoudal's Chouans will undertake that part.'

'In that case,' d'Hervilly condescended cavalierly, 'I am prepared to adopt the plan.'

There being no time to lose, Puisaye directed the attempt for the following morning.

Sir John's ships pounded Penthièvre with a hot continuous fire, under cover of which Cadoudal led three thousand of his Morbihannais to the assault.

From the heights, amid the grim megaliths of Carnac, d'Hervilly with his staff observed the action, and what he beheld disgusted him. The Chouans, prone on the ground, wriggling forward on their bellies in open formation, outraged his every sense of military propriety.

'What tactics are these?' He addressed his question to the Universe. 'Observe me those savages. Thus have I seen the Hurons on the Savannahs. I can almost imagine that I am back in America.'

A voice came to startle him: 'How regrettable that you are not.'

Doubting his ears, he swung about, and beheld a young man in a riding-coat of green, who had come to stand on the edge of the group of officers.

'Monsieur de Morlaix! What is your regiment, sir?'

The terrible voice and the terrible glances of the staff left the young man unperturbed.

'I have none. I am in civil life.'

'Then, what are you doing here?'

'Observing those very gallant fellows, admiring their tactics, and wondering that their virtues should be unperceived by a soldier.'

'Monsieur, you are an impertinent.'

'Monsieur, you are not civil.'

One of his officers laid a restraining hand upon d'Hervilly's arm. He aimed at creating a diversion, and chance supplied him with the means. 'Look, my Colonel! The fort is striking its colours. The tricolour is coming down.'

A burst of cheering came up to them from the Chouans below.

At this decisive effect of the British bombardment and in the excitement of the moment, d'Hervilly allowed himself to be drawn forward and down the slope.

That night, however, he stormed into the farmhouse quarters whence Puisaye was preparing to transfer himself.

'So, monsieur! We have reached the point at which you send a *spadassin,* a bully swordsman, to provoke me to a quarrel, to insult me.'

Puisaye straightened himself from the dispatch-box over which he had been bending.

'What's this?' His voice was sharp. 'Of whom do you speak?'

'Of that master-at-arms, Morlaix, who calls himself Marquis de Chavaray. You'll not deny responsibility for his outrageous conduct.'

'I will not trouble to do so. No. I will content myself with observing that I am not only well able but even accustomed to conduct my own quarrels. If you do not know that of me, faith, you know even less than I supposed.'

Passion seemed to deafen the Colonel. 'I desire you to understand that it is only because it might provoke a mutiny of your savages that I refrain from ordering your arrest and dealing with you as you deserve.'

Puisaye stared at him for a long moment in dumb surprise. When at last he found his voice again, it was only to say: 'Go to the devil.'

'Monsieur le Comte, I will not tolerate this offensiveness.'

'You have your remedy.'

D'Hervilly choked. 'You are fortunate, sir, that my duty to my King rises above my duty to myself. But I warn you that if there is more of this, even that may not prevail with me. And in any event, this is not the last you will hear of the matter. You are warned.' He stalked out.

Puisaye went in quest of Quentin.

'What have you been doing to d'Hervilly?'

Quentin told him.

'The fool has the effrontery to suggest that I sent you to put a quarrel upon him.' He was still white with anger. 'One day, when this business is over, I really think I shall have to give myself the trouble of killing Monsieur d'Hervilly. Pray remember that it is a satisfaction I promise myself.'

'I will bear it in mind. I have no wish to be taken for a bully swordsman.'

Puisaye took him by the shoulders. 'Child, there's no need to be resentful. I was not reproving you. How could I when it was so generous of you to espouse my quarrel?'

'Not generous. Inevitable. The man is an offence. Nor was I espousing your quarrel. I was making one of my own; for the pleasure of it; provoked by the creature's meanness.'

'Ah!' Puisaye smiled wistfully. 'Well, well! Better so.' He turned away. 'Yet I was so foolish as to hope it was the other way.'

'But why?'

'Why? Who knows? Perhaps because I am a lonely man, never lonelier than here and now, with all my plans in jeopardy, my command usurped, my authority undermined among these gentlemen whom I brought here. It warmed me a little to believe that I had won a friend to take up my quarrel for me.' He laughed. 'That is all. Think no more of it.'

'But I shall, sir.' Quentin was touched by that glimpse of a heart under the hard glitter. Puisaye's flamboyant exterior was suddenly revealed to him as a panoply of stoical gallantry. 'Your belief was not so wide of the truth, when I come to think of it. It was certainly d'Hervilly's cavalier conduct towards you that influenced mine.'

There was an amazing softening of Puisaye's proud, hard glance. 'You're a good lad, Quentin. You've a heart. You deserve well.'

'If there is anything in which I can serve you . . .'

'I need an aide-de-camp whom I can trust. Tinténiac and Vauban have their commands, and among the rest there's scarcely a man in whom I could venture to place confidence.'

'I am not a soldier, sir.'

'Nor yet a fool. You've proved your quality. You offer just what I most need.'

Thus simply the link was forged that drew these two men closer, on the threshold of a period that was to test Puisaye's fortitude more heavily than any other in all his chequered life.

Trouble began on the day after Fort Penthièvre was occupied by the regiment that still called itself of Dresnay, although Dresnay himself had refused to embark with it rather than serve under d'Hervilly.

From early morning along the narrow isthmus known as the Falaise, that links the Peninsula of Quiberon with the mainland, the retreating hordes from Auray began to stream. They were made up not only of Tinténiac's Chouans, but of all the peasants of the district, the fugitives, amounting to some thirty thousand men, women, children, old men, and priests; and they brought with them their possessions, so as to save them from pillage and destruction: their herds of bullocks, sheep, and goats, their carts laden with household goods, their provender, and even the sacred vessels from their churches. It was nothing less than a stampede before the Army of the Republic, known to be advancing upon Auray, which the withdrawal of the Chouans had rendered defenceless.

To these fugitives were added by noon those from the other outpost, of Landévan, in similar terror of the vengeance that might be wrought upon them for having harboured that vanguard of the Royal Army.

From the ramparts of Penthièvre, in which he had taken up his quarters, Puisaye, pallid and dull-eyed, his jauntiness all shed, observed this ceaseless stream of peasants in flight before an army which the ineptitude of d'Hervilly had permitted Hoche to assemble. To him it was a spectacle that heralded ruin. There was little hope that the opportunity so crassly missed would recur, or that they could revive in the peasantry the enthusiasm which must now be fainting from disillusion.

Once across the Falaise, the arriving hordes spread themselves through the peninsula, some five miles in length by two across, with its half-dozen villages and the township of Quiberon towards its southernmost end. Nor was there a welcome for them such as might have lightened their distress. The gentlemen from England had quartered themselves upon the villages and hamlets, occupying every house, and refusing to be crowded by these savages, whose presence seemed to offend their very nostrils. They must find what accommodation they could in barns or stables, whilst the great mass of them were left to encamp under the open sky. Fortunately the July heat made this exposure tolerable.

That brutal refusal to yield quarters to ailing women and delicate infants, and the haughty undisguised contempt of the *émigré* nobles for these unhappy peasants, was quick to breed bad blood between the Chouans and those whom a week ago they had welcomed as their saviours. Brawls were frequent, and it might have come to a pitched battle but for the efforts in which Puisaye spent his despairing energies. With him laboured loyally to the same end, if with the same heavy heart, his lieutenants, Tinténiac, Vauban, Boisberthelot, and Quentin, as well as the Chouan leaders, Cadoudal, Saint-Regent, Guillemot, and Jean Rohu; but of all of them none worked more ardently or savagely for the preservation of order than Quentin.

His repute had spread through the ranks of the *émigrés,* among whom there were several who, like Bellanger—now a captain in the Loyal Emigrant—and d'Hervilly, had frequented his Bruton Street academy. Then, too, it was known that he had killed Boisgelin, that magician of the sword, and that he had smashed the conference at La Prevalaye. At once feared as a swordsman and respected for the stout monarchism of which it was accounted that he had given proof, his interventions were never ineffective; and he seemed ever at hand to intervene. That he should make enemies and excite rancours was inevitable; but their open manifestations were rare, and he had learnt the trick of a cold, hard glance that could quell them.

Once only was he startled, and that was when the Vicomte de Bellanger, whom he had reproved for insolence towards a Chouan, ventured to address him as the Marquis de Carabas, the odious by-name bestowed upon him by Constant de Chesnières. Only two other men had ever used it to him hitherto, and by using it had disclosed themselves for Constant's agents.

Viperishly he corrected Bellanger. 'Chavaray, sir. Chavaray. That is my name. If you should again forget it, you shall be taught to spell it, letter by letter. And you will not enjoy the lesson.'

He swung on his heel, and was gone before the gaping Vicomte could commit a further rashness.

He went fuming back to Penthièvre, into Puisaye's quarters, to intrude upon an altercation that drove all personal grievances from his mind.

D'Hervilly, who had also moved into the fort and established his headquarters there, was the centre of the debate. Puisaye's other three lieutenants were present, besides the *émigrés* officers d'Allegre and Garrec.

Tinténiac was talking, his voice loud and emphatic, his slight figure quivering with vehemence. The burden of his news was that Hoche, moving upon Auray the moment he had word of the Chouan retreat, would pause there only until joined from Laval by Humbert, who had assembled another five thousand men. 'Once the junction is effected, an army twenty thousand strong will be upon us, and not another man in Brittany will rise to join the Royal standard.'

Vauban, a brisk, vigorous fellow, took up the argument. 'The error of our retreat from a position in which we should have been supported becomes apparent. Where Monsieur de Puisaye's bold plan would by now have placed us in possession of Brittany, we find ourselves all but trapped here, in a position of great danger.'

'Unless,' added d'Allegre, 'prompt action is taken.'

D'Hervilly, as Quentin could read in his dismayed countenance, had been brought to realize the danger, and was impressed. He had shed his habitual aggressiveness. Almost he seemed to excuse himself for the errors he now perceived. He had been reluctant, he explained, to lose touch with the sea before the arrival of Sombreuil's contingent.

'We'll be pushed into it now if we remain,' was Boisberthelot's blunt retort.

Puisaye, who had had more than his fill of arguments with d'Hervilly, remained silent and aloof. D'Hervilly addressed him. 'You express no views,' he complained.

The Count awakened into sarcasm. 'Is it possible that

they are sought? Is it possible that they are needed?'
He shrugged. 'The situation should be plain even to
you. The choice is between being thrust into the sea,
as you have heard, and doing now the difficult thing
that would have been so easy a week ago. March to
meet Hoche before he can make his junction with
Humbert.'

When d'Hervilly had expressed at length his resentment of Puisaye's tone and manner, he made the only
possible decision, and on the morrow led forth the
regiments of the Royal Louis and the Loyal Emigrant.

They marched with drums beating and white banners fluttering, to form the spearhead centre of an army
of which ten thousand Chouans under Tinténiac and
Vauban were to compose the ponderous wings. But
before Plouharnel was reached, d'Hervilly had word
that the junction of Hoche and Humbert was effected,
and incontinently, to the rage of the Chouans, he ordered a retreat without having burnt a cartridge.

Puisaye, with Cadoudal and Boisberthelot, was mar-
shalling the reserves that were to follow in support
when he beheld, from the heights of Carnac, the return
of the *émigrés* regiments, still marching with that admirable military precision which was a source of pride to
their fatuous commander. It was a source of horror to
Puisaye, and of frenzied rage to Cadoudal.

'Why,' roared the Chouan, 'was not that monster
swallowed by the sea before he landed at Quiberon to
ruin us? Name of God! Is he a poltroon as well as a
fool?'

Vauban was to come in later, raging: 'What is this
man? A coward or a traitor?' And he demanded angrily that d'Hervilly be brought to trial for high treason.

When at last d'Hervilly himself arrived, it was seen
that at least his arrogance had been diminished.

'We were too late,' he informed them.

Puisaye lashed him with his scorn.

'Too late for what? It is never too late to die; and
there was always death had you failed. It still remains.'

Stung by the rebuke, d'Hervilly recovered his spirit, and with it all his obstinacy. It was idle, he asserted, to advise him to go forth again; to urge that in the pass to which things were come, nothing remained but to try immediate conclusions with Hoche. There might be little advantage in numbers on the Republican side; but he did not choose to take their word that this would be more than counterbalanced by the fighting qualities of the Chouans. He was not impressed by their Chouans, a rabble of brigands without military sense.

In a measure as he proceeded he recovered all his old arrogance. Yesterday's debate was entirely forgotten. He insisted now that he had always been right to remain in touch with the sea, so as to await the further troops from England before going forward. He regretted the moment of weakness in which he had yielded against his better judgment to persuasion. But that should not occur again. He knew what he was doing. He was not to be taught the military art by dilettante soldiers. He would fortify himself at Penthièvre and there await the Republicans.

He did so, and as a result, less than a week later Hoche was able to write to the Convention: 'The Anglo-Émigré-Chouans are shut up like rats in a trap, in the Peninsula of Quiberon.'

It was no exaggeration. He had set up his batteries so as to be screened by the dunes from the guns of the British fleet. Then by an enfilading fire he had driven the Royalists from their entrenchments at Sainte-Barbe, at the mainland extremity of the isthmus. Thereafter he had himself occupied and fortified those trenches, which, stretching right across the isthmus, definitely closed the trap in which the Royalists were held.

Only when that operation was complete did d'Hervilly realize the threat with which they were now faced, although he may not yet have understood that it was a threat of ruin beyond redemption. It was left for Puisaye to enlighten him, and this in the unsparing terms which his frantic, heart-broken chagrin dictated. The Chouans, fully disillusioned by now on the score of these nobles whom they had hailed as liberators and in whom they had discovered only incompetence and a wounding arrogance, were beginning to desert. They were slipping away by sea in their hundreds, to land at unguarded points of the coast and make their way back to their native districts, whence their report of what was doing would sweep over the countryside, to quell what Royalist ardour lingered, and send back to the cultivation of their fields those thousands who had been standing ready to rise in arms.

Puisaye was a changed man in those days of his despair, his assurance broken by a fortnight of sterile strife with the usurper of his command. His urbanity had fallen from him, and because he realized the invisible mischief as plainly as the mischief that was visible, he brought d'Hervilly with rude violence also to realize it.

'We are stuck here on a rock in a rising sea,' he declared. 'That is where your vaunted military perspicacity has placed us. A small matter, by God, compared with the perfection with which your regiments deploy upon the parade ground. You're a born commander, my Colonel, for a box of leaden soldiers.'

D'Hervilly received his reproaches and his sarcasms in alternating humility and insolence. High words flew between them, and once in the heat of exchanged insults Puisaye's hand went to his sword. But it fell away again.

'That can wait,' he said. 'There's something else to do at the moment; or, rather, to undo.'

In the bitterness of his resentments d'Hervilly might have pushed his usurped authority to the length of ordering Puisaye's arrest. But he had the sense to perceive that in this he was in a stalemate. Such an act would exhaust the patience of the Chouans, who, perceiving where lay the blame, had abated nothing in their reverence of the Comte Joseph. The result, in the present temper, might well be the massacre of every émigré on Quiberon. Moreover, d'Hervilly could no longer count even upon an unquestioning émigré support. His incompetence was being laid bare to them by the events, and their perilous, besieged position was beginning to be assigned to it. Commonly now the members of his staff, whom he brought to support him in the councils that invariably ended in stormy altercations, were found to be in agreement with his opponents. The only man who remained unwavering, even in haughty defiance of reason, in loyalty to his chief, was the Vicomte de Bellanger.

Soon yet another peril began to make itself manifest. Overcrowded as Quiberon was, victuals began to run short.

D'Hervilly held a council in the orderly room of the fort, and with a half-dozen nobles upon whose support he could count, received Puisaye, whom he had bidden to it, and those whom Puisaye brought with him unbidden: the Comte de Contades, his chief-of-staff, Cadoudal as chief of the Chouans of Morbihan, and the Chevalier de Tinténiac. Quentin came too, as Puisaye's aide-de-camp, in a British red coat that was now the Royalist uniform.

D'Hervilly received them seated at his writing-table, his officers grouped about him. He looked askance upon Puisaye's following, but offered no comment, and went straight to business.

He touched upon the gravity of a situation in which supplies of food were failing, and fatuously invited them once again to approve his foresight in keeping touch with the sea, since by means of the British ships it should be possible to feed the peninsula. He would thank Monsieur Cadoudal, too, since he was present, to reassure the peasantry on Quiberon, and to employ their influence to see that calm was preserved.

Puisaye, grey-faced and worn, blear-eyed from sleeplessness, laughed savagely. 'Thirty thousand Chouan combatants, thirty thousand refugees, and some thirty thousand native inhabitants, besides the *émigrés* regiments. A hundred thousand mouths in all to be fed by the foraging of foreign sailors along a coast not only hostile but bare. I suppose, sir, that you make the suggestion seriously. That is why I laugh.'

It was but the beginning of another tempest.

Cadoudal, like a raging bull, advanced to the table's edge. 'The fact is, messieurs, that starvation is about to complete the work of General Hoche's other ally, Monsieur le Colonel here.' He glared into the yellow face of d'Hervilly. 'By God, sir, the Republic should raise a monument to you for the way you've served and saved it.'

Coming from a peasant, this was rather more than d'Hervilly's gentlemen could stomach, whilst d'Hervilly himself seemed to freeze where he sat. His glance went beyond Cadoudal.

'Monsieur de Puisaye, must I ask you to protect me from such insolences as this, or must I protect myself?'

'Protection!' Cadoudal raged. 'Who will protect us from you? Who will repair the mess your blundering pompous stupidity has got us into? Who will . . .'

'Quiet, Georges!' Puisaye admonished him, his hand upon that massive shoulder. 'Abuse will not serve.'

'This isn't abuse. It's the nasty truth,' Cadoudal retorted. 'My lads are at the end of their patience. They begin to ask me if they have come here to get themselves slaughtered for the satisfaction of a puppet-master. They may not march in step; they may not possess the secret of formations and all the other barrack-square trumpery that make the soldier in the eyes of Monsieur le Colonel; but, as God lives, they know something of fighting, which is what they came for, not to be penned up like sheep to await the butcher. Fighting seems the last thing in the design of Monsieur de Colonel.'

D'Hervilly leaned forward, silencing by a gesture the indignation of those who were his friends. His voice shook with the passion he suppressed.

'I do not dispute with you, Cadoudal. I do not even explain myself; for I owe no explanation to anybody.'

'That we shall see before all's done,' Cadoudal threatened.

D'Hervilly went stiffly on. 'I merely express in passing my deep resentment of a tone taken by a man in your position to a man in mine.'

Cadoudal laughed savagely.

'Let us come to what matters. Since those of you who know this Brittany and its resources are persuaded that there can be no hope of victualling, it remains only to cut our way out.' He reared his head in proud audacity. He became declamatory. 'We will deliver battle to this General Hoche.' He seemed to pause there for applause. Instead, all that the assertion brought him was another laugh of bitterness from Puisaye. D'Hervilly smote the table with his fist.

'Monsieur le Comte!' he thundered, in passionate protest.

'You must forgive me. I have a sense of irony. It is provoked when I hear you now proposing to do something that has become impossible after so obstinately refusing to do it whilst it was not only possible, but easy.'

'*Voilà!*' said Cadoudal. 'Now you have it, my Colonel.'

But d'Hervilly's dignity did not permit him to heed the Chouan. 'Do you say that it is impossible, Monsieur le Comte?'

'Utterly. To attempt it now would be to fling your men to death against the wall of iron which by your . . . *Enfin,* which you have permitted Hoche to build. Your last chance was at Plouharnel, when you decided wrongly that it was too late. Now, when it really is too late, you propose to do it. In the position which he has fortified at Sainte-Barbe, Hoche could hold you with half the men he has concentrated there.'

Bellanger came superciliously to the aid of his chief. 'That is an opinion, Monsieur le Comte.'

'An opinion,' sneered Vauban, 'with which every man of sense must agree.'

'I fear so,' Contades sighed.

Again d'Hervilly smote the table. Anger had robbed him of reason. 'Always am I opposed,' he complained. 'It has been so ever since I set foot upon this cursed shore. How is a commander to conduct matters against constant opposition?'

'That won't serve,' Puisaye answered him contemptuously. 'Until now you have always had your own way. And that is just what has landed us in this quagmire.'

'Are you afraid, Monsieur de Puisaye?' cried d'Hervilly, so blindly on his defence that he cared not what weapons he employed.

'Afraid? Of what? Of death? What else can I welcome now that all my labours have been wasted, all my plans wrecked by your folly? Death, at least, would spare me the shame of facing those who trusted to my word and my promises.'

'Would it not be better,' said Contades mildly, 'to leave recriminations? We have to recognize that we are in desperate straits, and . . .'

'And how we came into them,' Cadoudal interrupted.

'That will not help us to get out,' said Bellanger. He went on to tell them at pompous length that this was the problem to which they should address their minds, and ended by inviting Monsieur de Puisaye to tell them frankly what course he would advise.

Puisaye looked as if the question dumbfounded him. Then he took a deep breath. 'If, being in command, as the King and the British Government believe me to be, I could by folly and lack of foresight have placed the Royal Army in this trap, then here is what I should do.'

He advanced to the table and the large-scale map that was spread upon it. D'Hervilly, who had ground his teeth at the first of those words, stifled his retort in a desperate hope inspired by the sudden brisk change in Puisaye.

With rough impatience the Count pulled the map about to suit his ends. 'Approach, messieurs. You, too, Georges, and you others.' His glance, which seemed now to smoulder, held d'Hervilly as if to dominate him. 'One definite chance remains to repair the harm, to smash Hoche, and to extricate ourselves. But only one. And it will be the last. If adopted it should make possible again my original plan. It should revive the enthusiasm and stimulate once more the general rising that will enable us to march on Paris. Be warned, however, that should it fail, we are doomed. But then, doomed we certainly are unless we have recourse to it. And there is no reason why it should fail if each performs his part without falter or waver.'

He lowered his glance to the map, and set himself to expound. 'See. Here is Penthièvre. Here the fortifications of Sainte-Barbe with Hoche's Army of Cherbourg, thirteen thousand strong. We muster in all some twenty thousand men. Now, if we had twice that number, we could not hope to carry that position by a frontal attack; yet the men we possess would be more than enough to deal with Hoche if we could place him between two fires. This we can do. It is in our power to place him like a nut between the two limbs of a nutcracker, and so crush him.'

Dramatically he paused there, and looked at them. D'Hervilly in a fever of impatience cried out: 'Yes! Yes! But how to place him so?'

'Thus: let ten thousand men, the *émigrés* regulars and five thousand Chouans, who will have to bear the brunt of the fighting, engage him in front, whilst another ten thousand, brought round to Plouharnel, descend simultaneously upon his rear.'

D'Hervilly glared impatiently. 'You talk as if we enjoyed freedom of movement. How do we place a detachment at Plouharnel?'

'You but say the same thing in different words!' cried Bellanger. 'The problem, Monsieur le Comte, is how to get to Plouharnel.'

Cadoudal laughed. 'Puppies will be yelping.'

'By God, sir!' roared Bellanger, his chin thrust out. 'I take impertinences from no man. I'll . . .'

D'Hervilly's fist came down with a bang. 'Hold your tongues! Monsieur de Puisaye, if you please.'

'There is no problem,' said Puisaye. 'To leave Quiberon offers no difficulty. Men are leaving us every night by sea. We have no lack of luggers, and at need there are Sir John's sloops. We can convey our men to the coves of Poldu, and put them ashore there. Thence, through a country where every man is their friend, and without fear of interference by the Blues, since Hoche has brought every soldier in Brittany to Sainte-Barbe, they can make their way to Plouharnel.'

The intention and the means became clear, and for once, at last, a proposal of Puisaye's encountered no opposition. This was not only because d'Hervilly had been schooled and subdued by the events, but because the plan would rid him of the greater part of those Chouan auxiliaries whose barbarous ways were a perpetual offence to his fastidiousness, and would relieve by some ten thousand mouths a peninsula that otherwise must soon know the straits of hunger.

CHAPTER 3

Dalliance

LEST from the heights of Sainte-Barbe the activity of craft transporting the brigades from Quiberon should be observed by Republican telescopes and its purpose surmised, d'Hervilly insisted that the operation should be carried out at night.

Puisaye was scornful of the precaution. 'Will you still be interfering? And have you vision for one object only at a time? What shall it profit them if they see our luggers? What can they conclude but that the Chouans continue to desert us?'

Yet, although he accounted it a source of unnecessary delays, he yielded the point.

The council's final decision had been that the Chouans be put ashore in the creeks of Rhuis; that they assemble at Muzillac, and thence move in a wide cir-

270

cle, by Questembert, Elven, and the moors of Lanvaux, round Vannes, to come down upon Plouharnel.

With the limited number of luggers and sloops available, three nights were consumed in conveying the Chouan divisions from Quiberon. So that the embarkations, commenced on the night of the tenth of July, were not completed until that of the twelfth.

Cadoudal went in command of the first contingent, Guillemot of the second, and Saint-Regent of the third. In addition to the Chouans, the expedition included a company of the Loyal Emigrant. This was a political measure upon which Puisaye had insisted. He had been equally insistent that this company be under the command of Tinténiac, and d'Hervilly had yielded only with the condition that the Vicomte de Bellanger, who had proved his loyalty to him, should go as second in command. He had also designated the remainder of the officers. To Quentin the departure of the Chouans and of Tinténiac represented a danger of being parted from the only friends he counted in Brittany, and of being left at Quiberon with no associates but the supercilious *émigrés,* on whom he wasted no affection. He was therefore urged to seek Puisaye's permission to go with Cadoudal.

At first the Count frowned upon the request. 'You would be better here with me. You will be saved the hardships of an arduous march.'

Quentin accounted the objection frivolous, and said so. Puisaye reflected, and his brow cleared.

'Why, if you're set on it, I'll not deny you. Indeed, perhaps I ought to be glad to have you go when I remember La Prevalaye. You proved a stout representative then; and with these fribbles about him, Tinténiac may be in need of your support. Take care of yourself. But then Georges shall have my orders as to that.'

So it was with Cadoudal on the night of the tenth that Quentin departed from Quiberon.

The entire force was to be in Hoche's rear by dawn of the sixteenth, ready to fall upon it as soon as the guns were heard announcing the opening of the frontal attack. The last of the Chouans should be ashore at Rhuis by dawn of the thirteenth, and the entire army would then be ready to move upon its circuitous march of forty miles. Two days at need would suffice those hardy lads for this. But because of the *émigrés* and so as to provide for eventualities, Puisaye had rightly insisted upon a margin of twenty-four hours. Eventualities there were almost from the outset.

In order to avoid congesting the little town of Muzillac, and so as to cover at once the first stage of the march, Cadoudal brought his men on the eleventh by Festumbert to Elven, thus disposing at once of almost half the distance to their destination. There on the morrow he was joined by Tinténiac and the detachment of the Loyal Emigrant. Tinténiac reported that he had left Guillemot at Festumbert, and that they would come forward that night, whilst word had been left at Muzillac for the last division under Saint-Regent, so that he might follow as soon as his men were landed.

Tinténiac would have pushed on at once. Elven was too near to Vannes, where the Representatives Tallien and Bled with the Army of Cherbourg had taken up their quarters, and word of the presence of this Chouan army must inevitably reach them. Cadoudal attached no importance to it.

'It will have reached them already, anyway. But so far it will have told them little. They'll suppose us deserters. It is only when we leave Elven that our destination may be suspected from the direction we take. So here we'll stay until the last moment.'

The men were quartered partly upon the townsfolk, who made them welcome, partly in farmsteads about the foot of the uplands of Lanvaux. The officers had joined Cadoudal at the Inn of the Grand Breton, which was one of the houses of confidence upon which the Royalists relied.

There Quentin was at breakfast with Tinténiac and Cadoudal on the morning of the thirteenth, when Bellanger came into the room with a letter in his hand, and on his face the glowing smile of the bearer of good tidings.

'Chevalier, this has just reached me from my wife, who is at Coëtlegon. She writes that Charette, with between five and six thousand Vendéans, is expected there today, and that he will be eager to reinforce us if we resolve to pass that way. She adds that they will be proud at Coëtlegon to welcome the officers of the Royal and Catholic Army. In her confidence that we will accept her invitation, she is assembling there some of the loveliest ladies of Brittany, as eager as herself to honour the gallant gentlemen whose swords are to bring back the King.'

Hand on hip, the rather too handsome head thrown back, he seemed to wait for the applause. Instead three pairs of eyes surveyed him coldly, and then Quentin expressed what was probably in the minds of all.

'How comes Madame la Vicomtesse to send you a letter? How does she know where to find you, and the rest?'

He exhibited impatience of the stupidity that could prompt such a question. She did not know where to find him. But news of the landings begun two nights ago had already gone out through Brittany, and it was none so far to Coëtlegon. Her courier was passing through Elven on his way to Muzillac, but seeing the army, he had naturally inquired if by any chance the Vicomte de Bellanger happened to be with it.

'Plausible,' said Quentin. 'Almost too plausible to be convincing.'

Bellanger became haughty. 'What the devil do you mean, sir? Do you suppose I don't know my wife's hand?'

'You may know her hand. It's not her hand that's in question.'

'What, then, if you please?'

'Her knowledge, of course,' said Cadoudal. 'You've answered only half. How did the Vicomtesse know that you were to be with this army that has landed in Rhuis?'

'She assumed it, of course.'

'From what?'

Bellanger's hauteur soared magnificently. 'From her

knowledge that I am ever to be found at the post of honour.'

'That, naturally,' said Quentin gently. 'But suppose that, for one of the many reasons that might arise, you had not landed on Rhuis, what would have become of this very important military news?'

'That is impertinent.'

'No. No.' Tinténiac spoke at last. 'Pertinent. Most pertinent.'

Bellanger curled his full lip, and flung the letter on the table. 'Look at the superscription, Chevalier.'

Tinténiac read it aloud: 'To the Vicomte de Bellanger or the officer commanding the detachment of the Royal and Catholic Army at Muzillac.' He returned the letter, smiling. 'That, of course, makes everything clear.'

'Saving that Muzillac *was* to have been our place of assembly. Actually, it is not,' Quentin objected.

The Chevalier swept that aside. 'It would be easily presumed by anyone who knew that we were landing at Rhuis.'

'And how would that be known? If the news went forth when Georges landed his men, what grounds would there be for assuming that others were to follow and that a point of assembly was settled?'

'Faith,' growled Cadoudal, 'I think that wants answering.'

'The answer is that, as you see, it was assumed.'

'Does that satisfy you?' wondered Quentin.

'It would be well to be plain, Monsieur de Morlaix,' said Bellanger. 'So tell us what you are supposing.'

'I suppose nothing. I ask; and I do not find an answer.'

'I think I have supplied one. My wife appears to have assumed that which you conclude was not to be assumed. It's merely your conclusion that's at fault.' As if that were the last word on the subject, he turned again to Tinténiac. 'The important matter is that of Charette and his Vendéans. You can hardly neglect so valuable a reinforcement.'

'I don't intend to.' He looked from Cadoudal to

Quentin. 'It's a piece of unexpected luck. It makes doubly sure the defeat of Hoche. As soon as Saint-Regent arrives we march to Coëtlegon.'

Cadoudal was dubious. He thrust out a heavy lip. 'What need for that? It's eight or nine leagues to Coët-legon. Let the Vendéans join us here.'

Bellanger's face was clouded with haughty displeasure. 'That is boorish. It is hardly the gracious return this invitation deserves.'

'We are at war,' was Cadoudal's brusque retort. 'War is serious. Boorish, if you like. It doesn't leave room for empty courtesies.'

The Vicomte was all disdainful tolerance. 'I fear, sir, that we look at this from different angles. The view you express has never been that of gentlemen.'

'Which may be why the sansculottes have nearly made an end of them.'

'Come, come,' laughed Tinténiac. 'No need to dispute over it. We have time to spare. Coëtlegon doesn't take us far out of our way. We are not due at Plouhar-nel until Friday.'

'And you've to consider,' said Bellanger, 'that five thousand Vendéans marching by themselves might easily be beset and routed, and so lost to us, whereas, when incorporated with us, we shall make up an army that need fear no force the Blues could send against us.'

'That is unanswerable,' Tinténiac agreed. 'And, of course,' the pleasure-loving rascal added lightly, 'it would be detestable to disappoint the ladies. It is settled, then, that we go.'

Again he looked from Cadoudal to Quentin, as if inviting their agreement. But it was not forthcoming. Cadoudal ill-humouredly held that they had a definite objective, and should not be led aside by any lure. Quentin, even more hostile, accounted that too much remained unexplained to render these proposals acceptable. As a result, Tinténiac, wavering between his ever-ready gallantry and his sense of strict duty, decided to summon a council of all the officers to determine the matter.

But when Bellenger had left them, the Chevalier reproached his companions. 'You make difficulties where none need be made.'

'Whilst you,' retorted the downright Cadoudal, 'think too much of disappointing the women.'

Tinténiac took the reproof in good part, with a laugh. 'Of disappointing Madame de Bellanger,' he amended. 'Consider that she has not seen her husband for two years. And you should remember that, too, when you criticize the Vicomte.'

Quentin's lip curled in a smile. 'You suppose them in a fever to see each other, do you? At the back of all my mistrust is the knowledge that she is more deeply attached to Lazare Hoche than the Vicomte de Bellanger's wife has a right to be.'

Tinténiac took it flippantly. 'Hoche! Ha! An Apollo, they tell me. Your long residence in England has made you puritanical, Quentin.'

'Hoche commands the Army of Cherbourg.'

'Ah, bah! Love laughs at politics.'

Thus airily he dismissed the matter, and left it for the council to settle their course. At the meeting, Quentin's was the only voice raised against marching by way of Coëtlegon. He urged that being in sufficient strength without the Vendéan reinforcements, nothing could justify their turning aside from their very definite goal. Cadoudal, whilst warmly agreeing with him, would not press the point since they had plenty of time in hand. The remainder—and there were eight of them in all— found the Vicomtesse de Bellanger's invitation irresistible. One of them even went so far as to argue that acceptance was strategically sound, since, if they were under observation by Republican scouts, this turning aside would be entirely misleading.

So in full strength they marched out of Elven on the morning of the thirteenth, and by evening they came to Coëtlegon. The Chouans arrived there weary, dust-laden, and disgruntled. The stout boots received from England had rendered footsore these hardy men who never knew fatigue when barefoot or shod with clogs of their own making. Nor did they show a proper pride in the gaiters and red coats that had replaced their fustians and goatskins.

At the disposal of their chiefs Coëtlegon placed the outbuildings, whilst the men themselves were left to bivouac in the vast park. Beasts had been assembled for their nourishment, and some pipes of wine. But they were left the task of slaughtering and preparing their own meat.

The hospitality of the château itself was reserved for the officers of the Loyal Emigrant, and it was lavish.

Madame de Bellanger, a white radiance, with a string of pearls entwined in her ebony tresses and more than a touch of the new, revealing, *merveilleuses* fashion in her dress, came out upon the terrace to receive them, leading a train of damsels attendant upon her queenliness. They came with chatter and laughter in a gay excitement to greet these knightly gentlemen of the Old France, and there were even some resumptions of acquaintance.

Quentin's glumness was dispelled by the unexpected sight of Germaine de Chesnières in that fluttering frock, a Germaine whose amazed eyes had no glances for any but himself. He broke away from the group in which he had ascended the terrace steps and went straight to her. With a smile on trembling lips, she held out both hands to him.

'Quentin! I had not dreamt that you would be of the company.'

'Nor I that you would still be at Coëtlegon. I might have been less honest had I known.'

'Less honest?'

'The eagerness to behold you would have stifled the misgivings in which I came.'

'Misgivings?'

He was given no leisure to explain. The Vicomtesse had concluded the reception of a husband she had not seen for two years. It had been marked by a self-possessed absence of all transports. That duty briefly and decorously performed, she fluttered diaphanous upon them, to say in other words what Germaine had said already.

'My dear Marquis! That you should honour Coëtlegon again! An enchanting surprise.' Her smile was wide with delight, but he thought her eyes were wary.

'I have to thank the fortune of war. Whatever else it brings, surprises are never absent.'

'If all were as agreeable, we should not complain of war. Should we, Germaine?'

'Alas!' Germaine answered gravely. 'War is no matter for light-heartedness when those dear to us are engaged in it.'

'How solemn, child! And yet how fitting to be solemn!' She assumed solemnity herself. 'I think I laugh to keep myself from weeping. Oh, and because it is a duty that we owe to these brave ones, who offer their lives to the great cause. We must be gay, so as to make gay for them the few hours they spend with us. What else,' she added wistfully, 'can women do?'

On that they were dragged away to be merged into the glittering throng that was slowly trailing across the terrace towards the house, and thus robbed of the communion for which they hungered.

Tossed hither and thither when the hall was reached, Quentin found himself presently shoulder to shoulder with Tinténiac, who was deep in a battle of pleasantries with the lovely Madame de Varnil and her lovelier sister, Mademoiselle de Breton-Caslin.

With scant ceremony he took the Chevalier by the arm and drew him aside.

'*Mordieu!* What's this? Is the house afire?' demanded Tinténiac.

'I've a notion that it ought to be. Was there—or did I dream it—some talk of Charette and a force of Vendéans? If so, where do they hide five thousand men?'

'Oh, that! They are to arrive tomorrow.'

'The report was that they would be here today.'

'They are longer on the road than was expected. Not surprising.'

'And if they should not arrive tomorrow?'

'Eh? To the devil with your doubts. Of course they'll arrive. Meanwhile, the company is charming, and the charm of it will become more marked as the evening advances. We are to dance after supper. My dear Quentin, why so glum amid delights?'

'Delights were not in our programme when we left Quiberon.'

'There was nothing against refreshing ourselves upon the way. Good God, Quentin, I may be dead tomorrow, or the day after. Let us live whilst we live. *Dum vivemus vivamus.*'

The banquet when they came to it, an affair of fifty covers, seemed to revive those spacious days before the guillotine was invented. The free flow of the wine warmed heads and hearts that nature had not fashioned cool.

Afterwards, to the stimulus of an orchestra that the lavishly provident Vicomtesse had assembled, came the dancing that Tinténiac had so joyously foretold.

Outside in the park, the Chouans about their bivouac fires could see the windows ablaze with golden light, could hear the tinkling strains of dance music wafted to them on the tepid air. It set them wondering whether their days and nights of bandit warfare and their forest life had not been all a dream.

Cadoudal smoked his pipe on a bench by the lake, with Saint-Regent, Guillemot, and some other chiefs. Annoyed by the absence of Monsieur de Charette's Vendéans, he was deploring his weakness in not having more strongly supported the Marquis de Chavaray's opposition to this excursion. He had been unduly swayed by Tinténiac. The bravest of the brave, Tinténiac. But of notorious weaknesses, and too prone to dalliance.

He was exercising it now. Amid the shadows on the terrace, etched by the silver radiance of a half-moon, Madame de Bellanger's high, gaily wanton laugh tinkled intermittently to announce the amusement she found in the Chevalier's gallantry. For tonight she had made him her own. She had been at need to remind Bellanger that this was proper in a hostess towards her principal guest, when he had sentimentally complained of being neglected by a wife to whom he returned after two years of exile.

In that same mood of sentimental dudgeon, yet with unfaltering dignity, the Vicomte had carried his lament to his old friends, Madame de Chesnières and her son.

Constant, now fully restored to health and vigour, was eager to take the place that belonged to him in the Loyal Emigrant. He had hailed the arrival of the regiment at the very moment when he had been on the point of setting out for Quiberon so as to rejoin it. He soothed Bellanger with arguments which had failed when urged by the Vicomtesse. He stressed Tinténiac's high consequence and the need to do him honour, which was to be regarded as honour done the Royal and Catholic Army.

'But then,' said the Vicomte, 'I, too, am of some consequence. I am the second in command.'

'And there is no lack of honour waiting for you, too. Mademoiselle de Breton-Caslin, for instance, has eyes for no one else.'

It was one way of being rid of him. He took the bait, and soon they beheld him bowing from his stately height over that frail piece of loveliness.

Constant was loftily amused. Madame de Chesnières, with other preoccupations, did not share his amusement. Through her lorgnettes she scanned the dancing throng.

'I do not see Germaine. Where is she?'

'I do not see the Marquis of Carabas. Either it is a coincidence, or it is the answer.'

She bridled. 'You take it calmly.'

He made a gesture of indifference. 'War settles many things, and not only for causes and nations. This pestilent fencing-master, to do him justice, is not easily handled. Time enough to think of it when these hostilities are over. He may not survive them.'

'That is your way, is it not? You let others fight your battles. Why, then, did you enrol in the Loyal Emigrant? Are you perhaps immune from the very dangers upon which you found hopes for this fellow?'

'There is the name. You must see that, madame. If the Royalist cause should prevail, as we hope, how would a man of the House of Chesnières look who, being at hand and in health, had held aloof? I may possess the wisdom to avoid unnecessary risks, but I do not lack the courage to face necessary ones. Now that the regiment is here I have claimed my place. I am to join Tinténiac's staff.'

She sighed ponderously. 'I suppose you are right.' She became lachrymose. 'But you will not expect a mother to show enthusiasm. Armand's case gives me anxiety enough.' She looked up into the heavy, swarthy face. 'If I should lose you both, there will be none to dispute possession of Chavaray to this bastard of Margot's.'

'Is that what troubles you?'

'Constant!' It was an exclamation of fierce denial.

'Be easy. Armand is safe with Sombreuil's division, since, from what they tell me, all should be over before it arrives in France. He will be in time to reap the laurels which others will have cut.'

'If I could be sure of that!' Inconsequently she added: 'I wish Germaine would not continue absent. A headstrong, wilful girl. Instead of being a help and comfort to me in these dreadful times, she merely adds to my distraction. I am a very unhappy woman, Constant.'

He stayed to soothe her when she would have had him rescuing Germaine from her fencing-master, and thereby increased her irritation.

Meanwhile Germaine and her fencing-master were one of the few couples who paced the terrace, where the golden glow from the windows was merged with the silver radiance of the moon.

She intoxicated him with a sweet, gentle frankness that made amends for the pangs of earlier misunderstandings. 'I should be happy, Quentin, if I could forget tomorrow and what you go to do.'

'Yet if I were not going you would contemn my lack of a proper Royalist fervour.'

'Don't make a jest of it, even to punish me for my past unfaith. That was a school through which I went. I have come out wiser. I know my heart. And it is time I did. For in three months now, Quentin, my tutelage will be ended. I shall be free to dispose of myself, mistress of my fate.'

'And mistress then of mine.'

She stood still, to face him. 'Is that a promise, Quentin?' She was singularly solemn.

'Much more. It is an assertion.'

She may have accounted his tone too light. 'But I want you to promise it—whatever happens?'

'I could promise nothing more gladly. Whatever happens. But what is to happen?'

She drew a sigh of relief, and they moved on again.

'Who can say what will happen? Who can look more than a little way into the future? Let there, for us, be at least this one sure thing towards which we travel.'

'You give me pride and joy, Germaine.'

'Your first words to me today were of misgivings. What troubles you?'

He told her, and went on to speak of Puisaye's sufferings, of his strife with difficulties, and of the thwarting of his well-laid plans. 'The adventure in which we are concerned represents a last chance to undo the harm that's been done, to save his great conception from ruin. If he should fail him, it will break his heart; yes, and more hearts than his. The Royal cause will be sunk.'

'Monsieur de Puisaye is enviable to inspire such deep concern. For your concern is for him rather than the cause. I am a little jealous, perhaps, yet grateful to him for having made so stout a Royalist of you. I would that I had achieved it.'

'But, Germaine,' he protested, 'more than anyone alive are you responsible for my politics. Until the King comes to his own, I shall not now come to Chavaray, and I shall have no kingdom to offer you.'

282

'Must we talk of that again? Have I not convinced you of how little is the store I set by that?'

'That may be. But there's the store I set by offering it. It makes me fearful of everything that may jeopardize Puisaye's success. The light-heartedness of these gentlemen fills me with impatience. Even Tinténiac, hero though he is, all fire and valour, has a streak of frivolity that dismays me in our commander.'

Yet, when at last they quitted the terrace to rejoin the throng of dancers, he had not told her of the weightiest factor in the misgivings that were heavy upon him.

With Tinténiac and two of his lieutenants, Monsieur de la Houssaye and the Chevalier de La Marche, Quentin camped that night in one of the fine rooms of the château. It was late when they retired, too late for men before whom there was an arduous march on the morrow.

That morrow dawned still without sign of Monsieur de Charette and his Vendéans.

'It would be well,' said Quentin impatiently, 'to discover if they exist at all.'

He made one of a group consisting only of Tinténiac and his staff, which now included Constant de Chesnières and Cadoudal, who had come to join them on the terrace, where they conferred in the morning sunshine. Bellanger was quick to take up the challenge of that question.

'Is that an innuendo, monsieur?'

'No. A plain suggestion. Is someone fooling us? Whence was Monsieur de Charette last reported? It is time that we knew.'

They looked at one another, and their eyes were uneasy. Then the Vicomte answered him. 'The Vicomtesse will know. I will ask her.'

'No, no.' Quentin stayed him. 'It is perhaps no great matter after all. What is important is that we march without waiting any longer.'

Bellanger's laugh of scorn and wonder was joined by La Marche's in a minor key. 'With forty-eight hours before us, and the distance a mere matter of six or

seven leagues! Why, if we left here no earlier than
tomorrow night, we should still be in time.'

'In time for what? For fighting? Are men to be taken
into action at the end of a six-leagues' march?'

'Anyway,' said Tinténiac, 'we can afford to wait
another day. Better, indeed, that we do not set out
until tomorrow morning.'

'Better for whom? For what?' demanded Cadoudal.

'Better because our direction will not be known so
soon. There will be less chance of warning Hoche.'

Cadoudal lost his temper. 'And more leisure for
guzzling and dancing and apish gallantry here at Coëtlegon. Aye, messieurs, you may find me coarsely frank.
You may stare at me. But, by God, you'll not stare me
down. I'm no court fop to mince my words. I say what
I think.'

'But, I wonder,' lisped Bellanger, 'do you think what
you say?'

Cadoudal gave him a glance that was like a blow,
and continued to address Tinténiac. 'What is more, I
gave you the mind of my lads. They're not happy here.
They are beginning to ask more questions than I can
answer. Many of them left their fields to come to
Quiberon. They are reminding me that it is harvesting
time, and that if there's nothing better for them to do
than to bivouac here under the stars, as a guard of
honour for merry-making popinjays, they'd better be
getting back to their labours. This morning we found
that five hundred of them had gone. By tomorrow we
may have lost another thousand. Their tempers are on
edge from the treatment they had at Quiberon, and
they haven't much patience left. That's what I have to
say. Perhaps, Monsieur le Vicomte, you'll believe that
I think what I say.'

Tinténiac was gravely conciliatory. 'You may be
sure that it weighs with us, Georges. Yet, I ask you:
would it be reasonable to depart before the arrival of
these Vendéans, who are expected hourly?'

'Surely,' said Houssaye, 'it must not be that we have
come so far out of our way for nothing.'

'Devil take me if we should ever have come,' swore

Cadoudal. 'We do not need these reinforcements. We have enough without them.'

'Georges is right,' Quentin agreed, his tone hard and definite. 'Better sound the assembly, and take the road.'

A general display of heat was his answer from these men who did not love him.

'Do you give orders here?' Bellanger demanded. 'Since when?'

'I do not order, sir. I advise.'

'Your advice is not sought,' snapped La Marche.

'But it seems needed.'

Houssaye, who was the eldest and the gravest, eyed him sternly. 'Do you presume to advise experienced soldiers on matters that are purely military? You are a civilian, I understand.'

'But not on that account an idiot. The issue is a simple one. A child might pronounce upon it.'

'But we are not children,' drawled Bellanger.

'Then let us not behave as if we were.'

'I dislike your tone, sir. I find you insufferably impertinent.'

Tinténiac thought it time to intervene. 'No need for heat, sirs. The issue, as the Marquis says, is a simple one.' He turned to Cadoudal. 'Will it satisfy your lads, Georges, if we set out tonight?'

'I'ld prefer to go this morning. But I'll not argue it if you promise that we start at dusk.'

La Marche objected. That would mean that they would be at Plouharnel by morning, with twenty-four hours to wait for the attack and for Hoche to be warned of their presence there.

'Absurd!' Constant agreed with him. 'It is the way to lose all the advantage of surprise.'

'Sirs, sirs!' Quentin admonished them. 'Is it, then, necessary to make one march of it? We march five hours; we rest for twelve; then march another five or six, reaching Plouharnel at night tomorrow, and resting there again for eight or ten hours. Thus we go into battle on Friday fresh and unexpected.'

'You assume, of course, that Hoche has neither spies nor friends to inform him?' sneered Bellanger.

'Oh, no.' There was a bitter smile on Quentin's lips. 'I wish I were as sure of the existence of these Vendéans as I am that Hoche lacks neither friends nor spies.' It was plain to all that he left something unexpressed.

'I have observed in Monsieur de Morlaix,' said Constant, 'a disposition to see what does not exist, and to overlook what does.'

'What's in your mind, Quentin?' Tinténiac asked him.

He evaded the question. 'That the sooner we march, the sooner shall we repair the error of having come here.'

They were crying shame upon his ingratitude of the bounteous hospitality of Madame de Bellanger when the Vicomtesse herself descended upon them, drawn by the sounds of their altercation.

'Fie, sirs! Oh, fie! You'll wake the ladies. An ungallant return for their entertainment of you last night.' Over her shoulder she glanced up at the curtained windows. She came fresh and delectable in shimmering pink, a very emblem of the morning; in the courtly words of Tinténiac, a rose upon which the dew still lingered.

Bellanger, not to be outdone in gallantry, offered excuses for the altercation, blaming those who were so little sensible to the joys assembled for them at Coëtlegon as to be urging immediate departure.

She played archly at displeasure. 'Who are these heartless, insensible ones?'

'Monsieur de Morlaix is the chief offender.' Like Constant, Bellanger avoided allusion to him by his title. 'Newly admitted to military rank, he displays the impatient ardour of the neophyte.'

'On the score of his ardour we may forgive him. But what military necessity can exist for the impatience?'

'Why, none, madame,' said Tinténiac.

'Indeed, no,' added Bellanger. 'Because at dawn on Friday we are to be on Hoche's rear, for action in concert with . . .'

'*Morbleu,* man!' Quentin interrupted violently. 'Will you publish it to the winds of heaven?'

Forth pealed the silvery laugh of the Vicomtesse. 'Behold me, the four winds of heaven, who am more gentle than the gentlest zephyr.'

Tinténiac, whose brow had darkened at Bellanger's monstrous indiscretion, and so remained, now interjected gravely: 'These Vendéans that were to have met us here, madame? Whence were they reported to you?'

'From Rédon, four days ago. Monsieur de Charette sent a rider ahead with a letter begging the hospitality of Coëtlegon for them. They would arrive, he said, on Tuesday, which was yesterday. They have been delayed. But that they will arrive is certain. They should be here at any moment.'

'Did Charette say whither they were bound?' asked Quentin.

'Why, for the coast. To embark for Quiberon, so as to reinforce the army there.'

'An odd way to the coast from Rédon by Coëtlegon. That is rather to march away from it.'

'Is it?' She raised her brows. 'You must tell that to Monsieur de Charette when he arrives. He will probably answer that Coëtlegon offers a convenient encampment for his men, whilst he sends forward to make sure of the craft they'll need.'

'He could encamp at Muzillac, in sight of the sea. And from Rédon, Muzillac is only half as far as Coëtlegon.'

'How well you know the country! You must tell Monsieur de Charette this.' She was of an airy, smiling, playful impertinence. 'I do not pretend to fathom the reasonings of military men.'

'Nor should Monsieur de Morlaix,' opined her husband.

Tinténiac put an end to the discussion on a tone of authority. 'We will wait until nightfall. Then we march; with the Vendéans or without them.'

She was all dismay. 'You will leave us all disconsolate,' she complained.

Houssaye sighed. 'Alas! We bow to cruel necessity, madame.'

They began to drift away towards the house, with the exception of Quentin, who lingered with Cadoudal. He watched the little knot of men displaying themselves so gaily about that winsome lady, and he fetched a sigh of weariness.

'What do you think of it all, Georges?'

There was a heavy scowl on Cadoudal's big, blond face. 'That your questions hit the weaknesses of the story.'

'And that puts me further out of favour with these gallants. No matter, so that we march tonight.'

He went in to breakfast and to be, in the course of it, the butt of some jests on the score of his military perspicacity. These he contemptuously ignored.

They were still at table when a rattle of galloping hooves receding from the château made him attentive. They went, he observed, not northwards, by the avenue through the park, but by the road that ran southwards from the stables. It made him thoughtful, but he gave no expression to those thoughts even to Germaine when he came to walk with her later in the neglected garden.

For a while in her company he forgot his preoccupations. It was only upon returning to the house towards noon that he was startlingly recalled to them.

He found in the hall a gathering of officers and ladies about a dusty fellow, booted and spurred, whom Tinténiac was questioning.

He approached to listen, and in a moment had grasped the situation. This rider was from Josselin, with word that Charette was beset there by a Republican army corps under the Marquis de Grouchy, some eight thousand strong, which was on its way from Paris to reinforce Hoche. The Vendéans were entrenched in the town, but could not hold it for long. Unless relieved, they were doomed.

There was a silence of dismay when the last question had been asked and answered. Tinténiac stood with bowed head, stroking his chin in thought until suddenly the Vicomtesse spoke.

'How providential that you should be here!'

Tinténiac raised gloomy eyes. 'I do not perceive the act of providence, madame.'

'But, Chevalier, that you should be within reach of them. To Josselin it is less than twenty miles.'

Quentin, who had been thoughtfully considering the messenger, here interposed: 'And twenty miles farther from the goal which your husband has made known to you.'

'Did he?' In wide-eyed surprise she turned to the Vicomte. 'Did you? If you did I have forgotten it. But this . . . Ah, you cannot leave Charette and his brave fellows to be massacred. No Frenchman could do that.'

'If they are massacred it will be by Frenchmen,' Quentin reminded her.

Tinténiac looked round with troubled eyes. Vexation had turned him pale. 'We cannot discuss it here. Quentin, be so good as to summon Cadoudal. Bring him to us in the library, if madame will permit.'

CHAPTER 4

Mutiny

THAT staff conference in the library was stormy from the outset.

Tinténiac, seated at the writing-table, grave and stern, began, as it seemed, at the end by announcing a decision to the six who made a semicircle before him.

'Out there I spoke of discussion, merely so as to avoid one. This is not a matter in which I can be dragged into arguments, or listen to the opinions of the general. Actually there is nothing to discuss.'

'You mean, of course,' said Constant, 'that we must go to the relief of Charette.'

'I mean that we must not.' They would have interrupted him with protests, but he bore them down, displaying all that firmness of which under his foppish exterior the little man was capable. 'I mean that neither this nor anything else can alter the decision taken this morning. At nightfall we set out for Plouharnel, so that we may not fail to be punctual and fresh at the post of duty when Friday dawns.'

Quentin's sigh of relief was heard by all. 'Thank God for that,' he said, and so caused Bellanger to turn upon him sharply.

'Are you giving thanks that we leave these poor brave fellows to be murdered?'

La Marche was leaning across the table. 'You can't mean it, Chevalier. It is unthinkable.'

'What is unthinkable is that we should permit anything to interfere with our duty. If we fail in that, the Royalist cause is lost.'

'You mean,' Constant corrected him, 'that it may not be won.'

'And the difference?'

'It is considerable. Puisaye's attack may fail. But that need not mean his total defeat. After all, even without us he will still be in sufficient strength to hold his own against Hoche. And you forget that he is about to be reinforced; that the expedition under Sombreuil, with the British regulars, should reach Quiberon at any moment now.'

Tight-lipped, stern-eyed, Tinténiac answered him. 'I began by saying that I would not consent even to discuss this matter. But I will remind you of this. We did not leave Quiberon so that the Royalist army should hold its own, but so that the Republican army should be crushed. I deplore as deeply as any of you the misfortune to this corps from the Vendée. Yet as things stand, and if I am to be frank, in the interests of the Monarchy I am thankful that these Vendéans hold

Grouchy in play, since otherwise it might be in his power to prevent us from being punctually at Plouharnel.'

'That is inhuman!' Bellanger protested.

'It is war,' said Quentin.

'Not as Frenchmen understand it, sir.'

'You mean, not as you understand it.'

Tinténiac rose. 'Gentlemen, there is no more to be said. You have my orders. We march at nightfall.'

Constant thrust forward. 'Oh, but by your leave, Chevalier! A moment! There's a great deal more to be said.'

'Not to me.' Tinténiac held himself stiffly. 'I command this expedition. You will respect my orders, whatever your opinions.'

'I should not respect myself if I did.'

'Nor should I,' added Bellanger.

'You summoned us to hold a council, not to be arbitrarily ordered.'

Darker grew Tinténiac's brow. He looked from one to the other of them. Then his glance passed, sternly, challengingly, on. 'Is anyone else of that mind?'

The Chevalier de La Marche made a gesture of despair. 'It seems terrible to me not to succour these men who are within reach.'

'And, faith, that's my view,' said La Houssaye.

'It is also mine,' Tinténiac coldly agreed. 'But it cannot influence my decision. And you, Georges?'

Georges bowed his big head. 'You are in command, Chevalier, and the responsibility is yours. I thank God that it is not mine.'

'Even you!' Tinténiac's confidence seemed shaken. He permitted himself a bitter little smile. 'Is there not one of you, then, who sees eye to eye with me?'

'Oh, yes,' said Quentin. 'Cadoudal is mistaken. When he speaks of responsibility he is thinking of choice. Your orders leave you none. If you depart from them, there are no grounds that would save you from being court-martialled and shot.'

'You hear, sirs? It is a timely reminder for you all.'

'But it overlooks,' objected the lofty Bellanger, 'that there are duties imposed by honour.'

'Those,' Quentin answered him, 'I permit no man to teach me.'

'You never have permitted it, I suppose.'

Quentin smiled. 'If you suggest that I have, Vicomte, I shall be happy to argue the point with you at some other time.'

'Oh, at your pleasure, sir.'

'Meanwhile we leave the Vendéans to their fate,' said La Marche bitterly, whilst La Houssaye took his big head in his hands in a gesture almost hysterical. 'By God, it's too much,' he lamented.

'Certainly too much for me!' cried Constant boldly, feeling himself supported. He thrust forward. 'Let me have five thousand men, and I'l lead them forward myself to the relief.'

Tinténiac pondered him in indignant astonishment. 'You propose a folly, sir,' he said curtly.

'Why a folly?' demanded Bellanger. 'It's a solution, and it's the very least that we can do.'

'To weaken my force by half?'

'Momentarily only,' Constant insisted. 'Listen to me, please. Five hours to Josselin; five to return; eight for the remainder of the journey to Plouharnel. That's eighteen hours. We should make short work of the Blues once they are between us and the Vendéans. But allow six hours for the operation. That makes twenty-four in all. And from now to the dawn of Friday we dispose of thirty-six. That leaves us twelve hours for rest, without counting our reinforcement by the delivered Vendéans.'

'Your reckoning is fantastic,' Tinténiac condemned him, 'the programme crazy. Even if you could keep to it, which you never could, twelve hours would still offer no proper rest to men who had been so mercilessly used. Let me hear no more of it.'

'You underestimate the endurance of these Chouans.'

Tinténiac smiled on that. 'I've marched with them and fought with them. Of their endurance neither you nor another can teach me anything. They may seem made of iron; but even iron can bear only a certain strain. If you could bring these men to Plouharnel on time, weariness would make them useless there.'

'That is no more than an opinion.'

'So it is. But it is my opinion, and I permit none other to count in this. Why, my dear Constant, the least hitch, and your crazy timetable would be wrecked.'

'I will take the risk of that.'

'Oh, no. The risk would be mine. For the responsibility is mine.'

'Is that what you fear?' Bellanger taunted him.

The Chevalier's face flamed. But before he could answer the four of them were smothering him with protests, clamouring that he yield the point and accept the compromise that Constant offered.

Cadoudal held aloof, glum and surly, watching them from under his brows, and it was Quentin, at last, who went to the aid of his chief.

'Messieurs, hear me a moment.'

Scenting his opposition, they turned on him in fierce impatience.

'What can you have to say?' snapped Constant.

'Something that your obstinacy forces from me. That to let you have your way would be, perhaps, to let you walk into a trap. A trap that has been baited for us. What evidence do we possess of even the existence of these Vendéans? A letter is said to have come from Monsieur de Charette from . . .'

There Bellanger haughtily interrupted him. 'What do you mean, a letter is said to have come? A letter came.'

'Have you seen it?'

'My wife saw it.'

'So. Well. That was four days ago, she told us. Last Saturday. And the Vendéans were then at Rédon, a two days' march from here. Charette announced, I think, that they would be here on Monday. We arrive on Tuesday, and still they are not here.'

Again Bellanger interrupted him. 'Because they were held up by Grouchy at Josselin.'

'When? On Sunday, or Monday? But even if only yesterday, how comes it that we have no news of it until noon today? That is remarkable and interesting. It is also interesting that word of it comes only after we have announced that we march at nightfall, with or without the Vendéans.'

'What the devil are you insinuating now?' roared the Vicomte. 'What do you mean by "interesting"?'

'Consider.' Quentin spoke quietly, very deliberately. 'If these Vendéans had been imagined only for the purpose of detaining us until too late to keep our assignation at Plouharnel, would not the tale of their being beset at Josselin be a last resource to counter our resolve to depart tonight?'

'But what is this? What is this?' cried Bellanger, his wrath curbed by amazement. 'How much farther will you let your imagination run, sir? It is already sufficiently offensive.'

Tinténiac's brooding eyes were upon him. 'Have you nothing more than this, Quentin?' he asked.

'I fancied that I had already given you something. But, of course, there's more. There's this messenger from Josselin. Why does he come to Coëtlegon for succour? How does he know of the presence of an army here? Who sent word of it to Josselin? And when? And if anyone did, how came the news to get through the Republican lines to the Vendéans beleaguered in the town?'

'By God!' swore Cadoudal, whilst Tinténiac's glance was suddenly quickened.

'Faith! You are right. These are questions that need answering.'

'You begin to see.'

Constant broke in. 'To see what? What matters is that the news did get there. Thank God for it, since it must put heart of resistance into those poor devils. All the more reason why we should succour them.'

'Have you quite done, sir?' Bellanger asked Quentin. 'Or is there more in your sack?'

'There is still the messenger. He lied to you when he said that he is a man of Josselin. I happen to recognize him for a groom of Coëtlegon, whose name is Michel.'

They were stricken dumb whilst slowly the implication sank into their minds. Then Bellanger lost all his hauteur in sheer fury.

'Name of God! What are you saying?'

'It's plain enough,' said Constant. 'We are to believe, it seems, not only that there is a traitor here, but that the traitor is Madame la Vicomtesse herself. You dare to accuse her!'

'I accuse nobody. I merely state the fact. Whom the fact accuses is a matter for you.'

'Fact?' Constant retorted. 'Are you a fool or a rogue? Do you merely deceive yourself, or is it your aim to deceive us?'

'If you will decide I shall know how to answer you. Meanwhile, so as to quicken sluggish wits, there is something I should prefer not to drag in. But you leave me little choice.

'By what miracle does it happen, Monsieur de Chesnières, that Madame la Vicomtesse was able to offer you shelter here at Coëtlegon, and that having broken prison and with a price upon your head, you have been able to remain here for weeks immune from arrest? What privileges does Madame de Bellanger enjoy from the Republic that her house should be such a sanctuary? Find the answers to those questions, add them to the rest, and decide whether the sum does not justify my fears that the invitation to Coëtlegon was an invitation into a trap baited with these phantom Vendéans.'

'God's Blood! This is too much!' raged Bellanger. 'You must be mad. This is something that through my wife reflects upon my honour.'

'I merely state facts, undeniable facts, which it would be well to look into.'

With the single exception of Cadoudal, who swore again, by way of agreement, they stared at him in horror. Tinténiac appealed to him in tones of distress.

'My dear Quentin, this is entirely incredible.'

'Not so incredible as are to me these Vendéans, or

these Republican troops under Grouchy. I tell you, sirs, I do not believe there is a single Republican soldier this side of Auray.'

Bellanger was raging at him. 'You have said things that must be unsaid. At point of sword if need be.'

Tinténiac waved him aside. 'Point of sword never proved anything. That is mere brawling.' Then quietly and firmly he added: 'We wander into digressions. We open up matters beyond my present concerns, and these are more than enough for me. The rest must wait.'

'It cannot wait,' Bellanger fumed.

Constant abetted him. 'Of course not. A gross imputation has been made—an unpardonable affront to the Vicomte's honour.'

Quentin shocked them by laughing at Constant. 'Have not fingers enough been burnt of those you've employed to pull your chestnuts from the fire?'

Maddened by the taunt of that galling truth, Constant raised his hand to strike, when Tinténiac thrust himself between them.

'Not another word, on your lives! To what are we descending? Name of God! We seek the truth in the interests of ten thousand men, and you obscure it by your brawling. This conference is at an end. It has been too far prolonged. You have my decision and you will keep to it. You may go. Quentin, you will remain, if you please.'

But Bellanger would not be dismissed. 'The matter cannot end so,' he protested. 'I cannot submit to it.'

Constant would have supported him; but Tinténiac, at the end of his patience, waved them out peremptorily, and Houssaye, La Marche, and Cadoudal, obeying him, compelled obedience from the other two. They went almost physically propelled, but protesting to the end, and Constant's last words were a threat.

'Since you refuse to listen, Tinténiac, you may take the consequences; there are others who will not refuse, who will realize that our duty is at Josselin.'

'The fool,' said Tinténiac, as the door closed at last upon them. 'It seems that all that you have said has been wasted on that mulish mind. You heard him. He still rants of Josselin and these supposed Vendéans. Your facts may be few, when all is said, and they may be slender. But when bound together, they make a nasty bundle.' He dropped wearily into a chair. 'Is there more, or have you told us all?'

'You'll have gathered, I suppose, that Hoche is the Vicomtesse's lover.'

'Good God! Do you surmise that from the rest?'

'On the contrary. I surmise much of the rest from that.'

He related what he knew, and it went to deepen the Chevalier's gloom. 'I see,' he said. 'And Bellanger? What is his part in this?'

'The part of a poor, deluded cuckold, so sure of himself in his lordly fatuity that you cannot move him even by jealousy as you could another.'

They talked long on this, and might have talked longer but for the return of Cadoudal.

He came in tempestuously, breathless, his big face flushed.

'There's the devil at work,' was his blunt announcement. 'That animal Chesnières whom you've taken on to your staff is stirring up a hell's broth out there. He's haranguing the men in the park, inflaming them on the score of the Vendéans, calling for volunteers to go with him to Josselin.'

Tinténiac bounded to his feet. 'By God! Was that what he threatened? The madman!' He made for the door. 'Come on! I'll put him under arrest.'

Cadoudal caught him by the arm. 'You're too late, Chevalier. You'ld risk a mutiny. I've been telling you that since last night those lads have been ripe for any mischief, asking where is the Prince that was promised them, swearing that they are being cheated and betrayed. Only their faith in their own leaders, in Saint-Regent, Guillemot, and myself, and their love for you have held them in subjection. But they've been explosive as gunpowder, itching to be at the throats of somebody, and now this fool Chesnières has put a match to them.'

'What then?' Tinténiac shook his arm free of the Chouan's heavy grip. 'Am I to wait until they're all consumed? We must talk to them; do what we can to counter this sentimental poison.'

'But no violence, Chevalier, or they'll make a hell about us. No arrests or threats of arrest to exasperate them.'

They went off at speed, through the empty hall and across the terrace, without a glance for the ladies and the *émigrés* officers crowding the balustrade, spectators of what was taking place in the vast park below. A man's haranguing voice, high-pitched and penetrating, beat upon the air, and there, on horseback, sat Constant de Chesnières, bare-headed, gesticulating, above a swarm of red coats in that sparsely planted meadow. As they approached they made out the words of an oration that neared its close.

'Can we suffer the gallant Monsieur de Charette and those brothers in arms from the Vendée who were hastening to our assistance to be slaughtered by the Blues when it lies in our power to save them?'

Whilst a roar was answering him, Tinténiac drew close. A way through those dense red ranks had opened promptly to the orders of Cadoudal. But when the Chevalier would have mounted an ammunition-cart in Constant's neighborhood, Quentin wisely restrained him.

'Let Cadoudal,' he said. 'They'll understand him better.'

Cadoudal bounded up with the swift athletic ease that was surprising in so corpulent a man, and began at once to address them in their native Breton tongue.

The sneering smile with which Constant had greeted him faded as he perceived the advantage over himself which this gave the speaker.

But whilst Cadoudal's influence and authority over the majority were soon manifest, yet many there were who from their clamorous interruptions made it plain that the passions which Constant had fanned into flame were not so easily to be quenched. Perceiving this,

Constant returned to the attack when Cadoudal had finished. Unable to supply answers to arguments which he had not understood, he confined himself to the core of his appeal.

'It remains,' he cried, 'that five thousand of our brothers in arms are beleaguered in Josselin, and will be massacred by the *patauds* unless we go to their assistance. Let those who perceive in this a sacred duty take up their arms and follow me.'

Thus he flung into that seething crowd the elements of a violent contention between those who decided to go and those whom Cadoudal had persuaded that their duty lay elsewhere.

Constant, in the act of wheeling his horse, found Tinténiac at his stirrup, white and stern. His incisive voice cut sharply above the uproar.

'I should provoke a pitched battle if I attempted forcibly to restrain those you may have seduced into this mutiny. But, whatever the issue, I warn you that I shall bring you to answer before a court-martial at the earliest moment.'

Constant, in the momentary exaltation of his achievement and the sense of power it brought him, laughed insolently. 'You brought it on yourself by giving heed to that mountebank fencing-master of yours. For the rest, sir, if I deliver Charette, as I intend, you should know that there is no court-martial that will not hold me justified.'

'You think so? You'll think differently when you face a platoon.'

Without answering, Constant moved his horse slowly forward. A stream of men came winding after him through the main mass, swollen as it advanced by lesser confluent streams.

Tinténiac looked at Cadoudal with eyes of dull anger that plainly asked a question. Cadoudal, grey-faced, heaved his great shoulders in a gesture of helplessness.

'By Our Lady of Auray,' he groaned, 'you might as well try to dam a river with your two hands.'

CHAPTER 5

Grouchy's Division

THE secession, whilst lamentable enough to Tinténiac, proved less than he had feared. For this he had to thank Cadoudal and his Morbihannais. Amounting to almost half the Chouan total, they were not only loyal in themselves, but stout advocates of loyalty among the others. In the end it was found that rather fewer than four thousand had marched away with Constant, leaving Tinténiac with between six and seven thousand men.

Grimly, with Quentin and the three Chouan chiefs, but otherwise without a single member of his staff, the little Chevalier had stood at the side of the avenue to watch that mutinous departure.

Guillemot, whose contingent had suffered most heavily in defection, having vainly exhausted himself in seeking to stem the desertion, was now venting his impotent anger in a steady flow of imprecation.

At the last Constant had returned to the Chevalier for a final conciliatory word. That mention of a platoon had helped him to digest Tinténiac's threat. Having digested it, he was shaken in his assurance of what must be the military view of his action.

He drew rein and leaned over from the saddle, whilst the departing men swung briskly past without formation.

'When I return tomorrow, Tinténiac, you will condone what I do.'

The Chevalier returned him no answer beyond the stab of his stern eyes. Cadoudal, however, was less restrained, and he addressed that man of birth in the

300

second person singular, as if the better to mark his contempt for him.

'If you make the mistake of returning at all, you'll see the sort of condonation we shall have for you.'

Constant ignored him, and made another attempt with Tinténiac. 'Besides these lads, I shall bring back the Vendéans. Think of the great strength we shall then be in. If you will wait for me until noon, that will leave plenty of time for the march to Plouharnel.'

'And that's the species of fool you are,' said Saint-Regent. 'If only these animals realized it, not one of them would follow you a yard.'

And then Tinténiac was moved to add: 'All that I can promise you is that if you come back alive I'll bring you before a court-martial and have you shot for this.'

On that the rage simmering in Guillemot boiled over suddenly. 'Why wait? You damned, muddling, mutinous animal, this'll put an end to your buffooneries.'

He pulled a pistol from his belt, levelled it, and pulled the trigger. It would have ended the adventure there and then for Constant had not Quentin, acting upon impulse, caught Guillemot's arm and flung it upwards, so that the pistol was discharged into the air.

The report checked the flow of Chouans abreast of them. From those who perceived what had happened, there was a sudden threatening movement, averted and quelled, however, by Constant, who moved his horse so as to make a screen for Tinténiac's group, whilst with voice and gesture he urged the indignant Chouans away and on.

When that was done he looked down at Quentin, who with Cadoudal was still restraining the fierce Guillemot. His expression was one of frowning wonder.

'I am in your debt for that, Monsieur de Morlaix. Do me the justice to perceive that it's a debt I have not sought to incur.'

Quentin answered neither by word nor look, and at last Constant went off, riding slowly along the flank of the defiling column.

When the last of them had passed into the cloud of dust their marching raised in the avenue, Tinténiac sent off the three Chouan leaders to prepare their men for departure.

'I'll delay no longer. Better had I listened to you, Quentin, and not come. The place is unlucky to us. Still, though reduced in numbers by this piece of treachery, we should be in sufficient force to do our part. Anyway, we must attempt it, and there must be no more delays. We march as soon as the men have eaten. See to it.'

They went up to the terrace, and there the fluttering courtly throng closed about them, to plague them with questions as to what exactly had happened.

'A mutiny,' he answered shortly. 'Led by an imbecile I was fool enough to appoint only yesterday to my staff.'

Madame de Bellanger stood before him, the Vicomte towering dark and haughtily protective at her side. 'But, Chevalier,' she cried, 'he has gone to rescue the Vendéans. Can you blame him for that?'

'I can, madame. I do.' Abandoning ceremony, he swung aside, and raised his voice. 'Messieurs, we march in an hour. I have to request you to be ready.'

Madame was horrified. 'In an hour! That will scarcely leave you time to dine.'

The Vicomte supported her protest. 'Why this, Chevalier? What need for such sudden haste? We have time to spare.'

With nerves strained to breaking point, Tinténiac was curt. 'Those are my orders.' And he stalked on.

Quentin was following when Bellanger caught him without ceremony by the arm. 'What ails him? Are you responsible for this?'

'He does not like the air of Coëtlegon,' said Quentin dryly. 'It is not proving healthy.'

'Oh, Marquis!' cried madame, a lovely appealing figure of distress. 'I have neglected nothing the times permit, so as to make your sojourn pleasant.'

'On the contrary, madame. You supplied too much.

We did not come for pleasure. We came to incorporate a body of men which does not arrive.'

'*Mon Dieu!* And you blame me, I hear, for this misfortune. Appearances can terribly mislead us.'

'Make it clear to him,' said the Vicomte. 'It may moderate his offensive assumptions.'

'That is so unjust,' she complained. 'This man who came from Josselin—Michel—because he was once a groom here, you assume that he is still in my service. You forget the times in which we live, and the constant changes they bring.'

'I hope you are answered, sir,' said the Vicomte, looking down his nose.

'So foolish to suppose me to act with some dark, selfish motive. And not only foolish. Monstrous. Almost I could laugh.'

Quentin was non-committal. 'All this, madame, ceases to be of consequence, since we march at once.'

'It is to slight my hospitality.'

'The harsh necessity imposed by duty.'

He bowed in leave-taking. But Bellanger had not yet done with him.

'Hardly a gracious *amende* for your ungenerous opinions, sir.'

'I trust that the sequel will put me to shame,' he evaded, and so, at last, took himself off.

On the doorstep he came upon Germaine, her aunt in agitation at her side.

'They tell me,' said Madame de Chesnières, 'that my son has gone to the rescue of Monsieur de Charette, and, what is even worse, that his gallantry has earned him nothing but the reproof of your commander. That is a strange attitude in a Christian gentleman.'

He murmured the platitude of a soldier's first duty being obedience, and with a glance for Germaine, in which he sought to express all that her aunt's presence rendered unutterable, he escaped.

He found Tinténiac beset by a clamorous staff. In his desire for instant departure he was yet again being baulked by Madame de Bellanger's too bounteous hospitality. Reluctantly he was yielding to the insistence of his officers that it would be a climax of ungraciousness, and a gratuitous one, not to stay at least for the dinner which had been prepared. Having yielded, he was to discover delays in coming to table.

When at long last, some three hours after Constant's departure, they sat down, a gay, frivolous company, the Chevalier was in a fume of exasperation at the insouciance of his *émigrés*.

Whilst within doors they banqueted unhurried, outside, the Chouans, having consumed their bread and onions and some odd scraps left over from last night, waited impatiently to be gone.

Suddenly the laughter and chatter about the long table in the dining-hall was silenced by a shattering volley of musketry from the park.

As men and women questioned their neighbours with dilating eyes of alarm in faces suddenly blenched, a second volley roared a sequel to the first, to be followed by an uproar near at hand, above which rang the cry: 'To arms! To arms! The Blues!'

From one of the tall windows which he had reached almost at a bound, with a crowd of diners pressing behind him, Quentin saw a heavy veil of smoke rising along the belt of trees across the valley, a mile or more away. Nearer, in the middle distance, in the meadowlands, there was a stir and scurry of clamorous red-coated Chouans caught unawares in the open. Under the direction of leaders made frantic by surprise, the several companies were falling back out of range, forming ranks, and looking to their weapons, so as to meet this onslaught of an assailant as yet invisible. In their exposed position they were vulnerable to an enemy who attacked from cover. It was a reversal of the order with which these warriors were familiar, and they found it little to their liking.

The firing continued: heavy rolling volleys from the edge of the timber, answered by ragged bursts from groups of Chouans who had been caught within range, and who had dropped prone, according to those tactics which d'Hervilly had so contemptuously described as proper to Hurons, but without which they would now have been mown down in swaths.

Quentin heard Tinténiac's voice behind him, shrill and compelling.

'To your posts, gentlemen! We are attacked.'

The men melted from the group that pinned him where he stood, whereupon with scant ceremony he thrust himself free of the women who remained.

In the middle of the room, where all was now confused movement, he confronted Bellanger, who was buckling on his sword. The Vicomte's expression was unpleasantly sneering.

'Ah! Monsieur de Oracle! Not a Republican soldier, you said, this side of Auray.'

'I said some other things that it were better to remember.'

'And with the same authority.'

'Or the lack of it!' cried the Vicomtesse, standing tense and white just beyond her husband, a hand repressing the agitation of her breast.

'So I pray, madame,' he answered, as he sped on.

Near the door he came upon Germaine. She stood detached from a cluster of huddled, panic-stricken ladies. She was pale, but singularly calm. Their eyes met, and her lips parted in a little smile of wistful greeting. He drew close.

'Courage, Germaine. They cannot be in sufficient force to break through.'

'That is not what I fear,' she told him, with a touch of pride. 'God guard you, Quentin.'

He would have lingered, but outside the voice of Tinténiac was summoning them. 'Monsieur de Bellanger! Gentlemen of the Loyal Emigrant! To your posts!'

He bore her hand to his lips, and was gone, almost swept out by the sudden rush of *émigrés* who answered the Chevalier's call.

Sharp orders received them on the terrace and sent them off to their men, who were already mustering their ranks. To Bellanger, as second in command, fell the first directions.

'Vicomte, you will post your company yonder on the right, so as to be on the flank of the Blues when they debouch from the wood.'

'If they debouch, sir.'

'Away! Monsieur de La Marche, you will instruct Saint-Regent to form a left wing with his division. Monsieur de La Houssaye, be good enough to find Cadoudal. Order him with Guillemot to compose the centre. And let word go forward commanding those advanced men to fall back. They are getting themselves killed to no purpose. We must draw the Blues on out of cover. Hasten, sir.'

Bellanger's rich, sonorous voice came up to them from below, raised in command, and presently there was a rolling of drums, and the company of the Loyal Emigrant was marching to take up its station as steadily as if on parade, a spectacle to have satisfied the fastidious eyes of Monsieur d'Hervilly.

Volley was succeeding volley from the woods, and the veil of smoke steadily deepening until that distant belt of trees grew dim. In the short grass of the middle distance, red bundles lay still, to tell of the execution done.

From the summit of the terrace steps Tinténiac watched and waited, impatient until at last he saw that his order had gone forward.

The rash, futile, crawling advance of the foremost Chouans had been stemmed, and they were beginning to fall back, still wriggling along the ground.

Cadoudal arrived at speed and breathless. He had thrown off his coat, and the wet shirt clung to his sweating torso. But his spirit was as cool as his body was overheated.

'A lad of the district has just come in, who tells me that this is a division under Grouchy, some three thousand strong.'

'Grouchy! Then what has become of the Vendéans? It was Grouchy who pinned them at Josselin. My God! Has he destroyed them?'

'Impossible. He comes from Vannes. He was on his

way to join Hoche, and turned back, having winded us here. Thousand devils! That explains things, I think.'

'It should finally dispose of your faith in those Vendéans,' said Quentin. 'You'll begin to believe that we've been fooled?'

Tinténiac stared at him white-faced. 'By God!' he said through his teeth. 'Ah, but we'll have the truth of it when this is over. Do you suppose that fool Chesnières will have got too far to hear the firing?'

Cadoudal shook his massive head. 'Bah! He's been gone these four hours. He'll be a dozen miles away, more than halfway to Josselin.'

Quentin pointed. 'Look.'

Through the distant smoke that hung like a curtain upon the summer air, a long line of horsemen was emerging. It advanced, and halted clear in view. A second line followed it, and after that another, and yet another. 'Grouchy's Dragoons,' said Cadoudal. 'Guillemot is getting his bayonets ready for them.'

They could see Guillemot's men deploying into double lines at well-spaced intervals.

'Let us go,' said Tinténiac.

They went at a run to place themselves at the head of the body forming the centre, and composed mainly of Cadoudal's Morbihannais, at present held in reserve.

Before they reached their posts they heard a bugle sounding the charge, and presently came the drumming of hooves, muffled at first, but gradually swelling in volume, as three hundred horsemen, sabres flashing in the sunlight, charged down upon the Chouan lines.

Could d'Hervilly have seen the Chouans then it might have changed his views of their fighting qualities. Steady as veterans they waited, holding their fire until Guillemot judged the dragoons within range. Then from the foremost double line a volley of two hundred muskets smote the Blues. Falling men and stumbling horses disordered for a moment the rhythm of that charge. Before it was recovered, the Chouans who had fired flung themselves prone upon the turf, and over them, from the next lines, a second volley, deadlier

307

than the first, now that the range was shorter, renewed increasingly the cavalry's confusion. Then, like those ahead of them, these Chouans too lay prone, to allow yet a third fire to blast the Republicans, whereafter, instantly, all were on their feet; the three lines closed up, the front rank knelt, and bayonets bristled to receive so much of the remaining cavalry as might charge home.

But shattered to less than a third of its strength, the meadow strewn with men and horses, the air filled with the screams of beasts in agony and the lamentations of maimed men, what was left of the dragoons scattered widely and went off to re-form out of range.

That retreat, however, revealed a dense column of Blue infantry to the deployment of which the cavalry had served as a screen.

At Tinténiac's orders, Guillemot's men, falling back to right and left to reload, opened their ranks to give passage to Cadoudal's division, sent forward to engage this main body of the enemy.

That engagement, begun in murderous fire from both sides, developed into a bitter mêlée with cold steel, a wild, fierce confusion in which all strategic order was lost to both. If the Chouans suffered heavily at first from the Republican fire, they took a terrible revenge at close quarters with the bayonet. Steadily, but ever more quickly as their resistance weakened, the Blues were pressed back, until at last, towards sunset, being taken on one flank by the Loyal Emigrant, and on the other by Saint-Regent's division, they broke and ran, so as to extricate themselves from the closing grip of those pincers.

To cover the retreat and enable his infantry to restore itself to order, the Marquis de Grouchy, on a white horse, at the head of the remainder of his dragoons, charged down upon the flank of the pursuers, sabring fiercely; and actually with scarcely the loss of a man, he held them in check long enough to permit his foot to re-form.

When, the task accomplished, Grouchy rode his dragoons out of the press, the Chouans, themselves a disordered mob by now, were confronted with a line of Blues that, firm once more, met them with a fire that tore gaps in their too solid ranks, and then steadily retreated to new positions.

The Chouans of the centre, now entirely out of control, a furious horde maddened by blood-lust, incapable of concerted action, obeyed no attempt to restore them to order, but merely hurled themselves in rage against that steady blue wall that received them with fire and steel.

Their overwhelming numbers, however, far greater, no doubt, than Grouchy had reckoned or been informed, made it impossible to snatch from them the victory which was already won from an enemy whose only aim now was to retire in as good order as possible. Yet by such wild tactics as the Chouans were now pursuing that victory might be too dearly bought.

So as to make an end, Tinténiac led Saint-Regent's division, which had been out of this phase of the engagement, away towards the wood, and then down on to the Republican right flank, so as to turn it.

Grouchy, perceiving the aim of the manoeuvre, and fearing that it might be copied by the Loyal Emigrant on his other flank, formed his foot hastily into three sides of a square backed by the timber into which he proposed to retire.

A heavy discharge of musketry from Saint-Regent's men having thrown that right wing into disorder, Tinténiac, sword in hand, his coat torn, his face blackened, led in person a charge upon it before it could recover.

Quentin went with him, brandishing a musket which he had snatched up to replace his broken sword.

So impetuous proved the charge that it opened a gap in the face of the Blue square. The Chouans poured in, hacking and stabbing, and in a moment the Republican formation crumpled and broke up into fleeing groups intent only upon gaining the sanctuary of the trees. And now down upon them from the centre, like a torrent that has broken its dam, came Cadoudal's Morbihannais.

It was the end. The rout of Grouchy's division, which had taken the field some three thousand strong, with all the pride and confidence of regular soldiers, engaging a disorderly rabble, was complete. It remained only for the Republican commander to save what he could from the wreckage of his force. His survivors fled demoralized for cover, like panic-stricken conies, with that pursuing horde yelling upon their heels.

Tinténiac laughed in his hilarious excitement as he still led the men of Saint-Regent who had followed him. Laughing, he spoke to Quentin, who trotted beside him.

'That renegade Grouchy will have a fine account to render to his sansculotte masters for this day's work,' he jested, and on that jest he checked, spun half round, and crumpled into Quentin's arms which had been instinctively flung out to catch him.

On the very edge of the wood a fleeing Blue, almost one of the last of them, had turned and knelt and fired almost at random upon the pursuers, and the bullet had found Tinténiac's gallant breast.

The sansculotte paid for it with his life; for before he could regain his feet a Chouan was upon him and a Chouan bayonet had transfixed him.

Gently Quentin lowered Tinténiac to the ground. He went down upon one knee, supporting the body against the other. A ring of Chouans formed almost at once about them, and broke presently into lamentations when it was perceived who was the stricken man.

Quentin's hand was busy upon Tinténiac's breast. It came away drenched in blood.

The Chevalier looked up at him, his eyes momentarily puzzled and vacuous. Then the smile with which he had charmed so many broke upon the livid, powder-grimed face.

'I think this is the end of Monsieur de Tinténiac,' he said, and spoke lightly as if amused. 'A great moment, Quentin, and a victory won. I may depart with a calm mind.'

Quentin, with a strangling sensation, knowing him sped, could answer nothing.

The ring about them opened. Bellanger and La Marche stood over them in the gathering dusk.

'*Ah, morbleu! Quel malheur!* This is to pay too dearly for victory. Is the wound grave?'

Again Tinténiac smiled. 'Not grave. No. Just mortal. So that the King lives, what matter who dies?' The smile passed. 'You are in command now, Bellanger. On your life and honour see that you are punctual at Plouharnel.'

Bellanger bowed his head in silence, and in that moment was thrust aside almost roughly by a new arrival. It was Cadoudal, grimed and tattered from the fight. He fell on his knees beside the dying man.

'Chevalier! My Chevalier! *Mon petit!*' There was agony in his voice. 'You're not badly hurt. The good God could not permit that.'

'Ah, Georges!' It was a murmur of welcome. A feeble, wavering hand sought the Chouan's. Cadoudal grasped it eagerly, and bore it to his lips. 'My brave, great-hearted Georges, we'll hunt the Blues no more together. But you . . .'

He had made an effort to raise himself. The blood choked him. For a moment he struggled, coughing; then his head lolled sideways, and came to rest against Quentin's shoulder.

Cadoudal, on his knees, fell to weeping aloud with the passionate abandon of a child.

CHAPTER 6

❦

Bellanger in Command

LATE that night, in the library of Coëtlegon, five men sat in council under the presidency of the Vicomte de Bellanger, upon whom the chief command had now devolved. They were, besides the Vicomte himself, La Houssaye, La Marche, Quentin, and Georges Cadoudal.

From laying Tinténiac to rest in a grave beside the avenue, they had returned weary and heartsore to the château, to be feverishly greeted by ladies over whom had hung the terror of falling in prey to victorious sansculottes.

In contrast with last night's delights, there was grim work now for these ladies whom Madame de Bellanger had brought to Coëtlegon so as to lend gaiety to the gathering. The wounded were being borne in by their comrades. The château was rapidly being transformed into a hospital, and the services of the ladies were being claimed to minister to these poor fellows, to wash and dress their wounds, to nourish them, to quench their fevered thirsts, to cheer their spirits and ease their sufferings. They were proving themselves competent. Under the abiding frivolity of the old régime, their natures had undergone a steadying process through the sufferings of their class in the last few years.

The lovely Vicomtesse received the returning officers with a manner that admirably blended exultation in their triumph with sorrow for the sufferings at which it had been won.

Quentin, dishevelled, begrimed, and near exhaustion, met her smile with fierce, haggard eyes. 'How false,' he said, 'are the reports that come to Coëtlegon, and what a death trap it has proved!'

'How cruel to remind me of it!' she complained, in tearful desolation. 'Almost you make it sound like a reproach. And I meant so well.'

'I am sure of it. But for whom?'

He waited for no answer. He turned aside and staggered off across the hall, through which the wounded were being carried or assisted in a constant stream, until he came upon Germaine. With her was a Mademoiselle de Kercadio, who had been the betrothed of Boishardi, and wore mourning for him. This frail little lady, who had ridden sabre in hand into battle at her lover's side, was now in tears.

'It breaks my heart to think of Tinténiac, so brave, so gay. Boishardi loved him as a brother. How sorry he would be, especially for the treachery that doomed him. It calls for vengeance.'

'Treachery!' Quentin uttered a short, mirthless laugh. 'Whilst a third of us are gone to rescue imaginary Vendéans from Grouchy, Grouchy falls upon the remaining two-thirds. Who brought us word of the Vendéans? Who sent word of us to Grouchy, to bring him here?'

Both women stared at him in terror. 'Quentin!' cried Germaine. 'What dreadful thing is in your mind?'

'Just that. Just these questions. My suspicious nature requires an answer to them.'

In that fierce mood he came to the council, where he found no exultation of victory. Apart from the gloom occasioned by the loss of a commander so gallant and universally beloved as Tinténiac, there was the cost of that victory to be counted. Their casualties exceeded two thousand, a third of which was the number of the dead.

Out in the parklands, moving points of light, like will-o'-the-wisps, showed where the Chouans were at their grim work of retrieving the wounded and burying the dead.

The writing-table had been turned into a buffet by

the solicitude of the Vicomtesse, and was laden with wine and meats for the refreshment of these officers whose conference brooked no delays. In the high-backed chair that had been occupied by Tinténiac a few hours ago sat now Bellanger, morose and stern.

He bent a sullen glance upon Quentin, who was the last to arrive, and whom he would gladly have excluded had he dared, conscious as he was of his uncompromising hostility, galled as he was by the unavenged affronts which Quentin had put upon him. These, however, were matters that must wait. The command which had devolved upon him imposed duties from which no personal considerations must deflect him.

The sense of that command endowed him with more than ordinary prolixity. He was being eloquent. Even in this hour of gloom he must be finding sonorous words in which to expatiate upon what had that day been accomplished. A glorious instance, he described it, of matchless Royalist valour. He pronounced in emotional terms a brief funeral oration over the great leader whom he deemed himself unworthy to succeed—a confession which none mistook for a conviction—and he invited these gentlemen of his staff to offer suggestions for the immediate course of action now to be adopted.

Quentin, whose impatience had been growing under that flood of words, which offended his sense of fitness and intensified the ache of his lacerated nerves, was prompt to answer.

'What is to consider? Our course of action was laid down in Tinténiac's last words. He commanded us to be punctual at Plouharnel. It remains but to obey him.'

Bellanger afforded him a gloomy attention; then he looked at Cadoudal, as if to invite his comment.

The Chouan, still in ragged shirt and breeches, as he had fought, still in the grime of battle, sat apart, his elbows on his knees, his head in his hands, his fingers thrust through his tousled fair hair, his spirit mourning the bright leader he had followed with the unquestioning fidelity of a hound.

Seeing him thus, Bellanger's heavy glance passed on. 'Monsieur de La Marche?'

La Marche, who sat glowering into a glass of wine he held, looked up uneasily. 'As you've heard, we have our orders.' He spoke without conviction, and having spoken, drained his glass.

'And you, La Houssaye?'

'I agree that since we know Tinténiac's intentions, it is incumbent upon us to fulfil them as far as possible.'

'As far as possible. Exactly. But how far is it now possible?' He cleared his throat for the address that was to follow this exordium. But Quentin gave him no time to come to it.

'Tinténiac's orders apart, there is the purpose for which we left Quiberon. In spite of all that has happened, reduced as we are, that purpose must still be ours. Your clear duty, sir, is to give the order to march at dawn.'

'I am not asking to be told my duty.' The tone was acid. 'But I'll let that pass with the rest.' He waved it away with one of his long, graceful hands. 'Nothing remains but to march at dawn, says Monsieur de Morlaix. But with what, pray, are we to march? With half the force considered necessary for this enterprise? For that is all that now remains of the ten thousand that left Quiberon. Am I to march men who are wearied by a day of battle and a night of burying the dead? Can I march these men at dawn? Is that reasonable advice?'

'March them at noon, then. But march them tomorrow, so that we may still come to Plouharnel in time.'

'That is to answer only the half of my objections. There remains the question of our present numbers.'

'We must make them suffice. We have to remember that our function is to create a diversion by falling upon Hoche's rear. We are still strong enough for that:

315

to create confusion, compel that division of his forces which should enable the army of Monsieur de Puisaye to annihilate him.'

'At the price, no doubt, of our own annihilation,' said La Houssaye, faintly sarcastic.

'What then, so that the object is accomplished? It remains the only amend we can now make for all the blunders and worse that have brought us to this pass. And make it we must.'

That set them all against him; all save Cadoudal, who continued huddled in a seeming insensibility. In the scowling faces of the others, Quentin read his condemnation.

La Marche expressed it. 'By God, sir! Do you malign the dead? Do you dare to cast your foul censure on the generalship of Tinténiac?'

'I do not. And you know that I do not. My censure is for those who overpersuaded Tinténiac to come to this . . . to come to Coëtlegon; for those who resisted his will when, sensing danger, he was eager to depart; for Constant de Chesnières, who mutinously marched off a third of our men on a fool's errand, leaving us in diminished strength to bear today's attack. These are the errors, the wicked errors, for which we must accept the blame, and for which at need we must immolate ourselves, so that Monsieur de Puisaye may not be cheated of his victory.'

Bellanger sneered openly. 'I am not concerned to immolate what is left of this company for the sake of Monsieur de Puisaye.'

'Nor I,' said La Marche.

'My faith, nor I,' said La Houssaye.

Cadoudal seemed to awaken at last. He reared his great head, and glared at them from blood-injected eyes.

'Name of God! You sneer at the Comte Joseph, do you? Well, sneer your ignoble fill. But who the devil asks you to die for his sake? Are you all addleheaded?' His voice soared. 'It is for the sake of the King; for the sake of a cause in which a better man than any of us has given his precious life today. If you are not prepared to die for that, then, damn your souls, why did you not remain in England, or Holland, or Germany, or wherever else you've been idling, whilst we Bretons, who believed in God and the King's Majesty, have been bleeding freely these two years?'

Cowed and even shamed by that vehement outburst, they sat for a long moment in sullen silence, whilst Cadoudal sank back into his huddled attitude of dejection.

La Houssaye was the first to recover; but no longer to hector. 'You mistake us, Cadoudal. We are all prepared to die for the cause, else, as you say, we should not have come to France. What we are not prepared to do is to throw away our lives in vain undertakings.'

'To do our part at Sainte-Barbe is no vain undertaking,' said Quentin.

'Can you be sure of that?' Bellanger asked him.

'What does my conviction matter, or your conviction? For soldiers there is obedience, not conviction. And our obedience is due to the orders under which we left Quiberon, the orders confirmed today by Tinténiac.'

Bellanger sighed in controlled exasperation. 'It is not quite so simple. Things have changed since we left Quiberon. Give me leave, Monsieur de Morlaix! Arguments as to what may have changed them are beside the point. Things are not even as Tinténiac supposed them when he issued his last orders. For when he spoke he did not know the extent of our losses.'

'We still have men enough for what's to do,' Quentin insisted.

'That is merely your opinion.'

'It is also mine,' flashed Cadoudal.

Bellanger strove with his temper. 'What is yours, La Houssaye?'

'Definitely that we are too weak.'

'And yours, La Marche?'

'The same. Our only prudent course is to rejoin the force that followed Chesnières. Time enough then to consider our next step.'

'Time enough!' cried Quentin. 'That is what it may not be.'

Still with his long-suffering air, Bellanger expounded. 'We have heard two soldiers of great experience, and their view accords fully with mine. You, Monsieur de Morlaix, are becoming the victim of a fixed idea. You persist in overlooking that Puisaye is actually in greater strength than Hoche.'

'Without reckoning,' added La Houssaye, 'that by now he must have been reinforced by Sombreuil's division and the regulars from England. He will face the sansculottes in overwhelming strength.'

'You leave out of account the advantages of Hoche's fortified position!' cried Quentin, in despair. 'And, again, what if Sombreuil has not arrived?'

'You forget,' retorted Bellanger, 'that when Puisaye comes to attack, and finds that we are not in Hoche's rear, it will be for him to suspend the engagement.'

'What anxiety, monsieur, to discover reasons for neglecting duty!'

La Marche and La Houssaye turned indignantly upon Quentin. But Bellanger waved a hand to pacify them. He smiled acidly.

'We must continue,' he drawled, 'to bear with Monsieur de Morlaix's impetuosity and wild assumptions, however offensive, remembering that they are dictated by unreasoning zeal. Our aim must be to do the best for all concerned, and the immediate best is, clearly, to follow Monsieur de Chesnières to Rédon, so as to incorporate with ours not only his division, but also that of the Vendéans.'

'My God! Is it possible that you still believe in their existence?'

Belanger was lofty. 'Whether they exist or not can wait. We do know that three thousand Chouans exist between here and Rédon, and our first step must be to incorporate them in our ranks. When that is done we can consider what is to follow. So as soon as the men are fit to march, we set out for Rédon by way of Josselin and Malestroit.'

One last despairing attempt Quentin made to shape

the course of things. 'But it may be too late by then to do anything. In God's name, sir, summon at least a full council of all the *émigrés* officers and Chouan leaders, before you take so grave a decision.'

But Bellanger would not be moved. It is not impossible that the bitter resentment aroused by Quentin may have stiffened his obstinacy. 'The decision is taken. I am in command sir, and that responsibility lies with me.'

'The burden may prove heavy. Tinténiac promised Chesnières a court-martial for his insubordination. Beware lest you incur the same.'

The Vicomte rose, a tall figure of great dignity. 'You presume, I think, upon our patience.' He addressed the gathering. 'You have my orders. You will be good enough to communicate them to the quarters concerned.'

Cadoudal began to move towards the door. 'At least there's an end to all this fish-market chatter.' He overtook Quentin, and gripped his arm. 'These gentlemen from England seem all to be the good friends of General Hoche: Monsieur d'Hervilly in Quiberon and Monsieur de Bellanger here.'

'Monsieur Cadoudal!' Bellanger's voice was sharp and minatory. 'You are not respectful.'

Cadoudal turned upon him a face of sneering astonishment. 'By God! You've some discernment, after all.'

He rolled out, heavy-footed, and Quentin went after him.

CHAPTER 7

※⊱⊰⊱⊰⊱※

The Dupes

COOL and trim, a muslin fichu above her aproned petticoat, Germaine came from her labours of mercy with
the wounded, who lay in rows upon the straw that had
been carried into the handsome chambers of Coëtlegon.

Bruised in body and spirit, Quentin surveyed her,
sad-eyed. 'Can you minister to souls as well, Germaine?'

'To yours at need, I hope. I should not be the wife
for you if I could not.' Her glance was direct and
frank; her tender, generous lips were gently smiling.

'I should not be the husband for you were I not
conscious of my need of you.' He sighed. 'This is an
evil hour.' Briefly he told her of Bellanger's decision.
'Begun by deliberate malice, this betrayal is now to be
consummated by sheer obstinate folly. Whether he's
still deceived and deluded by that woman who is selling
us, I don't know. But the fool is marching us away
from the clear duty we were set when we left
Quiberon.'

'Quentin, this is all impossible. The appearances are
deluding you. I can't, I'll not believe this of Louise.'
She was so warm in defence of her friend that once
again he was driven to marshal his arguments.

Still they did not convince her. 'But all is surmise. It
must be. There can be no proof of any of it.'

'Proof enough. She is Hoche's faithful ally.'

'That is mad. Hoche? A sansculotte? The son of a
groom?'

'And the lover of the Marquise du Grégo,
Vicomtesse Bellanger. I am no evil tongue, Germaine,

to stain a woman's fame for the nasty joy of it.' He told her what he knew as a witness, and left her white and shaken.

'*Mon Dieu!* The shame of it. A groom's son; a champion of the *canaille.*'

'Oh, but a pretty enough fellow to please a more fastidious woman than the Grégo. A noble-looking animal, and laurel-crowned.'

'Don't, Quentin! Don't! It is all too vile. You make me ashamed; for if this is true, then we have profited by this vileness. Oh, yes. It explains a mystery. That is what has made it possible for Louise to offer us this secure shelter from pursuit.' Persuaded by that glaring fact, so suddenly perceived, she marvelled that any could resist persuasion. 'But isn't that enough to bring the Vicomte to reason?'

'Evidently not. I have been plain enough with him. In the interests of the cause I have spared him little. It has merely made me another enemy. Merely stiffened him in his mulish obstinacy. So, in spite of all, we march on this fool's errand; and God alone knows what will happen at Quiberon on Friday if we fail, as seems now inevitable, to be at our post.'

To comfort his distress she argued that to miss a victory was not necessarily to sustain a defeat. She reminded him that once the men at Coëtlegon were reunited with those who had followed Constant, they would be in strength to make themselves felt wherever needed. These were but the arguments that had opposed him in the council. That he permitted himself to take heart from them now served to show how the identity of an advocate may bear upon a plea.

'That, indeed,' he admitted, 'is all that can be said for what we do. Be it as it may, I have done all that was possible to a man in my place.'

'More,' she assured him. 'Much more. But for you the Royalist hopes would have been wrecked at La Prevalaye. The King shall come to know that he has had no more faithful servant than you. You,' she rallied him, 'who profess yourself without sentimental attachment to his cause.'

'That has been changed. Because I love you, I must love where you love.'

'As I must; and, therefore, hate where you hate. The shelter of Coëtlegon begins to stifle me. We must go. I must persuade my aunt to leave at once.'

This was to make him regret his frankness. 'To go whither?' he asked her.

Her eyes widened in sudden misgiving. Then, 'Back to Grands Chesnes, I suppose,' she said, but without conviction.

'You know that cannot be. Here in Madame de Bellanger's protection you are safe. Will you cast yourself into danger because she is what she is? There is no reason in that. Remain here until this time of trouble ends.'

'Knowing what I know? Despising her as I must? Practising a shameful opportunism?'

'There is no shame in using evil for purposes of good. Take advantage of that which it is beyond your power to mend or alter. Take advantage of it for my sake. I must know you safe. Do not add uncertainty and fear for you to what else my mind must bear.'

The disdain in which she had spoken fell from her. Her lip trembled. 'You'll never ask me to do anything more hateful, Quentin.'

'I shall never, I hope, ask you to do anything hateful once this nightmare is at an end.'

Across the hall Madame de Chesnières charged down upon the corner which they occupied. Her pale eyes were magnified behind the lorgnettes through which she surveyed them; her lipless mouth was tight.

'Ah, Monsieur de Morlaix!' Whether this was greeting, comment, or dismissal none could have told. 'Germaine, I have been seeking you everywhere. I shall go mad, I think. After all that I have suffered, after all the terrors of this dreadful day, I am deprived of my room, asked to share a cupboard in the attic with Madame du Grégo and Madame du Parc. It will kill me. A woman of my years!'

'Your room will have been taken for the wounded,'

Germaine patiently explained. 'There are so many of them. Poor unfortunates. And they suffer so.'

'Yes. Yes. But I? Do I not suffer? Is there to be no consideration ever for me?'

'It's an inconsiderate world, madame,' said Quentin, bowing, and so departed.

She stared after him through her levelled lorgnettes. 'Do you suppose, Germaine, he meant to be impertinent? I often suspect it in that young man. I never like the friends you choose. At your age mine were chosen for me. Alas! This Revolution has destroyed all the decencies of life. Where will it all end? I warn you that I cannot endure much more. I say so frankly. I wish that we had never left England. Better its fogs and mud and crudities than the life that we lead here. France is not fit for gentlefolk. Constant must arrange for our return to London. And now I hear these soldiers will be leaving us tomorrow. We shall be defenceless then; at the mercy of the *canaille*. It is all intolerable.' She was in tears.

'The Republicans did not trouble us before the Chouans came. Why should we be troubled when they're gone?' Germaine spoke with a tinge of bitterness that went unnoticed.

'But how can we stay here, in a house that has become a hospital?'

'We can tend those who remain, madame, and pray for the safety of those who go to fight our battles.'

Those prayers were to be needed by the weary men who set out at noon upon the morrow. Scarcely rested from the sad labours of the night, following upon their day of battle, it was demanded of them that they march. But for the spur of hunger and the knowledge that Coëtlegon was a platter they had licked clean already, it is unlikely that any power would have moved them. Their deceptively ready obedience was due to the urgency of finding food.

Over ten miles of empty moorland, in the torrid July heat, they dragged themselves to Josselin, leaving a trail of discarded red coats and stout English shoes to mark their passage.

Upon Josselin they came down late in the afternoon like a swarm of locusts. The place received them with apathy. It had undergone occupation, now by one, now by the other army, in the course of this internecine war. It had learnt the dismal lesson that the line of least resistance was the line of least suffering.

The famished Chouans fed greedily, drank copiously, and, relaxing in repletion and drunkenness, refused to budge another yard that day. Thus perished the last hope of those few who still remembered to what they were engaged.

And so the dawn of the sixteenth, which should have been so fateful to the Royalist fortunes, saw these men, whose post was on Hoche's rear, awakening from their drunken slumbers forty miles and more from the scene of action.

Quentin, watching the daybreak from a window of the house in which he was lodged with Cadoudal, heard in imagination the guns that would be opening Puisaye's confident attack upon Sainte-Barbe, beheld in imagination the ebbing of that high confidence, the angry increase of doubt, the despairing realization that Tinténiac's division was not at the post of duty, and, finally, the suspension of operations and the mortified retreat. Or, it was possible that Puisaye persisted, especially if the expedition under Sombreuil had arrived, and that thus reinforced he was able to defeat Hoche, and open the way into friendly Brittany. This, however, was too desperate a hope to mitigate his dejection.

The morning was well advanced before an orderly officer from Bellanger came to require Cadoudal to sound the assembly, and it was almost noon before they trailed out of Josselin, to resume the march upon Rédon, a march now purposeless and futile.

Progress was slow. The Chouans were sullen and depressed, as if sensing the uncertainty of their leaders, asking themselves to what purpose were they being trailed hither and thither in this fashion. Only the activity of their three chiefs, Cadoudal, Saint-Regent, and Guillemot, prevented a mutiny that would probably have begun in a massacre of the Loyal Emigrant. Instead the Chouans avenged themselves by being in their turn derisory of their supercilious associates. Lacking the stout resilience of the peasants and the hardening which in these guerrilla years they had undergone, the *émigrés* began to show signs of exhaustion at the end of a few miles, and to retard the progress of the whole. The Chouans jeered at them for women who should have stayed at the spinning-wheel, and left soldiering to men.

Quentin and the other officers who were now mounted rode to and fro along the struggling ranks, labouring to prevent open strife from embittering further the misery of that march.

At Malestroit, where they paused to forage, La Marche declared roundly to Bellanger that the Loyal Emigrant could go no farther that day.

'What, then, is to be done? We're still eight miles from Rédon. What is to be done?' Bellanger looked at those who were with him.

'It is of no consequence,' Quentin sourly told him.

'How? Of no consequence?'

'Nothing that you may do now can be worse than what you've done.'

'You are insolent. Insubordinate. I warn you that I will not suffer much more of it.'

'That also is of no consequence.'

'Very well, sir. It is very well. We shall see. Meanwhile, Captain de La Marche, if you are satisfied that the men of the Loyal Emigrant are too weary to go farther, you may quarter them here. I leave you in charge of the company. You will follow to Rédon by way of Peillac as soon as you are able. Cadoudal, you will appoint a half-dozen men you can trust to remain and act as guides.'

Cadoudal gave an ill-humoured assent, and Bellanger disdained to return to the matter of Quentin's insubordination.

The remainder being refreshed, the march was resumed, and with a half-dozen officers of the Loyal Emigrant who refused to be left behind, they came in

the summer dusk to the uncouth village of Peillac, where
they devoured bread and meat and guzzled the wine and
cider of the villagers with the careless vigour of
famished men. There, within a dozen miles of Rédon,
they sought news of Monsieur de Charette and his
Vendéans; but sought it in vain. At first the villagers
had spoken of an army moving in the district, which
had passed through Peillac two days ago, but it soon
became plain that this was the Chouan force under
Constant de Chesnières. And so, at long last, Bellanger's obstinate belief in the Vendéans began to break
down.

'If you should prove to have been right, Monsieur de
Morlaix?' he asked in his growing dismay.

'None will forgive you,' Quentin assured him.

'But the information was so precise.'

Quentin was in no mood for mercy. 'So were the
orders under which we should have been at Plouharnel
this morning.'

'Name of God! Why harp on that?'

'I understood you to ask my opinion.'

'That is not an opinion. It is a reproach; an impertinence.' His glance appealed for support to La Houssaye, who sat with them in the mean room of Peillac's
best house.

La Houssaye did not respond at all in the manner
that was desired. He wagged his big head in sorrow. 'It
begins to appear that we have been grievously misled.
It would certainly have been wiser to have kept to the
orders. Then none could have blamed you, whatever
happened.'

This was too much for Bellanger. After an amazed
pause, he bounded up. 'And that is all you have to say
to me! God of God! After urging me—you and La
Marche—to decide upon this step.'

'By your leave, Vicomte. We did not urge it. We
deferred to your plain wishes.'

'Do you think that subtlety will excuse you?'

La Houssaye bridled. 'I am not subtle, and I need
no excuse. I was not in command.'

'I see. I see.' Bellanger strode furiously about the

narrow room. 'I am to be flung to the wolves, am I? The responsibility was all mine, only mine, was it?'

'So I understood you to say, monsieur, at Coëtlegon.'

Cadoudal got heavily to his feet. 'This does not concern me. And I hate all quarrels but my own. Besides, I'm sick of the sound of your voices. I'll leave you, gentlemen, to your altercation.'

He stamped out of the hovel.

'You do not want me either,' said Quentin. 'And I am much of his mind.' And he, too, went out.

In the heat of his argument with La Houssaye, Bellanger scarcely heeded their departure.

So far, however, the Vicomte perceived only the shadow of the trouble that was in store for him. The substance of it overtook him on the following morning, whilst they were breaking their fast before taking the road again. He sat with La Houssaye and Quentin over a frugal meal that was being consumed in silence. They were not loving one another that morning.

To enliven their dullness the door was suddenly flung wide, and Constant de Chesnières stood on the threshold, looking in his swarthiness and wrath like an incarnation of the spirit of evil.

'Why are you here, you fools?' was his greeting.

Bellanger sprang up in amazement. 'Constant!' he cried. 'And the Vendéans?'

'The Vendéans?' Constant laughed unpleasantly. He came forward, leaving the door wide. 'They're south of the Loire, I suppose. A hundred miles or more away.'

'You mean that they retired from Rédon?'

'I mean that they were never there. Faith, Monsieur de Morlaix, you have been proved right.' He made the acknowledgment in bitterness, with a curling lip. 'We have been cheated by a foul piece of treachery. It aimed at dividing our forces, so that Grouchy might deal with us separately.'

Bellanger perceived here a spirit whose arrogance demanded a curb. He mantled himself in his loftiest manner. 'It is fortunate that your untimely heroics did not attract more men to join you in mutiny, or else we should have been in poor case to give Grouchy the warm welcome he received from us.'

For a spell Constant glared, speechless. Then his words came in a foaming spate; and the first of them betrayed the panic that was at the root of his wrath. 'God's Blood! I may be broke for this, or shot as Tinténiac threatened me. For I come back worse than if I had been defeated. My men have deserted. In disgust of the deceit that victimized us, they've just melted away: gone back to their harvests or to the devil. I have not three hundred left of the three thousand that followed me from Coëtlegon; and these are homeless bandit rogues who don't care where they go so long as they can plunder. That gives you the measure of my case. But, as I live, at least I had looked to you to stand by me now, as you stood by me when I proposed to go to the aid of those we were falsely told lay at Grouchy's mercy.'

'I stood by you?' Bellanger was flushed. 'Monsieur, I find myself with enough to answer for without that.'

'Would you have the audacity to deny it? And before these gentlemen who heard you? Here's baseness.'

'Monsieur!'

'Don't mouth at me, Bellanger.' Constant's livid face was convulsed with passion. He flung about the room, his breathing noisy. 'What the devil are you, then? Are you merely a fool? Noisy as a drum and just as empty of all but wind? Or are you the partner in treachery of your strumpet wife?'

Quentin sucked in his breath. Constant had discovered more, it seemed, at Rédon than the absence of Charette.

'My God, Chesnières, you are out of yourself,' La Houssaye protested, shocked. 'These words!'

'Let that silly cuckold answer them.'

'Oh, I shall answer you.' Even in that dreadful moment, Bellanger contrived to retain something of his histrionic manner. His face might be the colour of clay, but with head thrown back, his dark, velvety eyes under frowning brows were steady. 'You will realize, gentlemen, that for abuse so foul there is no answer in words. Monsieur de La Houssaye, have the complacency to perceive that I need a friend.'

Quentin rose and stood suddenly forward. 'Messieurs, it is not right, indeed most wrong, that you should engage in such a quarrel.'

Constant turned the blast of his wrath upon him. 'Ha! And now we're to have Monsieur de Carabas upon the code of honour. It's natural you should stand by this antlered imbecile. Birds of a feather. Impostors both. In his need of a friend I wonder he should not have called upon you.'

Quentin added to that madman's fury by a look of commiseration. 'For so poor a swordsman, sir, you have too rich a tongue.'

'I'm swordsman enough to meet a man who cannot answer me save with the sword.'

'Rant your fill,' said Bellanger. 'Rant your fill. The reckoning follows.'

'Bah! You shelter your villainy and your cuckoldhood in that. You cannot even deny it.'

'Deny what, sir, in God's name?'

'That your wife, the mistress of this Hoche, a stableman turned general, spread this snare for us so as to wreck the purpose for which we were sent from Quiberon. If you deny it I shall have the charity to believe that at least you are not her partner, but her victim like the rest of us.'

'There are things, sir, that dignity does not permit one to deny.'

'A cuckold's dignity! God save us!'

'*Sortons*,' said Bellanger. 'Let us go.'

But Quentin intervened again. 'A moment. Before you do this, Monsieur de Bellanger, you must know the quarrel you engage in. You are both dupes of this woman's treachery, and of the two it is you, Monsieur de Bellanger, who are doubly betrayed. How, then, can this be a cause of quarrel between you?'

The three of them were staring at him in different degrees of appalled surprise. 'It seems, then,' said Bellanger at last, 'that I am to have two of you on my hands.'

Quentin shook his head. 'There are several things for which I could kill you, Monsieur de Bellanger. But because your wife betrays you is not one of them. I will not meet you on such grounds.'

'On what grounds, then?'

'On none. I am in no need to prove my courage, and I should prove it as little by killing you as you will prove your wife's chastity by meeting Monsieur de Chesnières. Let us be serious.'

'You conceive that hitherto we have jested?'

'Carry your minds back to the council we held at Coëtlegon. I gave you then every hint I could that we were being betrayed. You derided me when I said that you would find the proof at Rédon, when I insisted that the Vendéans did not exist. You have found the proof, I think.'

'Proof of what?' Bellanger retorted. 'That my wife herself was duped if you will; but no proof that she duped us.'

'You forget the groom who brought the appeal for help. When I told you what I knew, you refused to investigate.'

'Of course he would,' sneered Constant, 'and the motive's plain.' Thus, in his blind rage, he smote at reason as it began feebly to raise its head.

Bellanger vowed that he would hear no more, and Quentin abandoned the effort to stem the evil course of things.

Outside they found the little square thronged and noisy. The three hundred who had come back with Constant were hemmed in by a seething, questioning mob.

Cadoudal, sweating profusely in the heat and mopping himself, met them almost on the doorstep.

'A fine consummation, sirs,' he mocked. 'To hold my men together after this will be like holding water in my two hands. Devil take me! It would have been better for all of us had you remained in England.'

Quentin drew him aside, and in a dozen words told

him what was afoot. He was not sympathetic.

'Excellent,' he said. 'Let them cut each other's throats by all means. A pity they did not begin sooner.'

Constant had found a friend in a Monsieur de Lantivy, of the Loyal Emigrant, and with Cadoudal clinging to Quentin, so as to see the sport, as he expressed it, the little group slipped out of the village unobserved. They found a quiet spot in a meadow watered by a brook that flowed to join the Arz. There in shirts and breeches, in blazing sunshine under the summer sky that was a dome of polished steel, the two men whose folly was chiefly responsible for the miscarriage of the expedition faced each other sword in hand.

It was a short engagement, surprising to Quentin in its result. Men of equal height and reach and vigour, Constant was cramped by natural clumsiness, and Bellanger incomparably the better swordsman. Yet whether his rage—a rage that may have been mingled with tormenting doubts—obscured his mind and wove a trammel for his limbs, or whether a streak of cowardice under all his bombast now made him falter, his blundering opponent ran him through within a few moments of engaging.

Thus, in the flower of his age, that rash, foolish man perished in defence of the honour of a faithless woman whose name was destined soon to become a byword for harlotry.

CHAPTER 8

❧❧❧❧

The Disaster

'HE WAS a fool to meet you,' was the rough comment of Cadoudal to Monsieur de Chesnières.

Constant sneered brutally. His success against a man held in some repute as a swordsman had gone to his head a little. 'I left him no choice,' was his vaunt.

'Indeed you did. But he was too much of a fool to perceive it. The Chevalier de Tinténiac promised you a court-martial for your insubordination. As the Chevalier's successor, Monsieur de Bellanger should have ordered your arrest and had you shot. It's what I should have done in his place. But, to be sure, I'm no fine gentleman with an oversensitive honour and a withered reason. And now the gentlemen of the Loyal Emigrant have elected you to succeed your victim. My faith, it rounds off the mockery.'

That is what had happened. The group of officers of the Loyal Emigrant who were with them had invited La Houssaye to assume command. La Houssaye, however, appalled by the disastrous shape that things had assumed, definitely declined the responsibility. After that, and in the absence of La Marche, their choice had fallen upon Chesnières, perhaps because they believed that, like Tinténiac, he was of influence with the Chouans.

Quite readily Constant had consented, and appointed his staff: La Houssaye, Lantivy, who had acted as his second, and Saint-Regent in the place of Cadoudal, who refused to serve under the new commander. La Marche was to be included when he rejoined with the main body of the Loyal Emigrant, left at Malestroit. Quentin, who more than any other now was to be regarded as Puisaye's representative, found himself excluded, and was content.

'Are there many more fools in your family like this cousin of yours?' Cadoudal asked him. 'To take command after what he's done to ruin the enterprise is to challenge fate. I'ld not willingly stand in his shoes when he comes to meet the Comte Joseph. Meanwhile, whether I march with him at all will depend upon whither he marches. The temper of my lads grows sour. They'll be led on no more fool's errands.'

The new commander's decision, however, was to make their way back to the army at Quiberon.

'The last decision I had expected from him,' Cadoudal commented, 'because there's sense in it.'

Upon that return journey they set out next morning, and at Malestroit they came up with the *émigrés* who had turned faint there. By evening of that Sunday, they were back to Josselin. The town, which had not yet recovered from the effects of their last passage through it, gave them a cool welcome, and seemed almost eager to present them with some ugly rumours.

News had come of a great battle two days ago at Quiberon, in which the Royal and Catholic Army had been routed. Confirmation followed on the Monday morning before they left. Yet they resisted belief. The Royalist attack had failed as a result of the lack of Tinténiac's simultaneous action. But they clung fiercely to the hope that this failure had been magnified by the tongue of rumour. That the Royal Army could have suffered the reported destruction was not to be believed.

Some of the Chouans, however, chose to believe it, and refused to go farther. They had been cheated, betrayed, ill-led, and treated with scorn by those whose betters they had come to fight. They had endured enough. The harvest was calling them, and they would go.

The end of it was that when that evening Constant rode up the avenue of Coëtlegon, where they were again to make halt, he was followed by no more than two thousand men, all that remained of the ten thousand that Tinténiac had brought there a week ago.

To Constant's vexation, the Vicomtesse was no longer at her château, and when he angrily demanded whither she had gone, only Quentin's bitter mockery supplied an answer.

'Seek her in Hoche's camp.'

In his disappointed vindictiveness, he does not appear to have been greatly concerned by the fact that his mother and cousin had also departed with the rest.

For there were no ladies now to greet them at Coëtlegon, to feast them and to languish for them. The château was abandoned by all save those wounded whose hurts were too grave to admit of their being moved, and some peasant folk who out of the charity of their hearts had come to nurse them.

Instead, they found there a half-dozen fugitives from Quiberon, officers of the Royal Louis, whom a Captain de Guernissac—a distant kinsman of the Grégos—had conducted thither into hiding.

They told a dreadful tale.

Even when d'Hervilly, realizing the dangerous situation into which his obstinate policy had brought them, consented to the adoption of Puisaye's plan, he still must be asserting himself by interfering with its execution. On the evening of the fifteenth, when preparations for the morrow's action were being concluded, the sails of Sombreuil's expedition appeared on the horizon. The five *émigrés* regiments that Sombreuil was known to bring represented at such a moment the most opportune of reinforcements. Yet d'Hervilly, in the madness of those whom the gods have vowed to destruction, would not consent that they be awaited. They could not disembark until the morrow, and that was the day for the dawn of which the attack upon Hoche was planned. Puisaye, waiting this timely arrival as an eleventh-hour gift from the merciful gods for their salvation, strenuously urged a twenty-four hours' postponement. As strenuously d'Hervilly opposed it, on the ground that Tinténiac's division would be due to attack from Plouharnel. Puisaye argued in the first place that Tinténiac's orders were not to stir until he heard the guns, in the second that if anything should have happened to delay or hinder Tinténiac, Sombreuil's division would so swell their strength that the Chevalier's absence would no longer cripple them. D'Hervilly, however, in a crowning act of folly, would not yield. Asserting for the last time his usurped authority of Commander-in-Chief, he insisted that the attack be carried out as originally planned.

For his further interference with the tactics of it he paid with his foolish life. He fell when an *émigré* regiment which he had ordered forward was annihilated by a gale of fire from four of Hoche's batteries.

The irony of it lay in that at the very moment that the last dispositions he had made procured his own death and ensured the ruin of the Royal Army, Sombreuil was casting anchor in the bay, bearer at last of clear instructions from the British Government. In these it was made definite that the British support had been given only on the clear understanding that the supreme command should be in the hands of the Comte de Puisaye. D'Hervilly was required to understand that his authority was straitly limited to the *émigrés* regiments, and he was ordered to take Monsieur de Puisaye's commands for all operations and in all matters concerned with general policy.

Had these definite orders reached Quiberon some twenty-four hours earlier, the situation might yet have been saved. When they arrived, death had already placed d'Hervilly beyond the necessity of answering for the disastrous presumption, the very last act of which had been one of the main factors in the Royalist ruin. The other had been the absence of Tinténiac from Hoche's rear.

Routed and hurled back behind Penthièvre, the demoralized Royalists had been driven thence again under the hammer blows of the Republicans.

Sombreuil and his five regiments, one of which was commanded by Armand de Chesnières, landing to support an army that had all but ceased to exist, found the

Peninsula of Quiberon become little better than a hospital. Caught in that *cul-de-sac* and constrained to own defeat, they capitulated to Hoche, and the Royal and Catholic Army of Puisaye's creation, upon which such high, confident hopes had been justifiably founded, ceased to exist.

With this dreadful tale those fugitives came to deepen the despair in which the remains of Tinténiac's division had staggered back to Coëtlegon. But it was hardly told in those terms; for Guernissac, like most of the *émigrés,* was a partisan of d'Hervilly, and hostile to Puisaye. So that when Cadoudal, who was of the audience, in a voice broken by grief, desired news of the fate of the Comte Joseph, Guernissac let loose his venom.

'Puisaye? The craven scoundrel was amongst the first to save his skin.'

'You lie,' said a voice that produced by those two words a dreadful silence.

'Who spoke?' blazed Guernissac.

Quentin stood forward. 'I did. I have some acquaintance with the man you defame.'

Constant intervened ferociously. The events had not improved his temper or his manners. 'Is it you again? Listen to me, you rascal, and understand. I am in command here, and I'll have no brawling. I'll make my authority respected. I've still power enough to place you under arrest if you attempt disturbances.'

'I wonder if you have,' put in Cadoudal. 'There are a few lads of mine who'll share Monsieur le Marquis' opinion, and at need defend it. The Comte Joseph's honour is not to be blown upon by any pimp who thinks himself a soldier. To hell with your scowls, my lad! They don't frighten me. I am Georges Cadoudal. If Monsieur de Puisaye is not master of Brittany today, if the army which only he could have raised is not victorious, it is because of the interference of such energumens as you, Chesnières, as d'Hervilly, as Bellanger and the rest of you strutting, posturing jackanapes.' He looked fiercely at Guernissac. 'Don't let me hear you adding lying calumny to the havoc your kind has made.'

'Calumny!' Guernissac was white to his thin lips. A tempestuous Gascon, lithely vigorous and swarthy as a Spaniard, he was quivering with anger. 'My man, I talk of what I know, of what I've seen. As these others.' His sweeping gesture embraced his fellow fugitives. 'Let me tell you of this precious Comte Joseph of yours. When all was in jeopardy and Quiberon a shambles, that poltroon abandoned us. He took a boat and fled to safety aboard one of the English ships. In his absence it was left for Sombreuil and Armand de Chesnières and some others to settle with Hoche the terms of the capitulation. Will you justify that desertion?'

'Justify it? I don't believe it.'

Then another officer, a middle-aged man named Dumanoir, took up the invective. 'We tell you that we saw it. Justified, it certainly can't be. But it can be explained. This traitor is in the pay of England; and England desires only the ruin of France. We all know that now. Why else should this sometime Republican have been supported by Pitt, who had refused to listen to the proposals of better men?'

'There were no better men,' Quentin answered him. 'Those others who went to Pitt had no proposals. They merely whined appeals.'

'So his friends may say. But when all is known, it will be seen that the perfidious Pitt employed him just so that our ruin might be accomplished.'

'You mean that until all is known, this fantastic falsehood is what you will choose to believe. It does credit to your wit.'

'Bah!' said Cadoudal. 'Let them stew in their nauseous vileness.' He stamped out of the hall, and Quentin, who so fully shared his feelings of disgust, went with him.

Outside Quentin asked him, 'What's to do now, Georges?'

At the moment Cadoudal had no answer for him. But it was not long delayed. The facts supplied it. Coëtlegon being in no case to feed the little army that had come to re-encamp there, it began almost at once to melt away. The greater part of the Chouans slunk off to their husbandry; others, enured by now to a life of banditry, sought again their forest lairs. Of the latter was Cadoudal, with a following of some three hundred men, all that remained him of his Morbihannais. For him there could be no return to civil life. He was so marked and notorious a rebel that to lay down his arms would be tantamount to suicide. He took himself off, with the announced intent to cross the Loire and join Charette, whose Vendéan army continued afoot there.

Quentin, with no notion of going into the Vendée, remained behind with Saint-Regent, who with a bare hundred of his lads lingered at Coëtlegon when all the rest of the Chouans had gone. He was inspired to this by the need to protect and nourish the wounded who still cumbered the château. He organized foraging parties, and it was only thus that the men of the Loyal Emigrant were provided with supplies. In addition, at Quentin's instances, he sent out scouts for news in general and in particular of the ladies of Chesnières. It was chiefly a torment of anxiety on Germaine's account that still retained Quentin at Coëtlegon. Until he knew what had become of her, it was impossible for him to dispose for his own future. But for that he must have quitted a place which on every count had become hateful to him. To the *émigrés* he had been an object of overt hostility ever since his hot defence of Puisaye, and only the fear of his sword kept that hostility circumscribed in its expressions. Feeling himself an outcast in that society, and himself despising it, he avoided it and consorted almost exclusively with Saint-Regent and his men.

As the days passed, the reports that came to Coëtlegon brought no comfort to its tenants.

Sombreuil and his *émigrés,* a long column of prisoners, had been marched in chains to Vannes, where the Representatives Tallien and Bled were dealing with them. These Royalists had capitulated to Hoche with the condition that their lives should be spared. But the politicians refused to ratify what the military had done.

338

They took the view that these men's outlawry as *émigrés* antedated their surrender as prisoners of war. They were being brought in groups to summary trial, and as summarily shot on the warren of Vannes.

One day news came that the venerable old Bishop of Dol and fourteen priests, together with Sombreuil himself, Armand de Chèsnieres, and some of their companions in arms, had been executed in a batch. They heard, too, that some three thousand Chouans had deserted to the Republicans. It was, indeed, the end of all hope, and the unfortunate Royalist remnant at Coëtlegon was brought to perceive that only flight remained.

Still harboured in despair and rage, these two hundred *émigrés* considered their plight.

For Quentin, however, there was relief. The same scout who brought in those grim details of the fusillades was actually the bearer of a letter from Mademoiselle de Chesnières.

In the character of an onion-seller, moving freely through the land, this peasant lad had penetrated as far as Saint-Malo, and there his ceaseless, shrewd inquiries had put him on a trail that led him straight to Madame de Chesnières and her niece. It might hardly have been so easy but that he found them lodged quite openly and under their own names at the house of a baker in the shadow of the square castle.

The hurried scrawl from Germaine of which he was the bearer had brought at once peace and vexation to Quentin's hungry soul.

She wrote of her ineffable relief to learn of his safety, and prayed him to continue to care for and preserve a life upon which her own depended. Next she reassured him on her own score. Passports had been obtained for her aunt and herself, through the interest of General Hoche, and they were at the moment of her writing on the point of boarding a ship for Jersey, whence it would be an easy matter to reach England.

He understood the prudence which omitted all allusion to the military and political tragedy which had overtaken the Royalists, and gave no hint of the channel through which the interest of General Hoche had been enlisted. He guessed it, as she knew he would, and in this lay the pang of vexation that leavened his thankfulness. There is a humiliating sense of meanness in the acceptance of help or service from one whom we despise. Yet this was the course he had himself urged upon Germaine, with his sophistry on the employment of evil in the service of good.

CHAPTER 9

The Court-Martial

QUENTIN sought Constant de Chesnières that same evening with the news of Madame de Chesnières' safety. He was moved by an impulse of kindliness to allay anxieties which he conceived must exist, and to bear tidings that might offer some mitigation of the mourning into which news of his brother's death must have plunged Constant.

Constant was displaying both mentally and physically a steady deterioration since the return to Coëtlegon. Brooding upon the disaster to which his folly had so largely contributed, aimless, without plans for the future or the will to form any, he was drinking heavily, and as a consequence grew daily more overbearing and quarrelsome.

He scowled upon Quentin's approach and, scowling, interrupted him at the very outset. 'You have, then, the presumption to correspond with my cousin?'

'We can discuss my presumption afterwards, if you wish. Let my news come first. It concerns madame your mother.'

They were alone together in that library which had

already been the stage of some fateful scenes, a room now dusty and disordered from the neglect and carelessness of its inquilines of these past weeks. The shards of a marble, knocked from its pedestal some days ago, lay where they had fallen on the Aubusson carpet that was stained with muddy footprints. A broken chair, in brocade and gilded wood, of the days of the Fifteenth Louis, hung in drunken collapse bereft of a leg. Books taken from their shelves to beguile the tedium of the *émigrés* lay tumbled where they had been cast by their careless readers. It was a room that presented an epitome of the state of the party of those who had confectioned it. Its erstwhile gracious, fastidious dignity had succumbed to the corruptive forces of misfortune.

Monsieur de Chesnières himself had undergone in his own person some similar dilapidations. Dishevelled, carelessly clad, his long yellow-satin waistcoat unbuttoned and wine-stained, his neckcloth soiled and crumpled, the big swarthy man presented a coarse, debauched appearance.

He leaned against the heavy writing-table, his full, malevolent eyes considering the trim, spare figure before him.

'How does madame my mother concern you?'

'She does not. But I conceive that she may be of some concern to you.' And briskly, so as to be the sooner done, he conveyed his news.

The momentary relief on Constant's face was presently followed by a sneer.

'We are fallen so low, then, as to be in the debt of a harlot for our lives.'

'Your mother's safety should be of more importance than the means by which she procures it.'

'Oh! You are to instruct me?' There was an ominous lift of the thick black brows. 'You would not perceive the presumption. It's no matter. I am obliged to you, sir, for the tidings, although there may be much that does not commend them.'

Quentin smiled. 'There is also so much about me

that does not commend itself that you will be relieved to hear that I am leaving Coëtlegon tonight.'

Constant's eyes opened in surprise, then gradually their expression became dark with malevolence. 'By whose leave, sir?'

'Leave! Is leave still necessary?'

'Do you pretend to forget that I command here?'

There was in this no new note to take Quentin by surprise. For days past Constant had been ranting on the subject of his authority, and becoming the more insistent upon it in a measure as it dwindled by the natural processes of disruption.

'That,' said Quentin placidly, 'is merely tiresome. What remains to command? A pack of fugitives?'

'You choose to be offensive. It will not serve. You do not help yourself.'

Seeing no profit in pursuing the discussion, Quentin shrugged, turned, and walked out of the room. But Constant went after him, as if in pursuit of a prey about to escape, and overtaking him just beyond the door, laid an arresting hand upon his shoulder.

A group of officers lounged dismally in talk at the far end of the hall. Three or four convalescents made another group on a bench near the main doors.

'I will remind you,' Constant was shouting, 'that insubordination in a soldier is a serious offence.'

But Quentin mocked him. 'Faith! I did not suspect that you realized it. Shall we be sensible?' He shook the hand from his shoulder. 'This wreckage of what was once an army is daily going to pieces. It is an army no longer, the *sauve qui peut* has sounded, and it is idle to pretend that any authority remains.'

'You will not find it idle. I will tolerate neither desertion nor insubordination.'

'Bah! You want to laugh.'

'By God! Must I order your arrest to show you that I'm serious?'

Quentin looked at him for a silent moment, steadily meeting the malevolence of his glance. 'Please be frank with me. What is the purpose of this comedy?'

'You'll find it no comedy, you impostor; you bastard!'

For just one second, Quentin, who took such pride in his ability to maintain calm under any provocation, completely lost control of himself. With the next heartbeat he recovered it. But by then the mischief was done. In that one blind, volcanic second, he had struck so hard a blow across Constant's face that, taken unawares and perhaps off his balance, Constant had gone over backwards, and lay stretched upon the floor.

Quentin stood over him, a smile on his white face. 'It was overdue,' he said. 'I have been curbing myself ever since I met you, Monsieur de Chesnières. But now that it has happened, I think that we shall have to go through with it.'

He had not heeded the quick approaching steps behind him, bringing the startled officers at speed from the far side of the hall.

'Yes.' Constant was gathering himself together. His tone was a snarl. 'You will certainly have to go through with it.' He stood up, displaying in a bruised countenance eyes of evil, mocking exultation that alone might have warned Quentin of what was about to follow. He addressed the officers. 'Messieurs, you arrive most opportunely. Monsieur de La Marche, be good enough to place Monsieur de Morlaix under arrest.'

La Marche, who held Quentin in no affection, was promptly obedient.

'Your sword, sir.'

Quentin stepped back, his face momentarily blank. 'Arrest me?' Then he laughed. 'This is fantastic. My quarrel with Monsieur de Chesnières is not only a personal affair, it is an old one.'

'A personal affair?' Above the eyes, whose exultation was maintained, the heavy brows were raised. 'I should be happy so to regard it. But that would make an end to all discipline. You'll not be ignorant of the consequences of striking a superior officer. There is no lack of witnesses. So the matter need not keep us long.'

Quentin's hand went by instinct to his sword. Instantly La Marche and another officer, named Du Cressol, laid hands upon him. Feeling himself firmly held, he wasted no strength in a futile struggle. Whilst these two retained their grasp, a third came to unbuckle his belt, and remove it with his sword.

Constant spoke softly. 'You have long curbed yourself, you say. So have I, with the patience of one who knew that sooner or later your insolence would overreach itself.'

'And,' added Quentin, 'with the guile of the coward who pursues through agents the gratification of his private rancour.'

Constant ignored the taunt. 'If you will come with me, messieurs, we will deal with this at once.'

He turned, re-entered the library, and went slowly to take his stand beside the writing-table, whilst the others followed with Quentin in their hostile midst. There were six of them in all, besides Constant himself: La Marche, La Houssaye, Dumanoir, that elderly warrior, Major de Maisonfort, Guernissac, and a youngster of subaltern rank.

'There are enough of us for a court-martial,' Constant announced, at which Quentin laughed. 'And since all of you were witnesses of the assault with which I have to charge the prisoner, the matter is simple. If you will preside, Monsieur de La Houssaye, we will dispose of it without waste of time.'

Quentin's air remained one of scornful amusement, although he had by now no illusions on the score of the trap into which he had stepped. Himself, he had supplied Constant with the means to settle the old account between them. He realized, too, his danger from the general hostility of these officers who were to form this mock court-martial, and do the will of this man who had pursued him with an enmity as relentless as it had been sly. Yet, having broken out of other snares as deadly that Constant had laid for him, he could not yet believe that he would not break out of this one.

Looking keenly about him in the silence that followed Constant's invitation to La Houssaye, he perceived that, saving perhaps La Marche and Guernissac, these men were actually startled by the service required of them. Whatever their hostility to Quentin, the code by which they governed their lives made them regard this primarily as an affair between gentlemen, for the settlement of which a gentleman should scorn to make use of his position, especially when that position was as indefinite as Constant's had been rendered by the events.

La Houssaye expressed more than his own stiff mind when after a pause he asked: 'Do I understand, Monsieur de Chesnières, that you make the blow that was struck a matter for a court-martial?'

Constant frowned upon him. 'I thought I made it clear.'

The little man's big face had lengthened. He still hesitated. 'Permit me to ask, monsieur, the nature of the quarrel in which he struck you.'

'What has that to do with it?'

'Something, I think. If the blow was struck in the course of a quarrel on personal grounds . . .'

He was harshly interrupted. 'I do not quarrel with my subordinates, sir. But since you ask, I must tell you that the matter was nowise personal. Monsieur de Morlaix was insubordinate. He had announced to me his intention to depart from Coëtlegon. When I refused him leave, and warned him that if he dared to go without it I should hold him guilty of desertion, he aggravated his mutinous conduct by striking me as you all saw.'

'Ah!' La Houssaye inclined his head. 'In that case I am at your orders.' He went to take his seat at the writing-table, and signed to the officers present to dispose themselves about him.

Dumanoir alone remained in charge of the prisoner.

Then Quentin, who remained outwardly composed, put a question to the president. 'In this farcical trial that you propose to hold, am I to have a friend? It is usual, I think.'

'Certainly. You may name any one of these gentlemen to act for you.'

'I should prefer the choice to be less circumscribed. I

am within my rights, I believe. I do not recall that I have found any of these gentlemen too friendly.'

'You may name anyone you choose,' La Houssaye conceded.

'I thank you, sir. Perhaps some gentleman will do me the kindness to find Saint-Regent and bring him here.'

Constant reared his head as if he had been struck. 'Saint-Regent? A peasant! That is inadmissible. You will confine yourself to your brother officers of the Loyal Emigrant.'

'I mistrust their brotherliness,' said Quentin placidly. 'By what rule of procedure must I confine my choice to them?'

Under his calm, hard eyes the president shifted uncomfortably. He looked at Constant, standing massively beside him.

'If the prisoner insists, we can hardly refuse. But I trust that he will not. He should have the grace to recognize that the Sieur Saint-Regent, a Chouan, a peasant, is hardly . . . ah . . . fitted to represent a gentleman born before a tribunal of his peers.'

'Of course not,' said Constant.

'A gentleman born, Monsieur le Président. I thank you for the description. But it was precisely for denying me that estate that I knocked Monsieur de Chesnières down, as any of you would have done in my place.'

'Ah, bah!' Constant exclaimed in angry impatience. 'What need for a friend at all, in so plain a case? What advocacy can possibly avail against that blow, witnessed and now admitted? This comedian merely wastes our time. Let us get on.'

'Here's an indecent haste to get me before a firing-party.'

Under the dominance of Constant, La Houssaye gravely shook his head. 'Indeed, sir, there is little to be tried, unless you should deny the remainder of the charge as formulated by our commander: that you proposed to depart, and were insubordinate when denied your leave.'

'If,' said Quentin, 'we are not to observe the ordinary forms of procedure, then this ceases to be a trial, and becomes a mere discussion. Speaking, then, not as an accused, but as one officer to another, Monsieur de La Houssaye, it is the fact that I did Monsieur de Chesnières the civility to inform him of my intention to leave Coëtlegon tonight with Saint-Regent's contingent.'

'Saint-Regent's contingent?' cried Constant. 'You said nothing of that.'

'True. I left it for Saint-Regent himself to tell you or not, as he chose. I confined myself to my own affairs.'

'You admit that when Monsieur de Chesnières refused you leave, you struck him?' asked La Houssaye.

'When he refused. But not because he refused. Because of the offensive terms in which he uttered the refusal.'

Now this gathering, as was to be seen, had been oddly and unpleasantly stirred by the intimation that Saint-Regent was about to withdraw a body of men which the *émigrés* had come to regard as their main shield and protection. The two hundred men remaining them would feel helpless indeed if deprived of the support of the hundred Chouans with Saint-Regent. Moreover, the peculiar tactics of the Chouans and their peculiar knowledge of the country and its fastnesses were things upon which the *émigrés* must count in a last extremity. The general indignation aroused by that threat of desertion was voiced by Guernissac.

'No terms, sir, could be too offensive. You and Saint-Regent are creatures both of that traitor Puisaye, and worthy of him.' With mounting fury the Gascon raged on: 'Rats that desert a doomed ship. Like Puisaye at Quiberon, so you and your brigand associate here make off to safety, leaving those you have betrayed to shift for themselves.'

It was a speech to whip up the passions of these men, and as Quentin looked round, his lip curved in scorn, he perceived the effect it took.

'Those we betrayed? Do you even know what you are saying? How have we betrayed them?'

347

Guernissac replied with violence. 'You betrayed them into following you, you and Cadoudal and this Saint-Regent and the rest of Puisaye's jackals.'

La Marche took up that infamous perversion of the facts, the more eagerly perhaps because he perceived in it a shield for himself and his associates.

'We were removed from Quiberon so that the Royalist forces might be weakened by being divided. That is the betrayal of which we are the victims, we and those others who remained to fall at Quiberon or were massacred in Vannes, whilst Puisaye has fled to England to receive his Judas fee, his price for all the rich French blood that has been spilled.'

Thus the passion stirred by Guernissac spread like a contagion through those present. One after another in varying terms of invective they repeated the substance of that accusation, which originally had been the Gascon's, so that in a moment the very ground of the trial seemed to have shifted. Only La Houssaye held judicially aloof. He let the storm rage on, waiting patiently until it should have spent itself.

Constant sat tight-lipped, content that the venom of the men who formed this haphazard court should ask nothing better than to do his will.

At last, a pause enabled Quentin to make some answer.

'Faith, sirs, this travesty of a tribunal leaves me wondering whether it claims to sit in judgment upon me, or upon the gentlemen who supplied you with the very coats you are wearing.'

That earned him a fresh onslaught, dominated by the elderly Maisonfort.

'Do you rally us with that? Is it because you are so much in that scoundrel Puisaye's secrets that you know the price he has had from that perfidious assassin Pitt to lead us to destruction?'

'The man is half an Englishman himself,' said someone, with the air of advancing a final proof against him.

'Of your charity, sirs,' Quentin protested. 'One charge at a time. At least make up your minds for what offence you are trying me. Is it for being half English, for having been associated with Monsieur de Puisaye, or for having struck the foul-mouthed poltroon who commands you?'

'You are to answer for all,' raged the truculent Guernissac.

La Houssaye beat upon the table in a belated attempt to restore some decency. 'Messieurs! Messieurs! We cannot now concern ourselves with matters on which there is no evidence before us.'

But Guernissac was not so easily silenced on the subject of his obsession. 'Do we lack evidence that Puisaye has sold us or that he was in the pay of England?'

'But, sir, we are not in judgment upon Puisaye. Whatever evidence we possess against him is not evidence against the prisoner.'

'Does this man's close connection with Puisaye count for nothing, his and his Chouan associate's, this fellow Saint-Regent who now proposes to desert us?'

La Houssaye began to show signs of distraction. 'This way, we shall never reach conclusion. We are here to deal with a charge of insubordination and violence.'

'Then why the devil don't you?' cried La Marche. 'What need to waste more time? Send him before a platoon, and have done.'

With political passions at boiling-point, the assent to this was stormily general.

'If you value your own skins, sirs,' said Quentin gently, 'you'll commit no such rashness. My fellow-traitor Saint-Regent and his Chouans might ask an unpleasant account of you for my assassination.'

'Do you reckon upon that?' Constant asked him coldly.

La Houssaye took it up. 'Are you threatening a wholesale mutiny so as to deter us? This, sir, is an aggravation of your offence. We are not to be intimidated in the execution of a clear duty.'

'Bear with him,' mocked Constant. 'It is the only defence he can offer.'

Under Quentin's cool appearance, alarm was stirring. His sense of being trapped increased. He began seriously to fear not merely sentence, but a swift execution before the Chouans could intervene. He assumed—and no doubt correctly—that Constant's aim would be to present Saint-Regent with an accomplished fact, secure in the support of the Loyal Emigrant and in the conviction that whilst Saint-Regent might possibly be reckless of bloodshed to rescue Quentin, he would hardly risk a pitched battle so as to avenge him.

La Houssaye was sternly addressing him. 'You can hardly realize the gravity of your position, or you would not treat the court with levity. If you have anything to say that will mitigate the charge which you do not deny, I offer you a last opportunity of doing so.'

Quentin, still with every appearance of ease, stood supporting himself with both hands on the back of a light chair. He smiled a little as he answered. 'What can I say that would prevail against passions so blind, against malice so determined? I should but waste the breath that I may need for something else. For this, for instance.'

On the word he swung the chair aloft, spun round and hurled it through the window, with a resounding crash of shattered glass. After it he sent a shout delivered with all the strength of his lungs. 'To me! Saint-Regent! To me!'

Then he was struggling in the grip of Dumanoir and La Marche, and a roar of voices filled the room. The young subaltern went to the assistance of the two who strove with him, and amongst them they bore him to the ground.

As he went down under their weight, he was cheered by the reflection that these fools by the noise they made could not fail to draw the attention he desired. Over the shoulder of La Marche, who knelt upon him, he saw that the door was opening. Then on a sudden hush that fell, he heard a voice asking, with a marked Breton accent, 'In the name of God, what is happening here?'

CHAPTER 10

❧❧❧

The Avenger

THE newcomer, a bulky fellow in baggy Breton breeches of soiled linen and green fustian jacket, a red nightcap drawn tight upon his fair hair, displayed to Quentin's amazed eyes the rosy countenance of Georges Cadoudal, whom he imagined miles away.

For a moment of mutual surprise the Chouan stood gazing at the *émigrés,* and they at him. Then Constant heaved himself up in truculence.

'What do you want here? What have you come back for?'

'By Our Lady of Auray! Here's a welcome for a brother-in-arms. What have I come back for? To bring you a visitor.' He turned his head and spoke over his shoulder. 'In here, Monsieur le Comte.'

A brisk step and the jingle of a spur rang on the marble pavement of the hall, and a tall figure in a long black riding-coat came to fill the doorway.

The gentlemen of the Loyal Emigrant looked as if they beheld a ghost. They may have believed they did. For it was the Comte de Puisaye who stood before them; the man so confidently reported to have fled to England. He was followed by Saint-Regent.

He swept off the round black hat that shaded his brows, swept it off with a characteristic flourish and tossed it spinning to a chair. His face now fully disclosed showed grey and haggard. But the commanding haughtiness of its expression had abated nothing. He bowed theatrically.

'*Serviteur,* messieurs!' There was a queer biting mockery in his metallic tone.

He came slowly forward, a riding-switch held across

351

his body in his two gloved hands, and his deep-set eyes pondered the group that sprawled on the floor beneath the window.

'What am I interrupting?' He looked round for an answer, but received none from those men, who continued to stare at him in a sort of awe.

Cadoudal thrust past him. 'Monsieur le Marquis! And was it you, then, who called for help?'

'Don't I look as if I needed it?' The three who had held him fell back before the Chouan's approach, and he sat up. 'Good evening to you, Monsieur de Puisaye. You ask what you are interrupting. You'll hardly believe it from the appearances, but it's a court-martial.' He came to his feet, none hindering him now, and dusted his garments. 'I stand charged with insubordination by gentlemen who certainly understand the crime.'

Puisaye considered them. 'A court-martial. Most opportune. Being assembled, perhaps you will now sit in judgment upon me. I am accused—so I am told by my friend here, Georges Cadoudal—of cowardice and treason.'

He paused there. Dominated by his masterfulness, uneasy under his scorn, not one of them ventured to answer him.

'Well, sirs?' He threw his hands apart in a gesture of submission. 'I am here. Which of you will utter in my presence the indictment with which I understand that you are so free in my absence?'

Then Constant found voice and courage to give the company a lead. 'Why you are at Coëtlegon you know best yourself. But if you think to carry things by insolence, we shall discover your mistake to you.'

'Why I am here? First, to prove by my presence that I have not fled to England, as is stated by loose-tongued liars.'

Here Guernissac, who felt himself directly challenged, made bold to answer him. 'At least you'll not deny that you fled from the fight, that you slunk off like a coward to the English Admiral's flagship. You'll not deny it to me, because I saw you go.'

Puisaye displayed no resentment. 'I went off to Sir

John's flagship, as you say. But not as you suppose.'
And Cadoudal behind him laughed in contempt of the
charge. 'I went off in the discharge of my duty; the
duty of a general to whom all played false. I went off
so as to persuade Sir John to stand in with his ships, in
a last hope that his guns might retrieve, or at least
check, the disaster of the day. And he might well have
done so. A frigate, in fact, did open fire on the Republicans, and was withering their battalions, when once
again the gentlemen of the *noblesse* of France betrayed
me. In contravention of my orders to stand firm, they
entered into a capitulation and sent word of it aboard,
demanding that the fire should cease.'

'That is your tale, is it?' Constant sneered.

'That is my tale. To their own undoing, as the sequel
proves, those gentlemen on Quiberon would no more
take my orders in the hour when I might yet have
saved them than they would take them whilst it was in
my power to lead them to certain and easy victory.'

At this there was some fleering laughter.

'It is in character, I suppose,' he quietly rebuked
them, 'that you should be amused by the consequences
to the King's cause of the incompetence, the ill-will, the
empty vanity, and downright treachery which are the
only qualities of which you gentlemen have given
proof.'

'Have you the effrontery to speak of treachery?'
Constant asked.

Puisaye looked at him, and there was a deadliness in
his cold, steady eyes. 'I have scarcely come to it yet. I
point to the fruits of it. That it has ruined me is
nothing; but'—and suddenly his tone was incisive as
the edge of a knife—'that it should have ruined plans
so long and laboriously laid, plans that I was years in
perfecting, and that it should have rendered null the
invaluable aid that none but I enjoyed the credit to
procure from England, is the tragedy for which the
Monarchy must pay.'

'Is that what you have come here to tell us?' was
Guernissac's truculent question.

'Because if so,' said Constant, 'you waste your time. You do not impress us.'

'Perhaps I shall before all is said. One reason why I am here is to prove to those liars who say that I fled to England that I am still in Brittany. I might have fled. Being aboard Sir John Warren's flagship, I might have returned with him. But there were duties here in France still to be discharged. There were events to be investigated, so that I may render a full account to the British Government should I ever reach England again.'

'That we can well believe,' sneered Constant, and found one or two to sneer with him.

Puisaye left the sneer unheeded. 'I spent five days in Vannes; in the lion's den, as you might say. I was there when Sombreuil paid with his life for the credulous folly of his capitulation. And with him went those others who had prevailed upon him to disregard my orders at the end, as my orders had been disregarded throughout this ill-starred adventure. Your brother, Monsieur de Chesnières, was amongst those whom I saw shot with him. The total of those massacred by the Republican fire on the warren of Vannes amounts, sirs, to some seven hundred.'

It drew a cry of horror from his audience.

'That holocaust impresses you, I see. I hope it brings you—you who are assembled here to sit in judgment upon insubordination—I hope it brings you to reflect upon the dreadful guilt of those who by their insubordination to me, the Commander-in-Chief of the expedition, whether treacherous or just blindly stupid, have procured the shedding of so much good French blood.'

'Who more guilty than yourself?' cried Constant.

'That is what I am here to tell you.'

'That blood cries to Heaven for vengeance,' raved Guernissac.

'To Heaven, no doubt. It cries also to me. Hear me yet a moment, sirs. There are amongst you here some officers of that division which left Quiberon under the Chevalier de Tinténiac, to be on Hoche's rear on the sixteenth at dawn.' He seemed to swell before them now with the just indignation that was in him, and his vibrant voice beat out the words deliberately. 'It was a last attempt to undo what the insubordination of an incompetent fool had done; and but for the failure of your division to keep that engagement it must have succeeded. Instead, to that failure are due the disaster of Quiberon, the rout of the Royal and Catholic Army, and the massacres on the warren of Vannes. What, I ask you, are the deserts of those responsible?'

He dominated them completely. Even the bitter Guernissac quailed under the sweep of a glance that made each of them feel not merely accused but guilty.

He resumed. 'Whilst down there at Quiberon we counted upon you in foolish confidence, you were making merry here in this very house to which you have now returned; like dogs to their vomit.'

There was a mutter of indignation at the insult.

'Don't bay at me,' he thundered back, and so silenced them again. 'Whilst we made ready for action, trusting that loyal to your pledge you would be on your way to take up your positions, you were feasting and dancing and toying with the women brought here by a treacherous harlot to beguile you.'

Here Constant broke through the spell that his just indignation, and their shamed sense of it, was weaving over them. 'I think there has been enough of this. If you know so much you will also know that Tinténiac is dead. It is a vileness to malign him.'

'It is not of Tinténiac that I complain. That was a loyal soul. As loyal as brave. Had he lived, the engagement had been kept.'

'You allude, then, to Bellanger. He, too, is dead.'

'By your hand. I know. And so he cannot answer for his part in his betrayal. But you, Monsieur de Chesnières, remain.'

'I?' Constant's dark eyes widened. He lost some colour.

'Can it be that I surprise you? Was it not your gross insubordination to Tinténiac in marching off with three thousand of his men that weakened the division and laid it open to the Republican attack in which Tinténiac was killed? Did not the events leading to the failure of this division to keep the engagement at Plouharnel follow out of that?'

There was no truculence in Constant now. A sense of peril invaded him, a sudden fear of this dominant man who towered before him like an incarnation of Nemesis. He faltered in glance and tone as he defended himself. 'I was deceived by lies that Charette and his Vendéans were at Rédon beset by Grouchy.'

'What lies could deceive a soldier who knew his duty, who had his orders?'

Constant stiffened. 'I am not to be browbeaten. What I did then I would do again in the like circumstances.'

'Do you dare to say so with the knowledge of an army destroyed and a wholesale massacre at Vannes in consequence of that mutiny?'

'Will you make me responsible for that?' Constant demanded, recovering in heat some of his spirit. 'Will you make me the scapegoat of your treachery and your ineptitude? It will not serve, Monsieur de Puisaye. I am conscious of having acted only as my honour demanded.'

'Honour!' Puisaye echoed, in withering scorn. 'You talk of honour, do you? Honour! Ha! In what do I find you here engaged? Having failed by other means—and you have had recourse to many—to extinguish a life that stands between you and your succession to the Marquisate of Chavaray, you contrive this comedy of a court-martial and employ these poor deluded dupes of yours to do your murder for you.'

There was no single outcry at this from those officers who might well have deemed themselves insulted. They remained mumchance, suddenly stricken by the charge; for it revived acutely their misgivings at the outset, their feeling that the matter was one for personal settlement between the parties, a feeling which had been overlaid and obscured by the political passions Guernissac had stirred up. With a painfully renewed consciousness of this, they looked at Constant, to see how he would receive that formidable accusation.

He stood tense and white, his hands working nervously at his sides. 'On that I give you the lie, sir,' he said. 'And I can prove it. None stands between me and that succession since my brother Armand's death. Certainly not this bastard who pretends himself the son of Bertrand de Chesnières.'

Puisaye's lip curled. 'He can pretend it so successfully that you find it necessary to have him murdered. But you lead me to digress with your talk of honour. My concern is with the military duty in which your failure has wrought such irreparable havoc. For that you must pay, Monsieur de Chesnières. I am here to exact it.'

'Pay!' Constant's face was momentarily blank. Then he masked his fear in bluster. He laughed. 'You hear this ranter, gentlemen, this impudent traitor in the pay of Pitt.'

But that was a pistol from which Puisaye had already shaken the false priming. There was no such response as Constant looked for. The company sat appalled, overawed.

'Leave my sins,' the Count commanded. 'At the proper time and in the proper quarter I will answer for them. At present you will answer to me for yours.'

'I do not answer to you. I am not on my trial.'

'It is perhaps unnecessary. You are already judged and sentenced. You will recall Tinténiac's words to you when you rode mutinously away with the Chouans you had seduced into following you. What were the exact words, Georges?'

Promptly Cadoudal quoted them: ' "If you come back alive, I'll bring you before a court-martial, and have you shot for this." '

That rehearsal had power to drive Constant's fear deep into his soul and to drain the blood from his dark face. But in the next heart-beat, remembering the predominance of his numbers, he took courage in the conviction that the men of the Loyal Emigrant would stand by him, right or wrong, in a trial of strength with

Puisaye. In that thought he recovered all his arrogance.

'You are singularly daring to come hectoring me here,' he said. 'As daring as I have been patient in listening to you. For whatever I may have done, like yourself, I will answer at the proper time and in the proper place.'

'I mean you to do so,' Puisaye answered him, and added: 'That time is now; that place is here.'

'You want to laugh. When I answer it will be to my peers. I do not recognize your authority.'

'There you state precisely your offence; the offence for which some thousands have perished.'

'Look you, Monsieur de Puisaye, there has been enough of this. I must ask you to withdraw and to leave Coëtlegon at once, counting yourself lucky that you are permitted to do so.'

Behind Puisaye Cadoudal loosed a laugh. 'What a cockerel! And how he crows! Name of a name!'

Puisaye took a step forward. 'Monsieur de Chesnières,' he said quietly, 'I have come to Coëtlegon to execute the sentence passed on you by the Chevalier de Tinténiac.'

The shock of this dissolved the spell that Puisaye had woven. There was a sudden stir, some murmurs, and a general rising. La Marche, Dumanoir, and Guernissac closed about Constant as if to protect him, whilst in a quavering, indignant voice La Houssaye expressed the thought of all.

'Monsieur de Puisaye, there is a limit to what we can tolerate from you. Whatever authority you may once have possessed in the Royal and Catholic Army has long since passed from you.' He rose. 'I summon you to depart. I warn you that you linger at your peril.'

An angry rumble followed to announce the gathering of a storm. Puisaye half turned. 'At my peril, Georges!' he exclaimed. He shrugged. 'There is no more to say.'

'It is well for you that you perceive it at last,' cried Guernissac, with a recovery of truculence that was doomed to instant extinction.

Cadoudal had moved to the door. He threw open both wings of it, and to their angry consternation those gentlemen beheld a mob of armed Chouans close-packed in the great hall. To a beckoning sign from him a half-score of them marched in at once.

'There is your man,' Cadoudal told them, pointing to Chesnières.

It produced a fierce clamour of oaths and shouts of 'Betrayal!' and 'Treachery!' Swords flashed out, and the *émigrés* about Constant stood in a posture of defence.

But Cadoudal had now taken charge. 'On your lives,' he admonished them, 'let there be no resistance, or we'll cut him out from amongst you with our bayonets.'

Behind the *émigré* group, Monsieur de Saussure, the subaltern, was opening one of the windows so as to escape, calling to his comrades to hold the brigands whilst he fetched the regiment.

'You'll provoke useless bloodshed,' Cadoudal warned them with phlegm. 'I have brought three hundred of my Morbihannais with me, and there are the men of Saint-Regent. We outnumber your company by two to one.'

Nevertheless, a brief resistance there was, with more Chouans pouring in from the hall to smother it. But for Puisaye's intervention, they would have indulged the ferocity which the foppish insolence of these allies had long since kindled in them. On his injunctions, however, they used the stocks of their muskets instead of the bayonets. The slender rapiers were beaten aside and broken, and whilst one of the Chouans was lightly pinked, there were some bleeding heads among his defenders before Constant was fast in the grip of his captors.

They dragged him, limp and trembling, before Puisaye, who, very tall and straight in his tight black coat, stood aloof from the scrimmage, with Quentin now beside him.

Cold, implacable, contemptuous, the Count waved

the wretched man away. 'You know what is to do, Georges.'

'My God! My God!' Constant was almost screaming in his terror. 'Am I to be murdered, then?' His eyes were wide, his olive tint was of a greenish pallor; the sweat glistened on his shallow brow.

Puisaye was unmoved. 'We have a priest with us,' he said. 'He shall give you the only comfort justice permits us to afford.'

'Justice!' raved the doomed man. 'You beast! You murderer! This is a pretext for your infamy. You butcher me to make succession safe for that bastard impostor there who has been your jackal!' He made a wild appeal to Cadoudal. 'Cadoudal! You at least are honest. Do you make yourself a party to this villainy? You will pay for it if you do, as that rascal will pay. You will be hunted for this by every Frenchman who counts himself a gentleman. Don't think that you'll escape their vengeance if you persist in this.'

'*Finissons!*' was all the answer he had from the Chouan, who waved his men out with their prisoner.

But still he struggled. 'At least hear me first, before you burden your soul with murder. I'll make it plain that this villain wants me murdered in the interest of Morlaix, an impostor who calls himself Marquis de Chavaray, a bastard who would rob me of my heritage. It's the truth, Cadoudal. I swear it in the face of death. In the face of death, do you hear? I can convince you if only you will listen.'

Still raving and struggling, he had reached the door. His late associates, ranged behind a line of Chouans, looked on in impotent rage.

Quentin's hand gripped Puisaye's arm.

Constant's violence, that oath of his, 'in the face of death,' as he had said, had filled him with a sudden fear. It brought him a sudden illumination, cast light for him into depths unsuspected hitherto. He bethought him of the inexplicable circumstances of his upbringing from infancy in England, by a mother in exile who concealed from him his rank and heritage; he recalled how oddly Germaine had begged him not to pursue his

claim to Chavaray, and how she had looked; in
remembering the answer, when he had swung to the
portrait of Bertrand de Chesnières, he was struck for
the first time by the age at which his putative father
had begotten him.

'Wait, sir,' he begged. 'In God's name, wait. Let me
hear what he may have to say. Let him explain himself.'

Puisaye did not move. 'He can explain himself to a
file of muskets.'

'But if it should be the truth that . . .'

'Peace! What have I to do with that?' He spoke in a
thunder of indignation that almost stunned Quentin's
bewildered wits. 'I execute the sentence passed by
Tinténiac. I punish the only one left of those responsible for the ruin of Quiberon.'

Leaving Quentin without an answer to this, he
moved away, stalking deliberately towards the line of
Chouans. Over their heads he spoke to the herded
émigrés.

'Messieurs, there is nothing more for you to do here.
The Loyal Emigrant has ceased to exist. The *sauve-
qui-peut* has sounded. Coëtlegon may at any moment
be invaded by the sansculottes; and after tonight there
will not be a single Chouan here to aid in its defence.
It is for you to scatter and make your way out of
France as best you can. Or you may cross the Loire
and join the army which Monsieur de Charette still
keeps in the field.' He signed to the Chouans to open
their ranks. 'I have no wish to detain you, sirs. You are
at liberty to withdraw.'

He made it plain that it was a command. La Houssaye, however, stood forward with an assumption of stiff
dignity.

'Monsieur de Puisaye, you will have to answer for
what you do in the case of Monsieur de Chesnières if
you persist. I exhort you to . . .'

'You waste your time, sir, and mine. Be thankful
that I am satisfied with Monsieur de Chesnières' expia-
tion, and that I do not deal similarly with those of you
who formed his staff. Be thankful, all of you, that I do

not call you to account for what was doing here when I came; for abetting the pursuit of a private vengeance. Go, sirs.'

La Houssaye pursed his lips, raised his brows, and flung out his arms in a gesture of angry helplessness. Then he led the way out. The others followed him, those who were whole assisting the three who had been damaged in the brief struggle.

CHAPTER 11

Margot's Child

IN THE spacious book-lined room whence all the others had departed, Quentin turned solemn, almost fearful, eyes upon Puisaye.

'Monsieur le Comte, I require to know . . . Are you sending Chesnières before a firing-party because of his dereliction of duty, or because of what was doing here when you arrived?'

Puisaye did not at once reply. His hands behind him, he paced away to the window and back before speaking, and then it was to evade the question. 'Since he deserves death on either count, what matter?'

'You answer too lightly, sir.' White and stern, Quentin's tone was one of reproof.

'Name of God! Why this concern? There have been attempts enough on your life by this Monsieur Constant. There was Boisgelin's, there was Lafont's; and no doubt there were others less apparent. It is time that Chesnières paid.'

From this Quentin took his answer, and it brought a vehemence into his manner. 'You are not required, sir, to pay my debts. I do not tolerate it.'

Puisaye raised his brows. His glance was sardonic.

'Be it so. He is being shot, then, for his insubordination.'

'You say so now. But you persuade me otherwise.'

'I persuade you?'

'Your tone, your attitude; oh, and things that have happened in the past.'

'You mean, of course, the attempts upon your life.'

'I mean other things. Above all what he said just now, swearing it "in the face of death." Would he go before his Maker with a false oath on his lips? Do you think I could tolerate to have this man put to death for my profit?'

'You would prefer him to live for your ruin. Very noble. But I tell you again that he is being shot for insubordination.' Puisaye came closer, and set a friendly hand upon Quentin's shoulder. 'Why torment yourself, child?'

Quentin answered him in dull resentment.

'Because there is so much in all this, so much about my own self, that I do not understand; things of which I have had no more than puzzling glimpses. I am struggling to see the truth behind the hostility of these cousins of mine.'

'Is that so difficult to understand, men being what they are? Chavaray is one of the noblest heritages in France, or will be when normal times return. It is not lightly to be relinquished by men who have always believed themselves heirs to it.'

'Why have they believed that? Didn't they know of my existence?'

'It is possible that they did not.'

'Ah! But only if my mother had concealed it, as she concealed from me that I was heir to Chavaray. Why? Why should a mother conspire to deprive her son of his heritage? I know of one only answer.'

'And that?' Puisaye was suddenly stern.

'Her knowledge that he is not entitled to it. If that were so, then what Constant swore is true. I am an impostor, a Marquis *pour rire,* a Marquis de Carabas, as he named me long ago.'

'Bah! Are you so easily imposed upon by assertion? Have you no evidence in your possession? You possess certificates, of your mother's marriage to Bertrand de Chesnières and of your own birth at Chavaray.'

'If that were all. But there are some facts to set against the documents. My father . . . Bertrand de Chesnières was in his seventy-fourth year when he married my mother, a girl of twenty. It was only seven years later, when he was past eighty, that I was born.'

'And then? You were born in wedlock. Your claim to the marquisate is legally unassailable.'

'Legally, yes. I have been told that that is precisely why the Chesnières assailed it in other ways.'

Puisaye's hand fell away from Quentin's shoulder. He stood back, pondering him from under frowning brows. 'Since when have you harboured such notions as these?'

'Since Constant made oath here before they dragged him out.'

'Pshaw! What is the fellow's oath worth? To what can he swear? To an assumption, a suspicion, like your own. On that assumption these Chesnières would have murdered you in one way or another. And you are so soft-hearted as to find it necessary to justify them, even at the cost of doing so little honour to your mother's memory.'

'Do you know of any reason why my mother should have run away from Chavaray after Bertrand's death, and gone to hide herself and me in England?'

Puisaye may have perceived that the question was rhetorical; but not on that account did he leave it unanswered. 'Name of God! Isn't it plain? To remove you from just such vindictiveness as that which has pursued you since you succeeded to Étienne de Chesnières.'

Quentin stared in surprise. 'That is what you assume?'

'It is what I know. You are to remember that, as I've told you before, I was garrisoned in Angers in those days, and I was intimate with the Lesdiguières.

That is why I took so deep an interest in you, Quentin, when once I had found you. That is why I sought to make a friend of you, or, at least, to be a friend to you. Listen now.'

He turned away, and thereafter as he talked, he paced the room in long, slow steps.

'Old Lesdiguières, who was intendant to the lords of Chavaray, was an ambitious old scoundrel who sacrificed his daughter to his cursed worldliness. The septuagenarian Bertrand de Chesnières, rheumy and gout-ridden, in an expiring flicker of a lasciviousness he had never learnt to curb, cast his bleary eyes upon your mother. Her crafty, vigilant father saw his chance to make a great lady of her. He handled old Bertrand with such villainous astuteness that, to the dismay of the old gentleman's family, they were married.'

Quentin, who had found a chair and sat huddled in it, elbows on knees and his chin in his hands, listened avidly, and missed no accent of the stinging bitterness in which Puisaye spoke, as if this were a tale which he found it impossible to tell dispassionately.

'Considering Étienne's crippled condition, Bertrand's nephew, Gaston de Chesnières, had long regarded himself as the heir. His brother Claude, the father of Germaine de Chesnières, made an eleventh-hour attempt to prevent the marriage. But Bertrand, even in his dotage, was not a man to be thwarted, and there was that old devil Lesdiguières at his elbow, to sustain and guide him.

'Afterwards, Gaston, the father of Armand and Constant, never lost an opportunity of humiliating and slighting the young Marquise. He allowed her to see very clearly what she might expect at his hands when once he should be Marquis of Chavaray and head of the family. For considering Bertrand's age and infirmities, he was at least confident that no issue of that marriage would ever interfere with his succession. When, some seven years later, your birth came to destroy his prospects, he made the country ring with the rage that possessed him. He went in fury to the courts, demanding that they should declare the illegitimacy of the newborn heir. When the courts confessed themselves powerless to interfere, he made appeal to the King. But the result was the same. Infuriated by these rebuffs, he went about vowing openly that he would take for himself the justice that was denied him.

'So far I was a witness of what I tell you. Of the rest I can speak only from what I learnt later and what is easily surmised. For my regiment was ordered overseas, to the Antilles, and I had gone with it. But it needs little imagination to conceive what a time of anguish must have followed for your mother. It endured for four years. Then Bertrand died, and she found herself utterly unprotected; for by then her father, too, was dead. Her terror of what might be done by Gaston and his sons, Armand and Constant, who were then in adolescence, must so completely have broken her spirit that she resolved to carry you beyond their reach and into hiding.'

At a standstill now, he paused there before concluding: 'Their conduct towards you since Étienne's death serves to show that the malevolence that drove her forth has been fully and bitterly alive in the house of Chesnières.'

Silence followed. Puisaye resumed his pacing, mechanically, his face dark with thought, his chin on his breast, as if he were looking physically into that past which his words had evoked. At last Quentin spoke.

'You are singularly well informed.'

'It so happens.'

'And yet there are gaps in the story.'

'Naturally.'

'Will you hear how my imagination fills them?'

The Count wheeled, squarely to face him, his glance keen and searching. Then a wave of his fine hand invited Quentin to proceed.

'When the Marquise, my mother, in those first childless years of her marriage was brought to fear what must happen in a widowhood that could not be long delayed, it might occur to her that her only chance of protection from that rancour, from being cast out, lay in the possession of a child. As a mother of the next heir after Étienne, of the next marquis, she will have supposed that her widowed position would be secure, unassailable.'

There was an interrogative note to his statement; and, having made it, he paused as if for a reply, watching Puisaye.

As none came, he resumed. 'It is not difficult to imagine that she may have had a lover of her own age, one perhaps from whom her father's damnable ambition had separated her. Don't you agree?'

'Proceed, proceed,' he was sharply bidden.

'The child came: the son so ardently desired. But the immediate consequences of his arrival would show her how grievously she had miscalculated. And so, as you have told me, when Bertrand de Chesnières died and she found herself defenceless, she was content to abandon everything for herself and her child, so that she might place him beyond the resentment of the men of Chesnières, whom she had thought so easily to cheat.'

He paused there, his eyes steadily upon Puisaye, who had not moved whilst he had been speaking. 'Do you not think, sir,' he asked, 'that that is how things happened?'

For once he observed signs of faltering in that man of indomitable self-assurance. 'I . . . I think . . . it may have happened somewhat in that fashion.'

Quentin leaned farther forward. Sharp as the crack of a whip came his next question. 'Do you know that it did?'

A deathly pallor gradually overspread the Count's haggard face, and then, as if his will snapped suddenly under stress, the answer came: 'Yes. I know.'

Quentin stood up, and for a long silent moment those two men confronted each other, eye to eye, something of dread in the regard of each. In that moment was resolved for Quentin the puzzle of the haunting elusive likeness presented by Puisaye to some countenance that he had seen. He knew now that it was his own mirror that had shown it to him.

He spoke, and the hoarseness of his voice surprised him. 'You mean, of course, that you are my father.'

Puisaye's countenance contracted as if from a blow. He sucked in his breath, and wrung his hands. 'Ah! God of God!' Then he recovered his poise. He lowered his head, and made a gesture of resignation. 'Impossible to deny it,' he confessed.

Quentin betrayed no excitement. 'It explains many things,' was his cool comment. 'Only the assurance that I was Bertrand de Chesnières' son can have prevented me from suspecting it.'

At that very moment the roar and crash of a volley of musketry made the windows rattle. He started half round. 'What was that?'

Terrible in his resumption of imperturbability, Puisaye answered him. 'The end of the last claimant that stands between you and the Marquisate of Chavaray.'

'My God!' Quentin's eyes were filled with horror. 'Was that why you had him shot? Was it?'

'Believe me, I should not have boggled at it,' the Count answered in cold contempt. 'But it was not necessary. I but executed the sentence passed by Tinténiac. Remember that. The fool has expiated an offence through which some thousands of lives were lost and a great cause has perished.'

'If I could believe you!' Quentin almost wailed in his angry distress. 'If I could believe you! But it will not serve.'

'What the devil is there to trouble you? Mordica! You have had no part in this. Your conscience may sleep in peace. My shoulders are broad enough to bear the burden of it. Be content that there is none now to dispute your title, Monsieur le Marquis.'

'Dare you say that? Dare you mock me with it, knowing that I have no right to it?'

'You are wrong. You have every right. A legal right that no one can dispute, and a moral right, earned by your mother's sufferings.'

Quentin uttered a short, loud laugh. He made a gesture as of thrusting something from him. 'I am the son of the man who has cleared away the last legiti-

mate Chesnières so as to make room for an impostor.
Is that something I could ever forget?' Passionately he
ran on: 'Sir, you would have dealt more fairly by me
had you told me this on that day when first you visited
me in London. You should not have assumed that I
take after my parents. You should have remembered
that it was possible that I might, after all, be honest.'

Puisaye had winced under the bitter taunt. Now an
ironical smile crept to his tight lips.

'I should be proud of you, I suppose. Not only for
this honesty of which you make a boast, but also for
the hardness you display. Fine, manly qualities both.
But is all that has gone to make you Marquis of
Chavaray to be thrown away? Are you not, after all,
lord of Chavaray by right of purchase? Had you forgotten? Or isn't that enough for this incorruptible honesty of yours?'

'Not as long as a Chesnières lives to inherit.' There
was a stern finality in his tone.

Puisaye's brows met over eyes that reflected only
pain. His glance seemed to burn its way into Quentin's
mind. 'Aye! You're an inflexible dog.' Then he
laughed, not without bitterness. He turned aside. 'I was
born, I think, for frustration,' he complained. 'I touch
nothing but it withers; no man has toiled more re-
lentlessly, planned more soundly, fought more daunt-
lessly. Yet in every endeavour of mine there has been
some incalculable adventitious factor to baulk me in
the end.' He resumed his pacing. 'Heart-break has
been my portion, from the day when as a young soldier
at Angers I saw your mother, whom I worshipped,
forced into repulsive nuptials with the senile Chavaray.
Through you I thought to avenge her fate; for it
seemed to me a sweet vengeance to set you back in the
place for which she bore you and from which she was
compelled by fear to remove you. I cherished the
thought that if she looked down on us from heaven, she
would feel herself repaid for her sufferings, and would
bless me with her approval for having played a father's
part by you: for having preserved you, guarded you,
and guided you to that heritage so dearly bought for

you by her. For ever since I so fortuitously discovered you that has been my lodestar. Even tonight, Quentin, my tutelary duty towards you is the main reason of my presence here. The punishment of Constant de Chesnières was no more than incidental. What really brought me was the knowledge of your presence and the hope to serve you whilst the power is still mine. How timely was my coming shows how well I was inspired.'

Quentin hung his head. 'Indeed, indeed, had you not come . . . It is I who would have been the target of that volley.'

'I comfort myself with that, and blame myself for my failure otherwise. I have talked too much, admitted too much. But my senses took me by surprise; my emotions weakened my will; temptation defeated me. For it was beyond my power to resist the temptation to acknowledge myself your father when you claimed me. What would you, Quentin? I am accounted hard. I have so accounted myself. But it has remained for my son to show me how hard a man should really be.'

'God knows you do me wrong, sir.' Quentin's voice almost broke on the words, and what more he would have said was choked in him. He advanced to proffer a hand, and the next moment found himself engulfed and crushed in the embrace of that towering, powerful man.

'Child! Child!' the deep rich voice was sobbing. 'Margot's child!'

CHAPTER 12

The Marchioness of Carabas

ON A MELLOW, hazy afternoon of late September, a post-chaise rattled down Bruton Street, bringing Monsieur Quentin de Morlaix home from his travels.

From the climax which his high adventure may be said to have reached that night at Coëtlegon, it had sped almost uneventfully to its close. For this his thanks were due once again to the tutelary offices of the Comte de Puisaye. Taking advantage of the established chain of communications, now as necessary as ever it had been, owing to renewed Republican activity in the West since Quiberon, and moving cautiously by night from one house of confidence to another, the Count had brought him safely to Saint-Brieuc, and there had shipped him aboard a contrabandist lugger for Jersey.

Puisaye himself had remained in France. 'I am not in the humour to bear reproaches patiently,' he had said. 'And nothing else can await me at present in England.'

The surmise was correct enough, although it was not with the English that the reproaches originated. It was the compatriots whose jealousy he had provoked, and who could not have failed him more actively had they deliberately set out to betray the Royalist cause, who laboured now to ruin him in reputation.

In reporting the disaster of Quiberon to the House of Commons, Mr. Pitt was able to assure his audience that at least no drop of English blood had been spilled, to which Mr. Sheridan for the Opposition retorted: 'Yes. But honour bled at all its pores,' a politician's silly insulting falsehood which placed a weapon in the hands of those French gentlemen who were clamouring that England had betrayed them, and that Puisaye had been the agent of this betrayal.

Had he foreseen this, Puisaye might have crossed to England with Quentin, so as to be at hand to answer calumny. As it was, he accounted it his duty to continue in France.

'Another chance may come to raise the country. I remain, to seize it if it does. I shall cross the Loire and join Charette. If I live, you shall see me again, Quentin.'

'You know where to find me,' Quentin had answered. 'If I can ever serve you, do not fail to call upon me.'

'Serve me! Should I take where I have so signally failed to give?'

'None lives who has given me more. From you I have had knowledge of myself, and twice you have saved the life which in the first place you gave me.'

'If that is a gift to rejoice in, may you continue so to find it.'

They had embraced on the shingle by the waiting cockboat, and as the seamen bent to their oars the stalwart figure, with hand upheld, gradually fading into the night, was memory's last abiding image of that indomitable man.

It alternated in Quentin's mental vision with the slim, straight wraith of Germaine, as he had last seen her at Coëtlegon in the moment of departure upon that fool's errand at Rédon; and this was a vision to arouse a yearning that was blent with sorrow and bereavement.

Puisaye, who had given him so much and sought to give him so much more, reckless even of honour, had lost her to him by the truth he had imparted. Yet Quentin would not have been without the pain this brought him, for then he must have lost also the memory of the sweetness, and this memory, he told himself, was something that would irradiate all his future, as the reality had irradiated the months that were overpast. It had all been a dream, he vowed; the dream of a fencing-master, who, being now awake, came back to be a fencing-master once again.

It was late afternoon when unannounced he stepped into the long panelled room of which he had been so proud, and which he had regarded as his kingdom in the days before he was summoned to his phantom heritage.

He was greeted by the ring of steel that once had been as music to him; for a single pupil still lingered at practice with O'Kelly.

Old Ramel, on a bench against the wall, sat strapping a *pointe d'arrêt* to the tip of a foil.

At sight of him standing there, so straight and slender in his long coat of bottle green, O'Kelly had lowered his point, plucked the mask from his fiery head, and, the pupil momentarily forgotten, had stood foolishly at gaze. Much as he had greeted him on a day a year ago did O'Kelly greet him now.

'Ah, now, is it indeed yourself, Quentin?'

'Myself it is, and thankful to be home.'

In an instant they were upon him, each wringing one of his hands, babbling a welcome that was incoherent with delight, whilst Barlow, appearing none knew whence, came sidling up with a broad grin on his priestly face.

'Faith, it's a homecoming,' said Quentin, his heart warmed by this affectionate reception.

'And have you come to stay, now?' O'Kelly asked him.

'I have. My roaming ends where it began.'

'Glory be! We're not the only ones that'll be delighted.'

There was one present, however, who manifested little delight. The pupil, abandoned and neglected, stared at them in haughty displeasure. O'Kelly, meeting at last that disapproving eye, was moved to laughter.

'Ah, now, my lord, it's in luck ye are. For here's the master himself, the great Quentin de Morlaix. And if there's a man in the world that can make a swordsman of you, sure it's himself.'

After his lordship had taken a slightly ruffled depar-

373

ture, and the three of them sat in the embrasured lounge, about the table on which Barlow had set the decanters as of old, O'Kelly gave him news of the academy. It prospered ever and was well attended, chiefly now by Englishmen, who did not forget to pay their fees like the impecunious French. Of these there were scarcely any left. All who could wield a sword had crossed to France in the early summer. Few of them, as Quentin knew, would ever return. As a result of that exodus, the academy had lost its character as a fashionable meeting-ground of *émigré* society.

'But there's a lady of the old days who's been here twice in the past week to ask if we had news of you. Mademoiselle de Chesnières.' O'Kelly was sly. 'Maybe ye'll remember her.'

Here was history repeating itself again.

'Maybe I do,' said Quentin, aware of quickened pulses; aware, too, that O'Kelly's eyes were intent upon him.

'I thought ye would,' said the Irishman, and that was all.

On the following morning, Quentin took up his share of the work of instruction as naturally as if there had been no interruption of it. In this he sought an ease of the heartache that oppressed him.

That the news of his return spread quickly through the clubs and coffee-houses was made manifest within the week by the appearance in the academy of old friends who had been in the habit of coming to practise with him, and by the daily enrolment of new pupils.

But these evidences of undiminished popularity, these harbingers of affluence, procured him no exhilaration, failed to cure him of the listlessness that closed down upon him when the day's work was done.

O'Kelly watched him with affectionate anxiety, yet never ventured to intrude upon that gloomy taciturnity.

The Irishman was alone early one morning in the fencing-room, awaiting the first pupil, whilst in the adjoining antechamber Barlow could be heard at work setting things to rights for the day, when the door opened and a slim, straight figure in dove-grey velvet confronted him. He was suddenly, instinctively uplifted. He sprang forward in welcome.

'Ah, come in with you, come in, mademoiselle. It's the glad news I have for you. He's come back.'

She swayed and turned so pale that for a moment he was scared.

'Do you mean that he's here?' Her voice trembled.

'Isn't that what I'm telling you? Glory be! Is it weeping you are?'

She wiped away the tear that had caused the question. 'It's for relief, O'Kelly. Thankfulness. I've been in such fear that he would never return. When . . . when did he arrive?'

'It'll be a fortnight tomorrow.'

'A fortnight!' Surprise, perplexity, displeasure crossed her fair face. 'A fortnight?'

'To be sure. Will ye go up, now, and take him by surprise?'

Barlow appeared in the doorway of the antechamber, drawn by the sound of voices.

'Let Barlow take him word that I am here.'

'Ah, that's never the way of it. He's up there all alone, at breakfast, with a black dog sitting on his shoulders. Sure, now, the sight of you'll scare the beast away forever. This way, mademoiselle.'

He led her through the antechamber, to a farther door that opened upon a staircase. 'Up with you, now. The white door yonder.'

Perhaps it was the mention of that black dog on Quentin's shoulders that made her so obedient. She went up, opened the door, and stood on the threshold of that pleasant white-panelled room, now filled with the sunshine of the October morning.

He was at table, with his back to the door, and supposing it to be Barlow who came, he did not stir.

Thus she was given leisure to consider him and his surroundings.

He wore a dressing-gown of dark blue brocade over his small-clothes. His head, with its lustrous, bronze-coloured hair as trimly queued as of old, was bowed in

375

thought, his chin buried in the high black military stock he wore for fencing. Before him the white napery of the table, the gleam and sparkle of silver and glass in the morning sunshine, and the bowl of late roses in the middle were so many expressions of his fastidiousness.

Her eyes grew moist and wistful as she pondered him, until at last he stirred. 'Why the devil do you keep the door open?' He glanced over his shoulder, and then in a swirl he was on his feet.

For a moment he stared, a consternation in his white face. Then, seeming to collect himself, he bowed.

'I am honoured . . . Marquise.'

The consternation was now with her. She rustled to him. 'Why, Quentin! What is this?'

'You should not have come,' he told her, his tone very gentle.

'Should I not? Let me rather ask you why you did not come to me. You have been home a fortnight, I am told.'

'I . . . I did not know where to find you.'

'Did you seek me?'

'I thought it would be better not to.'

She frowned. 'Because of Madame de Chesnières?' she asked. But she did not wait for an answer. 'Do you know the month and the year in which we live? I am of full age, Quentin, and mistress of myself.'

He was affectionately courteous. 'My felicitations, Marquise.'

'Marquise?'

'Of Chavaray.'

Through mounting, pained bewilderment, she made an attempt to smile.

'You anticipate. You have not yet made me that, Quentin.'

'Nor ever shall. For it will never be in my power to do it. That is why you are already the Marquise de Chavaray. In your own right.'

'I . . . I don't understand.' The perplexity in her eyes asked a fuller explanation. He supplied it.

'There has been—shall we say?—an error. I am not,

376

and never have been, heir to Chavaray. I am not Morlaix de Chesnières, and though I must continue to call myself Morlaix, I have not a right even to that name.'

To her quick understanding his aloofness ceased to be a puzzle. Her eyes grew compassionate and very tender. She set her hands upon his shoulders. 'Who has had the cruelty to make this known to you?'

'That I was an impostor?'

She shook her head. 'There is no imposture where there is no intent to deceive. And that you never had, as I long since assured myself.'

This was as a blow between the eyes to him. 'You knew, then?'

'I heard, long ago, a miserable, scandalous story.'

'And you never told me!'

'Why should I? What should I have told you? A piece of hurtful scandal, resting on surmises, which never could be proved, however true it might be. Was I to wound you with that? What mattered to me was that your honour was clean; that you had no suspicions even that your claims were not as just as at law they were and are unchallengeable.'

He looked at her in silence and humility, his glance full of wonder and homage.

'You have not told me how this knowledge came to you,' she said.

Gently he disengaged her hands. 'I keep you standing.' He set a chair for her.

'Will you be formal with me?' Nevertheless she sat, and heard from him the tale of those last events at Coëtlegon.

'You understand now,' he told her at the end, 'that you are mistress of Chavaray.'

'Do you mock me? It was last yours by right of purchase, and now it will be national property again, and likely so to continue until it falls into the hands of Republican buyers. We need not dispute possession of that ghostly heritage. Had it continued a reality, a man of your stubborn pride might have made it a barrier between us. So it's a dispensation of Providence that

377

for us it has ceased to exist.' She stood up again to confront him. 'There was a solemn promise you made to me at Coëtlegon; an oath you swore. You will remember.'

'Ah, but that was sworn by a man who believed himself to be Marquis of Chavaray, not by a man without so much as a name to offer, whose only marquisate, as your cousin Constant discovered long ago, is that of Carabas.'

She disdained all further argument. She possessed subtler weapons to subdue him to her will, and she had recourse to them. She came to put her arms about his neck, to smile with a winsome, conquering tenderness into his startled eyes.

'Another sweet dispensation of Providence,' she said, 'is that I was born to be the Marchioness of Carabas.'